THE ARTEMIS FILE

Also by Adam Loxley

The Teleios Ring

THE
ARTEMIS
FILE

Adam Loxley

Matador
9 Priory Business Park,
Wistow Road, Kibworth Beauchamp,
Leicestershire. LE8 0RX
Tel: 0116 279 2299
Email: books@troubador.co.uk
Web: www.troubador.co.uk/matador
Twitter: @matadorbooks

ISBN 978 1789018 738

A | British Library Cataloguing in Publication Data.

Typeset in | Adobe Garamond Pro by Troubador Publishing Ltd, Leicester, | UK

For Oliver & Guy

"A nation can survive its fools, and even the ambitious. But it cannot survive treason from within. An enemy at the gates is less formidable, for he is known and carries his banner openly. But the traitor moves amongst those within the gate freely, his sly whispers rustling through all the alleys, heard in the very halls of government itself. For the traitor; he speaks in accents familiar to his victims, and he wears their face and their arguments, he appeals to the baseness that lies deep in the hearts of all men. He rots the soul of a nation, he works secretly and unknown in the night to undermine the pillars of the city, he infects the body politic so that it can no longer resist. A murderer is less to fear. The traitor is the plague."

Marcus Tullius Cicero

One

G EORGE AMBROSE WIGGINS WAS A TALL, STICK-INSECT
of a man, as high as a hop pole and as thin as a rake, the
only concession to his otherwise lean and angular frame being the
large, round spectacles that perched on the end of his nose; two
bright and polished circles on either side of his face, like a pair of
luminous headlamps on a vintage Bentley.

By his own admission, George was a creature of habit, and
tonight was no exception. Every other Thursday was when
Margaret went to her book club; a regular get-together with a few
girlfriends to share a couple of bottles of wine, catch up on the
latest gossip and discuss books that she hadn't read. George used to
worry that they'd catch her out but of course they hadn't read them
either. Still, whether they were pretending or not the arrangement
suited George fine. It gave him the opportunity to drop into The
Red Lion on the way home from work, have a bit of banter with
Ron the landlord and enjoy a couple of pints of real ale before
wandering home to a microwave meal and some undisturbed
time in front of the telly. A bit of peace and quiet before Margaret
came rushing through the door, all flushed and talkative from the
evening's entertainment.

The Red Lion was something of an old fashioned establishment,
in fact in George's opinion it was the only proper pub left in
Tenterden which hadn't been turned into a trendy wine bar or even
worse, some kind of child-friendly, food-hugging monstrosity. All
the other so-called watering holes were full of under-aged kids
swigging tasteless, expensive lager out of designer bottles, or else
they were soulless, half-empty bistros frequented by tired, aspiring

families who thought that the height of fine dining was eating some sort of pre-prepared meal cooked in a box. *Still, thank God for the Red Lion*, thought George as he slurped the top off his pint of bitter. He nodded to a couple of locals who had congregated at the end of the bar and then wandered over to his usual seat, crossing his daddy longlegs into a comfortable position before settling himself into a pint of Harvey's and the evening paper. Satisfied that here at least the world was still as it should be he munched his way through a packet of crisps, swilled a mouthful of beer around his gums and then spent the next five minutes sucking his teeth as he read the day's news, completely oblivious to the comings and goings on around him.

It didn't take long for the pub to fill up, Thursday being a popular night for people to get a head start on the weekend. Within minutes a seemingly endless procession of customers had come through the door, most of them in twos or threes, all looking forward to a well-deserved drink and a good night out. The bar was soon packed with a loud and lively crowd, creating a real buzz about the place. Tenterden might have been a small, traditional market town but The Red Lion was definitely the place to be on a Thursday evening.

'You alright George?' asked Ron, as he walked past, clearing up the empty glasses and straightening a few chairs. 'How's life in the fast lane then?'

George looked up and gave him a half-hearted smile. Ron Stebbings always had been a sarcastic bugger. 'Not bad,' he replied. 'You know, scratching a living.'

Ron shrugged and wandered back behind the bar. He'd known George for four or five years now but wasn't exactly sure what he did for a living. He knew that he worked in London somewhere but beyond that he hadn't got a clue. Not a high paid city slicker, that was for sure. George was much too ordinary for all that financial services malarkey. *Maybe he works in a post room somewhere,* thought Ron before turning his attention to the crowd of locals who were waiting patiently to buy another round.

George went back to his paper and immersed himself in the evening news. It was always quality time as far as he was concerned. A precious moment of rest and relaxation in an otherwise hectic week. A chance to slowly unwind after all the machinations of commuting up and down to London every day. He was still engrossed in the paper, still enjoying his slow, leisurely pint when he became aware of a sudden movement in the chair opposite, the furniture clattering with the impact of someone sitting down hurriedly and then a distinctive waft of perfume floating across the table towards him. He looked up startled, wondering what the hell was going on.

'Oh my God, I think he's coming in. Do something, quick!'

George looked at the woman in complete bewilderment and not without some annoyance. The last thing he wanted was to be interrupted by some excitable female. She, on the other hand was still talking but wasn't looking at George at all, her gaze fixed firmly over his shoulder towards the front door and on someone about to walk in.

'Oh for God's sake, I don't believe it! He looks like Toad of Toad Hall!'

George twisted around and raised an eyebrow as he looked at the man coming through the door. Whoever he was he certainly did look a bit like Toad of Toad Hall. The guy must have been about forty-five, maybe pushing fifty years of age and the combination of an over-elaborate moustache, a loud and flamboyant bow-tie and a large-checked waistcoat stretched tight over a round and portly frame gave him a rather pompous appearance, all of it embellished by a large pink carnation proudly displayed in his lapel button-hole.

Suddenly the penny dropped. 'Blind date?' asked George, turning back to look at his uninvited guest.

The woman ignored him for a second, her attention still fixed on the man who was now standing at the bar, checking out the room, trying to find the person he had arranged to meet. She turned and looked at George properly for the first time and then nodded, rather sheepishly. 'Internet. Monamour dot com.'

George pulled a face, not sure what to think about that. He didn't know much about Internet dating but assumed it could all be a bit sleazy and not without some risk. 'Don't you have to post photos of yourself?' he asked, 'so you know what each other looks like?'

'I don't think his photo was taken very recently,' replied the woman with a rueful smile. 'Mind you, luckily for me neither was mine. Hopefully he won't recognise me.'

'I wouldn't be so sure about that,' said George, 'I think he's coming over...'

The woman looked up in panic, just in time to see Mr. Toad wandering slowly through the bar, clutching what looked like a double whisky and surveying the crowd of customers, hoping to spot his intended victim.

'Oh my God!' she whispered, leaning across the table as if George was now her new-found confidant. 'He looks even worse close up. Quick, do something. Talk to me.'

'Talk to you? What about?' asked George indignantly, still wishing that the wretched woman would just go away.

'I don't know...anything. Just act like we're a normal couple and start talking for God's sake!' And with that she leant forward again and took hold of his hand, as though they were two lovers having an intimate conversation.

George shifted uncomfortably in his chair. It was as much as he could do not to pull his arm away. It was years since he'd held a woman's hand. Not even Margaret's. It didn't seem right. And it certainly didn't feel right. He looked up briefly, just in time to catch a glimpse of Mr. Toad who was now approaching and staring at their table, probably trying to work out whether the woman was his blind date or not.

'Okay,' said George, unable to disguise the irritation in his voice, 'how about the offside rule. What's your view on that?'

The woman looked at him with incredulity. 'The offside rule? I'm a damsel in distress and you want to talk about football?!!'

'It's a very important subject,' replied George stubbornly, 'at least it is to most of the people in here...'

'Most people in here being men, you mean?' interrupted the woman, annoyed at George's tone.

'That's not what I said.'

'It's what you implied.'

'It's just a bit complicated.'

'Football?'

'Offside. In my experience...'

'Oh, spare me the patronising explanation, please!'

'There you are,' said George, a glint of mischievousness in his eye, 'we've only just met and we're arguing already. What could be more normal than that?'

The woman looked at him for a second and then smiled, suddenly realising that Mr. Toad had walked right past them, no doubt concluding that they were just another couple having a matrimonial row.

'I think he's gone now,' said George, checking over his shoulder just to make sure.

The woman smiled at him again and said nothing, the silence suddenly making George feel slightly awkward.

'Do you think I could have my hand back?' he asked, tugging gently to separate them.

'Oh, sorry.' The woman let go and withdrew her arm slowly, still staring intently at George across the table. 'I'm Laura, by the way.'

'George,' said George, not sure what else to say.

'Well, pleased to meet you George. And thank you, you've been very gallant. I owe you a drink.' Her handbag suddenly appeared from nowhere and within seconds a £20 note had been flourished. 'What's your poison George?'

George shifted uncomfortably again. Helping out a damsel in distress was one thing but having a quiet cosy drink with a woman he'd never met before was another thing altogether. How on earth was he going to explain that to Margaret?

'I'm fine,' he said, picking up his glass and draining the last dregs of his pint of bitter. 'Anyway, time I was going.'

'Nonsense,' replied Laura, giving him a firm but appreciative smile. 'It's the least I can do. Besides, we haven't discussed the offside rule yet, have we?'

'Another time, perhaps,' said George. 'Like I said, it's a bit complicated.'

'Well, I agree, it is now but it didn't used to be. A few years ago it was much more straightforward. You were offside simply because you were in front of the ball and nearer the other side's goal line than the second-to-last defender when the ball was passed to you. Unless of course you were in your own half, or if the ball was played from a throw in or a corner kick. But now they've introduced all this nonsense about being in an offside position but not interfering with play. No wonder the referees are confused. Not only have they got to make on-the-spot decisions about whether someone is level or not, they've now got to decide whether other players are interfering with play. It's a complete nonsense.'

George looked at Laura in stunned amazement, his jaw literally open in disbelief.

'What do you think George? Do you think it's a backward step?'

'I…er…um…definitely think it's a backward step,' replied George, somehow finding his composure. He was also looking at Laura properly for the first time that evening and to his surprise, starting to change his mind about her. The rather excitable, annoying female had suddenly turned into a very self-assured woman and one that he now realised was extremely attractive. She must have been about ten years younger than him, *about mid-forties* he thought to himself, and when she smiled, he noticed how the small laughter lines around her eyes somehow lit up her face and made her look all the more striking. She had blonde, shoulder length hair which had been cut into a casual, fashionable style and was wearing a tight, grey top and smart black trousers, both of which showed off her figure and made her look a lot younger. George hadn't taken so much notice of a woman in years. In fact he couldn't remember the last time he had done that but there was no disputing the fact; she looked absolutely stunning. And then there was the perfume. He didn't normally like women's fragrance; too many years sitting next to early morning commuters drenched in overpowering smells had made him almost allergic to the stuff but this one was completely different. Elegant, subtle, evocative.

'You have a very good knowledge of football,' he said, trying to think of something to say.

'I get it from my father. He really loved his football.'

'Well, it's certainly rubbed off.'

'I used to go to Highbury with him as a child. He was an avid Arsenal supporter.'

'Arsenal? I thought you said he loved his football?'

Laura grinned, the banter between rival supporters quickly established. 'Come on George, join me in a drink won't you? I was all set for a night out. I can hardly go home now, it's only eight o'clock. How about one for the road?'

George looked at his watch, thought better of it for a couple of seconds and then gave her a sympathetic smile. 'Go on then, I'll have a pint of Harvey's'

In the end Laura paid but George went up to the bar to get the drinks. Mr. Toad was still standing at the bar, still checking his watch periodically but increasingly looking like a man who had been stood up and was now drowning his sorrows. By eight-thirty George's "one for the road" had turned into two, and the guy at the bar had disappeared, presumably having given up on his blind date. By nine o'clock George and Laura were finishing their third drink, contemplating a fourth and getting on like a house on fire, in fact engrossed in each other's company like a couple of long lost friends. It was eventually nine-thirty by the time they left, George ignoring the less than subtle winks and innuendos from Ron and a few locals as he and Laura stepped out into the warm summer's evening.

'Sorry about that,' said George, buttoning up his jacket and feeling the need to apologise for the behaviour of his fellow drinkers. 'Some people have one track minds.'

'Don't apologise George. I thought it was quite funny actually. Anyway, it was really good to meet you. Thank you again for coming to my rescue.'

George hesitated, uncertain about how to say goodbye. Eventually he pushed his arm forward having decided that a formal handshake was the proper and gentlemanly thing to do. 'Not at all,' he replied, 'it was very good to meet you too.'

Laura couldn't help smiling at how old fashioned he was but the pair of them shook hands and then stood there in silence for a couple of seconds, each waiting for the other to make the first move.

'How are you getting home?' asked George rather awkwardly, trying his hardest not to sound as if he was offering her a lift. He wasn't sure how he was going to get home himself but driving a car after four pints of bitter was not an option.

'Oh, I can walk,' replied Laura, nodding in the general direction towards the end of the High Street. 'It's a nice evening and it's not far.'

George frowned. Tenterden was one of the safest places he knew but it was getting late. He didn't know how long it would take Laura to walk home and she seemed the sort of person who could probably look after herself but all the same, it didn't seem right to let a woman walk home alone in the dark.

'Actually, I need to get a cab,' he said. 'I live about a mile away. Why don't I drop you off on the way?'

It took them about five minutes to find a taxi and then only another few minutes to get to Laura's home, a smart, semi-detached property on a small modern development on the outskirts of town. George was quite relieved that the journey didn't take long. Although it had been his idea and he had been quite insistent that Laura shouldn't walk home on her own, for some reason he felt strangely uncomfortable sitting side-by-side with her in the back of the cab, as if it were somehow more intimate than spending a couple of hours drinking with her in the pub. *Stupid really*, he thought to himself. Nevertheless he let out a sigh of relief as the taxi pulled up outside her house.

'Here we are,' announced the driver, keeping the engine running but looking in the rear view mirror to check that he'd got the right address. 'Number 14. Is this it?'

George nodded and then waited for Laura to open the door and get out. He was all ready to give her a friendly wave, expecting her to shut the door and disappear when suddenly she leant back into the car.

'Please don't take this the wrong way George,' she said, sounding slightly apprehensive, 'but would you like to come in for a coffee?'

George shifted uneasily, not for the first time that evening. 'I'm not sure that would be a very good idea...'

'Oh, come on George, I'm not going to bite. It's just a cup of coffee.'

'No honestly, I really ought to be going.'

'But why? Where are you rushing off to?'

'Well, home obviously...'

'But it's not even ten o'clock. You said you wife doesn't get in until about eleven.'

George looked at his watch. Laura was right. It wasn't yet ten o'clock and Margaret wouldn't be home for at least another hour. The offer was certainly tempting. A bit of company and some interesting conversation would be a welcome change, much better than sitting on his own in front of the telly which is what he normally did when Margaret was out. He could do that any other night of the week. And a strong cup of coffee sounded like a good idea, particularly after four pints of bitter. Then again, what on earth would Margaret say? He could just about explain why he'd stayed in the pub and had a few drinks but going back to her house for a cup of coffee was completely different. No, the sensible thing would be to go home and then everything could get back to normal as soon as possible. He looked at Laura again, still leaning into the car, waiting expectantly for his answer. *Still, on the other hand, it's just a cup of coffee. What could be the harm in that?*

'What we doing then mate?' asked the taxi driver, still looking in the rear view mirror and getting impatient with all the dithering. 'Are we going onto the next address or what?'

For some reason the interruption helped George make up his mind. 'No, I'm getting out here,' he said, getting out his wallet and giving the guy a £10 note. 'Keep the change.'

The driver muttered something under his breath and then did a u-turn and sped off, not waiting to watch George and Laura walk up the garden path. Laura opened the front door and led George into a sitting room, while she disappeared into the kitchen.

'Make yourself at home George. I'm just going to put the kettle on. Tea or Coffee?'

'Coffee please,' shouted George. 'White, no sugar.'

He could hear Laura busying herself in the kitchen so settled himself into an armchair which was positioned to one side of a small fireplace, opposite a small two-seater settee. He looked around the room for a moment and admired the décor, particularly the combination of soft furnishings and subdued lighting which gave it a cosy, homely feel.

After a couple of minutes Laura appeared carrying a large tray and two mugs of coffee. 'There you go George,' she said, leaning forward and lowering the tray to his height, 'that's yours on the left.'

George looked up and carefully took the mug, making sure that he didn't spill any. He couldn't help notice that the effect of Laura leaning over him in her tight grey top left little to the imagination.

'I'm just going upstairs to use the bathroom,' she announced, putting her own coffee on a small side table. 'I'll be back in a minute.'

'Righty ho.' replied George, holding his mug in both hands and gently blowing across the surface. *Too many glasses of wine probably.*

A minute or so later, he heard her come back downstairs and turned to look at her as she came through the door. It wasn't what he was expecting. In fact it was the last thing he was expecting. She was still wearing the same high-heeled stilettos but instead of the grey top and the smart black trousers she was now wrapped up in a white fluffy dressing gown.

George looked at her and opened his mouth several times, as if he was going to say something, but nothing came out, his brain suddenly not connected to his mouth anymore.

Laura stood motionless in the doorway for a moment, watching the impact of her entrance on George's equilibrium. George meanwhile was still frozen in the chair, clutching the arms as if he were about to fall out and still trying desperately to think of something to say. Eventually she walked into the room and then slowly leant over him again, just as she had done with the tray of coffees. Her bottom lip pouted with pretend guilt. 'I'm sorry George, I've a confession to make. I got you here under false pretences.'

'Really?' George pushed himself back into the chair, trying to get some space between them but it was no use. The further he retreated the more she moved forward. All he could see was the top of her breasts, nestled gently inside the soft white dressing gown as she leant further and further over him.

Laura pouted again. 'Come on George, I'm sure it wasn't just a cup of coffee that you came back for.'

George squirmed again, trying his hardest not to look anywhere that he shouldn't. 'I'm sorry if I gave you the wrong idea Laura, I really didn't mean to ….'

'What's the matter George, don't you fancy me?'

'It's not that, it's just that I wasn't expecting…'

'Because I definitely fancy you George.'

'Really?'

'Can't you tell George?'

'Well, it's just I'm not very used to…'

'Can you tell now George?' she purred. And in the same breath, she suddenly undid the cord which had been tied around her waist and the dressing gown fell open, her smooth and naked body now leaning over him in all its wonderful glory.

George practically fainted on the spot. He tried to gulp as much fresh air as he could swallow and then actually shut his eyes for a second, hoping that it would all go away.

'Nothing to say George?'

'I…er…I'm…just not sure what…'

George's wittering was suddenly silenced by Laura kissing him passionately on the lips, her tongue darting into his mouth and across his teeth. Within an instant, the pheromones kicked in and his heart started pumping for all it was worth, just as the room started to spin.

After what seemed like an eternity he somehow managed to push her gently away. 'I…I think I need to use the bathroom as well,' he stammered, trying to ease himself out of the chair.

Laura smiled and took a couple of steps backwards, giving him just enough room to get out of the chair and escape. George practically ran up the stairs, found the bathroom at the top of the landing and quickly locked the door behind him. It took him a couple of seconds to fumble around and find the light switch, and then he sat on the toilet seat and put his head in his hands. What a bloody mess. What the hell was all that about? And how on earth was he going to explain this to Margaret!!!?

He sat still for a few moments, trying to think through his options and work out what he should do next. Then he looked up and noticed a reflection of himself in a mirror which was on the wall, just above the wash basin. Because he was still sitting on the toilet he could only see the top half of his head, which was shining brightly under the glare of the bathroom spotlights. He rubbed his hand over the bald egg-shaped scalp, a familiar action which always made the few remaining wisps of hair stand up to attention and made him look all the more comical. He couldn't understand how someone like Laura could possibly fancy an old duffer like him. He smiled quizzically to himself. But then again, maybe he should stop worrying and just let events take their course. See it as an opportunity rather than a problem. After all, it was hardly likely to be an opportunity that would ever come his way again.

George stood up and looked at himself in the mirror properly, smoothing down what little hair he had left and re-tucking his shirt into his trousers. Maybe he wasn't such an old duffer. Suddenly he spotted a bottle of perfume which was on a narrow shelf in front of him. He picked it up and out of curiosity squirted a small amount into the air. The effect was instant. It was definitely the same one. Evocative, seductive, haunting. He looked at the bottle again, an expensive piece of sculptured glass with the word "Serendipity" engraved across the front in stylish, flamboyant letters. *That's funny,* he thought, *that was the answer to one of the clues in the crossword this morning. It must be a portent.*

Downstairs, Laura was standing by the sitting room door keeping one eye on the landing to make sure that George was still safely locked up in the bathroom. She pressed the call button on the mobile phone, knowing it would be answered within seconds.

Less than a mile away, the guy with the over-elaborate moustache, the loud and flamboyant bow-tie and the large-checked waistcoat was waiting patiently on a barstool. He took the call as soon as it rang. 'How's it going?'

'He's ready. Hook, line and sinker...'

Two

THE NATIONAL GALLERY WHICH SAT MAJESTICALLY overlooking Trafalgar Square was one of London's premier cultural attractions, housing a collection of over 2,300 paintings and the fourth most visited art museum in the world. Charles Buchanan knew the place like the back of his hand, the labyrinth of rooms and stairwells a reassuring, familiar maze after years of exploring its varied and priceless collection. From late medieval works by the likes of Dürer and Botticelli to the impressionist movement of Monet and Cézanne, London's National Gallery was home to some of the world's great masterpieces. It took Buchanan no more than a couple of minutes to squeeze past the crowd of tourists on the front steps and find his way to Room 32, a large rectangular room on the north side of level 2.

He stood in the doorway for a moment, the paintings of the Spanish room behind him, and surveyed the room ahead. Tom Draper was already there, catalogue in hand, moving casually from picture to picture, mingling unnoticed amongst the other visitors. A warm, midweek day in July was always going to be relatively quiet but there were still twenty or so people in the room, an eclectic mix of European, Japanese and American tourists, mostly young couples complete with digital guides, cameras and mobile phones. Buchanan studied them carefully, checking each one in turn to make sure that they were genuine. The gallery was the perfect setting for a discreet, informal meeting but the nature of browsing and the prevalence of new technology meant that one could never be too careful. Some of them were wearing earphones which was always a risk but eventually he decided that they were all harmless enough.

Draper made the first move, working his way slowly along the south wall, studying each picture as he went before taking a seat on the large brown sofa facing *The Supper at Emmaus,* probably the finest example of Italian Baroque art in the whole collection. Buchanan waited a couple of seconds and then joined him, sitting in silence for a minute or two, neither acknowledging the other and both of them staring at the painting in front. In any event, Draper knew the rules of engagement. He always waited until Buchanan was ready. Pawn to E4…

'So, what do you think?' asked Buchanan eventually. As ever, the cut glass accent was unequivocal, the heritage undeniable. Marlborough, Balliol, Whitehall.

Draper nodded slowly, as if making a considered response, the pair of them still not looking at each other. 'I like it. Who's it by?'

Buchanan smiled to himself. Tom Draper's accent was in contrast pure 100% American; all baseball, apple pie and Kentucky bourbon. Somehow it sat perfectly with his complete lack of knowledge of all things cultural. Several years of living in London had done nothing to refine his accent and several years of visiting the National Gallery had done nothing to refine his taste either. 'It's a Caravaggio. You can tell by the dramatic treatment of light and shade.'

Draper nodded again. 'I've heard of Caravaggio.'

'Most people have.'

'The guy's good.'

'I'm sure he'd be pleased to have your endorsement.'

Draper smiled, acknowledging the gentle teasing. 'What's it called?'

'*The Supper at Emmaus.* It depicts the moment when Jesus reveals himself to two of his disciples after the resurrection.'

'It's fabulous.'

'I agree. There's another version in Milan but this one is far superior.'

Draper continued staring at the painting, mindful that most of the visitors were now at the other end of room. Time to change the subject. 'Thanks for coming.'

Buchanan held up his palm, brushing away the gratitude. He didn't know what Draper wanted but he knew it must be important.

Draper checked over his shoulder a couple of times just to make sure that they were out of earshot and then lowered his voice. 'We have a situation.'

'Go on.'

'Lots of panic back home.'

'Washington?'

'Langley. I've been recalled.'

Buchanan leant back into the leather sofa and crossed one leg over the other, casually brushing the nap off his trouser leg as he feigned indifference to perfection. 'Sounds like you've got a problem.'

Draper said nothing but stared vacantly into the distance. He was thirty-eight years of age. Pushing forty. After five years of living in London he'd adjusted to the lifestyle. He liked it here. His wife was happy. The kids were settled. Going back to the US wasn't a problem, it was an absolute disaster.

Buchanan tried again. 'Anything I can do?'

Draper put his head in his hands. There wasn't anything anyone could do. Somebody somewhere had stamped the decision. The bags were packed. They were flying out on Sunday. His whole life was about to turn upside down and there was nothing he or anyone else could do about it. He turned and looked at Buchanan for the first time, realising that he would probably never see him again. No more discreet meetings, no more guarded conversations, no more alliances and mutual interests. He put his hand in his jacket pocket and took out a small coloured plastic stick.

'I thought you might be interested in this.' Draper quickly checked that no one was watching and then passed the memory stick over.

Buchanan pocketed it in a single, swift movement. 'Thanks. What's on it?'

Draper gave him a wry smile. 'Call it a parting gift.'

'I'm usually wary of people bearing gifts.'

'I thought that was just Greeks?'

'Especially Greeks. And Americans of course.'

'Make an exception. This one is worth keeping.'

'Valuable?'

'Priceless.'

Suddenly Draper stopped, conscious that a couple of tourists, German by the sound of it, had sat down on the sofa immediately behind them, facing the opposite wall. He switched the conversation instantly. 'Are there any other Caravaggios here?'

Buchanan pointed towards the wall in front of them. 'The picture on the right. *Boy Bitten By A Lizard*. It's a much earlier work.'

Draper looked briefly at the smaller painting to the side and then nodded back towards *The Supper at Emmaus*. 'I prefer that one.'

'Most people do.'

'It's also better than the one you showed me last time.'

'Remind me.'

'*Mr and Mrs* something...'

Buchanan smiled to himself. '*Andrews.*'

'Whatever, I prefer this one. It's much better.'

'Different. Not necessarily better.'

Draper nodded, conceding the distinction. He looked at Buchanan again and studied him carefully, wondering whether anyone really knew the person underneath the cool and polished veneer. On first impression he was the quintessential English gentleman; eloquent, refined, sophisticated with a casual, understated confidence in everything he did. Even his appearance was straight out of Jermyn Street. Despite his 55 years of age, his tall lean frame and distinguished grey hair still gave him a classic, almost aristocratic bearing. From the hand-made tailored suit and old school tie to the solid gold links and the monogrammed signet ring on his little finger he was every inch the archetypal, cultured mandarin; a product of public school, private clubs and old city dining rooms. A bastion of middle England and traditional, conservative values. But underneath it all there was a detachment; a cold, calculating indifference born out of years of navigating the political minefield that twisted back and forth between Westminster and Whitehall. A survivor of more governments, coalitions and cabinet reshuffles than he cared to remember. And while the faces changed and the civil servants braced themselves for the next, inevitable round of spending cuts, Buchanan quietly got on with managing Vector, a discreet and powerful intelligence operation free of any government oversight or ministerial control. Clandestine, ruthless and very, very effective.

Eventually Buchanan looked up and glanced over his shoulder. The Germans had finally stood up and were moving down the gallery.

Draper took the cue and dropped his voice again. 'Does the name Damien Ross mean anything to you?'

Buchanan shook his head. 'Who is he?'

'Apparently he's one of ours.'

'Never heard of him.'

'Neither had I until last week. He disappeared off the face of the earth about ten years ago.'

'And?'

'And suddenly he turned up three weeks ago and all hell has let loose.'

Buchanan raised his eyebrows. That would explain why Langley were getting so agitated. No wonder they were in a panic. 'So where's he's been?'

Draper shrugged. 'No idea. It's a complete lockdown. I tried to pull his 201 file and hit a brick wall. Two days later I'm being repatriated.'

'Coincidence?'

'Plausible deniability.'

Buchanan grimaced. Only the CIA could invent a whole new vocabulary. *Two nations divided by a common language.* He checked his watch. He needed to be somewhere else. 'Anything else?'

'Ross turned up in London. I just wondered if you'd heard anything?'

Buchanan shook his head again. 'Nothing. Not a whisper.'

'Never mind, just a thought.' Draper nodded towards Buchanan's jacket pocket where his leaving present was now safely kept. 'Last week Ross made a brush pass in St. James's Park. The surveillance footage is on the stick.'

'Thanks. What was he handling?'

'Well, that's the problem. We tailed the courier and picked him up as soon as he left the park. The envelope was empty.'

Buchanan frowned. That certainly didn't make any sense. 'And the courier?'

'Nobody. Just an innocent mule paid to sit on a park bench and collect a package. Recruited in a pub round the corner.'

'And Ross?'

'We followed him back to a flat in Knightsbridge. The address is on the memory stick. He's been under surveillance ever since.'

Buchanan frowned again and then patted his pocket in appreciation. 'Well, thanks. I'll let you know if we come up with anything.'

'Not me. I've got to fly.' Draper glanced back at the Caravaggio for a second and then gazed slowly up and down the room, taking his time to catch one last look at the large Italianate marble columns, the green fresco wallpaper, the polished herringbone floor and of course the stunning masterpieces in gilt frames hanging on the walls. This was going to be his last time. No more visits to the National Gallery. No more lessons in cultural appreciation, courtesy of Charles Buchanan. Fairfax County, Virginia was going to feel like Hicksville compared to this. God knows how his wife and kids were going to adjust. He turned and looked at Buchanan who had stood up and was waiting to leave. Draper also stood up, conscious that they were about to part company.

'Anyway, thanks for all your help Charles.'

'Likewise.'

'And good luck.'

'And you. Have a safe flight.'

Draper hovered awkwardly for a moment, not sure how to actually say goodbye. 'I suppose a handshake would be inappropriate?'

Buchanan looked him straight in the eye. 'Totally inappropriate.' And with that he turned and headed towards the door, not bothering to look back as he walked out. Tom Draper was a decent enough guy but at the end of the day he was just another faceless CIA officer; here today and gone tomorrow. Most of them were ten a penny. And none of them could be trusted of course. Dealing with the Soviets was easy by comparison. At least you knew where you stood. The challenge was always managing the Americans. Plus the bloody French of course.

Buchanan made his way to the front of the building and slipped out through the front doors into the bright summer sunshine. It was nearly midday and London as usual was packed full of tourists, a constantly moving throng of bright colourful clothes and noisy, unintelligible chatter. He thought for a moment about waiting around the corner just to make sure that Draper had left behind him but in the end thought better of it. Draper wasn't smart enough to meet anyone else. Besides, the clock was ticking and he had things to do. He checked his watch again. He could go back to the Greenhouse, which was just a short walk along Pall Mall, or he could go on to Boodles, his club in St. James's and maybe get an early spot of lunch. He stood on the steps of the gallery and thought for a moment. Lunch was tempting but the first thing he needed to do was make a call which meant going back to the office. He needed to use a secure landline and it was best to strike while the iron was hot.

He walked briskly along Pall Mall, past the Haymarket on his right and then turned left into Waterloo Place, the noise of traffic soon disappearing behind him. His office, known to everyone that worked there as the Greenhouse, was a large gated property in Carlton Gardens, the cul-de-sac at the end of Carlton House Terrace; a street of white, stucco-faced Georgian properties that sat majestically on the south side of Pall Mall, overlooking St. James's Park.

Buchanan swiped through the security entrance and quickly made his way up to his office on the first floor. He closed the door behind him and walked over to his desk, a large, twin-pedestal antique finished in English burr walnut with gold gilt inlay and dark green leather insert. He picked up the phone, not bothering to sit down and immediately hit one of the speed dials. He had no idea where Carlisle was but it made sense to try his office first. Besides, he had a private, direct line which he knew would be answered in seconds.

Less than half a mile away, at number 70, Whitehall, Sir James Carlisle was ensconced in his office, working his way through a pile of ministerial papers with strict instructions to his office staff to field all calls and make sure that there were no interruptions. It was with some surprise therefore that less than half an hour into what was meant to be a free, undisturbed afternoon the telephone on his desk rang. He looked at it in disbelief for a moment, wondering whether to ignore it or not, but then after a couple of rings picked it up with undisguised irritation. 'I thought I said no calls?'

His secretary at the other end wasn't fazed for one moment. Joyce Wilson, a thirty-year, career civil servant had dealt with them all in her time. Compared to some of the people she'd worked with, managing a rather irritable Cabinet Secretary was all in a day's work. 'It's Charles Buchanan. He says it's urgent.'

Carlisle frowned. There weren't many people he would allow himself to be interrupted by. Number 10 obviously, plus the Palace of course. But Buchanan was one of only a handful of others. He let out a long, exasperated sigh. 'Okay, put him through.'

Buchanan sensed that he hadn't called at a good time. He cut straight to the chase. 'James, we need to talk.'

'What about?'

'Damien Ross.'

'Damien Ross is dead.'

'That's what we thought. Not any more.'

There was a silence at the other end of the phone, the impact of Buchanan's news taking a moment to sink in. Carlisle was suddenly processing as fast as he could, trying to work out the implications of Ross still being alive.

'Are you sure?'

'Our cousins are. They've got him under 24 hour surveillance.'

'But they haven't talked to him?'

'Not yet.'

Carlisle pulled a grim face. No wonder Buchanan had called him. Time was of the essence.

'Not a difficult decision then Charles.' More a statement than a question.

'No, not really.'

'I'll leave it with you then.'

'Fine.' Buchanan put the phone down. The decision on Ross was inevitable. He just needed someone else to make it. Now he needed someone else to execute it. Literally. Which meant selecting the right person was going to be critical. Once upon a time that would have been easy. An obvious decision. He thought momentarily about choosing someone else but then thought better of it. The risks were too high. Much better to keep things under the radar. It had to be Craven. Despite everything that had happened it had to be him. Besides, it was time to move on, an opportunity to draw a line under the past. God knows, the silence had gone on long enough. He picked up the phone again. There was no point in hanging around. They needed to get to Ross before anyone else did. Time to get to work. *"Cry havoc and let slip the dogs of war; That this foul deed shall smell above the earth..."*

Three

NUMBER 36, ORCHARD DRIVE WAS A LARGE FOUR bedroom detached house, a typical 1930s pre-war property with round bay windows, a traditional arched porch and a solid oak door complete with original *art deco* glass and polished brass letterbox. Craven stood by the front gate and gazed up and down the street, looking at the well-maintained gardens and the rows of immaculately cut hedges, a symmetry of clean, straight lines shimmering in the warm, July sunshine. In any other part of the country this would be expensive but affordable housing, at least for the professional classes, but here in North London it was something that only the most affluent could aspire to. What struck him most was how quiet and peaceful it all seemed. In the distance he could hear the sound of someone using a power saw and also the faint barking of a dog somewhere but otherwise everything was still and tranquil. There was something reassuring, almost comforting about English suburbia, as if regardless of what was happening in the world outside the indefatigable residents would make sure that life went on as usual, uninterrupted and unchanged, sweeping their drives, pruning their roses, mowing their lawns. *"If I should die think only this of me: That there's some corner of a foreign field that is forever England."*

Craven walked up the garden path and rang the doorbell, an old-fashioned tubular chime which resonated long after he had pressed the button. Within seconds he saw the outline of someone coming down the hall, their silhouette getting larger as they approached the front door. He waited a moment and fiddled with his collar, just as the door was opened by a neat middle-aged woman of indistinguishable appearance; medium height, medium build, with features that were neither plain nor overly attractive. Even her hair which was medium length was somewhere between blonde and brunette. In fact everything about her was in-between and shouted ordinary. She smiled and stepped back a couple of paces. 'Mr. Craven I presume. Come in.'

Craven smiled back and stepped inside the hall, waiting a moment for her to shut the door behind him. She stared at him for a second, thrown momentarily by his demeanour which was slightly disarming; the natural, self-assurance of someone who was entirely comfortable with himself. Either that or it was the six-foot lithe frame, chiselled features and deep brown eyes which were distracting her. Inevitably, the rugged good looks were ageing a bit after forty or so years but the impact was still pretty much the same. He held out his hand. 'Mrs. Wallis. Sorry I'm late.'

'Not a problem. Come through Mr. Craven, can I get you a cup of tea or coffee...?' She turned right into what was obviously the living room and Craven followed behind her. As he entered the room he stopped short, his mouth literally open in surprise.

'...or something stronger perhaps?' she added, ignoring the look on his face. Most people reacted like that the first time.

Craven looked at his watch. It was barely midday. He held up his hand to decline. 'A bit early for me thank you but a coffee would be nice. Black, one sugar please.'

Mrs. Wallis disappeared into the kitchen and Craven stood in silence, staring up and down the room. He didn't actually want a cup of coffee but that was often the case, it was the established ritual that most people went through, the usual offer and polite acceptance to smooth the greeting of complete strangers. Besides, it gave him time to look at the room in more detail. Craven knew nothing about art, particularly modern art, but instinctively he knew that the work in front of him was of the highest quality and probably worth a small fortune.

The room was large and rectangular but looked as though it had once been two smaller receptions, probably dark and cluttered living rooms with tiled fireplaces, wooden picture rails and Bakelite door furniture. Now it was completely the opposite, in fact as modern and contemporary as one could imagine and in absolute contrast to the traditional exterior of the house. Everything was decorated in clean crisp white and the interior design was completely minimalist; a solid wood floor in light Nordic ash furnished predominantly with white leather sofas and smoke-grey glass tables. But it was the art that really captured the room. Huge, square, unframed canvasses of bright vibrant colours plus elegant, stylish, multi-coloured glass sculptures and modern aesthetic ceramics in muted, urban tones. Craven looked at each of the pieces in turn, unsure about exactly what the compositions were meant to be but fairly sure that this was a serious and impressive collection.

After a couple of minutes, Mrs. Wallis returned carrying two cups of coffee, putting one on a glass table beside one of the white sofas and holding the other as she sat down on the sofa opposite. 'Are you an art lover, Mr Craven?'

Craven turned round and gave her an apologetic smile. 'Sorry, more of a Constable man I'm afraid. Although I have to say, this is a stunning collection.'

'Thank you. It's my husband's really. He's very proud of it.'

'He must be a serious collector,' said Craven, sitting down and picking up the cup of coffee.

'Yes he is. We have a gallery actually, so it's more of a vocation really.'

'Oh, I didn't realise. Local?'

Mrs Wallis gave him a knowing smile. Most people thought that. 'It's in the West End. Bloomsbury to be more exact. Near the British Museum…'

Craven took a sip of coffee and nodded in appreciation. No wonder they were loaded.

'…David wanted to call it the *Wallis Collection* but the lawyers wouldn't let him.'

Craven smiled politely, the joke completely lost on him. He looked around the room again. 'Well, he's certainly got an eye for talent.'

Mrs. Wallis raised an eyebrow. 'Well he's certainly got an eye for something Mr. Craven. Unfortunately that's why we're here.'

'Oh.'

'Yes, I was rather hoping that David's midlife crisis was going to involve buying a motorbike, or maybe learning the guitar and joining a rock band. Unfortunately he's been a bit more predictable than that.'

'Ah, I'm sorry.'

'I'm sure it's not an uncommon situation in your line of work?'

'No, unfortunately not.'

'And your background Mr. Craven? I assume you were in the Police Force or something?'

Craven tried not to show his disgust. Being taken for an ex-woodentop was about as insulting as it got, although these days it seemed to be an occupational hazard. The market was full of them. Cynical, lazy, barely educated ex-coppers trying to supplement their over-inflated pensions by relying on old-boy networks and doing as little as possible. It was positively galling. And it was certainly a situation that made him question whether he had made the right decision, usually when he was up to his ears in some dull and tedious domestic case, trawling through the underbelly of peoples' sad and parochial lives. If this was what going freelance was all about he was going to have to think again. He was trained in special operations for God's sake, a reconnaissance and intelligence expert who had spent most of his life working undercover behind the Eastern Bloc. And here he was, in the middle of English suburbia, listening to yet another squalid tale of deceit and betrayal. He gave Mrs Wallis a wistful smile, unable to hide the faint reminiscence in his voice. 'I was in the Security Services. Fifteen years.'

Her face lit up momentarily, her interest suddenly sparked by the thought of spooks and international espionage. 'Security services? As in MI5?'

Craven hesitated. It wasn't something he could particularly talk about. Once you'd signed the Act it applied for life. Besides, even if he could talk about it no one had ever heard of Vector. It didn't mean anything to anybody. In fact, other than the PM and the Joint Intelligence Committee it was pretty much off the radar to everyone else. Barely anyone in Whitehall knew it existed. He put the cup and saucer back on the coffee table and leant back into the sofa. 'Not exactly. But similar. Unfortunately it's classified so difficult for me to say very much.'

Mrs. Wallis held up her hand in apology. 'Of course, stupid of me.' Then she looked down for a second, suddenly embarrassed by the situation. 'I'm sorry, this must all seem very sordid and mundane in comparison.'

Craven gave her a sympathetic smile. 'Not at all. As you say, it's not uncommon. But are you sure that your husband is having an affair?'

Mrs. Wallis lifted her head up and took a moment to regain her composure. Suddenly she looked resolute, proud, dignified. 'We've been married for a long time Mr. Craven. You get to know each other very well after all those years. I'm absolutely certain.'

'And any idea who it might be?'

'I assume it's one of his protégés.'

'Protégés?'

'My husband specialises in spotting brilliant young artists, preferably while they're still at Art College. It means he can buy or commission work at very low cost, which means the margins can be significant. Astronomical in fact if they really take off...'

Craven raised his eyebrows. It sounded like a smart strategy.

'...and it's a mutually beneficial arrangement. New artists find it difficult to get any sort of exposure, let alone commercial success.

The sponsorship of a West End gallery can be career defining for them...'

Craven nodded. It was all making perfect sense. In fact he wondered why more people didn't do it.

'...but I trust you get the picture Mr. Craven. A middle-aged man constantly surrounded by young ambitious art students, all of them competing to get his attention and secure his patronage.'

Craven nodded again. 'And I assume a lot of the students are young attractive females?'

'Most of them are between 18 and 25.'

Craven blew out his cheeks. It sounded like a complete nightmare. Or maybe the opposite. The guy must have been walking around with a permanent erection. *Lucky Bastard.* 'And do you just want me to find out what's going on?'

Mrs. Wallis frowned, clearly not keeping up with Craven's line of thinking.

'Limited surveillance and simple research should be enough to confirm the situation. I ought to be able to establish the facts and get you a name, address, basic bio-data within a few days. But if you wanted photographic evidence, for...' Craven hesitated, not quite sure how to phrase things. He didn't want to assume anything.

'For divorce proceedings you mean?'

It was Craven's turn to look embarrassed. 'Exactly. Photographic evidence for a court case would need to be built up over a period of time. It would mean a lot more surveillance which could be expensive.'

Mrs. Wallis gazed around the room for a moment as if to accentuate the point. 'Cost is not an issue Mr. Craven. My husband will be paying...'

Craven nodded in acknowledgement. Mrs. Wallis was a lot tougher than she looked.

'...besides, he'll only deny it. I'm not sure about divorce Mr. Craven but I think I would prefer absolute proof.'

'Of course. And any idea which of his students it might be?'

Mrs. Wallis shook her head. 'I'm afraid I haven't a clue. I don't know their names and he's very careful with his paperwork and his mobile phone these days.'

Craven shrugged. 'Not to worry, I just thought you might be able to point me in the right direction.'

'Although come to think of it, I do know one thing about her. Wait there a second.' Mrs Wallis stood up and left the room, having obviously just remembered something. Craven stood up and stretched his legs. He could hear her moving around upstairs, presumably in one of the bedrooms. Within a few moments she was back again, holding what appeared to be a crumpled white shirt. She held it out, indicating to Craven to take it from her.

'My husband's shirt from earlier this week. A late night viewing he said.'

Craven took the shirt and turned it over carefully, not exactly sure what he was meant to be looking for.

'Smell it Mr. Craven. If that isn't proof that he's up to something I don't know what is.'

Craven put the shirt up to his nose and breathed in hard. Even after a few days of being in a linen basket the fragrance was still quite strong. 'Not his aftershave then?'

'It's a woman's perfume. And it's definitely not one of mine.'

'Do you know what it's called?'

'There are hundreds of perfumes Mr. Craven. I recognise probably no more than five or six.'

'That's a pity.'

'But the girl on the cosmetic counter at House of Fraser knows virtually all of them. I took the shirt down there yesterday…'

Craven smiled. He could just imagine Mrs. Wallis marching into her local department store and getting the girl to identify it for her.

'…it's called Serendipity. Apparently it's very exclusive and very expensive.'

Four

F RANCORELLI'S IN MINT LANE WAS AN OLD-FASHIONED
family concern, one of the last surviving greasy-spoon cafés in
the City of London. For most people it was a drab and uninviting
place, a combination of unhealthy food and poor service, with
an ambience and décor which would have been more at home in
the 1960s. In fact the interior had hardly changed in the last fifty
years. The metal tables and thin plastic tablecloths were relics from
a bygone age, each one furnished with a sticky, dog-eared menu
propped up between two small salt and pepper pots. Once upon a
time the bare emulsion walls were a bright sunshine yellow but the
years had taken their toll; the daily diet of fried food and cigarette
smoke fading everything to a dreary, brownish hue and the feel-
good backdrop now just a distant memory. But for George it was
an absolute godsend, an oasis of proper, no-nonsense English grub
sold at reasonable prices in a world full of fast food, branded coffee
shops and fluorescent sandwich-bars. What he liked most of all
was that when he ordered a cup of coffee that was exactly what
he got, not some convoluted interrogation about skinny lattés,
cappuccinos or flat whites. And the food, a range of omelettes, fry-
ups or anything on toast was exactly to his liking. Freshly cooked,
piping hot and served with decent helpings.

The original owner, Francorelli, had long retired, probably to
the warm Italian hills of San Gimignano or some other Tuscan
village, the café now run by his nephew, Dino, who managed to
continue the tradition of slow, indifferent service with apparently
effortless ease. For a Wednesday lunchtime the place was fairly
busy, mostly a collection of builders, delivery drivers and like-

minded office workers. George wandered up to the counter and looked at the specials board hanging on the back wall, checking that it read the same as it always had done; half a dozen culinary options advertised in faded flowing chalk, probably written years ago.

'Hello George,' said Dino, appearing from the kitchen carrying some loaves of bread. 'You alright?'

'Not bad Dino. You?'

'Oh, you know, living the dream.'

George smiled. Dino had the most fabulous dry sense of humour, honed to perfection from years of serving his working class clientele. In some ways he was more English than Italian. George exchanged a bit of banter about Chelsea, Dino's adopted team, and then ordered a bacon sandwich and a mug of tea. His favourite seat at the back of the café facing the front door was already taken, so he picked one half-way down the right-hand wall and settled himself down for a quick read of the paper before the food turned up.

Or at least he tried to. In truth he'd already flicked through it but there was nothing much of interest, or at least nothing that he hadn't read before. Just the usual crisis in the Middle East, speculation about the impact of the UK economy on house prices, and the latest discovery that some common or garden food which was previously thought to have fantastic health properties was suddenly bad for you. Same old, same old...

But it wasn't really the newspaper that was the problem. George just didn't have the concentration for reading at the moment. Ever since his assignation with Laura last week he'd been in a permanent state of anxiety. He shivered as the memory of it flooded over him again. God knows how he'd managed to crawl back in without Margaret waking up but luckily she'd been dead to the world. And miraculously she'd also believed his story about a late night lock-in at The Red Lion; half a dozen grown men unable to resist the temptation of illicit drinking after hours. *"Boys will be boys.*" Sure, it looked like he'd got away with it but what if he bumped into Laura again? Pushing his trolley around the supermarket or standing in the butchers. She only lived round the corner. How stupid was that, to do it on your own doorstep? Talk about a lucky escape. And then there was the guilt of course; the absolute, despicable shame which was not an emotion that George had ever experienced before. He and Margaret had been absolutely loyal to each other for over thirty years. She deserved better than that. Much better. He put his head in his hands. He'd been a complete bloody idiot. *"There's no fool like an old fool."*

All of the tables were set for four so George was used to sharing, in fact it was a frequent occurrence. Francorelli's had a loyal and regular customer base so it was usually busy by one o'clock. Sometimes it would be another lone diner which normally resulted in a nice quiet conversation-free meal but sometimes it was two or three people together, which meant it was loud and talkative, making George feel as though he was in the way. On many occasion he had bolted his lunch just to get away from the mindless drivel that he was forced to listen to. For some reason, today was busier than usual and it wasn't long before he was interrupted by someone wanting to sit down.

'Excuse me, do you mind if I join you?'

George looked up and saw a middle-aged man dressed in beige, casual trousers and a white, button-down collar shirt, carrying a rucksack in one hand and a map of London in the other. Obviously a tourist. His English was perfect but the accent was hard to place; East European or Scandinavian possibly. George gave him a polite smile, palming a gesture towards the two empty seats opposite him. He would have preferred a table all to himself but at least it was someone on his own.

'Turned out nice again,' said the guy pulling out a chair and sitting down.

George nodded and mumbled something in agreement, determined not to get into a conversation if he could help it.

Immediately his head dropped back into the newspaper as he pretended to concentrate on the day's news again.

'What's the form then?' asked the man, picking up the menu and studying it carefully, 'do they come to you or do I have to go and order?'

'It's counter service,' replied George, still trying to keep his responses to a minimum. Where the hell was Dino with that sandwich?

The guy pulled a face as if were unimpressed and then squinted at the specials board, trying to read it from a distance. Eventually he stood up and walked over to the counter. George flicked through the paper again and was just on the point of asking how much longer he would have to wait when suddenly Dino appeared with his lunch, accompanied by a bottle of brown sauce.

'That looks good,' said the guy returning to the table a minute or so later. He pulled out the empty chair next to the wall and put his rucksack on it before sitting down opposite George.

George nodded and gave him a smile, his mouth full of white bread, bacon and PG Tips. Some fat had dribbled down his chin, which as a result was now greasy and shining brightly under the interior lights.

The man smiled back. 'You've got some on your chin.' he said, pointing towards the offending spot.

George picked up the napkin and wiped it around his mouth. 'Thanks,' he said, before taking another bite out of the sandwich, the fat dripping onto the plate below.

'You look a picture,' laughed the guy, 'I wish I had my camera with me.'

George shrugged and went back to his paper; he was getting fed up with this. All he wanted was to be left alone and enjoy his lunch. So what if there was fat running down his chin? That was part of the enjoyment of eating a bacon sandwich wasn't it? In fact it was almost obligatory. The last thing he needed was some smartarse commentary from an interfering tourist. And anyway, what sort of tourist would come to London without a camera? The bloke must be a complete idiot.

'A shame really,' continued the man, 'it would have finished off my collection nicely. The perfect ending to a perfect montage...'

George looked up from his paper and scowled across the table. What the hell was he talking about?

'...the final close-up. All that self-indulgent gratification, dribbling down your chin as you savour the excesses of life...'

'I've had enough of this,' said George, pushing his empty plate to one side with as much contempt as he could manage. He wiped his mouth with the napkin again and then pushed his chair backwards to get up. 'Enjoy your lunch, I'm off.'

'...still, I suppose I've got enough photos of you George, one more won't make any difference.'

George suddenly stopped, half-way between sitting down and standing up, his mouth open in stunned surprise. He looked at the guy in disbelief.

'This one for instance,' said the man, leaning over to his rucksack and taking out a large white envelope, 'I have to say you take a really good picture George.' He pulled out what looked like a number of photographs and passed the top one across the table.

George sat down gingerly and looked at it, a 6" x 8" colour photo of him in front of his house, a shot clearly taken in the morning as he was leaving for work, the front door and garden path behind him. The date and time were printed in small digital letters in the bottom right-hand corner. He frowned in confusion trying to work out what the hell was going on.

'Or this one maybe,' added the guy, passing over a picture of George arriving at work, the name of the office block, Empire House, clearly visible above the large glass revolving doors. The date and time confirmed that it was taken later the same day. Suddenly the comment about a perfect montage was starting to make sense.

'What do you want?' asked George, suddenly realising this was serious.

'This one is particularly good…' continued the man, ignoring George's question and passing over another photo, this one taken outside The Red Lion later the same day. George looked at it in dismay, an unmistakeable shot of him and Laura standing outside the pub, deep in conversation.

'…although I have to say this is my favourite. I think the camera really loves you George. What do you think?'

George winced as he glanced at the next photo. It was a picture of him standing in Laura's bedroom, absolutely stark naked other than for an unbuttoned shirt, Laura kneeling in front of him in flagrante. It left nothing to the imagination. Suddenly his mind was racing, trying to keep up with a chain of events which were out of his control.

'But I think the *pièce de résistance* George has to be this one. I think they call it the "money shot" in porno…'

'I know what it's called,' interrupted George, waving away the final photo. He didn't need to look at it. He knew exactly what it was going to look like.

'What was it Wilde said? *"It was like feasting with panthers; the danger was half the excitement."* Is that what it was like for you George?'

George stared across the table and said nothing. He'd read enough about Oscar Wilde to know what the bloke was talking about. Wilde had ostensibly rented rooms as a hideaway in which he could write in peaceful seclusion from the distracting hubbub of family life in Tite Street but in reality they had served as a lair for his undisturbed assignations with grooms, telegraph boys and other renters. The illicit indulgences of a serial hedonist. The comparison was ridiculous.

'What's the matter George?' asked the guy, leaning back into his chair with the smug, self-satisfied grin of a man who had just cornered his prey. 'Lost your tongue?'

'What does she want?' asked George, cutting straight to the chase, recognising that there was no point trying to deny anything.

'What does who want?'

'Margaret. If it's a divorce just bloody well say so. There's not much I can do about it.'

The man laughed. 'This is nothing to do with Mar…' He stopped mid-sentence as his lunch suddenly appeared.

'There you go,' said Dino putting the plate and mug on the table in front of him, 'one bacon sandwich, one tea.'

'Thanks,' said the guy picking up the mug and taking a quick slurp.

'You want any sauces, mustard?'

'No. I'm fine. Just the brown sauce. Same as George.'

'You two having exactly the same then?' observed Dino, slightly bemused that someone who he thought was just a passing stranger knew George's name.

'Yeah, snap,' said George, with as much sarcasm as he could muster.

Dino wandered off and the guy started tucking into his sandwich. George sat patiently, saying nothing. He knew he didn't have any option but to sit there and wait until the guy was ready.

'Very amusing George,' said his visitor eventually, also wiping the napkin around his mouth as he finished eating. 'Very apposite in the circumstances.'

'What?'

'"Snap". Very droll. They said you had a way with words.'

George gave him a thin smile. The bloke had a way with words himself. Not many people used the word "apposite" in general conversation, at least not in Francorelli's. George leant back into his chair, trying to adopt the casual body language of someone less worried than he actually was. 'So, who are you then?'

'Who I am isn't important George. What's important is what you're going to do for me.'

'Which is what?' George folded his arms across his chest, an involuntary defensive gesture which he always adopted when he was trying to stand his ground. He didn't like being organised at the best of times. Being told what to do by a total stranger was a complete anathema to him.

'The details are in here,' replied the guy, leaning over to his rucksack and pulling out another envelope, a brown one this time. 'It's all self-explanatory.'

George took the envelope and opened it, pulling out the contents, two sheets of A4 stapled together. He scanned them quickly and raised his eyebrows in surprise. He didn't know what he was expecting but he wasn't expecting that. 'And if I don't?'

The man shrugged and said nothing. The inference was clear. As long as George cooperated, his little secret would remain exactly that.

'And afterwards?' asked George, scanning the paperwork again. 'Is that it?'

The guy nodded. 'As far as we're concerned, yes. But if I were you, I'd take some holiday and disappear for a few days. A lot of people are going to be looking for you.'

'What if something goes wrong? What if I can't do it for some reason?'

The man was already standing up, zipping up his rucksack and getting ready to leave. Suddenly he put his palms on the table and leant across it, the threat as cold and menacing as his body language. 'Failure isn't an option George. Otherwise there's only one person going to be looking for you. And that person's going to be me…'

Five

I T DIDN'T TAKE CRAVEN LONG TO REALISE THAT HE'D MADE a mistake. Driving back across London on a warm sunny afternoon was meant to be a straightforward leisurely journey but this was turning out to be a complete disaster. The Commercial Road which ran all the way from Whitechapel to Limehouse was for some reason gridlocked and he'd moved no more than five yards in the last five minutes. He slumped back in the driver's seat and rested his elbow on the open window, cursing for the umpteenth time at the lack of air-conditioning. It was one of the hottest days of the year and the heat was practically bouncing off the tarmac. Summer in the city. He closed his eyes for a second, wishing that he was somewhere else. The line of cars snaked ahead of him as far as he could see, a nose-to-tail queue of idling engines and on-off brake lights. Everyone going somewhere, no-one going anywhere.

Craven checked his watch. This was taking ages. Still, there was nothing he could do about it. Everyone was in the same position. *Time for a smoke. Be patient and maybe it will start moving in a minute.* He leant over to the glove box and suddenly his day went from bad to worse. The cigarette packet was empty. He must have smoked the last one when he walked back to the car in Muswell Hill. Immediately any good intentions about being patient went out the window. He couldn't think of anything worse than being stuck in a traffic jam and suffering from nicotine withdrawal. He quickly scanned the row of shops ahead and spotted a small newsagent's about a hundred yards up the road on the right-hand side, the tell-tale boards on the pavement advertising cold drinks and ice cream. The traffic in front started to inch forward so he made an instant decision, indicated left and pulled up on a double red line.

He crossed the road and walked the hundred yards or so towards the shop, checking as he went that he had enough change. About halfway there he noticed that there were some youths hanging around outside, looking as though they were up to no good. Summer had finally arrived and most of London was in t-shirts and shorts. These three were wearing hooded tops and what looked like woollen scarves across the front of their faces like makeshift masks. Bad luck and trouble all rolled into one. As he got nearer he tried to work out how old they were; sixteen or seventeen maybe, but these were no innocent teenagers. There was something menacing about them and they seemed agitated and pumped up, as if they were on the point of deciding whether to do something or not. Craven was no more than ten yards away when suddenly two of them burst through the front door leaving one guy standing on the door step, acting as some sort of sentry.

Craven stopped up short and looked at the guy who was standing with his back to the pavement, peering through the closed door and checking the progress of his two mates inside. In his right hand was a baseball bat which was twitching backwards and forwards, a sort of nervous, involuntary signal to anyone who might be stupid enough to get too close. Craven thought about turning back there and then; the last thing he needed was to get embroiled in some sort of urban gang war or petty street theft. There would always be another shop further along the road, probably less than a couple of minutes away. Besides, he wanted to get home and he was already late. Better to move on and not get involved. But then again, he was dying for a cigarette. And anyway, why the hell should he? He wanted one now. Easy decision then…

He walked up to the hoodie on the doorstep and gently tapped him on the shoulder. 'Excuse me mate, I want to get through.'

The kid turned around and looked at him without expression, two large, white eyes staring out from inside his hood, his nose and mouth still covered by the scarf. He said nothing but raised the baseball bat slightly, the message unequivocal. *Fuck off or you'll get this.* Then he turned back and peered through the door again.

Craven took a deep breath. He tried one last time. 'Come on sonny, get out the way. I haven't got time for this.'

The kid turned around and glared at him again, still saying nothing. He raised the baseball bat and clenched it harder this time. *You really want some of this?* Craven took a step backwards and raised both hands in surrender, palms facing outwards. 'Okay, I get the message.'

The hoodie gave him a final defiant stare and then turned back to the door. In the same instant, Craven stepped forward, lifted his right foot and then stamped down the kid's left leg, starting at the calf muscle and stomping as hard and as deep as he could down into his ankle.

The kid screamed as the searing pain literally took his breath away. In the same instant his leg gave way and his body twisted and buckled under its own weight. As he turned and collapsed on one knee Craven kicked him hard in the bollocks. Not some sort of flimsy, placed-it, penalty-kick from an overpaid Premiership footballer but a proper, old-fashioned conversion kick with all the power and follow through to send a rain-soaked rugby ball hurtling through the posts. The force of Craven's kick practically lifted the hoodie off the floor at which point he screamed again, dropped the baseball bat, and then hit the deck in a crumpled, groaning heap.

Craven looked at him in disgust. By now the kid had curled himself into the foetal position, trying to protect as much of his body as he could. In the space of a few seconds his world had literally turned upside down. One minute he was the ace; the main man with the arrogant swagger, protecting the crew. The next second he was hugging the pavement, blubbing like a girl. And then it got worse.

Craven picked up the baseball bat, flexed his body and then swung it a full 360 degrees, smacking it hard into the kid's right knee, a strike delivered with such speed and ferocity that the sound cracked and ricocheted off the pavement. The kid let out another blood-curdling scream as his kneecap shattered and the pain ran up his spinal cord and back down his leg again. Fifteen seconds and it was all over. Even if he was brave enough to try and retaliate he wasn't in a position to do anything about it. He wouldn't be able to stand properly for a couple of weeks, let alone walk. Craven kicked him again hard, just to make sure that he wasn't going anywhere and then walked up to the shop front and opened the door.

The shop was narrow and deep, a long central aisle leading to a counter at the far end. On either side, running the length of the store were shelves stacked full of biscuits and crisps and all kinds of overpriced, unhealthy junk food. In one corner was a large red refrigerator full of bottled water and fizzy drinks and in the other, a rack cluttered with newspapers and magazines. The whole place smelt damp and stank of cooked food. Craven could see the cigarettes and tobacco behind the counter. He could also see the altercation at the far end of the shop which was still in full swing.

The place was in absolute bedlam. The two hoodies were jumping up and down either side, left and right, of an Asian guy who was standing behind the counter trying to protect his till and all three of them were screaming and shouting at the top of their voices. The kid on the left was holding a large long-bladed knife which he kept jabbing towards the shopkeeper while his mate repeatedly kicked the front of the counter, both of them screaming and threatening all sorts of violence and retribution.

To his credit the Asian guy was standing his ground. From somewhere he'd found a long piece of wood which he was now brandishing in defiance, shouting back as loud as he could to demonstrate that he wouldn't give up without a fight.

None of them heard Craven walk into the shop, in fact it wasn't until he was practically standing behind the two hoodies that the guy behind the counter was the first to notice him. He suddenly stopped shouting and then all three of them stopped and stared at Craven in disbelief; a six foot, forty-year-old stranger casually standing there carrying a baseball bat. A baseball bat that two of them had seen before. The chaos and mayhem of the previous few seconds all of a sudden dissolved into stunned, frozen silence. Everyone waiting for someone else to make the first move.

Craven ignored the two hoodies and continued looking at the shopkeeper. 'Twenty Marlboro please mate.'

The guy stood motionless for a second, completely thrown by Craven's remark.

'Soft pack if you've got it.' Craven nodded towards the cigarettes on the shelves behind the shopkeeper's shoulder. *Come on mate, get a move on.*

Eventually the guy stirred and reached behind to get the cigarettes. Then he hesitated, not quite sure what to do next. He put them gingerly on top of the counter. He couldn't lean over and pass them to Craven because the two hoodies were standing between them. And Craven wasn't making any attempt to move closer to him.

Craven nodded. 'Thanks. How much is that?'

The guy shook his head. 'On the house.'

'Thanks.' *Good answer.*

'You're welcome,' replied the guy, still confused by what was going on. 'Anything else?'

Craven thumbed over his shoulder to the front of the shop. 'You could call an ambulance for the pussy on the pavement.' Then for the first time he turned slowly and looked at the hoodie on his left, still clenching the knife and staring pure hatred back at him. Craven gave him a sarcastic smile and then nodded towards the counter. 'Pass me the cigarettes, boy.'

The kid twitched and rocked back and forward on his toes, clenching the knife even harder. Craven could almost see his nostrils flaring beneath the scarf, as if he was about to explode. Either that or he was trying to decide whether to make a move or not. At the same time his mate on the right was starting to look nervous, the Mexican standoff clearly not to his liking. After a moment he turned as if to pick up the cigarette packet. Craven glanced at him and raised the baseball bat slightly, indicating to stay where he was. Then he looked at the hoodie on his left again, a long cold stare, deep into his soul. The threat was silent but it was absolute, ruthless, unequivocal. *Pass me the cigarettes or I'll rip your fucking throat out.*

The kid hesitated for a second. All his instincts, all of his feral upbringing telling him to attack. It was two against one for God's sake. And he had a blade. But there was something about Craven, something about the way he stood which unnerved him. Eventually he leant forward, picked up the packet with his left hand and then turned and offered them over. Craven leant forward, also holding out his left hand but just at the point when he was going to take the cigarettes, he let them drop and suddenly grabbed the kid's thumb, bending it inwards and pressing as hard into the joint as he could.

The effect was instant. The kid howled in absolute sheer pain and dropped to his knees, his eyeballs practically bursting out of their sockets. One pressure point and he was completely disabled, instantly dropping the knife and begging Craven to stop. Craven ignored him and pressed even harder. Then he turned to the hoodie on the right who was rooted to the spot, a look of fear and bewilderment on his face. He had never seen his mate like that before; on his knees, begging like a dog, and now he was suddenly penned in with no means of escape. Craven was in front of him blocking the aisle and the Paki was behind him, still holding the piece of four-by-two.

Craven flexed the baseball bat again. 'Pull down your hood and take off the scarf.'

The kid stood motionless, frozen in panic, not sure what to do.

Craven twisted his left hand which had the effect of twisting the left arm of the first hoodie who was still squirming under his grip, still screaming at the top of his voice. Now he was practically lying flat on the floor with his arm locked out straight, his elbow facing upwards. Craven tried again. 'Pull down your hood or I'm going to break his arm.'

Still the kid froze and didn't move. Complete terror on his face.

Craven shrugged and lifted his right leg as if to stamp down on the hoodie's elbow. The arm was about to snap in two like a matchstick and they all knew it. The kid screamed and braced himself for the excruciating pain that was coming next. Craven was just on the point of no return when suddenly the second kid shouted something and everything stopped. Then he pulled down his hood and unwound his scarf, unable to stop his hands trembling as he clutched it nervously in front of him. Craven looked at him; a long slow stare just to make sure that the kid understood that he was going to remember his face. Which was all bollocks of course. Craven couldn't tell one black kid from another. They all looked the same to him, other than this one was probably no more than fifteen or sixteen and was so terrified that he was practically wetting himself.

'Good. Now pass me the cigarettes.' Craven nodded towards the packet which was still on the floor. The kid instantly bent down and picked it up. In the space of a few seconds he had transformed from vicious thug to obedient teenager.

Craven pocketed the cigarettes and then stood to one side slightly, making just enough room to get past. 'Now piss off, before I change my mind.' The kid looked at him and hesitated for a second, reluctant to leave his mate behind but then suddenly put his hood back up and literally ran out of the shop.

Craven waited a moment and then looked at the hoodie again, still writhing in pain on the floor. He contemplated smacking him with the baseball bat, just to teach him a lesson but in the end decided that he'd had enough. Besides, there was no point in hanging around. He'd got what he came for. He turned around and looked at the newsagent, still holding the piece of wood and still in a state of shock at what had just happened. 'You okay?'

The newsagent nodded, unable to speak for a moment.

'Sure?'

He nodded again, this time smiling in gratitude. Craven had just saved his bacon.

'You should get yourself some CCTV. Or an attack dog. Or better still, both.'

'I will. Thank you.'

Craven smiled back at him, more in sympathy than anything else. Protecting your business let alone your wife and family was probably a normal occurrence in this part of London. He took one last look around the shop and then made his way back to the car, still carrying the baseball bat and smoking a cigarette as he walked. He tossed the bat onto the back seat and flicked the cigarette butt into the gutter. Then he got in the car, turned on the ignition and was about to ease back into the line of stationary traffic when his mobile suddenly burst into life. He picked it up and frowned, the screen confirming that it was a private call, number withheld. 'Hello?'

'It's me.'

'Obviously.' Craven turned off the ignition. It was a long time since he'd spoken to Buchanan, in fact he wasn't sure that he'd ever speak to him again. But the opening exchange hadn't changed in over fifteen years. No names, no pack-drill. Everything on the assumption that somebody somewhere was monitoring every word.

'Where are you?'

'London. Commercial Road.'

'Classy.'

'It has its moments.'

There was a pause at the other end as Buchanan hesitated, uncertain about how to approach the subject. Craven was never the easiest person to deal with. After Teleios he was going to be even worse. 'Still freelancing?'

'What else would I do?'

'And busy?'

'As a bee.'

Buchanan paused again. Time to get straight to the point. 'I need to talk to you.'

'We're talking now.'

'I meant in person.'

'Why?'

'Something's come up.'

'Like I said, I'm busy.'

'This is important.'

'It must be if you're ringing me.'

'Are you interested or not?'

Craven took out another cigarette, using the pause to full effect. He flipped open the lid of the Zippo lighter and thumbed the wheel in one swift movement, the smell of petrol catching his senses as it always did. He took a long drag and blew a thin stream of smoke out of the window. 'Give me a clue. What's it about?'

'Not on the phone.'

'It could be a waste of time.'

'It's triple C.'

Craven raised his eyebrows in surprise. Triple C was practically unheard of. The last thing he wanted to do was turn around and drive back into London but suddenly he was curious. In fact he was dying to know what was so important that it had prompted Buchanan to call him after all this time.

'I'm on my way home. I'll drop the car off and get the DLR back in. I should be back about four.'

'Fine. I'll meet you at four. In the Garden? Usual place?'

'No, you can come to me. Waldron Court, Number 9.'

'Where's that?'

'You'll find it. Ask for a copy of *The Conquistador*.'

Buchanan scribbled the address down. It sounded like a bookshop.

'See you later.' Craven tossed the mobile onto the passenger seat and started the car again. He didn't know what Buchanan wanted but one thing was for sure. Whatever it was, it was going to have deceit and betrayal written all over it...

Six

M AURICE DAMPIER WAS A SMALL, URGENT LITTLE MAN, A bundle of wired, nervous energy at the best of times but this afternoon he was particularly tense as he sat outside Charles Buchanan's office, anxiously waiting to be called in. He checked his watch and then tapped his feet impatiently, wondering for a moment if he had got the wrong time. Buchanan was a stickler for punctuality so it was unusual to be kept hanging around. In fact it was positively unheard of. In almost ten years Maurice could hardly remember him being late for anything, at least not by more than a couple of minutes. And that was only once in a blue moon. He checked his watch again and then fiddled nervously with the memory stick which was in his jacket pocket. Something wasn't right. The meeting was meant to be at three o'clock and it was already nearly quarter past.

Jean Pettipher looked up from her desk and stared at him over the top of her glasses, the ubiquitous half-moon spectacles balanced on the end of her nose. She took them off for a second, letting them dangle from the bright, gold chain which she wore around her neck and gave him a reassuring, sympathetic smile. 'He knows you're here Maurice. He shouldn't be long.'

Maurice shifted uneasily in his chair, trying to get comfortable without looking as though he was actually slouching. It reminded him of sitting outside the headmaster's office all those years ago, trying to straighten his tie and smooth down his hair as he waited to be questioned about some indiscretion or another. 'I could come back later if that would help?' he offered.

Jean shook her head. 'He's just on the phone. He should be finished in a minute.'

Maurice nodded in acknowledgment and fiddled with the memory stick again. Something was obviously going on. Whoever Buchanan was talking to it sounded like it was an important phone call. Something major must have kicked off which meant that it was probably connected to the surveillance footage. It was too much of a coincidence to be anything else. Everything they handled at Vector was classified but suddenly this was on another level. Not that Buchanan ever gave anything away but this was different. The security rating was unprecedented. Maurice looked at his watch again just as the door behind Jean Pettipher suddenly opened with a flourish.

'Maurice, sorry to keep you waiting,' said Buchanan, standing in the doorway. 'Come on through.'

Maurice jumped to his feet and quickly followed him into the room. As always he stood politely in front of the desk, resisting the temptation to sit down until invited to do so. Buchanan pointed towards one of the soft leather armchairs and then sat in the desk chair opposite, pulling out a grey manila file from the middle left-hand drawer, the word "Artemis" written discreetly in small letters on the front cover.

'So, how are you Maurice?'

Maurice hesitated, not sure whether this was just polite small talk or something more meaningful. He opted for the former. 'Fine, thank you Charles. You?'

Buchanan said nothing, his attention drawn back to the file which he opened slightly, carefully scanning the top document inside. Maurice leant forward and noted the name on the front cover, and also the triple C rating stamped in the bottom right-hand corner. Years of working at Vector had taught him the advantages of being able to read upside down. Frankly, these days it was the only way he got to find out what was going on. Still, that was situation normal for the likes of Maurice. Only the Landscapers, the intelligence officers closest to Buchanan were allowed into the inner circle. Plus Jean of course. Jean Pettipher had been there as long as anyone could remember and knew absolutely everything.

The word "Artemis" meant nothing to Maurice but he logged it anyway. Sooner or later he would get into a discussion with someone and then casually slip it into the conversation, as if he were privy to more information than he actually was. Invariably that was when people opened up and started to talk, comfortable in the assumption that he was already in the loop. It was like dropping a pebble in a pond and then watching the ripples unfurl. Anyway, there was no point trying to work it out now. Artemis was probably just a random word without any specific origin or meaning. Besides, it was the security rating that really intrigued him. Vector used the same four document classifications as the rest of the security services; Restricted, Confidential, Secret and Top Secret but in truth the nature of their work meant that they rarely dealt in anything that wasn't Top Secret. Virtually everything that came across Maurice's desk was classified as *"material which would cause exceptionally grave damage to national security if made publically available,"* which is why Vector had its own rating for special assignments. Maurice had only seen a triple C rating once or twice in his whole career and now suddenly there it was, stamped in red ink on the front of an innocuous looking grey file.

Eventually Buchanan looked up and stared at him across the desk. 'Have you reviewed the footage?'

'Yes,' replied Maurice, shifting uncomfortably in his seat again. He always found the leather armchairs in Buchanan's office a bit too soft for his liking. 'We've been through it in fine detail.'

Buchanan nodded. He knew what that meant. Maurice and one of his lab rats would have trawled through it in slow motion, frame by frame. Several times over probably. 'We?'

'Me and Ian Spence. No-one else has seen it.'

Buchanan nodded again. Spence had the highest security clearance. 'And?'

Maurice shrugged. 'Looks pretty straightforward to me. A standard brush pass made in broad daylight. Do you want to see it?' Maurice pulled the memory stick out of his pocket and held it up, underlining the offer to watch it there and then.

Buchanan hesitated for a moment, conscious of the time and his next appointment with Craven. 'How long is it?'

'16 minutes, 43 seconds.'

'Can we get it on a decent screen?'

'Upstairs is best.'

Buchanan closed the file again and put it back into the middle drawer, making sure that he locked it before they left. 'Right, come on then, I've got twenty minutes.'

The pair of them stood up and made their way up to one of the meeting rooms on the first floor, a smallish, rectangular room equipped with light modern furniture and a high tech screen on the far wall. Buchanan chose a chair close to the screen while Maurice closed the blinds and then sorted out the technology. It took him a couple of minutes to set everything up, finally loading the memory stick onto the computer. 'Do you want me to fast-forward it?' he asked, standing poised with the remote control in hand, 'or shall I run it from the start?'

'Let's see it from the beginning,' replied Buchanan. He had enough time to watch it all and anyway it was always good to get a feel for these things before the action started.

Maurice pressed the play button and suddenly an image appeared on screen, a slightly grainy picture of a park bench on a warm summer's day, clearly filmed at some distance, the effect of which accentuated any minor shakes so that the whole thing appeared slightly amateurish, as if shot on a cheap camcorder.

'Jesus, is this as good as they can manage?'

Maurice smiled to himself. Buchanan hadn't actually told him who had carried out the surveillance but it was obviously the Americans. Every firm had its own signature and this one was definitely CIA.

Buchanan leant forward and watched the film intently. Even without much detail he could tell that it was St. James's Park, probably shot sometime close to midday looking at the shadows. The camera was positioned a long way back, presumably using a zoom lens so the sound was almost non-existent, or what sound there was related to the vicinity close to the camera rather than to the park bench which was being filmed. There was the occasional sound of shuffling feet or rustling foliage but otherwise the footage was pretty much silent. Whoever was operating the camera had tried their hardest to get the bench as close-up as possible but clearly the lens was on its limit, there was a reasonable view of the path either side.

Maurice sat down and watched the film for what must have been the eighth or ninth time. He knew that nothing happened until about four minutes into the sequence but watched it patiently again, knowing that Buchanan wanted to see the whole thing. The park was busy, with large numbers of people scattered on the grass enjoying the warm summer's day; some reading books or newspapers, some eating lunch, but most just lying on their backs or on their stomachs, soaking up the sun. There were also a lot of people walking through the park, criss-crossing on the numerous paths which meandered from one side to the other. Some were obviously office workers using it as a shortcut between appointments as they strode through at pace, suited and booted with no time to spare. But the majority looked like tourists or locals with more time on their hands, strolling at a leisurely pace and enjoying the day.

In the distance were a number of groundsmen all dressed in the same stone coloured jeans and green polo shirts complete with local authority insignia, some tending the borders and others emptying rubbish bins and generally keeping the place tidy. Buchanan peered at the screen again, trying to see if any of them looked like CIA officers but it was impossible to tell from that distance. Nothing happened for the next couple of minutes and then just as he was thinking about asking Maurice to fast- forward everything a young guy came into shot from the left of frame and walked purposely up to the park bench and sat down, his back towards camera.

'That's the mule,' said Maurice, just to make sure that Buchanan knew who was who. Buchanan nodded but said nothing. He didn't need Maurice to tell him that. He hadn't seen Damien Ross for a long time but one thing was for sure, the guy that had just walked into view wasn't him. Buchanan kept watching the screen although there was no activity for a while. The guy sat pretty motionless on the left-hand side of the bench, other than looking up from time to time as someone walked past, obviously not sure who he was meant to be meeting. It was exactly as Tom Draper had described; just an innocent pawn recruited from a local pub, no doubt tempted by the offer to earn a few hundred quid. Cash in hand, no questions asked. Buchanan smiled to himself. The guy must have got a real shock when the Cowboys turned up, all pumped up and trigger happy.

The film rolled on for another few minutes with again, not much happening other than an endless procession of people walking past the bench, some of them couples arm in arm or deep in conversation, some with small children invariably skipping ahead or lagging behind and some on their own, walking purposefully to their next destination. Buchanan studied them all. It wasn't uncommon for couriers to walk past the target once or twice, just to check out the lie of the land but he couldn't spot anyone that looked suspicious. Besides, the camera was too far away to make out any detail. Just a collection of ordinary people living their ordinary humdrum lives.

It was after about eight minutes that another guy came into view, strolling nonchalantly from the right hand side of the frame, wearing what looked like blue jeans and a casual, lightweight jacket, carrying a folded newspaper. Almost without hesitation he made his way towards the bench and sat down on the right-hand side, as far away as possible from the guy at the other end.

Nothing unusual about that I suppose, thought Buchanan. In fact it would have been more unusual had they sat closer together. The park was full of strangers sitting as far apart as possible on the same bench. 'Is that the courier?' he asked, looking across at Maurice who had his head down, scribbling some notes onto an A4 lined pad.

Maurice looked up and nodded. 'Yes, that's him. Anyone we know?'

Buchanan shrugged and said nothing. There was no need for Maurice to know anything. In fact the fewer people that knew the better. He leant forward again, trying to see if he recognised Ross but he couldn't be sure. The long, tousled hair looked familiar but the camera was too far away and besides, too many years had gone by. He probably wouldn't recognise him now if he passed him in the street.

Ross sank back into the park bench, crossed one leg over the other and then opened the newspaper. Within seconds he appeared to be engrossed in reading, turning the pages occasionally and apparently oblivious to the guy sitting at the other end.

'The exchange is coming up now,' said Maurice after a couple of minutes, more than familiar with this section of the film.

Sure enough, having read the newspaper for about two minutes, Ross put his right hand in the inside left-hand pocket of his jacket and then pulled out a brown envelope which he placed in the middle of the bench, equidistant between himself and the other guy. The movement wasn't particularly fast but it was so smooth and precise that Buchanan almost missed it, as if he were watching a magician's sleight of hand; knowing that a trick had just been performed but not sure how it had happened.

'Just run that section again please,' he asked Maurice, studying the film intently.

Maurice duly rewound the film and they watched the sequence again. In retrospect there was nothing magical about the pass, just the accomplished finesse of someone who had spent years perfecting discreet, clandestine exchanges, probably practised in the cold grey parks of Helsinki, Vienna or Bucharest. Buchanan smiled to himself. Not unlike someone else he knew.

The guy at the other end of the bench wasn't quite so subtle. In fact not subtle at all. Almost immediately he stared at the envelope and then shot a quick glance at Ross who had returned to the newspaper, his head once again buried in the daily news. Within seconds the guy had reached over, picked up the envelope and was now walking away, exiting the scene left of frame and heading towards Birdcage Walk. Whoever was operating the camera must have had strict instructions not to follow him, the lens still fixed firmly on the park bench and on Ross.

'That's about it,' said Maurice, picking up the remote control as though it was all over, 'not much else happens after that.'

Buchanan held his hand up indicating to Maurice not to stop anything. 'Let's just run it to the end Maurice. See what happens next.'

Maurice shrugged and put the remote control back on the table. Buchanan peered at the screen again. Something else had to be going on otherwise it didn't make sense. In fact it didn't make any sense at all. Why on earth would Ross suddenly turn up in London after all these years? And why the hell would he give somebody he'd never met an empty envelope?

Ross read the paper for about another minute and then put his hand in his right-hand jacket pocket and pulled out a pack of cigarettes and a lighter. Buchanan saw the flash of blue and white and almost caught the smell of the Gitanes wafting across the screen. There were many distinctive things about Damien Ross but his love of red wine and French cigarettes was almost legendary. A product of too many years spent in Paris.

Ross smoked the cigarette which took about three or four minutes and then he stood up and stubbed it out on the gravel. Then he put the newspaper in the rubbish bin next to the bench, buttoned up his jacket and walked away, right of frame. This time the camera followed him, obviously under strict instructions to stick with him for as long as possible. The camera started to pan to the right as Ross walked along the path, heading towards the exits on The Mall. A number of people passed him coming the other way but otherwise nothing happened. Ross didn't stop to speak to anybody. He just carried on walking, becoming a smaller and smaller figure in the distance until eventually he rounded a corner and disappeared.

The camera stopped for a moment and then panned slowly left, retracing the path that Ross had just walked in reverse, until it centred back on the park bench again which was still unoccupied. The film ran for about another ten seconds and then it went blank.

'That's it,' said Maurice, pressing the stop button on the remote control. 'Like I said, just a straightforward brush pass.'

Buchanan stared at the blank screen and said nothing.

'Problem?' asked Maurice, sensing that he was trying to work something out.

Buchanan stayed silent for a moment and then gave him a tired, frustrated look. 'The envelope was empty, which must mean it was a decoy. I was rather hoping the surveillance would show us the real drop.'

Maurice raised his eyebrows. Typical bloody Buchanan. All you ever got was half a story. 'I wish you'd told me,' he said, unable to hide the irritation in his voice. 'I could have looked out for something.'

Buchanan held his hands up in apology. 'Well, it doesn't make any difference now. It's pretty obvious how they managed the exchange. The problem is it took place off-camera.' He pushed his chair backwards and then stood up. 'Thanks for your help Maurice.'

'Obvious?' asked Maurice, still in catch-up mode.

Buchanan leant over and picked up the remote. He switched the film back on and pressed the fast-forward button, trying to get to a particular point in the sequence.

'If the envelope was blank,' he said, still pressing the remote control, 'it must have been to fool the Americans which means there had to be a second drop. It could have happened as he left the park of course, once he was out of sight, but I don't think so. Look at this.' At the same moment the film on screen started up again, just at the point where Ross rounded the corner and disappeared from view. As before the camera paused for a moment and then panned slowly left, retracing the path back to the park bench where it stopped with just the final ten seconds of the film to run. Buchanan hit the pause button with the empty bench frozen in the centre of the screen.

'Notice anything?' he asked, looking at Maurice across the table.

Maurice stared at the screen and frowned, trying to see something other than just an empty bench, using his years of professional experience to spot the minutest of clues. Then it hit him. Right in the centre of the screen. Buchanan was right. It was obvious.

'The newspaper's gone,' said Maurice pointing towards the rubbish bin next to the bench. 'Two minutes ago it was sticking out the top of that bin.'

Buchanan nodded and smiled to himself. It was classic. A text-book, old-fashioned dead drop. Straight out of the cold-war operations manual. He hadn't seen something like that in years. Ross had decoyed the empty envelope to a complete stranger and all the time the real exchange was hidden in the newspaper, probably another envelope taped to the inside. While all the Cowboys were following Ross or jumping all over some poor innocent mule, all someone had to do was walk up to the bench and take the newspaper out of the bin. They must have banked on the camera following Ross and knew that they had about a minute to pick it up. Not long, but long enough.

'That's very impressive,' said Maurice looking across at Buchanan.

'Yes, it is,' said Buchanan, handing back the remote control, 'but unfortunately it doesn't really help. It doesn't tell us who picked it up.'

'Wait a minute,' said Maurice, ignoring Buchanan's intention to leave. 'There was something we spotted earlier. I just didn't think it was significant.'

Buchanan hovered by his chair, uncertain whether to sit down or not. He had a meeting with Craven and needed to get a move on. But then again, it sounded as though Maurice might be onto something.

'In theory,' continued Maurice, 'anyone could have walked up to that bin, anybody within a 360 degree radius who was about a minute away...'

'Go on.'

'...but your man passed about half a dozen people as he walked out of the park. Half a dozen people walking the other way, heading directly for the park bench.'

'So?'

Maurice had his head down, furiously scanning his notes on the A4 pad. 'So, one of the benefits of doing forensic analysis is that we took detailed notes of everyone who appeared on screen and in particular, everybody who walked past the bench, right from the point when the film began...'

'And?'

'...and one of the people who he passed on the way out, had walked past the bench about ten minutes earlier, just after the first guy had sat down. Plausible if they were going in the opposite direction, walking back to where they had come from but they were going the same way, passing the same spot in the same direction, right to left, as if they had just done a complete circuit. I didn't think anything of it before but maybe it's significant.'

'Reconnaissance, you think?'

Maurice shrugged. 'Could be.'

'Let's have a look at him,' said Buchanan, suddenly impatient to identify the suspect.

'It's a "her" actually,' replied Maurice rewinding the film for about thirty seconds. 'In fact there she is,' he added, pointing to the person frozen on screen, an attractive middle-aged woman with blonde shoulder length hair wearing a tight grey top and smart black trousers, both of which showed off her figure and made her look a lot younger.

'Anyone you know?' asked Maurice.

Buchanan shook his head. This time he wasn't playing games. But he intended to find out. *"O serpent heart hid with a flowering face! Did ever a dragon keep so fair a cave?"*

Seven

E VEN FROM A DISTANCE GEORGE COULD TELL THAT THE house was empty. He'd only seen it once before and that had been in the dark but as he walked up the garden path it was obvious that Laura, or whatever her name was, had disappeared. Not that there was any certainty that she had lived there at all of course. All sorts of explanations were now running through his mind, most of which were just too incredulous for words but then again, after the lunchtime incident at Francorelli's almost anything was possible. One minute he was living an ordinary humdrum life and the next minute he was acting like some sort of furtive criminal. He checked his watch, wondering how long he had to wait before he could go home. There was no way he could turn up unannounced at 4.00 o'clock in the afternoon. Margaret would think that there was something wrong with him, or that he'd been fired. Mind you, by tomorrow morning that was a distinct probability. Once his handiwork was in the public domain all hell was going to break loose. Still, explaining to Margaret why he had suddenly booked a few days holiday wasn't going to be that easy either. He'd just spent an hour on the train trying to think of a plausible explanation for that but had come up with absolutely nothing, or at least nothing that Margaret wouldn't see through in about ten seconds flat. He needed to come up with something good and he needed to come up with something quick.

George stepped gingerly onto the front border and pushed his nose up to the bay window, cupping his hands either side of his face to shield his eyes from the glare which was bouncing off the glass. The lounge was absolutely empty except for the pale cream carpet and the green and gold curtains which had been drawn the other night. Everything else had completely gone. Every stick of furniture, all the lamps and pictures, all the books and photo-frames had completely disappeared. George stared at the room in disbelief. Today was Wednesday and it was less than a week ago that he was sitting in that very room, quietly drinking a cup of coffee, completely oblivious to what would happen next and how his whole world would turn upside down. He stepped away from the window and then tried the front door, ringing the bell a couple of times but without any real hope that it would be answered. Then he bent down and peered through the letterbox, a few pieces of junk mail on the hall carpet confirming his worst fears. Laura Whatshername had definitely done a bunk.

George stood up again, his hands on either side of his hips as he slowly straightened his back. That was the problem with being so tall. Any bending over gave him instant backache. He was just contemplating what to do next when the front door of the house on the left, number 12, opened and the next door neighbour appeared, obviously curious about what he was up to.

'Are you looking for Richard or Sarah?' asked the woman, a typical Tenterden resident; all twinset, Waitrose and W.I.

'I'm looking for the lady who was living here last week,' said George, 'although I think her name is Laura.'

'Oh her,' replied the neighbour, unable to hide the disapproval in her voice, 'I didn't know her name, she was only here a couple of weeks...'

George looked at the woman in surprise. What sort of person lived somewhere for just a couple of weeks?

'...in fact it was more like ten days. She moved in about two weeks ago and moved out on Monday.'

George looked back at the house in disbelief, as if staring at the front door would somehow provide an answer as to what the hell was going on.

'She turned up with a van full of furniture,' continued the neighbour, 'and then ten days later it was back again, taking everything away. I've never seen anything like it.'

'I don't suppose you remember which removal firm it was?' asked George, suddenly sensing an opportunity to follow up on something.

The woman shook her head. 'It wasn't a proper removal van. It was just a large white van. I don't think it had any markings.'

George turned back and looked at the front door again, remembering his visit from the previous week. Everything was looking much more ominous and disturbing than he had ever imagined.

'Do you know where she went?' he asked.

The woman shook her head again. 'I didn't speak to her. In fact I don't think anybody did. Well, no one other than Sam of course.'

'Sam?' asked George, his interest suddenly sparked by her last comment.

'Sam the plumber. I saw his van parked outside last week. I expect she had to call him out.'

'Sam Waterman?'

'That's him. You know him then?'

George nodded. 'Yes, I'm local. Thanks for your help.'

He left the woman on the doorstep and started walking back towards the High Street. He knew Sam Waterman all right. He'd hardly forget a plumber with a name like that. He'd used him for plumbing jobs a few times but more importantly, Sam was one of the regulars at The Red Lion. George didn't know him that well but he certainly knew him well enough to ask him a few questions and possibly ask a favour.

He checked his watch again. He had a couple of hours to kill before he could go home. The Red Lion was an option of course but it was a bit early to start drinking and anyway, Sam wouldn't be in there yet. He wandered off towards the town to pass some time. Most of the shops would be open for another hour or so.

Tenterden was a small market town on the edge of the Kentish Weald, renowned for its picturesque High Street which ranked amongst the finest in the country. The broad tree-lined thoroughfare and adjacent lanes boasted a range of quirky, independent stores which allowed visitors to experience shopping as it used to be, full of antique, craft and special gift shops, all in a relaxed and welcoming environment. It even had a steam railway, a tiny museum and lots of old-fashioned tea rooms, plus of course a variety of pubs and inns and plenty of places to eat.

Like most prosperous towns in the south-east Tenterden also had a lot of estate agents, the buoyant UK market and the demand for desirable housing somehow providing enough income to support a large number of them in the same location. Most of them dealt mainly in properties to buy and sell, the core activity for any real estate firm but unusually one of them dealt exclusively in the rental market. It was located on the right hand side of the high street as George approached it from East Cross, not far from the town hall. He stood outside the window for a minute, scanning the numerous photographs, about thirty in all which filled the display from top to bottom, each one accompanied by a brief description and the monthly rental price. It took him only a few seconds to spot what he was looking for, the picture of the front of Laura's house looking exactly as it had in real life only a few minutes earlier. In the top, right-hand corner was a small triangular sticker which read "Now Let". In fact about half the properties seemed to have been snapped up. Either business was booming or Armstrong Bachelor were keeping old transactions on display to make things look busier than they really were. Either way they seemed to have cornered the market for property rental. If anyone wanted to rent something in the Tenterden area, this was clearly the place to go.

George went inside and found a small office crowded with four desks and several filing cabinets but just one person, a middle aged woman sitting inside the door on the left-hand side.

She looked up from her computer screen and gave him a forced smile, seemingly not pleased to see a late afternoon customer.

'Sorry to bother you,' said George sensing that he had called at a bad time.

Suddenly her shoulders relaxed and she gave him a warm, genuine smile. 'Sorry, my fault. Just struggling with technology.' She nodded accusingly at the computer screen on her desk and then looked back at George. 'How can I help?'

'I was interested in one of the properties you've got in your window. Bedford Close.'

The woman frowned. 'Number 14?'

'That's it.'

'It's already let I'm afraid. Was there anything else you were interested in?'

'Not really,' replied George, 'but I've just been round to look at Bedford Close and the house is empty again.'

The woman gave him a sympathetic look. 'We only let it a couple of weeks ago. I expect the new tenants haven't moved in yet.'

'I've just spoken to the next door neighbour,' said George, standing his ground, 'she said they moved in about two weeks ago and have definitely moved out again. Perhaps it was a short-term let.'

The woman frowned again and turned back to her computer screen. 'I'm sure it was a six month let.' She shuffled the mouse a few times and then pressed a number of keys on the keyboard, more out of frustration than in any hope of getting a response. 'If I could get this blasted thing to work I could check for you.'

George watched her for a second and then had an idea, 'Would you like me have a look at it for you?' he offered. 'I'm quite good with computers.'

The woman looked up at him, not quite sure what to say. Part of her knew that it was inappropriate but on the other hand she needed to get some contracts finished before she went home, which at the moment wasn't looking very likely.

'No, that's very kind of you,' she said eventually, 'I'm sure I'll be able to sort it out.'

'Honestly, it's not a problem,' replied George, trying not to push his luck too hard, 'it should only take a minute.'

The woman stared up at him again, still uncertain about whether to say yes or no when suddenly a phone on one of the other desks rang, the interruption jolting her into making a decision.

'Thank you,' she said, standing up and walking over to the other side of the office, 'that would be very kind if you could. Help yourself. I'll just take this call over here.' She picked up the phone and without sitting down took the call, all the time looking back across the room at George.

George slipped into her vacant chair and quickly opened the Task Manager and unfroze the computer. The woman continued looking at him so he frowned at the screen and pressed a few keys, pretending that he was still trying to fix things. After a couple of seconds she turned round to look at the property photos in the window behind her, still talking to the customer on the other end of the phone. 'I'm sorry, we've got a problem with our computer at the moment. Give me a second and I'll dig out the particulars from the file.' Then she put the handset on the desk and went over to one of the filing cabinets, turning her back on George to pull open one of the drawers.

George saw his chance and opened the folder marked "Properties" and then the sub-folder which was named for the current year. The files were sorted alphabetically which meant that Bedford Close was near the top. He double clicked on it and a spreadsheet opened with all the details of number 14. He thought momentarily about emailing it to his home address but instantly decided against it. The woman was pulling a file out of the drawer which meant that in a few seconds she would be picking up the phone again and probably facing back in George's direction. He didn't have time to attach the file to an email, let alone type in his own email address and then delete everything after he'd sent it.

He scanned the spreadsheet as quickly as he could. He reckoned he had about five or six seconds to spot as much information as he could. The name Laura Taylor jumped out at him and also an eleven digit mobile number. George had no idea whether the number was real or not but had just enough time to scribble it on a scrap of paper before the woman perched her backside on the desk opposite and stared across the room at him again. George closed the spreadsheet and folders and then gave her the thumbs–up as he pushed the chair back under her desk. She took another minute or so to finish the call so he waited patiently, still wanting to know how long the house had been rented for.

'Have you really fixed it?' she asked as she moved back into her seat.

George smiled at how surprised she was at him solving something so simple. It hadn't taken him a minute. In fact it hadn't taken him ten seconds.

'Thank you so much,' said the woman shuffling the mouse again to check that everything was working properly, 'Now then, let's look up Bedford Close for you.'

It took her no more than a few moments to open the folder that George had just closed and confirm that indeed, the property had been let for six months. 'With an option to extend on a rolling one month contract,' she added.

George sighed and gave her a disappointed look, as though he had really hoped that it would be available. In reality he was still trying to work out the implications of someone taking out a six month property rental knowing that they would only use it for a couple of weeks, specifically to entice him into a compromising situation. He didn't have a clue what this was all about which was a paradox really, given what they had asked him to do. He didn't really understand that either but the lengths that they had gone to were worrying. This wasn't some casual, amateurish operation. It felt like something organised, professional and all very sinister.

'Oh well,' he said, 'thanks for checking.'

'No, thank you,' replied the woman, still appreciative of his help.

George stepped outside and immediately took out the scrap of paper. He thought about ringing the phone number there and then but in the end decided against it. Much better to wait and do it once he'd thought about what he was going to say. And that was assuming it was answered of course. There was still a possibility that the number wasn't real and that the last fifteen minutes had been a complete waste of time. He tapped it into his mobile, just in case, and then wandered off towards The Red Lion. Time for a beer and some quiet reflection on the day's events. See if he could work out what the hell was going on.

'Evening Ron,' said George as he walked through the front door, looking around the bar to see who else was in. It was practically empty. The afternoon crowd had gone home and the early evening drinkers hadn't turned up yet. *Probably still at work, or on their way home.*

Ron glanced at his watch and gave him a quizzical look. 'You're early George. Half Day?'

'Something like that,' replied George, 'Has Sam been in?'

'Sam the plumber?'

George nodded.

'Not yet. Pint?'

George nodded again. There was no point waiting with a thirst. He watched as Ron carefully pulled a pint of bitter and then found himself a quiet table in the corner where he could sit and think in peace. Try and work out what his next move was going to be. He could always go to the police of course but it was probably too late for that. Besides, it would mean letting the cat out of the bag regarding his indiscretion with Laura which was not an option he wanted to consider. He shuddered as he visualised having to tell some spotty-faced adolescent copper all about it, the whole situation no doubt becoming the day's entertainment in the local police station, everyone gossiping about it in the canteen. He'd be a complete laughing stock. Mind you, that was going to be a breeze compared to Margaret finding out. George shuddered again. No, the only option was to sort it out himself. He wasn't sure how yet but it was only a matter of time. He enjoyed nothing better than a good puzzle and this was one puzzle that he was definitely going to work out.

The pub slowly filled up and eventually Sam Waterman came in and ordered his usual pint of lager, exchanging a few words with Ron before picking up his glass and wandering over to where George was sitting.

'Evening George, you alright?'

'Not bad Sam. You?'

'I'm good thanks,' replied Sam, pulling out a chair. 'Ron said you wanted a word.'

George took another swig of beer and waited for Sam to sit down and do the same.

'I'm trying to get hold of someone,' said George deciding to cut straight to the chase, 'who's proving a bit difficult to track down. I heard you did a job for them recently and might have their contact details.'

Sam frowned as he took a mouthful of lager and then settled the glass carefully into the centre of a beer mat. 'Who's that then?'

'Laura Taylor,' replied George, trying to make it sound as though it was just a routine business enquiry. 'Number 14, Bedford Close.'

Sam's face broke into a broad grin, a glint of mischievousness in his eye. 'Oh her. I heard all about you and her George. What's happened then? Has she run off with the baby?'

George tried to stop himself from blushing and fidgeted in his seat for a second, running a finger inside the collar of his shirt which was suddenly feeling tight.

'Very funny. I just need to get in contact with her, that's all.'

'Like a couple of lovebirds is what I heard,' said Sam, still grinning from ear to ear. 'Apparently you left here the other night having both had a skinful. What we all want to know George is what happened after that?!'

George fidgeted again, trying hard not to give anything away. 'Don't be ridiculous, nothing happened after that.'

'That's what you say…'

'That's because it's true.'

'…or maybe you don't remember.'

'There's nothing to remember. It was just an innocent drink.'

'So why do you want her number then?'

George stopped, his mouth open as he tried to think of an explanation. Nothing came out. Sam grinned at him from across the other side of the table, enjoying the gentle teasing. It wasn't often anyone got the chance to get one over on George.

'I promised to call her,' said George, eventually coming up with something that sounded vaguely plausible, 'with the details of a restaurant that we'd been discussing.'

'What, you promised to call her but she didn't give you her phone number?' Sam's voice was getting higher and more disbelieving by the second. And the grin was getting even wider.

'I lost it,' said George, trying to think on his feet and wishing that he'd never started the blessed conversation.

'So why don't you just pop round her house and give it to her?' replied Sam, turning the screw as he lured George closer towards checkmate. 'Figuratively speaking of course,' he added, unable to stop himself from laughing.

'I don't know where she lives,' replied George with as much righteous indignation as he could manage. 'Like I said, it was just an innocent drink.'

Sam took a sip of lager and relaxed back into his chair, the look on his face now one of smug satisfaction. 'But you just told me where she lived George. 14, Bedford Close you said.'

George gawped in silence for a second and then put his head in his hands. What a bloody mess. So much for sorting things out himself. He couldn't even hold his own with the local plumber. He looked up at Sam who was still staring at him across the table. Suddenly honesty looked like the only policy.

'She's done a bunk.'

Sam frowned. 'I thought she'd only just moved in.'

'She had. Two weeks ago.'

Sam moved his beer to one side and then leant into the middle of the table, the grin now replaced by genuine concern. 'Are you in trouble George? Look, what you do in your private life is up to you. Consenting adults and all that...'

George said nothing, not wanting to confirm or deny anything.

'...but if there's anything I can do, just ask.'

George smiled at him in appreciation. 'Thanks Sam. I just need to get in touch with her, that's all.'

Sam nodded. He didn't understand what was going on but it was obviously something serious. Time to stop mucking about. 'I had to go round there and fix the boiler. They've all had boiler problems in Bedford Close. Cowboy builders...'

George took a slurp of beer, still saying nothing.

'...but I was busy when she called so she had to leave a message on the answer phone. I had to ring her back so I've probably still got the number in the mobile.' Sam leant back into the chair as he struggled to ease the phone out of the pocket of his jeans.

'How did she pay?' asked George, instinctively knowing what the answer was going to be.

'Cash,' replied Sam, scrolling through the phone log, 'but there's nothing unusual about that these days. Here it is. Taylor, Bedford Close.'

George took the mobile and looked at the number. It was exactly the same one that Armstrong Bachelor had. 'And you called her back? It's a real number?'

'Of course it's a real number. Why wouldn't it be? Ring it if you like.'

'No thanks,' said George, handing the phone back. 'I'll do it later.'

'I'll ring it now,' offered Sam, 'just to prove it to you.'

George watched in horror as Sam pressed the dial button and put the handset to his ear. 'I'll pretend I've left something at the house, a screwdriver or something. That should...' Sam stopped mid-sentence and then frowned at the screen display. 'That's funny,' he said, 'it says "Number Discontinued".'

George said nothing but stared into the distance. Suddenly he knew that it was hopeless. There was no way that he was going to be able to contact Laura. She'd covered her tracks far too effectively for that. Which meant that he was running out of options. If he wanted to sort this out he had to do something that persuaded them to contact him, something that would flush them out. He drained the last dregs out of his glass and put it carefully on the table. Disappearing for a few days and keeping his head down was certainly tempting but suddenly he had other ideas. He was going to do the exact opposite. And he had a plan. A brilliant, audacious plan which would be like unleashing a Tsunami. *"Sometimes when fortune scowls most spitefully, she is preparing her most dazzling gifts."*

'You want another pint George?' asked Sam, picking up his empty glass.

'No thanks,' said George standing up. 'I've got things to do.'

Eight

I T TOOK BUCHANAN SEVERAL MINUTES TO FIND THE
right address, a sleazy, run down sex shop in a narrow alley
at the top end of Rupert Street, a typical seedy establishment
located deep in the heart of Soho. Buchanan had worked in
London all his life but that was exclusively in the area around
Whitehall and St James's, the safe and familiar world in which
he lived his discreet and privileged life. In fact he seldom strayed
beyond the streets of Westminster and the Royal Parks, living
his cultured existence between the flat in Pimlico and the
Greenhouse in Carlton Terrace. Soho was not somewhere that
he felt comfortable at all. As far as he was concerned it had
always been a shady underworld full of clip joints, degenerates
and organised crime. Not to mention the gay area in Old
Compton Street of course which he had only ever wandered
into by accident, or if needing to cut through from Covent
Garden to Mayfair in a hurry. It was like being on a different
planet let alone being in the same city.

He cringed as he stood outside the shop and stared at the
garish pink neon sign, advertising the name SEXUS in large,
bold letters and then looked at the window display, a collection
of DVD's, brightly coloured sex toys and cheap, tacky costumes.
In the corner of the window was a bald and faded mannequin,
all chipped and battered as though it had been recovered from a
skip, wearing what looked like a combination of imitation leather
and shiny black plastic. Buchanan stared at it in disbelief. How
anyone could find this stuff erotic was totally beyond him. It was
like dressing up in a black bin liner and a dog collar.

He walked past the shop several times, partly to make sure that there was no surveillance but mostly out of embarrassment at being seen. Only Craven could pull a stunt like this. Satisfying himself that the coast was clear he eventually took the plunge, parted the multi-coloured beads which were hanging in the doorway and then stepped inside.

If the outside of the shop was not to Buchanan's taste then the inside was even worse. He looked around the room in dismay. The interior was a dim, depressing eyesore; a gloomy, windowless room with filthy grey walls, a shiny brown floor which felt slightly sticky under foot and a pair of dull, fluorescent strip lights, one of which flickered and buzzed in the middle of the ceiling. The stock was mostly DVDs, thousands of them neatly stacked on shelves which ran the length of one wall on the left, all the way up to the counter at the far end. On the opposite wall were a number of shelves with magazines and then a hanging display and several cabinets full of sex toys and other paraphernalia; a collection of plastic, rubber and God-knows-what in a myriad of shapes and different colours. The whole place smelt of WD-40 and pizza deliveries, a sad and pathetic reality to the lure and promise of the neon advertising outside.

Buchanan looked at the guy at the far end of the room, leaning on the counter and reading what looked like a newspaper, seemingly not interested in what was going on around him. He certainly didn't seem interested in what was happening on the small television which was fixed to the wall above the counter, angled towards the front door so that all the customers could watch it. Not that they seemed particularly interested either. There were just two other people in the shop, a youngish guy in a t-shirt and jeans looking at DVDs and an older guy, suited and booted looking at magazines. Buchanan smiled to himself. It was the perfect meeting place. Nobody wanting to be seen and nobody looking at anybody else. Even if something happened no-one was going to admit to having been there.

He stared at the screen for a moment, a stick-thin teenager with improbably large breasts wearing nothing but a pair of white stilettos and a pearl necklace pounding up and down on a young male stud, his mate at the other end ensuring that her cries of ecstasy were limited to a series of choking, muffled grunts. Buchanan shuddered at the sheer vulgarity of it all, a bacchanalia of pneumatic, pumping flesh.

From a distance the guy behind the counter looked slightly ethnic although it was difficult to tell with his head bent over. He was certainly short and wiry, with dark hair and an olive complexion but that didn't really mean anything, he could have come from anywhere. Besides, Buchanan wasn't sure who ran Soho these days. Once upon a time it was the Maltese and Greek Cypriots, protecting their business interests with a mafia like regime but that was years ago, long before the East Europeans moved in and took control of everything. One of the Triads had spread its wings from Chinatown but generally they didn't venture much beyond Gerrard Street, much preferring to police their own kind. *Birds of a feather*. Buchanan decided that the guy was probably Albanian, or Turkish maybe. There was only one way to find out.

He walked up to the counter, conscious that his appearance stood out a mile; handmade suit, cutaway collar, old school tie, double cuffs with gold links. Or maybe it didn't. Perhaps they had customers like him every day of the week. He stood patiently for a moment, waiting for the guy to stir himself out of the sports page.

'Do you have a copy of *The Conquistador*?' he asked, his accent cutting through the room like a knife through butter, his neck and nostrils pointing slightly upwards at the sheer distaste of it all.

The guy looked at him for what seemed like an eternity and then nodded towards a door behind the counter. 'Upstairs, room on the left,' the accent equally cultured. More Tunbridge Wells than Tbilisi.

Buchanan raised his eyebrows in surprise and then went through the rear door and up a narrow stairwell until he reached a small landing at the top, one door on the right overlooking the back of the shop and one door on the left, overlooking the front. He opened the door on the left and immediately saw Craven sitting at a small wooden table in the centre of the room, staring intently at his mobile phone.

'Craven.'

Craven looked up and nodded towards the seat on the other side of the table, making no attempt to stand up or offer a warmer welcome.

Buchanan pulled out the chair and slowly eased himself into it, his movements deliberate and precise as they always were. The pair of them stared across the table at each other, neither saying a word for almost a full minute.

'So, how long have you been using this place?' asked Buchanan, eventually breaking the silence.

'Years,' replied Craven, closing his phone and putting it in his pocket. 'In fact I was using it when I worked for you.'

'Well, it has a certain ambience I suppose,' said Buchanan, nodding towards the television fixed to the wall in the corner of the room, the sound turned down but otherwise identical to the one downstairs. The film was showing exactly the same sequence, the extract obviously on a loop.

Craven looked at the television briefly and then shrugged. 'You get immune to it after a while.'

Buchanan raised his eyebrows again, not convinced. 'And who is the guy on the front desk. A drone?'

Craven nodded. 'Henry. Graduate entrant. They rotate them every three months.'

'To stop them getting bored presumably.'

'Or addicted.' Craven allowed himself a faint smile, the first sign of any humour.

Buchanan smiled back. Craven was the best agent he had ever had. The distance between them had gone on far too long. Time to try and repair things. 'So how's business?'

'Business is good. Too busy, mostly.' Craven touched the wooden table for luck and then as if to accentuate the point, the phone in his pocket jumped into life. He fished it out and looked at the number flashing on the screen, throwing Buchanan an apologetic glance. 'Hello?'

'Mr. Craven?'

'Speaking.'

'It's Mrs. Wallis, we met earlier today.'

'Yes. Is everything alright?'

'I just wanted to let you know that my husband called to tell me that he's going to be working late again tonight. Another late night viewing apparently.'

'Ah…'

'Exactly. I just thought you should know. In case you could check it out?'

'Of course, leave it with me.'

Craven ended the call and put the phone back in his pocket. 'Sorry about that.'

'Problem?'

'Opportunity.'

Buchanan smiled to himself. Sparring with Craven was just like old times. He put his hand inside his jacket pocket and pulled out a small piece of paper, folded into a perfect square. 'I mentioned that we have a little gardening job that we need some help with.'

'We?'

Buchanan hesitated, choosing his words carefully. 'Let's just say it's a broad coalition of common stakeholders.'

Craven cringed. The management speak was unbelievable. Maybe Deloitte had finally managed to infiltrate the security services. 'Go on.'

Buchanan leant forward and passed the piece of paper over. Craven unfolded it and looked at the contents, the address and postcode of an apartment in Knightsbridge. No other details.

'Pruning?'

'Dead-heading. Can you remember the details?'

Craven nodded, passing the paper back across the table, the protocol established and unchanged for as long as he could remember. Nothing traceable. 'So, who is it?'

'Nobody you know. Damien Ross. An ex Cowboy.'

'Ex?'

'It's a long story.'

'I'm all ears.'

'Another time.'

Craven shrugged. 'You got any ID?'

'Nothing recent. Male, five-ten, one brown eye, one blue.'

'I wasn't planning on getting that close.'

'Be creative. When can you do it?'

'Is it urgent?'

Buchanan gave him an old fashioned look. That was like asking whether the Pope was catholic. Of course it was urgent.

Craven held his hands up, acknowledging the stupidity of the question. 'I can recon tonight, finalise tomorrow.'

'Good, thanks.'

'You want me to ask him anything?'

'No.'

'Nothing at all?'

'Nothing at all.'

Craven shrugged again. 'Anything else I should know?'

'He might be under surveillance...'

'Great.'

'...some of his ex-colleagues. They might be trigger-happy.'

'Perfect.'

'So look out for yourself.'

Craven gave him a knowing smile. He always looked after himself. That was the golden rule. Rule number one. *"The skies are painted with unnumber'd sparks, they are all fire and every one doth shine, but there's but one in all doth hold his place."*

Nine

THE ABACUS ART GALLERY WAS SITUATED TOWARDS THE top end of Fielden Place, a smart narrow thoroughfare within a stone's throw of the British Museum, full of chic and trendy shops, antique dealers and an assortment of popular restaurants, bars and contemporary cafés. The whole street had a buzzy, cosmopolitan vibe and its proximity to Bloomsbury and its easy access to Soho and Covent Garden meant that it was a much coveted and fashionable address.

Craven pushed the door open and stepped inside, a small brass bell jangling above his head. He took a moment to look around the room and raised his eyebrows in surprise, a sense of déjà vu suddenly kicking in. The interior of the gallery was much like the house in North London, in fact the look and feel were almost identical; solid wood floor, crisp, white walls and large unframed canvases of contemporary, vibrant colours. Craven smiled to himself, the guy must have wondered where he was sometimes, particularly if he nodded off when the place was quiet. But maybe that was what he wanted, perhaps work was just an extension of his home life. Or maybe it was the other way round. Either way the similarities were striking. Except for one thing of course. Number 36, Orchard Drive didn't include a young, nubile art student hanging onto his every word.

Craven looked at the girl at the other end of the gallery, talking to a middle aged guy who was obviously Wallis. Even from a distance Craven could tell that she was stunning. Probably in her late teens or early twenties, petite and slim with long blonde hair and dressed in that casual, coquettish way that only teenagers or students can get away with; frayed denim jeans, a cropped white top which showed off her slender waist and bellybutton, and wearing an assortment of rings, silver bracelets and friendship bands. The guy looked up momentarily and nodded at Craven, acknowledging his presence as a potential buyer. The girl on the other hand continued talking, deep in conversation and seemingly unaware that anyone had even walked into the shop.

Craven nodded back and then started to look at the exhibits, making his way down the left hand side of the gallery, trying as much as he could to look like a genuine customer. In truth he didn't have a clue about modern art but it did occur to him that the prices looked pretty reasonable, particularly for central London. *One of the benefits of Wallis' art student strategy presumably.* After a couple of minutes he had worked his way down the left-hand wall and crossed over to the opposite side, passing Wallis and the girl who were still standing in front of a desk at the far end of the shop. Again, the guy looked up and smiled at Craven.

'Just shout if you need any help.'

Craven smiled back. 'Sure, will do.' He glanced briefly at the girl again, trying to read the body language between her and Wallis but there was nothing discernible about it. Certainly she seemed to be totally absorbed in whatever they were discussing, continually holding Wallis's gaze while she playfully twisted a strand of blonde hair but maybe she was just trying to hold his attention. Not that she needed to try too hard. Definitely another benefit of the art student strategy as far as Craven was concerned. He moved about half way up the other side of the gallery when he became aware that the girl was leaving and that Wallis had walked up behind him.

'See anything you like?'

'Oh, lots of things I like,' replied Craven turning round and nodding appreciatively around the room, 'not that I really know what I'm looking at. I'm afraid I don't know much about modern art but you've got some lovely pieces here.'

Wallis smiled and hesitated before offering the correction. The last thing he wanted to do was make a customer look stupid but in his experience people were generally interested to learn about the subject.

'Actually, strictly speaking it's contemporary art. Modern art is work produced between about 1860 and 1970. Anything after that is classified as contemporary.'

Craven smiled, picking up a round, glass bowl in front of him. 'Well, whatever it's called you've certainly got some nice stuff. I particularly like this.'

Wallis nodded approvingly. 'You've got good taste. Glass is a tricky medium, a lot of it tends to be fairly amateurish in that craft-fair sort of style or else it's mass produced without much emotion. I only stock high quality, independent work which means you get beautiful design at very affordable prices.'

'Who's it by?' asked Craven, turning the bowl over to see if there was a name on it.

'It's Moda Glass, made by a guy called Chris Walters in Somerset. You can see the craftsmanship in it and the care that's been taken. That one is a mixture of different glass; transparent, opaque, semi-transparent and iridescent, all fused together via a double firing process which gives it that fabulous eclectic but harmonious feel.'

'It's wonderful. How much is it?'

'That one is £149. That's very competitive for a unique design of that quality.'

Craven nodded slowly as if considering whether to purchase it or not. Inside he was wincing. He did actually like the piece but there was no way he could spend a hundred and fifty quid on a glass bowl. His father would have killed him. Besides, he wasn't there to buy anything. He'd only come in to find out what time they were closing.

'I'll give it some thought,' he said. 'I might pop back later. What time are you open to?'

'Six-thirty,' replied Wallis, not looking the slightest bit concerned at not closing a sale.

'Okay, I might see you later.' Craven put the bowl back on the display unit and left Wallis to it, the small brass bell jangling above his head as he walked out, exactly as it had on the way in. He crossed the road looking for somewhere he could wait until the gallery shut, somewhere with a good view of the shop-front and preferably with a seat so that he could wait in relative comfort. There were two options; a pub which was immediately opposite and a small independent café a few yards further up the road but still with a decent view of the entrance.

The Rising Sun was a typical old fashioned London boozer, a slate grey Victorian building with ornate brickwork and original engraved windows. The pub was busy but not crowded, some people sitting at tables and chairs and others congregated around the bar, an odd mix of tourists, locals and commuters on their way home. A few people, mostly smokers, were standing outside, pint in one hand, fag in the other. Craven poked his head around the door and smiled, the high ceilings and dark interior reminding him of the sort of place that his father used to drink in years ago, when all the men drank brown ale or light and bitter in the days before lager was even invented. A big old Wurlitzer jukebox sat in the corner, a huge fat sound swelling out of the speakers, filling the room with vintage chords and warm lush strings. It was like stepping back into the Fifties or Sixties. Craven glanced over at the bar and saw the familiar black and cream Guinness tap, nestled in between half a dozen pull-handles advertising a variety of real ales. It was certainly tempting but not a good idea. He had about an hour to wait and in his experience surveillance and alcohol rarely mixed, in fact they really didn't mix at all. *Another time perhaps*. Besides, whilst he could stand outside what he really wanted was somewhere he could sit down and rest his feet. It had been a long day and it was far from over.

The Granary Café, about fifteen yards up the road however was perfect. In contrast to The Rising Sun it was bright and modern, and more importantly it had a few tables and chairs scattered on the pavement outside. Craven ordered a black coffee, picked up one of the complimentary newspapers and then lit a cigarette and settled himself down for a well-deserved break, all the time keeping one eye on the gallery across the road.

After about ten minutes he took out a small digital camera and focussed it on The Abacus shop front. With maximum zoom it gave him a decent view of the door and of anyone going in and out. He wasn't sure what he was meant to be looking for but it was better to be prepared. Mrs. Wallis had been adamant that her husband was going to be late home again this evening and that she didn't believe for one moment his explanation that he was going to yet another late night viewing.

Craven drank the coffee as slowly as he could and flicked through the newspaper, trying not to get too absorbed in the news but at the same time trying to blend into the surroundings. Just another tourist enjoying a well-earned rest at the end of a busy day. A number of people stopped outside the gallery and a few went inside, presumably drawn by the window display or tempted by the competitive pricing. He fired off a few shots with the camera, just in case, but intuitively he knew that none of them were anything to worry about. Years of surveillance had given him an instinct for these things and this lot were all genuine customers, just a bunch of innocent people enjoying the buzz of Bloomsbury on a warm, summer evening.

After a further ten minutes he ordered a second coffee and lit up another cigarette, inhaling the smoke with obvious pleasure. How people could drink coffee without smoking at the same time was completely beyond him. The fact that society pilloried nicotine as an anti-social drug but happily promoted alcohol, with all its medical and social consequences was a mystery to Craven. In fact it was a paradox which made him really angry. He was just on the point of rehearsing the argument in his head again when he noticed a man and woman across the road. At first glance they looked just like any other ordinary couple but suddenly there was something about them that made him suspicious.

Everyone else had wandered up to the window and then hesitated, or taken their time before deciding whether to go in or not; the typical body language of people, particularly couples, who were window shopping. Casual, relaxed, impromptu behaviour. These two were different. The woman, an attractive looking middle-aged blonde had walked purposefully up to the front door and was now peering through the glass as if checking to see whether anyone was inside. Her partner on the other hand, a slightly older guy with a large portly frame was standing on the pavement facing the other way, scanning up and down the road as if checking to see who else was in the area. Or maybe he was looking for someone specific. Either way, it made it impossible for Craven to pick up the camera and take a photo of him, the guy was practically staring straight at him from the other side of the road. Like Billy Bunter, standing on a touchline.

Craven took another long drag on the cigarette and raised his newspaper again, managing to keep it at a height where he could just about see the front door, or at least the top half. Just enough to get by. After a few seconds he saw the door open and the head and shoulders of the blonde woman step inside, and then the door close behind her. He lowered the paper and looked at his watch, as if deciding whether to make a move or not. He had no idea whether this had anything to do with Wallis or not but something didn't feel right. And it certainly didn't look right. The round, portly guy had now moved a few yards up the road but was still obviously on lookout, checking up and down the road every few seconds and keeping a frequent eye on the gallery. Craven picked up the camera and as soon as the guy was looking the other way, took two or three quick shots, putting the camera back on the table before he turned round again.

Suddenly Craven had a dilemma. His intention was always to follow Wallis when he left the shop; see where he was going and more importantly find out whether he had arranged to meet someone else. The alternative, if somebody called to see him, was to follow them so that he could find out where they went afterwards, which hopefully would lead him to a name and address. Simple, straightforward, routine surveillance. He did it every day of the week. But now he wasn't so sure. He couldn't work out what these two had to do with Wallis having an affair but the only way to find out was to follow them as soon as they left. But all his instincts were telling him that something else was going on in the shop right now. And what he really wanted to do was go over there and find out for himself.

Craven stubbed out the cigarette and drained the last dregs from the cup of coffee. It was stone cold but the caffeine still kicked in. He decided to give it another minute. If the woman came out in the next sixty seconds he would follow her wherever that led him. If she didn't come out, he would go over and pretend that he was popping back in to look at the glass bowl.

Then he gazed across the road again and noticed that the sign hanging in the front door looked different. He couldn't actually read from that distance but it looked as though it had more letters than before, as if it read "CLOSED" rather than "OPEN". He picked up the camera and quickly zoomed in on the front door. Sure enough, someone had turned it round; presumably the woman when she went in, or possibly Wallis had done it himself. Either way something was definitely going on. Craven slid the camera into his pocket. Time to move.

As he stood up he noticed that the fat guy across the road was staring back at him, a confused frown on his face as he tried to work out why someone was taking photos of the front of the gallery. He was also holding a mobile phone to his ear, presumably warning his partner that they were being watched. Craven moved as fast as he could but before he reached the kerb the front door of the shop swung open and the woman appeared, clearly in a hurry to leave. She shot a quick glance at Billy Bunter and then looked across at Craven, their eyes locked in a cold, hard stare. Craven had the camera back in his hand and quickly took a couple of shots but without any time to properly focus or even make sure that she was in frame. Within seconds she was moving away, both her and the fat guy disappearing into the crowd of tourists. Craven stuffed the camera back into his pocket and then sprinted across the road and ran into the gallery.

At the far end of the room Wallis was slumped in his chair, not forward, face-down across his desk but backwards, with his head stretched over the back, as if he was staring up at the ceiling. Even from a distance Craven could tell that he was dead, the bright red mark around his neck and the bulging eyes confirming that he had been strangled.

Craven took a closer look at him, just to make sure that there was no chance of resuscitation but it was too late. He'd seen a lot dead people in his time and for whatever reason Wallis had suddenly joined that list. The deep red mark around his throat had all the hallmarks of a garrotte; a simple, effective method favoured by security services all over the world and one that was absolutely fatal. Providing enough pressure was applied and crucially, maintained for long enough after the victim stopped breathing, the end result was guaranteed and totally irreversible.

Craven returned to the front of the shop and locked the door. The last thing he needed was someone walking in on him bending over a dead body. Then he quickly scanned the area around Wallis, trying to see if there were any clues as to what had happened, and more importantly, why? The computer was still switched on and the desk had a few papers on it but it didn't look as if anything had been disturbed; everything looked neat and tidy and still in its place, as if the attack had taken Wallis totally by surprise. Craven stared at the computer again. Maybe the woman was standing behind Wallis, looking over his shoulder at the computer screen when she suddenly pulled out the garrotte and strangled him. No warning, no face-to-face confrontation, therefore no time to react. Just a squirming, thrashing, victim, still sitting in his chair, probably desperately trying to get his hands inside the cord and catch his breath while all the time getting weaker and weaker, slowly drowning for air. All of which meant that Wallis probably knew his attacker. He was hardly likely to let a stranger stand behind him, looking over his shoulder. Customers normally stayed the other side of the desk, even if he was showing them something on the computer. After all, he could always swivel the screen round. So who the hell was she?

Craven pulled the camera out of his pocket and switched it on, quickly flicking the switch to look at the pictures that he'd taken. The first few were of a number of different customers that had gone in and out of the gallery. The next couple were of the fat guy standing across the road, unfortunately looking away from the camera but both of them reasonable shots that would blow up nicely. The next photo was of the woman as she came out of the gallery but the speed of her movement meant that the whole picture was blurred and only part of her was in frame. Not a lot of use and not surprising given how quickly it had been taken. The next shot wasn't much better. More in focus and more towards the centre of frame but she was virtually hidden by another pedestrian walking right to left in front of her. Craven wasn't sure whether he had managed to take another photo but optimistically pressed the arrow button and then smiled as the final picture appeared on screen; a perfect shot of a blonde, middle-aged woman staring straight at the camera. Her facial expression said it all. *Who the hell are you?*

Craven studied the picture, trying to see if he recognised her but there was nothing there. Just an anonymous, attractive, middle-aged blonde. Not that he was particularly interested in middle-aged blondes but in this case there was definitely something about her that really interested him. In her right hand was a dark-blue plastic file, the see-through type with an envelope and popper closer which were popular for carrying A4 documents. He was absolutely sure that she didn't have it when she went in.

The desk had a small pedestal on the left hand side with three drawers. Craven quickly opened and closed each one in turn but there was nothing of interest in any of them, just an assortment of papers, books and stationary. Behind the desk was a small grey, metal filing cabinet with just a couple of drawers. He opened the top one which had a lot of hanging file dividers running from front to back, in each of which was a see-through plastic file, just like the one that the woman was carrying. Except in this case these were all red. Craven took one out and opened it. Inside was an A4 photograph of a painting and then some papers relating to the artist, some background notes on the painting itself and then some documents recording the original purchase by Wallis and the subsequent sale by the Gallery. In short, the full provenance on one piece of art. He put the file back and then opened the second drawer. More file dividers, in each of which were more see-through plastic files except in this drawer these were mostly green, save for a couple towards the back which were blue. Craven took out the green file from the first divider. Even without opening it he could see that it was a picture of a vase. He took out another one which had a picture of a glass bowl, just like the one he'd been looking at earlier. Wallis obviously had a neat and tidy filing system. Red for paintings, green for ceramics and glass. So what was blue?

At the back of the drawer were two dark-blue plastic files either side of an empty file divider. The penultimate file was missing and it was the only one in the whole cabinet that wasn't there. Craven took out the last file and undid the popper to look at the contents; photocopies of a series of black and white photographs, all framed in minimalist black frames. Craven didn't need to look at the notes to work out what they were. Sure, they were taken a long time ago when everyone looked very different from how they looked now but they were unmistakably photos of Mick Jagger and The Rolling Stones; previously unseen, original pictures taken over fifty years ago, capturing a rawness and naivety which was destined to quickly disappear with chart success and global popularity. Craven put the file back in the divider. It looked like Wallis also dealt in rare, valuable, photographs, although probably not that often given the number of files. Maybe an opportunistic purchase as and when something interesting came up. All part of the contemporary brand presumably. He took out the other blue file just to make sure. This time an old black and white photo of George Best sitting in a club, or a cocktail bar somewhere, London or Manchester probably, one arm draped around an attractive looking girl in a mini-skirt and the other hand cradling the obligatory glass of champagne.

Craven closed the drawer, a suction of air rushing out as he slammed it shut. And then it hit him. Not an instant, punchy, in-your-face kind of impact but the faintest wisp of something tugging at the back of his brain, a fragment of something that had been there before. He stood in silence for a second, waiting for the sliver of recognition to wash over him, the cue already dissolved into nothing. He breathed in slowly and closed his eyes. And then it came to him. *Serendipity...*

Ten

Maurice Dampier hovered by Jean Pettipher's desk as he waited for her to check the diary, the door to Buchanan's office closed firmly behind her. She clicked the mouse a couple of times and quickly scanned the screen to see his availability.

'He has a 9.30,' she said, looking up at Maurice as she took the spectacles off the end of her nose, 'and then he's back-to-back until about 4.00. Can it wait until then?'

Maurice shuffled uneasily on the spot and checked his watch. It was already 9.15. There was no way it could wait until the afternoon.

'No, not really,' he replied, 'could I see him now?'

Jean gave him a sympathetic smile. 'I don't think so. He's already running late and he needs to leave in five minutes.'

'I only need five minutes.'

'I'm sorry Maurice. He'll be reading papers for the JIC meeting. He won't want to be disturbed.'

Maurice shifted from one foot to the other again, looking more and more anxious by the second. 'It really is important, I wouldn't ask otherwise.'

Jean stared at him for a moment, trying to work out what she should do. Poor old Maurice. Everything in his mind was always urgent. There was always something that couldn't wait. Although perhaps today was different. There was definitely something about him that made her wonder. Something that for once might be serious.

'Trust me,' he said, brandishing a folded newspaper and shaking it slightly to emphasis the point, 'it's much more important that he reads this rather than some boring committee papers.'

Jean looked at him in surprise. She'd never seen Maurice look so agitated. Or so assertive. 'Wait here a second,' she said, standing up and walking over to Buchanan's office. She knocked gently on the door and then leant into it, putting her ear against the wood to listen for any response. Within moments she had disappeared, shutting the door behind her.

'You've got five minutes,' she said, reappearing about thirty seconds later and giving him an efficient smile, 'but I warn you, he's not in a good mood.'

Maurice smiled back. 'Thanks Jean. I owe you.'

Jean waved away the flattery and returned to her desk, leaving Maurice to go into Buchanan's office, the door still open. As usual he stood by the desk, waiting to be invited to sit down.

'What is it Maurice?' asked Buchanan, not bothering to look up from his papers, clearly irritated that his preparation was being disturbed.

'Have you seen the *Chronicle* today?' asked Maurice, holding up the newspaper in front of him.

Buchanan shook his head. 'No. Why, what's happened?'

Maurice put the paper on the desk, the back page folded twice so that the lower, outside quarter was face up. 'It's the crossword. Someone's trying to tell us something.'

Buchanan stared at the paper in disbelief. He thought Maurice was going to alert him to a breaking news story or some journalistic exclusive, something important that he ought to know about before his meeting with the Joint Intelligence Committee. But instead he was talking about a crossword puzzle. *What on earth is he going on about?*

'10. Across,' said Maurice. '"*Secret scramble to flight-path.*" Six letters.'

Buchanan continued staring at the paper, seeing nothing other than a grid of black and white squares, his train of thought still occupied by the security dossier that he'd just been reading; a detailed account of right-wing terrorist cells in Eastern Europe.

He looked up in frustration. 'Just get to the point Maurice, I need to go in a minute.'

'Scramble,' said Maurice, 'is crossword code for an anagram, meaning the letters are mixed up.'

Buchanan sighed in impatience. *I know what an anagram is.*

'An alternative six letter word for "secret" is "covert", an anagram of which is "vector." Vector is the flight-path of an aeroplane. It's a very clever clue. *"Secret scramble to flight-path."* Simple and complex in just four words. Very efficient.'

Buchanan stared back at the newspaper, imagining the letters filled into the first row of horizontal boxes. Maurice was right. It was a well-constructed clue. And an appreciation of crosswords was something that they both knew a lot about. In fact it was more than an appreciation, it was a fascination which had been an integral part of the culture of the security services for as long as anyone could remember. The whole organisation was steeped in tradition, a proud heritage that went back to its formation in 1919 and continued to this day, with a distinguished history that included the halcyon period of the 1940s and Bletchley Park, the forerunner to GCHQ. The ability to do crosswords was almost part of the selection process back then, a pre-requisite for any aspiring young code-breaker wanting to help the war effort. Many of the men and women who broke the apparently unbreakable Enigma code were crossword fanatics. In fact it was only a slight exaggeration to say that crosswords, and specifically the *Daily Telegraph* crossword, played a crucial role in helping Britain win the war.

In January 1942, a series of letters to the *Daily Telegraph* claimed that the paper's crossword wasn't hard enough, the assertion being that it could be solved in a matter of minutes. In response, Mr. W. A. J. Gavin, the chairman of the Eccentric Club, suggested this be put to the test and put up a £100 prize, to be donated to charity in the event that anyone could do it within an allotted time. Arthur Watson, the paper's then editor, arranged for the competition to be run in the newsroom on Fleet Street. Five people beat the twelve minute deadline, although one, the fastest, had misspelled a word and was disqualified. The puzzle was then printed in the next day's edition, 13th January 1942, so that the general public could also have a go. There the matter might have rested but unknown to the *Telegraph* and the contestants, the War Office was watching. Stanley Sedgewick, one of those who took part, received a letter several weeks later marked "Confidential" inviting him as a consequence of taking part in the *Daily Telegraph* Crossword Time Test, to make an appointment to see Colonel Nichols of the General Staff on a matter of national importance. Mr. Sedgewick, and several others who took part that day ended up working at Bletchley Park, breaking German military codes. Whether it was solving a simple cipher, or cracking something as complex as the Enigma machine, the Bletchley code-breakers were a group of unconventional thinkers, making links between letters and words that others failed to see by deploying creative, lateral thinking and pattern recognition. And crucially, also by regarding the whole process as mental combat; a personal battle of wits which involved getting to know the enemy and getting inside the mind of their opponent.

No-one was sure about the provenance of the name Vector anymore, its origin now lost in the mists of time but Buchanan felt fairly sure that somebody, one of his predecessors perhaps or maybe a long-forgotten Minister had been a crossword fanatic and had come up with the name as an anagram from the word "covert." He picked up a pen and carefully wrote the word VECTOR into the first set of blank squares, looking up at Maurice again when he had finished.

'I assume there's more?'

Maurice nodded. 'Try 16. Down. It's pretty obvious.'

Buchanan looked at the paper and read the clue; *"Greek deity in à la carte mistake."* He winced almost immediately as the answer jumped off the page, the word "Artemis" barely hidden in the middle of the sentence. Suddenly he realised why Maurice had interrupted him. All thoughts of the JIC agenda had now gone out the window. This was much more important, in fact it was an absolute crisis. Seeing the word VECTOR in a crossword wasn't on its own an issue of course but seeing it alongside the word ARTEMIS was a different matter altogether. His mind raced back to the Second World War again, this time to 1944 and to the *Daily Telegraph* crosswords which were published between 2nd May and 1st June 1944. Over a period of several weeks these contained the words Overlord, Utah, Omaha, Neptune and Mulberry, all of them code words for aspects of the D-Day landings which took place on 6 June. Overlord was the code word for the overall operation, Utah and Omaha were codenames for American landing beaches, Neptune the code for naval operations in the invasion and Mulburry the secret name assigned to the floating, pre-fab docks the invasion force would use.

The crossword setter, a teacher called Leonard Dawe, was questioned by Military Intelligence but after extensive interrogation was declared not to be a spy, the explanation being that he'd used words suggested by the schoolboys that he taught and that one of them had been taking notes from listening to American servicemen billeted near his house. Luckily, no one in Germany made the connection and the D-Day landings went ahead as planned. Bletchley Park's code-breakers played their part in misdirecting the Germans to discount Normandy as a possible landing zone but the coincidences in Leonard Dawe's explanation were just jaw-dropping and to many the whole incident remained an unsolved mystery to this day. Suddenly Buchanan was looking at something very similar, except this time the key words weren't spread over several weeks; it looked as though they were all going to appear in the same edition.

'You'd better sit down Maurice,' said Buchanan, carefully writing the word ARTEMIS into the second row of squares. Maurice eased himself into one of the soft leather armchairs just as

Jean Pettipher stuck her head around the door and tried to catch Buchanan's attention. She pointed at her watch and mouthed 'you need to go now,' trying to instil a sense of urgency in her boss.

Buchanan looked up and shook his head. There was no way that he could leave now. 'Can you ring through my apologies,' he replied, 'I'm going to be late. In fact I may not get there at all.'

Jean nodded and reversed out of the room, wondering what on earth Maurice had said. She'd seen all sorts of crises and emergencies over the years but she'd never known Buchanan miss a JIC meeting before, certainly not at short notice.

'Have you filled it all in?' asked Buchanan, turning back to Maurice and looking at the paper again.

'Almost,' replied Maurice. 'We've worked out about half the clues but should have it finished shortly.'

Buchanan smiled to himself. Most people in the department were extremely bright but the analysts that worked for Maurice were an arrogant bunch who definitely thought they were a cut above the rest. Completing a cryptic crossword was something that they would want to use to prove their intellectual superiority so it was guaranteed they'd be trying to solve it as quickly as possible. And crosswords were still the ultimate challenge. A computer could solve a Sudoku puzzle within seconds but a cryptic crossword could only be cracked by a combination of intelligence, lateral thinking and human ingenuity.

'We think the whole thing has been compiled for a purpose,' continued Maurice. 'Most of the answers reference this department and its operations.'

'Most?'

'There are a few which we don't understand.'

'Show me,' said Buchanan, twisting the paper ninety degrees so that they could both look at it sideways.

'Well, this one for example,' replied Maurice, leaning forward and pointing to one of the columns at the top of the grid. ' *"This Scottish region without the C word."* Four letters.'

Buchanan stared at the page, trying but failing to make any sense of the clue. All cryptic crosswords were constructed on traditional rigid rules known as Ximenean, after the great Observer crossword setter Ximenes but it still required an empathy with the compiler. Buchanan couldn't get on the same wavelength as this guy at all.

'The word "*This*",' replied Maurice, feeling slightly superior that his boss found it so difficult, 'refers to the crossword. So "*This without the C Word*" is simply the word "*Ross*", which is the name of a Scottish region. We just don't know what the connection is. Unless it's just a random word of course.'

Buchanan stared at the page, his mind racing. It wasn't random at all. Maurice was right. Someone was trying to tell them something. The question was, who and more importantly, why? And how the hell did they know about Vector and Artemis and Damien Ross? At the moment Buchanan didn't have an answer to that but it was clearly a message. He needed to find out what was going on as a matter of urgency. It was ironic really. Suddenly he had his own puzzle to work out.

'Does the word "*Ross*" mean anything to you?' asked Maurice, noticing that it had triggered some sort of reaction.'

Buchanan looked up from the paper and stared into the middle distance, trying to decide whether to tell Maurice or not. He wanted to keep Ross's identity secret, certainly to restrict it to as few people as possible but he couldn't really conceal it from Maurice anymore. It was time to bring him up to speed.

'He was an agent who worked on Artemis.'

'One of ours?'

'CIA. He disappeared about ten years ago.'

'Disappeared?'

'Exactly that. One minute he was one of their brightest stars, the next minute he'd completely vanished.'

'Defected?'

Buchanan shook his head. 'That's what we thought. There was a sighting in Moscow after he left but beyond that absolutely nothing. Complete radio silence. After a couple of years we assumed he was dead.'

Maurice nodded his head up and down slowly, wondering whether there was any connection between Ross and the surveillance footage from the Garden. He didn't know of course but it didn't stop him trying to work it out.

'Do we know who the compiler is?' asked Buchanan, suddenly clear about what their next move should be.

'They all work under pseudonyms,' replied Maurice. 'The *Chronicle* has two. One called Credo and one called Xerxes. This was compiled by Xerxes.'

'Xerxes?'

Maurice shrugged. 'A lot of them like their names to begin with a cross. It's kind of traditional.'

'And Credo?'

'An anagram of Coder, presumably.'

Buchanan nodded. It was obvious really. 'And Xerxes. Do we know his real name?'

Maurice checked the notes that he had with him. 'George Wiggins. He's been there about fifteen years.'

Buchanan almost burst out laughing. No wonder the guy had changed his name to Xerxes. George Wiggins wasn't exactly the most cosmopolitan moniker for a crossword compiler. He sounded more like a butcher, or a general builder. 'Well, we'd better get round there and pay him a visit. Find out what the hell's been going on.'

'I called them earlier. He's disappeared for a few days. He booked some last-minute holiday yesterday.'

Buchanan raised his eyebrows. That was pretty much confirmation that the guy was implicated. 'Well, I'll get someone onto it.' He slid the paper across the desk. 'Thanks Maurice. Let me know as soon as you've finished it.'

Maurice stood up, taking his cue to leave, just as Jean poked her head around the door again.

'A present from one of your team,' she said, looking at Maurice and handing over another copy of the newspaper, the completed crossword clearly visible on the back page. Maurice passed it straight over to Buchanan who quickly scanned the answers to see if they included some of the words that he was most worried about. It was worse than he thought. They were all there, plus some others that he hadn't thought even possible. It was absolute dynamite.

'Oh, and a message,' continued Jean. 'You were after a Mr. Wiggins who's gone on leave for a few days? Apparently he's just turned up at work.'

Eleven

Unlike its competitors, the *Chronicle* had remained true to its heritage, resisting the temptation to move to Wapping or some other low cost, high production facility, much preferring to trade off its reputation as the last remaining national newspaper still publishing from its historic location in Fleet Street. A strategy which was proving to have some success, the paper enjoying a recent resurgence in circulation and the great British public as always a champion for the underdog, particularly one that stuck to traditional, commercial values. And Vinny Goldman, editor for the last ten years was also the last of a dying breed; a larger than life character with a huge, imposing frame and personality to match, in fact something of a legend in the UK newspaper industry where he was feared and respected in equal measure.

Vinny had joined the *Chronicle* nearly forty years ago as a junior clerk, a sixteen year old tearaway from Bermondsey without a single qualification to his name but with a streetwise determination to succeed which was second to none. Over the next thirty years he worked his way up the organisation and gradually took control of every part of the firm, conquering the news desk, then the print unions and then finally the boardroom with a combination of unwavering self-belief, ruthless ambition and sheer bloody hard work.

Vinny's appearance, a combination of loud striped shirts, bright red braces and classic, polka-dot ties was straight out of the 1980s, a style which he had worn unchanged for as long as anyone could remember. In many respects he enjoyed the impact that his sartorial choice conveyed, complementing perfectly his reputation as a brash and intimidating workaholic, a persona that he was more than happy to promote. Amongst his contemporaries, the chalk pinstripe suit, the chunky gold rings and the fat, unlit cigar clutched permanently in his right hand became synonymous with Vinny's status and achievement as the King of Fleet Street; the last great personality in a long line of newspaper magnates.

Vinny's office was on the first floor of Empire House, a large rectangular room occupying the south-west corner with windows on either side and glass partitions into the open plan office so that he could keep an eye on everything. To say that Vinny's management style was autocratic and old fashioned was something of an understatement. He knew all about delegation of course, and "management by objectives" and all that other namby-pamby motivational theory but as far as he was concerned the only way to run a business properly was to know exactly what everyone was up to and to personally make as many decisions as possible.

Vinny eased himself back into his chair and smiled with satisfaction at the morning's front page, the headline *Lotto Layabout Loses Millions* summing up perfectly the story of a young, working class lottery millionaire who in the space of nine months had managed to squander the lot on gambling, drunken parties, expensive cars and even more expensive women. That was the sort of news that the great British public wanted to read about, a bit of unashamed Schadenfreude, not some depressing story about war or famine in parts of the world that nobody really cared about. He flicked through the pages, checking for any news stories on his favourite themes; illegal immigrants, gypsies, dole cheats, and of course, lazy good-for-nothing obese people who were getting free weight-reduction surgery on the NHS, all courtesy of the hardworking tax payer. Vinny wanted to see at least one news item from one of those categories in every edition and all the journalists and editorial staff knew they were expected to deliver on that. He quickly scanned the sports pages and then tossed the paper into the waste bin beside his desk. Last night's edition was good copy but it looked like today was going to be a quiet day for news. Still, something was bound to turn up. It normally did.

Vinny was just musing on what editorial items they might have to pull from the reserve bin when Bob Thompson, his sub-editor and one of his most loyal and trusted employees walked in, his shirts sleeves rolled up and his top button and tie undone as they always were. Vinny looked up and gave him an efficient smile.

'Bob. What's happening? Anything on Brighton yet?'

Bob shook his head. The Tory conference was in full swing but there was nothing out of the ordinary to report. The *Chronicle* would run a double page spread on the key speeches but otherwise it was all pretty dull.

Vinny looked at him in disappointment. 'What, not at least one MP shagging his researcher or fiddling his expenses?'

Bob smiled. 'Oh, there's plenty of that going on but I thought you were interested in news.'

Vinny gave him a knowing look and then stared out the window, the skyline of the West End in the distance. Something needed to break, otherwise they'd have to re-run some old article about the latest fad in diets or fitness regimes.

'About the only interesting thing this morning,' continued Bob, 'is some mysterious caller wanting to come over and speak to George. Some sort of government official...'

'George?'

'...at least I think that's what they said, I'm not absolutely sure.'

'George who?'

'George Wiggins.'

'Wiggy?'

'Yeah. Apparently someone over at Whitehall wants to speak to him.'

Vinny shrugged. 'Well, they're out of luck, George is on leave.'

'He was. He came in this morning.'

Vinny looked across at Bob, his journalistic brain suddenly kicking into gear. That was the trouble with Bob. He was good at his job but he was a production man at heart. He just didn't have the DNA of a proper hack. Vinny on the other hand had a journalist's instincts coursing through every fibre of his body, a product of having spent over forty years sniffing out stories that all of his competitors had missed. Already he was processing the fact that some faceless bureaucrat wanted to see George, and that George had suddenly turned up at work on the first day of his holiday. The chances of those two events not being connected had to be pretty remote.

'Where's he live?' asked Vinny.

'George? Kent I think. Not sure where.'

'Not round the corner though? It's not like he can just pop into the office when he feels like it?'

Bob shook his head. 'No. I'm sure he has a long commute.'

Vinny turned round and looked out the window again, trying to work out whether this was something or nothing. 'So why do they want to speak to him?'

Bob shrugged. 'Dunno. One of the girls on reception took the call. Hayley, I think.'

Vinny continued staring out the window, the sun-glistened office blocks signalling another hot, summer's day. 'Right. Well let's get her up here. Find out what's going on.'

Bob disappeared, returning a couple of minutes later with a young, nervous looking girl in her early twenties, clutching a lined notepad and pen. Given her age she was surprisingly old-fashioned, dressed in plain, dowdy clothes which gave her a shapeless and mousey appearance.

Vinny looked up and gave her an encouraging smile. 'Hello Hayley, how are you luv?'

Hayley gave him a hesitant smile back, still uncertain as to why she'd been summoned. Not many people at her level got called into Vinny's office. Not unless they were in trouble. 'Fine thanks Mr. Goldman.'

'And how's your Mum? Still dancing?' Vinny prided himself on knowing all of his staff. Hayley had only worked at the *Chronicle* a short while but her mother had worked there for over thirty-five years, in fact right up until her retirement a couple of years ago. Maureen had a passion for ballroom dancing which was the love of her life.

Hayley's face eased into a more natural smile. 'Always dancing. Off to Blackpool next week.'

Vinny smiled back. 'Good, good. Now tell us about this call you took this morning. Someone wanting to speak to George.'

Hayley's body language relaxed as she realised why she'd been called in. She quickly glanced at her notepad and turned the top page over.

'I took the call just after I got in, about 8.45 I think. The man said he was ringing from the Department of Work and Pensions and wanted to speak to whoever compiled our crosswords.'

'He didn't ask for George by name then?' asked Vinny, instantly sensing that something wasn't right.

'No. I told him that we had two people and he said he wanted to speak to the one that used the name Xerxes. I gave him George's name but told him that he wasn't in.'

'And what happened after that?' asked Vinny.

'Nothing. He rang off.'

'Did he leave a name or number?'

Hayley suddenly blushed, her cheeks instantly turning bright red.' Sorry Mr Goldman. He did leave a name but I didn't write it down...'

Vinny raised his eyebrows.

'...it all happened so quick. He did leave a number though. So when George came in I rang it back to let them know. I also told George and gave him the number as well.'

'And what happened when you rang them back?'

'Nothing really. A woman answered so I just left a message with her.'

Vinny looked across at Bob and exchanged a knowing glance. If the call was genuine then someone from the Department of Work and Pensions would have known George's name. The whole thing didn't make sense. This was nothing to do with George's employment or pension. It sounded like it was something to do with George being a crossword compiler. And specifically, the compiler called Xerxes.

'Maybe they like his work,' said Bob, reading Vinny's mind, 'and want him to do something for their house magazine.'

Vinny gave Bob a withering look which conveyed more than words could ever say. As explanations went it was absolutely pitiful. He turned back to look at Hayley whose face was starting to look less red. 'And have you still got the number?'

Hayley nodded and circled the number on her notepad, tearing it off and passing it over to Vinny.

'Thanks,' said Vinny, indicating that she could go. 'Oh, by the way, what did George say?'

Hayley turned around, halfway through the door. 'Nothing really, he just shrugged. He looked a bit...I don't know...preoccupied.'

Vinny looked back at Bob as Hayley made her exit, the question unspoken but the body language clear enough.

Bob shrugged again. 'I don't know. Maybe he hasn't paid his pension contributions.'

Vinny gave him another scathing look and then bent down and fished the paper out of the waste paper bin. Every bone in his body was telling him that this had nothing to do with George's pension. Or his employment for that matter. Vinny looked at the crossword on the back page but it meant absolutely nothing to him. He disliked cryptic crosswords. He always had done. He couldn't think of anything more meaningless than trying to work out the twisted, convoluted way that someone else's brain worked. Well nothing except for jigsaw puzzles of course. Spending hours on end putting something together in order to make a picture that somebody else had deliberately cut up beforehand was about as moronic an activity as he could think of. But crosswords weren't much better. Everything he hated about them was now staring up at him from the back page of his own paper. An empty grid of black and white squares and a list of impossible, unintelligible clues.

'Why don't we just ask George?' suggested Bob. 'He must know what's going on.'

Vinny practically snorted in derision. 'George? George has been a compiler for as long as I can remember. His whole life is a bloody puzzle. I haven't had a straight answer out of George in years...'

Bob smiled to himself. That much was certainly true. No-one could ever accuse George of being an open book.

'...no, let's ring this number first and find out who's at the other end.'

Vinny picked up the telephone and pressed the numbers into the keypad, his fat fingers stabbing each button with determination. The call was answered within seconds.

'Jean Pettipher.'

'Oh, good morning,' said Vinny, putting on his poshest voice, 'who am I speaking to please?'

'Jean Pettipher,' replied Jean, 'can I help you?'

'I meant, which department am I speaking to?' said Vinny, trying to get straight to the point.

'Which department are you after?' replied Jean, her response smooth and unruffled. She'd played this game many times before.

'I'm not sure,' replied Vinny, deciding that honesty was the best policy. 'Somebody on this number rang here this morning wanting to speak to a member of my staff. I just wanted to confirm that it was a genuine call.'

'And you are?'

'Vincent Goldman. Editor at the *Chronicle*.'

Bob smiled to himself again. Vinny always puffed his chest out when he introduced himself as the boss. *Working class boy done good.* His mother must have been proud of him.

'That would be Mr Dampier,' said Jean. 'Would you like me to put you through?'

'Yeah, why not.' Vinny's accent slipped back to its Bermondsey origins, the East End vowels lurking somewhere in the bottom of his throat.

'Hold a second please,' replied Jean, her voice still purring with effortless efficiency, 'I'll just check for you.'

The phone went silent for a few moments and Vinny stared across the desk at Bob, his body language conveying that he'd been put on hold.

'I'm afraid Mr Dampier is not available at the moment,' said Jean, suddenly back on the line, 'Can I take a message for you?'

'Not really,' replied Vinny, unable to hide the irritation in his voice. 'I'm just trying to establish who he works for.'

'Mr Dampier is an associate. He's not affiliated to any particular department.'

'What the hell does that mean?' said Vinny, starting to lose his patience.

'It means that he's an associate,' replied Jean, her response still calm and measured. 'Which means he's not affiliated to any particular department.'

'Are you deliberately trying to be obtuse?'

'Not at all Mr. Goldman. I'm being extremely clear.'

'Perhaps I can have your address then,' said Vinny, deciding to try a different approach.

'Of course. P.O. Box 4176, Whitehall, London...'

'I meant your office address,' interrupted Vinny, finally losing his temper and any sense of decorum, 'not your postal address. I want to know what department you work for, not where to send a fucking letter!'

The phone went silent at the other end. Jean Pettipher took a deep breath, her professionalism overriding any natural instinct to react. At the same moment, Hayley poked her head nervously around the door and passed Bob a piece of paper, another sheet of lined notepad, this time folded in half. She reversed out of the room as Bob unfolded it and quickly read the message. *"George has just gone. Back on holiday."*

'Mr Dampier is not available,' replied Jean, her voice firm and authoritative. 'You can leave a message for him, or you can call back later. Alternatively, one of his colleagues is on his way to your offices to see Mr. Wiggins. You can ask him if you prefer.'

'Don't worry, I will.' said Vinny, still irritated by her tone. 'What's his name and when's he coming.'

'His name is Craven,' replied Jean, 'he should be with you later this morning.'

'Good. Well you can tell your Mr. Craven that I'll be waiting for him and that if he wants to speak to a member of my staff he'll need to deal with me first. And I expect him to cut all this bureaucratic crap and provide some straight, bloody answers!'

Jean smiled to herself at the other end of the phone. 'Of course, I'll let him know. I'm sure you'll find him very responsive.'

George pushed through the revolving door and walked down the steps to the front pavement, the difference in temperature between the air-conditioned building and the heat outside hitting him as if he'd opened an oven door. Today was going to be another scorcher, the long, hot summer showing no signs of abating. As usual, the traffic on Fleet Street was clogged in both directions, a seemingly endless line of cars crawling east to west from St Paul's to Trafalgar Square, and exactly the same back the other way.

George checked his watch. It was nearly ten o'clock. Time that he was out of there. He didn't know how long it would take before someone reacted to the crossword but he assumed it would be fairly quick. There was no point in hanging around. He didn't have a clue what any of this was all about but he intended to find out, and that meant he needed some time and space to do some proper research; some good old-fashioned journalistic digging. The sort of stuff he used to do all those years ago before he was side-lined into features and then into crosswords. In fact the sort of work that once upon a time he really enjoyed and was really good at. Proper investigative journalism.

George took the rucksack off his shoulder and fished out the map. There was no point in getting a taxi or waiting for a bus, the traffic was solid in both directions. Quicker to walk, particularly with his long stride. Or at least part of the way. He slung the rucksack back over his right shoulder and took the phone out of his pocket. He checked to see whether there were any messages and then switched it off. The last thing he wanted was for anyone to trace him until this was over. Well, nobody except those that he wanted to find him. George didn't know who they were, or how many were involved in whatever was going on. But one thing was certain. By tomorrow morning all hell was going to break loose. Everybody was going to be looking for him... *"Tis slander, whose edge is sharper than the sword, whose tongue outvenoms all the worms of Nile, whose breath rides on the posting winds and doth belie all corners of the world..."*

Twelve

CRAVEN STOOD OUTSIDE THE FRONT DOOR AND PAUSED for a moment before ringing the bell. Despite all of his experience in covert operations, often in life and death situations, suddenly a conversation with a middle-aged woman in English suburbia seemed daunting in comparison. Much scarier than meeting some shadowy contact in a cold, grey square in Bucharest, unsure about which side they were really working for and always at risk that they would suddenly blow his cover or pull out a revolver. That was a walk in the park compared to what he was about to do next. He took a deep breath, pressed the bell and waited for what seemed like an eternity before the door opened.

The woman who eventually appeared looked like Mrs. Wallis but was a slightly younger version. The similarities in appearance, particularly the ordinariness were striking. *Obviously a relative, Probably a sister.* She gave Craven a brief, enquiring smile as she held the door ajar, half open but ready to close it at any moment.

'I'm sorry to bother you,' said Craven, 'could I speak to Mrs. Wallis?'

The woman shook her head without hesitation. 'I'm sorry, she's not available.' Already the door was starting to close.

Craven put his hand up, trying to stop her from actually shutting it in his face. He thought momentarily about sticking his foot in the door but decided that was probably too aggressive. Much better to explain why he was there.

'It's really important,' he continued, 'it's in connection with her husband...'

The woman stopped and eyed him suspiciously, trying to decide whether to continue the conversation or not. For all she knew he could be one of those gutter journalists, snooping around trying to get an exclusive.

'...I met Mrs. Wallis yesterday. It will only take five minutes.'

'It's not a good day,' she said curtly, opting for as few words as possible.

Craven put his hand up again. 'I know. I was at the gallery yesterday. It was me who called the police.'

The woman looked taken aback for a second but continued staring at him, still trying to decide whether to let him in.

'If you could tell her it's Mr. Craven. I'm sure she will want to see me.'

'Craven?'

'Yes. I was here yesterday.'

'Wait there a second.'

Craven waited patiently while she disappeared down the hall, the muffled conversation giving no clue as to what they were saying. She returned about a minute later and pulled the door back, stepping aside to let him in.

'Five minutes Mr. Craven. She's not in good shape.'

'Of course,' replied Craven stepping over the threshold. 'I just need a quick word.'

'Quick would be good. I'm Penny by the way. Fiona's sister.'

Craven nodded in acknowledgement and then followed her into the living room, the crisp white walls and the minimalist decor somehow feeling less homely that it had the day before. Fiona Wallis was perched on the end of one of the white leather sofas, her body shrunk into a huddled V shape, her wrists resting on her knees and her hands clutching a ubiquitous, crumpled tissue. She looked up momentarily and gave him a weak smile, her eyes red and sore from a sleepless night of crying and howling at the world. Craven looked at her, unsure about what to say. What on earth did people do in circumstances like this that had any real meaning. He'd only met her once and hardly knew her husband at all. Any condolences were just going to sound like platitudes.

'Would you like some coffee Mr. Craven?' asked the sister, sensing that someone needed to break the ice.

'No, I'm fine thank you,' replied Craven, grateful for the opportunity to say something but not wanting her to leave the room. He didn't fancy speaking to Mrs. Wallis on her own. Besides, he wasn't planning on staying that long.

He walked over and sat down on the other end of the same sofa, turning his body to face her. He paused for a moment, making sure that she was composed before offering his condolences but the words tailed off into nothing. There wasn't really anything meaningful he could say.

Fiona Wallis looked up and gave him another weak smile, the tears still welling up in her eyes. 'And to think yesterday I was worried that he was seeing someone else. I'd let him see whoever he wanted to if I could just have him back.' And then she burst into tears again, the sobbing becoming uncontrollable for several minutes.

Craven looked awkwardly around the room, the only thing he could think of rather than stare at a grieving widow; a woman whose whole world had turned upside down but was desperately trying to hold it together. Suddenly the fabulous art hanging on the walls looked more like a shrine than a collection. Penny knelt down in front of her sister, clasping her hands and trying to give what comfort she could.

'I understand it was you who called the police?' said Fiona Wallis, eventually managing to compose herself again.

'I went to the gallery,' replied Craven, 'just to check everything out.'

'And it was you who found him?'

'Yes. But I was there earlier in the afternoon. That's what I wanted to tell you…'

Fiona Wallis turned and looked at him, the frown indicating that she didn't understand what was going on.

'...I saw him about half an hour earlier and he looked absolutely fine. I wanted to let you know that I don't think your husband was having an affair.'

'It's a bit late for that Mr. Craven,' interrupted the sister, 'I don't think any of that really matters now.'

Craven saw the flash of anger in Fiona Wallis's eyes, the words spoken through clenched teeth and her body suddenly shaking with a new found energy. 'It might not matter to you Penny but he was my husband and it means a great deal to me. In fact it means absolutely everything right now!'

'I know it's no consolation,' continued Craven, 'but I don't think your husband was having an affair. I think the late nights were connected to something that he was buying, or maybe selling and that he was killed in connection with a business transaction. I think the perfume belongs to someone he was dealing with.'

'Hopefully not what the police think he was dealing,' interrupted Penny, looking across at her sister with concern.

'The police?' It was Craven's turn to frown and look confused.

'Drugs,' explained Penny. 'The police said it was drugs related.'

'Don't be absurd!' exclaimed Fiona Wallis, losing her temper again. 'David would never have anything to do with drugs.'

Craven frowned even harder. 'Drugs? Are you sure?'

Penny shrugged. 'We can't believe it either. Apparently his pockets were stuffed full of cash. And several packets of white powder. Cocaine they think.'

'It's ridiculous,' continued Fiona Wallis. 'Absolutely ridiculous! David didn't even like taking Paracetamol. What do you think Mr. Craven? Did you notice anything?'

Craven was barely listening to her. It was the oldest trick in the book. Eliminate a target and then stuff their pockets full of cash and narcotics to make it look as though it was drugs related. Give the local woodentops something easy to work with and deflect them from looking for the real motive. How on earth they could fall for it was completely beyond him. Anyone who knew anything about the drugs world knew that a body, dead or alive, got stripped of anything of value within seconds. Cash and powder were the only real currency on the streets and nobody with half a brain cell was going to give up the opportunity to make a profit. Dog eat dog. He looked across at Fiona Wallis, looking back at him, hoping for some words of comfort. He gave her a sympathetic smile, uncertain about what to say. This was none of his business. The job that he'd been hired to do had suddenly collapsed and the last thing he needed was to get involved in something the police were crawling all over. Besides, he was already behind schedule on the assignment that Buchanan had given him and now there was another one to follow up on. Suddenly he needed to get over to Fleet Street as quickly as possible. Craven checked his watch. He'd only come over to give Mrs. Wallis some words of comfort about her husband and he was already beginning to regret that. Time he was going.

'I'm sure the police will work it out,' he said, standing up and making it clear that he was about to leave.

Fiona Wallis looked up at him, her face crestfallen in disappointment. All her intuition told her that he didn't believe it either. She really wanted to try and persuade him to stay but she didn't have the strength. She let out a long, defeated sigh. 'Well thank you for coming Mr Craven. That was very kind of you.'

Craven looked back at her, something in her demeanour stopping him from simply walking out. One minute she thought her husband was having an affair, the next minute he was being accused of being a drug dealer, neither of which were probably true. She was never going to get him back but her prospects of clearing his name also looked pretty slim. Whatever future they had planned together had been cruelly taken away but at least she deserved the chance to know the truth. If he left now that wasn't going to happen. The police had a body, enough evidence to fill a charge sheet and a long list of low-life suspects that they were just waiting to convict. Cue impressive increase in crime statistics and less dross on the streets.

'I'll see you out,' said Penny, also standing up.

'Did your husband ever deal in photographs?' asked Craven, suddenly changing his mind.

'Sometimes,' replied Fiona Wallis, looking up at him expectantly. 'Not very often but occasionally if something interesting came up. Why?'

'And I suppose the police have taken his computer and all his records?'

Fiona Wallis nodded, still not sure where the conversation was going. 'They took his laptop from the gallery last night and all his books and accounts...'

'That's a pity.'

'...although David was very particular about his admin. He backed-up everything just in case there was a problem. It's all on a separate hard drive.'

'And is that at the gallery?'

'No, it's in his office.'

'Office?'

Fiona Wallis swivelled round and pointed to the wall behind her. 'His study really. It's next door...'

Being a commuter for most of his life, George was very familiar with London railway stations but unfortunately Paddington wasn't one of them. Cannon Street, Charing Cross, and to a lesser extent Blackfriars had all been regular destinations for him over the years but Paddington wasn't a station that he really knew at all. Built in the first half of the nineteenth century and designed by Isambard Kingdom Brunel the site had been the London terminus for the Great Western Railway and it's successors since 1838. Today it provided the majority of commuter and regional services to west London, the Thames Valley region and long-distance intercity services to south west England and south Wales. It was also the

London terminus for connecting services to London Heathrow Airport which meant there was a constant flow of passengers back and forth as well as the usual rush of commuters at either end of the day.

George stood on the concourse and stared at the departure boards in front of him, trying to work out which platform his train went from. The journey across London had taken longer than he had planned, a combination of too many tourists clogging up the Underground and George not being exactly sure where he was going. All of which meant that he was running late. And he still needed to buy a ticket and then find a newsagent to get a newspaper. He quickly scanned the schedules across platforms 1 to 12, advertising services to major destinations such as Bristol, Cardiff and Plymouth. Eventually he spotted what he was looking for; the 11.20 to Great Malvern, leaving from Platform 7.

If locating the correct platform was complicated, buying a ticket was even worse. The queue for the ticket office was long and slow so George reluctantly decided to use one of the ticket machines, a confusing algorithm of unclear prompts and complex options. By the time he had finally conquered the technology he only had a couple of minutes left to buy a paper and catch the train. He dashed over to the nearest kiosk, grabbed a copy of the *Chronicle* and literally ran down the platform as the guard watched him board, arm already raised and whistle in mouth.

Still, the one good thing about catching a late morning train was that it was practically empty. George had no difficulty finding a table with four empty seats, perfect for getting everything prepared before he arrived. He put his rucksack on the seat by the window and then plonked himself next to it, putting the paper face down in front of him so that he could see the crossword on the back page. He smiled to himself. It was a long time since he'd had to buy a copy of the paper. The office was obviously full of them but stupidly he'd forgotten to take one with him. It was also a long time since he'd composed a crossword based on someone else's answers. He hadn't done that since he was first in the job, God knows how many years ago.

The next thing he did was take out his mobile phone again and check it for any missed calls or text messages. There were none which was good news. That meant that Margaret was on her way to her sister's and that nothing untoward had happened. The house was locked up and if anybody came looking for him they would find no-one at home. Time to disappear. George switched off the phone and just to be double sure took the back off and took out the SIM card, putting everything safely into one of the zipped pockets in his rucksack. The chances of anyone tracing his whereabouts were now pretty much zero.

As they started to pull out of the station he took out the piece of paper which he'd printed off the night before, listing all the stopping stations en-route. The train headed north west towards Oxfordshire calling at Slough, Reading, Oxford and then Hanborough before reaching Charlbury at 12.36. After that it wound its way onto the Cotswolds, through Moreton-In-Marsh and Evesham before eventually reaching Worcester and then finally Great Malvern. That meant it was about an hour and a half to Charlbury. More than enough time to work out what he was going to say to Albert.

Then, as the train started to heave itself through the grey, sprawling suburbs of west London he took out a pen and started to fill in the crossword. If he was going to update Albert he needed to do that as quickly as possible and frankly, the crossword was as good a place as any to start. He stared at the first clue again, admiring the simple elegance of his handiwork, "Plaster for Helen's lover (5)". He often liked to start his crosswords with something fairly simple and they didn't come much simpler than that.

In fact it was this answer that had really unlocked the puzzle for him last night. George had spent most of his life composing puzzles so it hadn't taken him long to work out some of the connections. He didn't understand all of it of course but a few hours of simple research on the Internet had given him a good idea what this was all about, at least the context if not the detail. But now the magnitude of what he was involved with was starting to worry him. In fact it was beyond belief. Still, given the subject matter the decision what to do next was easy. There was no one better qualified to solve the rest of it than Albert.

George quickly filled in the rest of the answers and then folded up the paper and put it to one side. The train was starting to make him feel drowsy so he leant back and rested his head on the seat and closed his eyes, letting the soporific rhythm wash over him as he dozed in and out of sleep. He wasn't sure where all this was leading to but one thing was certain; it wouldn't take Albert long to work everything out and once he had, that was when the fun and games would really begin. *"Why then to-night let us assay our plot; which, if it speed, is wicked meaning in a lawful deed..."*

Thirteen

IT WAS LATE MORNING BY THE TIME CRAVEN GOT OVER TO Fleet Street. Vinny Goldman was still in his office, reading some draft editorial copy for the day's edition when Maxine, his long-suffering PA stuck her head around the door to tell him that there was someone in reception wanting to see him. Vinny looked up, clearly irritated by the interruption. It was nearly two hours since the conversation about George and the mysterious caller and Vinny had moved on since then. He was now absorbed in reviewing the pre-production schedule and the last thing he wanted to do was stop half way through just to see some faceless bureaucrat who didn't even have a proper appointment. Probably a Snodgrass in a pinstripe suit who spent his whole life in some sleepy backwater, keeping his head down and licking the end of his pencil. Vinny made a mental note that they ought to run an article on the billions of pounds of hard working taxpayers' money which was being squandered every year on gold-plated final salary pension schemes for tens of thousands of civil servants. It was an absolute scandal. A bunch of overpaid, over-protected administrators who contributed nothing to the real value creation of UK plc. At least the MPs were trying to change things for the better, even if you didn't agree with all of their policies. But the scribes and scriveners in Whitehall seemed determined to undermine every initiative simply to maintain the status quo. A breath-taking, unashamed, self-serving strategy and all at the expense of the great British public. It was outrageous.

'We've told him that George isn't here,' said Maxine, still hovering in the doorway, 'but he says he wants to see you.'

Vinny's shoulders slumped forward in tired frustration. What had seemed mildly intriguing a couple of hours ago was now no more than a harmless coincidence. He had more important things on his mind and had no intention of wasting his time on an uninvited visitor, particularly one that hadn't come to see him in the first place.

'Can't someone else see him? What about Bob, or Steve?'

'Bob's in a meeting,' replied Maxine, 'and Steve's over at Canary Wharf. Besides, he wants to see you.'

'Well he's out of luck. I'm busy. Tell him to come back another day when George is here.'

'We've tried that. He doesn't seem to want to take "no" for an answer.'

'Well get security to throw him out then!' shouted Vinny, starting to lose his temper. 'Then he'll get the fucking message!'

Maxine gave him a scathing look as she turned and left. Putting up with Vinny's temper was part and parcel of doing the job but she still objected to his language. Not that it made any difference of course. *"You can take the kid out of Bermondsey..."*

Downstairs, Craven was waiting patiently on a red leather sofa, browsing through a glossy magazine which as far as he could tell was mostly full of adverts for expensive-looking luxury goods. He flicked his way through it and then tossed it back on the coffee table in disbelief. What sort of person would pay three and half thousand pounds for a watch or a handbag, just because it was made by some supposedly designer brand? It was ridiculous. Mind you. So was this appointment. A wild goose-chase probably; trying to catch up with some bloke called George Wiggins who liked to call himself Xerxes and had suddenly disappeared on holiday. It sounded like a complete waste of time. What Craven really wanted to do was follow up on the name and address that he'd taken from Wallis's computer that morning and talk to the guy who'd sold him the photos. The photos that were now missing and which were simply recorded as "14 x PH. M. D&D" in Wallis's filing system.

That was much more important than sitting around waiting to see some clapped out old journalist who now wrote crosswords for a living.

Craven looked up as a security guard approached him, a guy of a similar sort of age and height and build, except in this case not quite as fit, the larger waistline a product of too many night shifts sat glued to a bank of CCTV monitors, no doubt stuffing himself with junk food and guzzling endless mugs of tea. *Probably an ex-copper* thought Craven. Most of them were ideally suited to a job like that. Slow, lazy and not very bright. That's why most of the security jobs were filled by the Old Bill but hardly any by ex-servicemen. You wouldn't catch anyone from the Paras or the Marines sitting on their backside all day. Either way, the guy was built like a cushion.

'Mr. Craven?'

'Yes.' Craven quickly stood up, expecting to be escorted to the Editor's office.

'I'm afraid I have to ask you to leave sir.' The chin jutted upwards as the guard stood with his feet slightly too far apart, keen to exert his authority.

'Why is that then?' asked Craven, trying not to sound too confrontational.

'It's not a discussion sir,' replied the guard. 'This way please.' He held his arm out, indicating towards the revolving door at the front of the building.

'I'm simply asking why I have to leave,' replied Craven, standing his ground and quickly weighing up the situation. Frankly it wouldn't have taken him more than a couple of seconds to disable the guy, his stance alone was just inviting a well-timed kick in the bollocks. But an altercation was the last thing that Craven needed. He wanted to get inside the building and creating a fracas in the main foyer wasn't going to help him do that. Besides, the two girls on the reception desk, one plain and one pretty, were watching the exchange from across the lobby. They'd be on the phone calling for more security or dialling 999 in a matter of seconds.

The guard lent forward slightly, the faint smell of stale smoke engrained in his uniform wafting over. The eyes peered out from under a cap worn too low and then he dropped his voice slightly, as if to give the message more effect. 'Either you leave now sir, or I will have to throw you out.' And then he gave Craven a brief sarcastic smile as if to say, *and trust me sir, that would be an absolute pleasure.*

Craven stared back at him. *Prick.* The temptation to simply smack him in the mouth and jump over the turnstiles was overwhelming but Craven could see the receptionists behind them, still watching with curiosity. Clearly not many people got thrown out of Empire House. He needed to come up with a strategy and he needed to come up with one quick.

'The exit is behind you,' persisted the guard, nodding towards the door behind Craven's back.

Craven put his hands up in defeat. 'Fine. I'll come back another day.' Then he turned and walked out, lighting up a cigarette as he left. He stood on the front steps for a couple of minutes, enjoying the smoke and contemplating his next move. There were two basic options to get into a building unannounced; in disguise or unnoticed in a crowd. He had the ability to do either. The question was, which one was more likely to be successful? He stubbed out the cigarette butt and then walked back to his car which was parked five minutes away on a side street heading north towards Holborn and Chancery Lane. When he got there he opened the boot and looked at the array of stuff which he always carried with him, an assorted collection of clothes and other gear designed to get him in and out of even the most inaccessible places. Camouflage wasn't about making yourself invisible, it was about making yourself blend in and look the same as everyone else.

He smiled as he picked up the white lab coat and moved it to the back of the boot. It wasn't what he was looking for but it reminded him of how many times he had simply wandered into a hospital and been able to walk practically anywhere he wanted to, just by wearing a plain white coat over his normal clothes. It was so easy it was unbelievable really. He quickly rummaged through everything and found the fluorescent jacket with the word "COURIER" on the back. All he needed to do was put on the motorcycle helmet, pick up the clipboard and the small brown parcel and he was ready to go. A special delivery for Mr. Goldman which needed a personal signature would get him access straight to the guy's office. Problem was, it wouldn't give him a lot of time once he was inside. Plus there was always the risk that the over-zealous security officer would ask him to take off the helmet before letting him through reception. No, on reflection perhaps plan B was the better option.

Craven took off his jacket and quickly put on a tie, a light pullover, and then a different coloured jacket. Then he changed his shoes, brown this time instead of black. A small detail but maybe enough to make a difference. Finally he put on a pair of spectacles with clear, glass lenses and then ruffled his hair into a different style. Well, no style at all really but again, hopefully enough to make him unrecognisable, at least in a crowd. By the time he had walked back to the office it had gone 12.00 o'clock. Perfect timing. No one really sure about who was still in the building and who had already gone out for lunch. He positioned himself on the other side of the road, just a few yards opposite the main entrance. Then he took out his phone, dialled 999 and told the girl on the other end that he could see smoke billowing out the top of Empire House in Fleet Street but that he couldn't hear any fire alarms and that all the staff still seemed to be inside. Within about thirty seconds the fire alarms went off and a few moments later a seemingly endless stream of people came pouring out of the front door, mostly smiling and not in a hurry, everyone assuming that it was either a drill or just another false alarm. It was always a drill or a false alarm.

Craven watched them from across the other side of the street, a motley collection of office workers with no defining style or common characteristic amongst them. Not casual and trendy like the staff in Covent Garden but equally not suited and booted like the traders and money-makers in the City. A sort of nondescript, inhomogeneous bunch of desk jockeys who worked in that indistinct hinterland halfway between the West End and the Square Mile. He twisted round and smiled as he caught a reflection of himself in the shop window. He blended in perfectly.

It was clear that there were two separate muster points. One group of staff had assembled to the side of the building heading towards St Pauls while the other group had crossed over the road and were clogging up the pavement further down towards Temple and the Law Courts. Within a couple of minutes Craven could hear the sound of sirens and then for the next ten minutes it was the well-rehearsed process of everybody waiting outside while the fire service searched the building before confirming that it was all clear to go back in.

Craven wandered over the road and casually joined the back of the first group, just ahead of the second group who were crossing the road behind him. In effect he was in the middle of hundreds of staff who were all trying to get back in the building, all of them snaking their way through a couple of small glass doors either side of the slow revolving door which had been locked shut. As usual, the turnstiles in the reception had been left open but lots of staff were opting to use the stairwells rather than join the queue at the lifts. The security guard was nowhere to be seen, taking the opportunity to have a quick cigarette and a bit of banter with the fire crew. Uniforms sticking together.

Craven stuck close behind a cluster of three young girls and tailgated behind them as they went through the door to the stairs on the west side of the building. There were four flights up to the first floor, at which point a number of the people in front of him went through another security door to the office while the remainder kept on climbing, obviously to the floors above. Craven didn't have a clue where Vinny Goldman worked but he didn't see the point in climbing stairs unnecessarily so tailgated through the first door, likewise holding it open for the person behind him. Anyway, it wasn't going to take him long to find out.

Vinny Goldman was still sitting in his office, still reading through a pile of papers. He hadn't bothered to go outside. Maxine had told him that it was probably a false alarm so he'd decided to stay put and take his chances. Besides, if he went outside he'd have to wait with everyone else on the street which meant having to act like he was one of them, or God forbid, even talk to people. *Jesus.* That was easy in the safety of his own office, sat behind a large desk where he was clearly the boss. Everything on his terms. But not outside in the real world, hanging about on the pavement, having to make small talk to people he didn't know. He didn't look up when he heard his door close, assuming it was Maxine or Bob returning from the fire drill.

'Mr. Goldman?'

Vinny looked up, startled. 'Who are you?'

Craven said nothing but continued turning the small chrome knob that closed the blinds in the office windows.

Vinny stood up. 'What the fuck are you doing?'

Craven finished closing the blinds and walked over to Vinny's desk, standing on the opposite side so that they were facing each other. 'Craven,' he said stretching out his arm to offer the perfunctory handshake. 'I understand you're expecting me.'

'Piss off,' said Vinny. 'I'm calling security.'

He leant forward to pick up the phone but as he touched the receiver Craven smashed his fist down onto Vinny's wrist, the fragile structure of eight carpal bones shattering in an instant. The sound hit Vinny's ears a millisecond before the shearing pain ran up and down his spinal cord and hit his brain. He gasped in absolute shock as his face drained white but before he could scream, Craven wrapped his hand several times around Vinny's tie which was hanging down towards the desk and in one swift movement jerked him forwards off his feet. Suddenly Vinny was lying prostrate, face down on top of his own desk, his feet off the floor and his arms thrashing about like a beached whale. Craven wrapped his hand around the tie a couple more times until it dug into Vinny's neck and then waited as he watched his face quickly turn from ashen grey to bright beetroot red.

'Now then,' said Craven, 'are we going to have a polite conversation or am I going to have to teach you some manners?' He released his grip on the tie slowly so that Vinny had enough air to give a reply.

Vinny looked up at him, a gasping, bloated fish caught on the end of a hunter's line. The sensible response was to acquiesce. Live to fight another day. But he was Vinny Goldman, the streetwise kid from Bermondsey who didn't take shit from anybody. He gave Craven a defiant look and said nothing.

Craven screwed his right hand another ninety degrees which had the effect of digging the garrotte deeper into Vinny's neck. Several minutes of this and he would stop breathing. Then he held up his left hand, spreading his fingers and rotating it clockwise and anticlockwise, admiring the sheer brilliance of its dexterity, a perfect design developed by nature and millions of years of evolution. Most people thought that unarmed combat was all about power and strength whereas in fact it was all about knowledge and technique. The wrist was one of the most vulnerable bone structures in the human body. Disable the wrist and you disabled the enemy. A man with two broken wrists couldn't wipe his own arse, let alone feed himself. Craven spread his fingers apart as wide as possible and looked at the webbed pieces of skin that connected each finger to the one next to it. Vector had perfected the art of "flipping," a quick and simple procedure where the skin between each finger was cut with a pair of secateurs and then the hand was ripped apart, straight down the middle, simply by taking two fingers in each hand and pulling them in separate directions. Unlike a broken wrist, the resulting flipper was never going to repair, the threat of which was enough to extract information from even the most resilient and well-trained opponent.

Craven looked back at Vinny who had now stopped struggling and was starting to look like a man drowning, his body going limp and his world going black. Craven let go of the tie and pushed him hard so that he slumped back into his chair. He was hardly a threat, just a fat, obstinate obstruction who refused to get out of the way. Besides, he was too shocked and exhausted to cause any trouble.

Vinny looked back at him, desperately trying to undo the top button of his shirt so that he could breathe properly. Not easy with one hand, the wrist on his right hand already blown up to twice its normal size.

'What's going to happen now,' said Craven, easing himself into the chair opposite Vinny, 'is that you're going to tell me everything you know about George Wiggins. I want to know where he lives, where he eats, where he drinks, who he talks to, where he goes on holiday and most importantly, where I'm likely to find him now.'

Vinny scowled at him across the desk but eventually nodded, realising that he didn't have any option. 'And then what?'

Craven gave him a cold smile, already looking forward to the exchange that was going to take place. 'And then you're going to call security and ask them to escort me out of here…'

Fourteen

THE 11.20 FROM PADDINGTON ARRIVED ON TIME, pulling into Charlbury station dead on 12.35. Charlbury was a small town in the Evenlode valley, about six miles south of Chipping Norton on the edge of the Wychwood Forest. With a population of around 3,000 it was no more than a large village really but it benefited from having a main line into London which meant that it was a popular destination for commuters and for tourists visiting the Cotswolds. George picked up his rucksack, stepped down onto the platform and then made his way through the small ticket office to the parking area outside. Albert was already there, leaning on his motor, smoking a roll-up and grinning like a Cheshire cat.

'Afternoon George. Made it then!'

'Hello Albert,' said George grinning back. 'You been here long?'

'Five minutes, that's all,' replied Albert, flicking the roll-up across the car park. 'Come on then, give us your clobber and we'll go and get some lunch.'

George smiled to himself. He knew what that meant alright. Four or five pints of real ale and a packet of crisps probably. Albert had always been an incorrigible old rogue and he doubted that retirement had changed his lunchtime drinking habits very much. Or the evening ones for that matter. Albert took George's rucksack and put it on the back seat. Then he opened the driver's door and slid in while George opened the passenger door and squeezed in the other side, twisting round to put on his seatbelt. The car was an old Ford Mondeo which had seen better days. God knows how many miles it had on the clock. Clearly Albert wasn't squandering his hard-earned pension on flashy motors.

'Travelling light then George?' said Albert, nodding towards the rucksack on the backseat.

'Just twenty-four hours,' replied George, 'or maybe a couple of days at the most. I just need to lie low for a while. I'll tell you all about it over lunch.'

'Okey dokey,' said Albert, turning the key in the ignition. 'Come on then Sally, let's get to the pub.'

'Sally?' asked George, frowning at Albert's turn of phrase.

Albert tapped the dashboard gently with affection. 'I call her Sally, after Sally Gunnell...'

George groaned, he knew it was going to be another one of Albert's outrageous jokes or anecdotes.

'...she's not much to look at but she's a good runner.'

George shook his head in despair as Albert drove out of the car park and turned left onto Forest Road, all the time chortling to himself.

'Where we going then?' asked George. 'Burford?'

'Of course,' replied Albert, 'no point in living in the best place in England and spending time anywhere else. What do you fancy? The Lamb or The Bay Tree?

George didn't mind. Both of them were fabulous pubs. To find two next door to each other was really unusual but because they were both exceptional they created enough trade for each of them to survive. In fact, such was their reputation that they were always busy and always in demand. Mind you, being located in Sheep Street, the most desirable location in Burford didn't hurt. Albert wasn't wrong about it being the best place in England either. It was a personal, biased view obviously and there were lots of contenders for that particular accolade but George had to agree, Burford was hard to beat. Wonderfully unspoilt with beautiful Cotswold architecture, exclusive shops and galleries plus one of the top twenty churches in the country, Burford was the perfect place to visit and stay. In fact only recently it had been ranked sixth in *Forbes Magazine's* list of Europe's Most Idyllic Places To Live. How an old reprobate like Albert had managed to end up there was beyond him.

It took them about twenty minutes to drive the ten miles or so to Albert's cottage in Green Lane. They parked the car outside and then walked up the High Street, crossing over to Sheep Street about half way up the hill. In the end they chose The Lamb, for no reason other than they spotted an empty table which meant they could get a seat. The pub was still busy though, full of people enjoying the welcoming atmosphere and the extensive selection of wines and local ales. With its 600 year old stone-flagged floor, four log fires and an extensive menu The Lamb attracted a healthy trade in locals and tourists alike. George settled himself down at a table by the window while Albert stood at the bar and ordered two pints of bitter.

George stared at him from across the bar, laughing and joking with a few locals while he waited to get served, his presence suddenly lighting up the room and everyone hanging onto his every word. It was fascinating. George suspected that he was also a regular at The Bay Tree next door, and probably a few other pubs in Burford as well. Albert was one of those people who never took life too seriously and as a consequence was always popular, no matter where he was or what company he was in. He had this amazing ability to walk into any room, even a room full of strangers, and within seconds be the centre of attention, beguiling everybody with his humour and his infectious personality; a genuine raconteur who was liked wherever he went. Well, everywhere except at the *Chronicle* of course where he had been a complete maverick; a brilliant investigative reporter who delivered some of the most sensational scoops ever published but someone who broke the rules and drove his bosses mad on an almost daily basis. George also doubted whether Albert had ever planned anything in his whole life, his success as a journalist being largely a product of spontaneity and intuition rather than from any structured or methodical approach. He had probably ended up in Burford completely by accident and was almost certainly spending his retirement in the same carefree spirit, enjoying an unfettered day-to-day existence free of any routine, plans or commitments. Of course, he had been a complete nightmare to manage, often the nemesis of senior management and all those sourpusses in HR but as far as George was concerned Albert was the most naturally gifted journalist he had ever worked with. And more importantly, his closest and most trusted colleague. There were others who worked harder of course, or who were more ambitious but none of them were as talented as Albert. Albert was a complete one-off. Authentic, original and very unpredictable.

'There you go George,' said Albert walking back from the bar, 'one pint of Old Hooky. First of the day.' Albert put the glass carefully on the table, taking care not to spill any and then sat down in the chair opposite.

'Cheers,' said George, picking up the glass and clinking it against Albert's. 'Good to see you.'

'Cheers,' replied Albert, taking a long pull of his pint and settling it down in the middle of a beer mat with a satisfied sigh. 'Now then, you'd better tell me what all this is about. Sounds like you're in a bit of bother.'

'You could say that,' replied George, also taking a slurp of beer. 'Not sure where to start really.'

Albert grinned. 'Well, start at the end then George. Always the best place to start in my opinion.'

George smiled. Typical Albert. Exactly the opposite to what most people would have said. He leant over and picked up his rucksack which was lying on the floor beside him. He unzipped one of the pockets and pulled out the newspaper. 'Today's edition.' he said, passing it across the table.

Albert frowned, wondering what on earth could be in the news that had got George into so much trouble. He glanced at the front page assuming it must be something to do with the headline *Lotto Layabout Loses Millions.* He stared across the table at George in confusion, his imagination suddenly racing ahead with thoughts of lottery scams and counterfeit tickets. What on earth had George got himself mixed up in?

George shook his head. 'Not that. The crossword on the back page.'

Albert frowned again and turned the paper over, his eyes instantly locating the black and white grid on the lower outside quarter. George leant back in his seat and picked up his glass, swallowing another large glug of beer. It was going to take Albert a couple of minutes to take it all in and George was starting to feel a bit peckish. 'I'm going to get some crisps.' he said, standing up and fishing out his wallet. 'You want some?'

'No thanks,' replied Albert, still engrossed and not looking up. He was working his way through the crossword, scanning each clue and answer in sequence, noting the connections in his head as he went.

George disappeared to the bar and waited patiently to get served, the staff rushed off their feet trying to keep up with the lunchtime trade. He glanced back at the table, Albert's head still buried in the paper. George knew that he was going to have to tell him the whole story which meant disclosing everything, including the bit about Laura. Nothing would make sense otherwise. He wasn't looking forward to that part at all. Knowing Albert, he'd want to know all the gory details and George wasn't in the mood for that. Besides, he'd been trying to forget about that particular episode, as if it hadn't really happened.

Albert continued working through the crossword, his reaction changing from initial intrigue to astonishment and then to complete and abject horror. He'd never seen anything like it. Or rather he had. Some of it he didn't understand of course but the vast majority was horribly familiar, a collection of names and places which brought it all flooding back; him trying to uncover the most sensational story of his whole career and everyone else including his own editor trying to close him down.

'Sour Cream and Chive,' said George, returning a couple of minutes later and dropping a packet of crisps on the table next to Albert's glass. 'It was either that or Beef and Onion.'

'I thought I said "no"?' said Albert, looking up.

'You did,' replied George. 'I ignored you.'

'Whatever happened to Cheese and Onion then, or Salt and Vinegar?'

'Dunno,' replied George, sitting back down and opening his packet. 'Probably went the same way as Spangles, Woolworths and Green Shield Stamps.'

Albert smiled. Then he lent forward, his face suddenly serious and his voice lowered. 'Bloody hell George, do you know what this is?'

'I think so,' replied George. 'I don't understand all of it but I did some research last night. That's why I rang you.'

'It's dynamite George. Absolute twenty-four carat, gold-plated bloody dynamite...'

'I know.'

'...in fact it's probably worse than that. This could be fatal George, and I'm not joking. People have died because they got too close to this.'

George said nothing, the seriousness of the situation suddenly hitting home. He picked up his glass again and drank several large mouthfuls of beer. Getting drunk wasn't going to solve anything but right now it didn't seem such a bad idea.

'Did you write this?' asked Albert, pointing his finger accusingly at the crossword.

George nodded and then leant forward and pointed to the name Xerxes at the bottom of the page. 'I wrote the clues. After someone else provided the answers.'

'Bloody hell George, what possessed you to do that? How on earth did you get involved in something like this?'

'It's a long story,' replied George, starting to look a bit sheepish.

'Well you'd better tell me all about it,' said Albert. 'And this time you'd better start from the beginning.'

George picked up his glass and drained the last dregs of his pint. Then he took a long, deep breath. *"Peace, cousin, say no more and now I will unclasp a secret book, and to your quick-conceiving discontents I'll read you matter deep and dangerous, as full of peril and adventurous spirit as to o'erwalk a current roaring loud on the unsteadfast footing of a spear."*

Fifteen

Jermyn Street, in London's West End was first established in 1664 when Henry Jermyn, the 1st Earl of St. Albans and former Ambassador to Paris and The Hague obtained a grant from Charles II to develop a residential neighbourhood in the area known as St James's Field. The completed development quickly flourished, the street bustling with houses, lodgings, hotels and taverns and dominated by the beautiful Church of St. James's designed by Sir Christopher Wren. It also became a fashionable address from the outset, its distinguished residents over the years including the likes of Sir John Churchill, 1st Duke of Marlborough; Sir Isaac Newton; William Pitt; Sir Walter Scott; the poet Thomas Gray; William Gladstone and William Makepeace Thackeray.

Tailors started appearing in Jermyn Street in the early nineteenth century so it had been a purveyor of sartorial elegance for over 300 years. Today it was world renowned for shirt-making and continued to be an iconic shopping location, retaining the original essence of gentlemen's style and still a quintessentially British experience. Though he did not live there, a statue of Beau Brummell stood at the end of the street at the junction with Piccadilly Arcade, embodying its elegant clothing heritage and values.

As far as Charles Buchanan was concerned there was no better street in London. Aside from all the resident shirt-makers it had by far the biggest selection of gentlemen's requisites anywhere in the country, including hats, handmade shoes, leather goods, shaving brushes, colognes, braces, collar stiffeners, objets d'art and fine wine. Alfred Dunhill, purveyor of luxury goods first took premises on the corner of Jermyn Street and Duke Street in 1907 and was still there, as was Ivan's & Trumper's, the famous barber to crowned heads and the aristocracy; cigar shop Davidoff; and the eccentric New & Lingwood, still the best department store that Buchanan had ever been in, squeezed into just one and a half shops but somehow managing to stock almost everything a man could ever need. Jermyn Street even had it's own 70-seat theatre, the smallest West End theatre in London.

Many an afternoon Buchanan would take an idle stroll and immerse himself in the Lucullan indulgence of A l'Ecu de France, the nostalgic whimsy of The Cavendish Hotel or the cheese-perfumed ambiance at Paxton & Whitfield, Britain's oldest cheese shop which had traded with royal warrants since 1797. But of all the varied and eclectic retailers, Farreau & Marney was by far his favourite. The gentlemen's outfitters had been a discreet but influential presence on Jermyn Street for over a hundred years, offering its customers an unrivalled shopping experience which was refined, prestigious and very exclusive.

Buchanan stood by the front of the shop just inside the Georgian bay window, browsing through the shelves of handmade shirts but all the time keeping one eye on *Maison Blanc*, the small French bistro on the opposite side of the street. A decent enough restaurant but not one of his usual haunts and not somewhere he had been to for a while, hence his early arrival and the cautionary reconnaissance standing in Farreau & Marney's window. And it was certainly not a venue where he had ever contemplated holding a covert meeting before. A discreet conversation at The National Gallery or in St. James's Park was one thing but a lunch appointment at a West End restaurant was something different altogether. Not something Buchanan was comfortable with at all.

The street was busy with lots of shoppers heading backwards and forwards, the majority walking past the restaurant and only a few bothering to stop and look at the menu which was hanging in the window. One couple, laden down with carrier bags eventually went inside but otherwise the front door remained firmly shut. Buchanan continued watching from his vantage point, making only a half-hearted attempt to look as though he was actually interested in buying something. The manager and his assistant didn't seem to mind. Buchanan was a loyal and valued customer and if he wanted to stand at the front of their shop and look out of the window then that was fine by them. All part of the discerning, unobtrusive service.

It was after about 10 minutes that Buchanan noticed someone walk purposefully up to the front door of *Maison Blanc* and go straight in. The sighting lasted only a matters of seconds, his lunch date certainly not hesitant about where they were going. Buchanan checked his watch. It was 1.00 pm which meant they were punctual. In fact they were dead on time. Also not someone who was bothered about whether they were the first to arrive. Confident, decisive, independent. Exactly the profile he had read in the intelligence file only an hour earlier. He waited another five minutes, just to make that there was no monitoring party behind then put the shirt that he was holding back into the pigeon-hole shelving, nodded a curt goodbye to the manager's assistant and walked out and crossed over the road.

The effect of the bright sunny day made the interior of *Maison Blanc* seem dark and gloomy and it took Buchanan a couple of seconds for his eyes to adjust. The dining room looked as though it was half-full, a small number of professional people discussing business over lunch and a larger number of tourists who had no doubt been shopping in Jermyn Street and had discovered the place by accident. Despite its reputation as a bistro the presentation was more like a five star restaurant, the tables covered in crisp, white linen tablecloths and dressed with high quality crystal glassware and silver cutlery. At the centre of each one was a jug of water and a small vase of fresh, coloured flowers. The Maître d' checked Buchanan's reservation and then directed him to a small round table at the back of the room, perfectly located for a private, discreet conversation.

Christine Michaels was already there, scanning the menu and sipping a glass of sparkling water, complete with ice and lime. She looked exactly as Buchanan had imagined; tall, slim and middle-aged but appearing younger with perfect cheek-bones and a translucent skin quality that so many Washington and New York women seemed to have. The white silk blouse and charcoal trouser suit gave her a classic, understated appearance but at the same time looked as though it had cost her a thousand dollars. The overall appearance was immaculate. A sharp bob cut meant that there was not a hair out of place and her nails were manicured to perfection, her body free of any jewellery other than a single platinum bracelet which slid softly onto her right cuff as she held up her hand to greet him. She gave him a thin, dead smile, not bothering with any pretence about special relationships or entente cordiale. They both knew exactly where they stood and that was invariably on opposite sides.

'Charles. Thank you for coming.'

'My pleasure,' replied Buchanan, maintaining a civilised veneer and gently shaking her hand. 'Sorry I'm late.'

'Heavy traffic?'

'Something like that.'

Buchanan pulled out a chair and sat down, all the time trying to hold her gaze and read her mind. The accent was hard to place. Boston possibly, or maybe Providence. Definitely more New England than New York.

Michaels leant over and picked up the wine list which was lying on the edge of the table. 'Can I get you a drink? A glass of wine perhaps?'

'Not for me thank you. I don't normally drink during the day.'

'Neither do I but I'm making an exception today.'

'Really? Why is that?'

'How about a Chablis? Something crisp as it's lunchtime.'

'Water will be fine thanks.'

'Nonsense. I can hardly drink on my own. Red or White?'

Buchanan stared back at her across the table. She was exactly as the file described. Cold, single-minded and ruthless. A lifelong CIA officer who had dedicated her whole career to the security service and who had little time for anything or anyone else. He suspected that she had to do a lot of things on her own. And not just in the kitchen either. 'A glass of white then, thank you.'

'Excellent. Chablis?'

Buchanan shrugged. He wasn't a lover of white Burgundy. A glass of Pouilly Fumé would have been more to his taste but it seemed ungracious to object. Michaels attracted the attention of a waiter and ordered a bottle of *Jean-Marc Brocard Grand Cru Bougros*. The waiter nodded obsequiously and disappeared, wine list in hand. Buchanan raised his eyebrows in appreciation. Not only did she have impeccable taste, the French accent was pretty much perfect. Definitely not your typical, provincial American.

'Well, it's good to meet you,' said Buchanan, picking up his napkin and folding it across his lap. 'When did you arrive?'

'Yesterday,' replied Michaels, 'I flew over on the red-eye.'

'Heathrow?'

'Terminal 5. Although I'm surprised you have to ask.'

Buchanan gave a self-deprecating shrug. Not that she was probably fooled for one moment. Christine Michaels had been on GCHQ radar since she'd checked into JFK on Tuesday morning. 'I don't think we quite have your expertise in surveillance.' he added, trying to maintain the charade.

Michaels looked up over the top of the menu and gave him a scathing look. 'On that point we are agreed. If you're going to carry out surveillance it's much better conducted undercover...'

'Of course.'

'...and if you're going to stand in a shop window pretending to be a customer you could at least move about a bit, otherwise you risk looking like a tailor's dummy.'

Buchanan smiled to himself. If anything, the intelligence file had underestimated how blunt she actually was. He held his hands up in mock embarrassment. 'My apologies for any misunderstanding. Just a little retail therapy as I was early.'

Michaels sneered at him in disbelief. 'I take the monitoring for granted. It's just the lack of competence that surprises me. Or then again, maybe it shouldn't.'

Buchanan stared at her across the table, resisting the temptation to tell her exactly what he thought of her. He'd dealt with some obnoxious people in his time but she was definitely up there with the worst. Still, there was no advantage in that. They were playing poker, not snap. The pair of them paused as the waiter arrived to serve some bread and then take their order. Buchanan ordered *Les Cuisses De Grenouille De Provence* followed by *Magret de Canard Sauce Cerises*. Michaels ordered *Coquille St Jacques De Printemps* followed by *Cabillaud A La Garniture Bourguignone*. The wine arrived within minutes, appropriately chilled and left by the table in a large bucket of ice.

'Anyway, thank you for coming,' said Michaels, picking up the jug of water and pouring a large measure into Buchanan's glass, 'particularly at such short notice.'

'Not at all,' replied Buchanan picking up the glass and taking a small sip. 'Much more civilised than sitting on a park bench.'

'Or traipsing round The National Gallery.'

Buchanan raised an eyebrow. It was unusual for contacts to reveal their meeting places. Even the Cowboys who generally couldn't be trusted didn't do that.

'I always insist on a thorough debrief,' continued Michaels, picking up a piece of bread to stave off her hunger, 'particularly before re-posting.'

'Clearly.'

'Anyway, he was very complimentary. He appreciated the cultural education as well as the relationship.'

'Well, let's hope it made a difference.'

'I doubt it. He's probably watching MTV and eating burger and fries as we speak.'

Again the pair of them paused as the waiter arrived to serve the first course, also enquiring to see if they wanted him to pour the wine. Michaels nodded her agreement and then took a small drop to taste, allowing the waiter to pour a decent measure into both glasses.

'So, is this just a general chat,' asked Buchanan, picking up his wine and taking an appreciative mouthful, 'or did you have something specific you wanted to discuss?'

Michaels shrugged nonchalantly. 'I just thought it would be good to meet and say hello.'

'Well, that's very thoughtful of you.'

'Although as we're here, there is one thing we could quickly cover.'

'Go on.' Buchanan waved a hand towards Michaels inviting her to continue. He was now eating the frog legs served on a yellow pepper compote with grilled courgettes, roasted vine tomatoes and aubergine flan, all drizzled with sauce vierge. Concentrating on the food but at the same time listening to her. Two pleasures at the same time. Delicious food plus the amusement of hearing about someone else's problem. Exquisite.

Michaels took a precautionary glance around the room to make sure that no-one could hear their conversation and then lowered her voice.

'Draper. Did he say anything to you when you met?'

'Often. That was the whole point.'

'I meant before he left. The last time you saw him.'

'Not particularly. Why?'

Michaels picked up her own glass and took an equally appreciative sip. The temperature was causing the glass to mist and form rivulets of cold moisture which were running over the surface and down the stem. The wine tasted clean and crisp. 'I thought he might have mentioned something.'

'He mentioned a lot of things. Anything specific?'

'A prodigal son.'

'Prodigal, as in back in from the cold?'

Michaels picked up her knife and fork and started eating the fresh king scallops, served on roasted garlic and saffron mash with buttered peas, broad beans and asparagus shoots. She said nothing and controlled her body language, determined not to give anything away.

Buchanan allowed himself a faint smile and relaxed back into his chair, using the pause to full effect. Time to shift the balance. 'I think you should get to the point. I assume we're talking about Ross?'

Michaels hesitated and then lowered her voice even further, almost to a whisper. 'What do you know about Ross? Did Draper mention him?'

Buchanan shook his head. 'Not really. Who is he?'

Michaels wiped the corners of her mouth with her napkin and then folded it neatly into a triangle and replaced it carefully across her lap. 'Well, if you don't know who he is, then we don't have a problem...'

'Good.' Buchanan was now clearing his plate. The cuisine in *Maison Blanc* was definitely better than he remembered. 'It's always nice to have a problem free day in my experience.'

'...although if you did know him, we wouldn't want any interference.'

'Interference?'

'Interference. It's a common enough word I think?'

Buchanan gave her a cold, hard stare. 'I know what interference means.'

'Good. As long as we understand each other.'

Buchanan picked up his glass and took a long, slow drop of wine, the crispness of the dry, gunflint after-taste merging with the hint of mineral on his palate. This was always the moment he savoured most. He would have preferred the Pouilly Fumé of course, more rounded and much more subtle but no matter, it was Michaels's choice so it was the perfect accompaniment. 'I think we understand each other perfectly...'

'Good.'

'..although as far as Ross is concerned, I suspect it may be too late.'

Michaels frowned and then suddenly leant forward, the words spoken through gritted teeth. 'What do you mean it might be too late?'

Buchanan circled his wine glass on the table top and then took another small sip, taking his time and choosing his words carefully. 'Ross is a broken asset and on British soil. We reserve the right to deal with that.'

'You will do no such thing!'

The two of them glared across the table at each other, the silence amplified by the noise of the other guests around them. Michaels reached over and pulled the bottle of wine out of the ice bucket, not bothering to try and stop the excess water dripping all over the tablecloth. She poured a large slug of wine into her own glass and then leant forward and offered the same to Buchanan. He raised his hand, politely declining any more. She shrugged and stuffed the bottle back into the ice.

'Ross is a liability,' continued Buchanan, still maintaining a calm and nonchalant manner. 'We need to deal with that.'

'We're already dealing with it.'

'Really?'

'Really.'

'I don't think so. Our parish, our responsibility.'

Michaels sank slowly back into her chair and stared across the room, looking at nothing in particular. The situation was spiralling out of control and she needed to pull it back. She fiddled nervously with the bracelet for a moment, trying to think of something to say. 'We need you to back off.'

Buchanan shook his head. 'Not possible.'

'This is important. Critical.'

Buchanan shook his head again. 'Not possible. Like I said, it's probably already too late.'

'This will go all the way up. Diplomatic recall.'

Buchanan paused. Michaels was looking genuinely agitated. The cool and polished persona had started to slip but it wasn't surprising really. She'd only just arrived and a diplomatic recall was about as bad as it could get. There was obviously something going on with Ross which he didn't understand. He toyed with his empty glass again, thinking through the options, contemplating what he should do next. Eventually he made a decision. 'I might be able to call things off.'

'That would be good.'

'We would need assurance…'

'Of course.'

'…about contagion…'

'Naturally.'

'…and confidentiality.'

'Absolutely.'

'I would need to make a call.'

'Go ahead.'

Suddenly the waiter appeared out of nowhere and started to clear away the dirty plates. Buchanan leant back and refilled his glass of water, all the time watching Michaels across the table, watching her every movement like a hawk. After a moment she stood up, picked up her handbag and disappeared towards the toilets on the other side of the restaurant. A few seconds later his mobile phone burst into life. He answered it immediately. 'Hello?'

'It's me.'

Buchanan checked the number to make sure but Maurice's voice was unmistakeable. London, middle-aged, Jewish. 'Obviously. Everything okay?'

'Loud and clear.'

'She didn't see you then?'

'No. Too busy watching you in the shop window.'

'I should hope so. I was practically waving at her.'

'We dropped it into her handbag. They'll dry clean her later but it's Russian. They won't be sure where it came from.'

'Good. What's she doing now?'

'Calling Langley. They're going to lift Ross straight away.'

'Predictable.'

'Do you want me to do anything?'

'No leave it with me. I'll handle it.'

Buchanan ended the call and immediately dialled another. Craven answered it within a matter of seconds. 'Hello?'

'It's me.'

'Obviously.'

'Where are you?'

'Knightsbridge. That gardening job. I'm outside the flat now.'

'Good. Just thought you ought to know, the cavalry is on its way.'

'When?'

'Now…'

'Great.'

'…so get on with it. And make it snappy.'

Sixteen

CRAVEN SWITCHED THE PHONE ONTO SILENT AND THEN put it back in his pocket. The last thing he needed was it suddenly ringing unannounced. Then he leant into the wall and slowly poked his head out beyond the corner, managing to get a glimpse of the black Audi saloon parked one hundred yards up the road. The question was, what to do next? Buchanan's message was quite clear; the cavalry were on their way which meant that the two Cowboys in the car, a couple of birdwatchers doing the daytime shift were going to get a call in any moment. No time to lose. But did he have enough time to deal with Ross before they moved into action, or did he need to take them out first?

He pulled out a packet of cigarettes and flipped open the lid on the Zippo lighter. He reckoned he had a couple of minutes to make a decision and a quick smoke always helped with the thinking process. He lit one up and took a long drag, the nicotine kicking into his central nervous system in a matter of seconds. The risk of leaving them in the car was that they started to move just a minute or so behind him. He would hardly have time to get in the flat, let alone deal with Ross. The alternative was to disable them first but that would take several minutes and for all he knew there could be another carload of Cowboys on the way, all tooled up and ready for action. He took another drag on the cigarette. Neither option was ideal but he didn't have a lot of choice. Somebody somewhere was about to press the go button and the clock was ticking.

Craven unzipped his jacket and took out the pistol, turning it over in his hand to feel the balance. The Glock 23 was the compact version of the full size 22, half an inch shorter and almost 100 grams lighter when fully loaded which meant that it was easier to use and easier to conceal. It was no surprise then that it was the weapon of choice for the FBI and countless enforcement agencies across the globe. He snapped open the magazine and checked the thirteen rounds of .40 calibre bullets, the smell of oil and gunmetal reminding him of another time and another place. Then he stuffed it back into the holster and zipped his jacket about halfway up, just enough to conceal the fact that he was carrying but open enough to draw it quickly.

He took a final drag on the cigarette and stubbed it out on the path. And then he stopped. Suddenly it hit him. Maybe there was a third option. And possibly a better one than the other two. After all, trying to disable a couple of trigger-happy Cowboys who were on red alert wasn't going to be easy. For one thing he hadn't worked out how he was going to get close enough to the car without them spotting him. He could hardly just stroll up and tap on the window. And he certainly didn't have time to go round the block so that he could approach them from behind. Not that it would have made a lot of difference. They'd be watching both ways and were bound to see him before he got within striking distance. In fact trying to neutralise them while they were inside the car wasn't really an option at all. The risk of something going wrong was much too high. But the alternative, which was to go in the building now and hope that he had enough time to deal with Ross before they moved in behind him wasn't that attractive either. He'd be looking over his shoulder all the time, covering his back and even worse, he wouldn't be in control of the situation. He'd be at the mercy of luck and chance, everything his years of training and experience had taught him to avoid. Craven's third rule of fieldwork. *Luck is what happens when preparation meets opportunity.* No, what he really needed to do was get them in front of him so that he could see what was going on. Let them do all the hard work with him following behind. Twist the situation around to his advantage. That way he wouldn't be under any pressure and could pick his moment.

He was just starting to work through a plan when he heard the sound of the car engine start up. That had been a regular occurrence every half hour since about ten o'clock this morning. It was now early afternoon and the temperature was pushing 30 degrees. Clearly, winding the windows down wasn't enough to stop them getting hot and bothered, stuck inside a metal box all day with the sun streaming through a glass windscreen. Hence the engine being run for five minutes every half hour to turn on the air conditioning. But something in the engine noise made Craven think that this was different. Either they were leaving or they were moving the car closer towards the block of apartments. Probably to park it right outside so that they could make a quick getaway Again, he eased his head around the corner of the wall, just long enough to see the Audi pull away from its parking space and crawl along the road towards him. Definitely not leaving. They were making their move.

Craven sprinted to the front door and pressed the button for flat number six. That was the problem with apartment blocks these days, especially in the pricier parts of London. Everybody was worried about security which meant that it was almost impossible to get in without an appointment. God knows how the postman managed to deliver anything or how the gasman managed to read the meter. Still, thank goodness for the reconnaissance last night. He'd spent nearly ten minutes trying to find someone to open the door and it was only after patient, methodical, perseverance that he'd finally found the woman in flat number six; ageing, lonely and practically housebound. Happy to let him in but also keen to have a chat on the doorstep. Now he needed to get inside in a matter of seconds before Micky and Pluto turned up. He pressed the button again, this time three short bursts in quick succession, trying to convey the urgency through his fingertips. Then he heard the squeal of brakes as the car pulled up outside. Almost immediately, the intercom crackled into life, the voice exactly the same as it had been yesterday; frail, slow and hesitant.

'Hello?'

'Mrs. Clements?'

'Yes?'

'It's Mr. Watkins. I called round yesterday and you kindly let me in.'

'Oh yes?'

Craven could hear the Cowboys getting out of the car, two doors slamming in quick succession. They were practically seconds away from walking up the steps and coming up the path. 'Sorry to bother you again Mrs. Watkins. Could you let me in again please?'

'Yes dear. Back so soon?'

Craven didn't wait to reply. As soon as the lock buzzed he pushed the door open and stepped inside, the sound of footsteps getting louder behind him. He wasn't sure whether they had seen him or whether they were still on the section of path that was out of sight, curving away from the building down to the road but either way he couldn't take the chance. His original plan was to go up the stairwell to the fifth floor, one floor above Ross's flat and then circle down behind them. But now he had to rethink. If they had seen him enter the lobby only seconds ahead it would look suspicious if he suddenly disappeared. It risked putting them on their guard, which could be fatal. Much better to play it cool and act like a normal tenant.

The lobby was a long rectangular space which other than a large pot plant near the entrance and a fire extinguisher fixed to the wall was devoid of any furniture. The lift was situated half way down the right-hand wall and typically for small, residential blocks was the only one. Craven stood in front of the lift doors and stared up at the illuminated numbers above his head, pretending that he was checking which floor it was on. In truth he hadn't pressed the button yet. He didn't want it to arrive before the cavalry turned up. He could see them out the corner of his eye, hovering outside, trying to work out the intercom. He waited a moment and then walked over and opened the door, just enough to talk to them and check their credentials.

'I'm not meant to let you tailgate but who are you after?' he asked, giving them a friendly smile and putting on his best Brummie accent. It was about the only one he had ever perfected but it came in useful now and again, normally when he wanted someone to think that he was harmless. The whole subject of dialects had evolved into something of a science in recent years, the location strategies for call-centres now determined as much on the perception of regional accents as on infrastructure, logistics or the availability of staff. No one was going to buy anything from someone with a scouse accent for example, not unless they were extremely stupid. In truth, the West Midlands accent wasn't that effective for selling either but there was something about it which sounded naive and slightly comical, which was therefore disarming. The perfect foil to a pair of cynical, suspecting CIA officers.

The two guys on the doorstep looked at Craven and relaxed slightly, the smiling face and the Brummie accent working its charm.

'Thanks,' replied the first guy standing nearer the door, 'we were just trying to work out how to get in.'

'Who are you after?' repeated Craven, standing his ground and maintaining the role of responsible tenant.

'Number 25,' replied the guy. 'Fourth floor.'

Craven smiled again as he pulled the door open. 'Come on then. I suppose I can let you in. You don't look like you're going to pinch anything!'

'Not today,' replied the guy, making some attempt at humour.

Craven walked back to the lift and pressed the button. It looked as though it was on the top floor which meant it was going to take a moment or two to arrive. 'I ought to take the stairs to be honest,' he said, 'they're a free gym really.'

The guy smiled back at him but said nothing, clearly not wanting to get into any more conversation. A few seconds later there was a bell like "ding" indicating that the lift had arrived and then the doors opened very slowly. Definitely not the fastest lift in the world.

Craven stepped inside and pressed the button for the fifth floor. The first guy followed behind but his partner who up until then had remained silent gave him a knowing look and nodded towards the stairs at the end of the lobby. 'I'm just going to make a call. I'll catch you up.' The first guy nodded back and pressed the button for the fourth floor.

Craven knew what that meant alright. Textbook building sweep. The first guy, probably the senior, would head straight towards the target while his backup would check all the doors and exits, including the stairwells. Making sure that the coast was clear and that they knew all the options if they needed a quick getaway. Contingency in case something went wrong. The lift trundled up to the fourth floor and as soon as the doors opened the Cowboy got out. Craven pressed the button again for the fifth floor and waited for the lift to make its slow ascent. As soon as it arrived he darted across the landing and headed straight for the stairwell at the back of the building. His whole plan now depended on him getting to the floor below before the second guy turned up. Suddenly there was an opportunity to pick them off separately which he didn't want to lose. He stood at the top of the stairs and listened for a moment. He could hear the sound of footsteps on concrete slowly getting louder, someone making their way up. It sounded as though they were still a long way off. Clearly the guy had taken his time to do a thorough check of the ground floor.

Craven raced down the stairs, twelve steps down to a u-turn and then another twelve down in the opposite direction to the fourth floor, a black, metal handrail following his descent on the right-hand side. He could still hear the footsteps making their way up from somewhere below. Quick decision. Wait on the fourth floor and risk the noise of any altercation spilling onto the landing or continue down to the third and risk bumping into the guy on the stairs? Craven kept going, taking the steps as fast as he could. He reached the door for level three just before someone reached the u-turn below to climb the last flight up to the same point. Craven pressed his back against the wall, the recess just deep enough so that he was out of sight. He held his breath and stood absolutely still, his heart thumping loudly from the sudden exertion. The guy didn't bother looking left as he walked past, less than a foot away from Craven as he turned to make his way up the final two flights to the floor above. Nor did he see anyone lurking in the shadows.

Craven stepped out as soon as the guy turned at the top of the stairs and tapped him sharply on the shoulder. Much better to have some multiple bone structures to aim at rather than the back of his head. The guy wheeled around, his hand instinctively reaching for the pistol which was stuffed into his waistband in the middle of his back. He only needed two seconds to react but he didn't get even one. Craven had clenched his right fist into the vertical position, with the thumb and forefinger at the top and then swung his arm upwards with as much force as he could, like a sledgehammer driving into the underside of the guy's chin. The force of the blow smashed his lower jaw upwards with such ferocity that it pushed some of his bottom teeth up and over his top row, so that his mouth was suddenly wedged shut in sheer, excruciating pain. His eyes bulged in absolute terror as Craven swung a huge, conversion-kicking boot into his testicles and then smacked him hard, this time on the side of his head, squarely on the temple. The guy reeled and stumbled backwards, collapsing onto one knee as his world started to turn black and spin. Still his instinct was to try and get out his pistol. Craven stood over him, watching his fumbled attempts to coordinate himself and then hit him again, this time firing a series of vicious rabbit punches into the side of his face. The sheer ferocity of Craven's attack shattered the guy's cheekbone, the impact of which knocked him senseless as he toppled over and lay motionless in a crumpled, groaning heap.

Craven removed the guy's pistol and checked it out. A Beretta 96 semi-automatic which was standard CIA issue. Chambered for the 0.40 S&W cartridge with double action on the first round and then single action on subsequent rounds. He turned it over in his hand, feeling the perfectly balanced weight and admiring the cold-hammered forged barrel, the dovetailed-mounted front sight and the machine chequered grip, all furnished in Beretta's corrosion resistant Bruniton finish. It was a work of art. Not as good as the Glock 23 in Craven's opinion but it was a close run thing. He snapped open the 12-round magazine and stuffed it in his pocket, safe out of harm's way. Then he took out some plastic cable-ties and tied one around the guy's wrist, not too tight to cut off his circulation but tight enough so that it wouldn't come off. Then he dragged the semiconscious body back to the middle of the stairwell and threaded another tie through the metal rail, looping it through the handcuff on the guy's wrist so that he was permanently anchored to the staircase. Now all he needed to do was get up to the fourth floor and tackle the first Cowboy before he came looking for his mate.

Doubling back up the stairs was Craven's quickest route but using the lift was his safest bet. Slower and less covert but less chance of bumping into someone coming down the other way, wondering where their partner had got to. He walked onto the landing and pressed the button several times in succession, impatient to get up to Ross's flat and find out what was going on. About thirty seconds later he got out at the fourth floor, spotting Ross's apartment about ten yards down the corridor on the opposite side. Even from a distance he could tell that the door was open. Either Ross and his CIA visitor were still inside or both of them had already left. He took out the Glock and crept up to the front door, taking care not to make any noise or sudden movement. He stood still for a moment, trying to peer into the hallway and listen for any sound of life inside. There was nothing. Absolutely nothing other than a wall of heat coming out of the apartment which was like opening an oven door. It was mid-summer and 30 degrees outside but inside the flat it was even hotter. Somebody had put the central heating onto constant and wound the thermostat up to max. That meant only one thing. And definitely not what Craven was expecting.

He pushed the door gently with his foot and stepped inside, the hall long and narrow with two doors on the left and one straight ahead. Craven held the Glock in both hands and kept close to the right hand wall as he inched his way towards the room at the end, the door to which was slightly ajar. Again, he stood still for several seconds, listening for even the faintest sound of life but there was nothing. Absolute silence. After a moment he nudged the door forward and stepped into what looked like a combined living and dining room, with a small kitchen leading off the far end. The place was immaculate, furnished in an elegant, contemporary style but it was clearly empty. If Ross lived here he wasn't leaving clues for anyone. The temperature however was even hotter than in the hallway. The boiler was probably in the kitchen somewhere which meant that it was even worse at this end of the flat. Craven could see the thermostat on the living room wall, the green light indicating that it was switched on, but resisted the temptation to turn it down. Somebody was going to be crawling all over everything before the day was out, looking for DNA and fingerprints. Besides, there was nothing here of interest. Either Ross was the tidiest person in the world or the place had already been swept.

He turned and went back into the hall, the two rooms now on his right hand side, presumably one bedroom plus a bathroom. He stood with his ear to the first door and waited a moment, just to make sure. Then he dropped his arm onto the handle and eased it open. It took him a couple of seconds to scan the room and work everything out. Firstly, because the bathroom was so small and the door had been shut, the temperature was actually several degrees hotter than in the living room. In fact it was unbearable. But it was like that for a reason. The higher the temperature, the faster Ross's body would decompose. Standing up in the middle of the bath was a huge, luggage holdall; designer brand with gold plated zips which were closed and fastened with a small padlock. Craven didn't need to open it to work out what was inside. It was obviously stuffed with something which was bulky and very heavy. And anyway, the smell of rotting flesh was starting to permeate through the fabric. He stepped forward a couple of paces and leant over the side of the bath, just to get a closer look. That was when he felt the cold, round steel of a revolver in the back of his neck. He froze instantly, not daring to move a muscle.

'So, where did you come from?' The voice was unmistakeable. Cowboy number one.

'Birmingham,' replied Craven, putting on the Brummie accent again and maintaining his statue-like position.

'Very funny.' The end of the barrel prodded a couple of times into the nape of his neck. 'Put the gun on top of the bag.'

Craven hesitated, desperately trying to think how he could buy himself some time. All he needed was a few seconds and an opportunity to turn around. The pistol jabbed a couple more times, the guy clearly getting impatient. Craven leant over and put the Glock on top of the holdall, very slowly and very deliberately. He guessed what that was all about. At some point someone was going to find Ross's body, stiff and contorted, all zipped up inside some designer luggage with Craven's revolver nestling on top; a crowning, unmissable clue served up on a plate. But it was the guy's first mistake. Craven could still reach the Glock from there. Much better to have dropped it on the floor and then kick it to the other side of the room. *Fifteen-love.*

'Good. Now you can tell me what the hell is going on...'

Craven smiled to himself. Second mistake. Should have disabled him there and then. *Thirty-love.*

'...you went up to the fifth floor. Suddenly you get out of an elevator that came up from the floor below.'

'Lift.'

'What?'

'Lift. In England we call it a lift.'

'Really...'

'You say tomato...'

Smartarse.

'...I say tomato.'

The revolver dug deep into Craven's neck again, this time with a force which felt like the guy was about to lose his temper. 'Fine. Let's call the whole thing off.'

Craven put his hands up in defence and stood absolutely still, trying to balance the point at which he pushed the Cowboy into losing control without actually pulling the trigger.

'So who are you. Five or six?'

Craven paused. He understood the question of course. MI5 or MI6 but there was no point in answering, at least not honestly. The guy wouldn't believe him. 'Six,' he said eventually 'and if we could get out of this sauna I'll tell you why we're here...'

'We?'

Craven shrugged. Bait taken. *Forty-love.* '...so I wouldn't advise standing with your back to the door.'

The guy paused, suddenly thinking through the logistics. The Brit was right. He wasn't in a great position. Besides, the heat in the bathroom was suffocating and the suggestion to move to another room was tempting. Quick decision then. 'Put your hands behind your head and walk backwards out of the room. Very slowly.'

Craven did as he was told, clasping his hands on the back of his neck and then reversed very carefully out of the room, following the Cowboy who had also walked backwards into the hall. Now they had a choice. Which way to turn? A long, narrow corridor with a door at either end, both of which were slightly ajar. The Cowboy turned and stepped backwards a couple of paces so that the front door was behind him. Craven turned the other way with his back to the sitting room, the two of them staring at each other for the first time since they had been in the lift. The guy still holding the pistol and still with the upper hand.

'So, start talking. And make it quick.'

Craven shrugged again. 'What do you want to know?'

'Where's my buddy?'

Craven looked at the him intently and then suddenly glanced a millimetre to the right and over the guy's left shoulder. Literally for a millisecond but at the same time nodding his head towards something in the distance. 'You mean him?'

It was the oldest trick in the book. Instinctively the Cowboy glanced round to see what was behind him. It was only a split second but long enough for Craven to spread the two fingers on his right hand into a V shape and then stab them as hard as he could into the guy's eyeballs. The effect was instant. He let out an agonising howl as he stumbled backwards against the wall, his world suddenly dark and his eyes full of searing, throbbing pain. In the same instant Craven stamped down hard on his left ankle and smacked him straight in the mouth. Hard, fast and with maximum follow through. Within a couple of seconds the guy had slumped to the ground, his brain scrambled in pain and his body momentarily disabled. Craven leant over him and then stamped on his wrist, the small, fragile bones shattering under the weight of his boot. Which meant taking the gun off him was like taking candy from a baby. It was going to look perfect sitting on top of the holdall in the bathroom; a crowning, unmissable clue served up on a plate. *Game, set and match.*

Seventeen

'So, what do you think Albert?' George was sitting at the kitchen table, the newspaper spread out in front of him while Albert was leaning against the worktop, waiting for the kettle to boil.

'Dunno,' replied Albert, putting three spoonfuls of tea into an old, china tea pot. 'I recognise most of the words but not that one. Doesn't mean anything to me.'

George stared back at the crossword and at the clue he had written for 10. Across, *"Secret scramble to flight-path."* Then he looked at the answer, VECTOR, which he had filled in earlier and smiled to himself. He wasn't that far off retirement himself but there was life in the old dog yet. That was a clue to be proud of. Even the most hardened of crossword fanatics would take time to crack that one. But what on earth did VECTOR mean? That was a different puzzle altogether.

'Nice clue though,' added Albert, leaning over George's shoulder as if reading his mind. 'Very devious.'

'Thanks,' said George, pleased at Albert's comment. Not many people appreciated the art of compiling crosswords anymore. Times had changed. The world was full of all sorts of fancy word and number puzzles these days. Every paper was full of them. Even the Chronicle had a four page centre spread on a Saturday to keep its readers occupied over the weekend. But it made the old-fashioned crossword look a bit tired and out of date.

'It's a nod to a famous clue from the past,' continued George. 'In fact one of the most famous ever written.'

'Really? Which one was that?' asked Albert, pouring the boiling water into the tea pot.

'I have to say,' replied George, ignoring Albert's question, 'for someone who can't even cook you're very fussy about how to make a cup of tea.'

'Quite right,' said Albert. 'Freshly filtered water, loose leaf tea, a temperature controlled kettle and always use a second warming pot. One for brewing and one for serving. And never use anything other than porcelain cups. You won't find any of that industrial tea bag or ceramic mug malarkey in this house!'

'You should write a book about it one day,' said George, laughing at Albert's organisation and attention to detail. It was completely at odds with the way he lived the rest of his life.

Albert shook his head. 'George Orwell already did that. Anyway, what's your famous clue then?'

'It's "*Gesg.*" Nine and four letters.'

'Gesg? What sort of clue is that?'

George grinned. 'A very good one. A classic in fact.'

'No idea,' said Albert, taking the lid off the teapot and giving the contents a quick stir. 'What's the answer then?'

George grinned again. 'I'm not telling you. That's the whole point. You have to work it out.'

Albert sighed as he poured the contents of the brewing pot into the second teapot, carefully using a silver strainer to catch the large, loose leaves. He'd never had much time for crosswords. Not that he didn't have the wherewithal of course. His ability to unravel a complex problem, or connect a series of seemingly unrelated pieces of information was second to none. He'd spent most of his career doing that. It was just that he'd always been more interested in solving real life puzzles. Things that really mattered and which made a real difference. Not wasting his time in a make-believe world full of made-up clues and artificially constructed answers. He looked across at George, a friend and colleague he had known for over thirty years. Poor old George. What a way to spend half your working life; constructing little black and white puzzles to entertain a load of people he would never meet and who had nothing better to do with their time. And what on earth had he got himself caught up in now?

'I'll give it some thought,' said Albert unconvincingly, as he brought the teapot over and placed it carefully in the middle of the table. Then he picked up the newspaper and scanned the crossword again. 'Although I'd much rather try and work this out.'

'Any ideas then?' asked George.

'Not really,' replied Albert, concentrating on a couple of answers that he still didn't recognise. 'I worked on this story for over a year and thought I knew everything there was to know about it. But there are a few things here that I've not seen before.'

'Like VECTOR?' said George, pointing to 10. Across.

'Exactly. Don't remember that one at all.'

'Maybe you've forgotten. It was a long time ago.'

Albert gave him an old fashioned look. 'I'm not bloody senile yet George. I think I'd remember a word like that.'

George put his hands up in defence. 'I'm just saying, the memory fades over time. It would be good to look at your notes again, that's all.'

Albert picked up a small white jug and poured two slugs of milk into each of the cups. George was right. It was definitely a long time ago. In some respects it felt like only yesterday but in others it seemed like it was from a different world, a faint recollection from somewhere in the dim and distant past. That was the problem with getting old. Every year seemed to go quicker than the last and before you knew it, twenty years had tumbled by without you really noticing. So whilst he recognised most of the words, his memory of how they all fitted together was now a little hazy. Another look at his notes from all those years ago would certainly be helpful.

'Milk first?' asked George, suddenly interrupting Albert's train of thought.

'Absolutely. It protects the bone china from the hot water. Don't believe all that modernist rubbish about putting the milk in afterwards.'

George raised his eyebrows in surprise. That was completely opposite to what he'd always been told. Still, Albert seemed to know what he was talking about.

'You might be right,' continued Albert, now pouring out two cups of tea, 'but my stuff was probably thrown out years ago. No chance of finding it now.'

'I'm not so sure,' replied George. 'Everything is scanned and indexed on computer systems these days but all the old stuff was boxed up and archived off-site. I've got loads of old files stored in a warehouse somewhere.'

'What, and they never throw them away?'

George shrugged. 'Dunno. But I doubt it. Don't suppose anyone bothers to think about it. Once they're off-site they're out of mind.'

'And do you know where this place is?'

George shook his head. 'No, but I know someone who does.'

'Who's that?'

'Maureen.'

'Maureen Green?'

'Exactly. Maureen knew everything that went on at the *Chronicle*.'

'I thought she'd retired.'

'She has. But she'll remember.'

'She might have moved.'

George smiled to himself. That wouldn't be a problem. Hayley worked there now. Even if Maureen had moved she wouldn't be hard to find.

Albert frowned, obviously not convinced. Then he picked up the paper again, hoping for a flash of inspiration as he scanned the crossword for the umpteenth time. He had no idea what VECTOR meant but the word ROSS looked like it was the name of someone. Someone obviously connected to the whole story. In fact it was hard to believe that it could be anything else. He racked his brains, trying to think of the names of all the bit-part players from all those years ago but it was no use. His mind was a complete blank. And 12. Across was exactly the same. Not only didn't he understand the answer, he didn't understand the clue either. 'What's this one mean?' he asked, pointing towards the middle of the page?

George twisted his head round to see which one Albert was looking at and smiled to himself. He wasn't surprised. In over twenty years he'd never written a clue for that word before. It had no doubt appeared in a general knowledge crossword from time to time but never in a cryptic one. In fact given that he wasn't able to change any of the answers, it was the hardest one that he'd had to write. 'Actually, I'm quite proud of that,' he said a bit defensively, 'that was really difficult.'

'I don't get it. *"It's a bunch, an unattached President."* What does that mean?'

'It's an anagram of the words *"a bunch an."* said George, looking slightly uncomfortable. He knew it was the most tenuous clue in the whole crossword.

'And the unattached President?'

'Buchanan was the only President of the United States who was a confirmed bachelor, so the clue works on two levels. It's an anagram of *"a bunch an"* as well as having a factual root.'

Albert put the paper down in disgust. How anyone was meant to work that out was beyond him. Still, the important thing was at least they knew what they had to do next, which was find out who Ross and Buchanan were. Trying to work out what VECTOR or ARTEMIS meant was nigh on impossible, they were just individual words which could have stood for anything. But having names and real life people to try and identify was much more promising. Something tangible to follow up on. The incident had remained unresolved for over twenty years and most of the other information in the crossword was in the public domain, or at least known to the journalists and everyone else who worked on the story. All of which suggested that if something was about to break, identifying Ross and Buchanan might be the key to unlocking the whole mystery. Maybe, after all these years there was finally a chance of identifying who was actually responsible.

'So, tell me again George,' asked Albert, picking up his cup and taking a small sip of tea, 'what did this bloke look like.'

'The one in the cafe?'

'Yes. Describe him again. What did he look like?'

George picked up his own cup and took a large gulp as he tried to remember, replaying the meeting and the conversation in Francorelli's back through his mind. Something he had done at regular intervals since it had happened. 'Not much to say about him really. Middle aged, or late thirties at least. Medium height, medium build. He was very ordinary looking.'

'There must have been something,' said Albert in frustration. 'Everybody has something that is distinctive about them.'

George shrugged. Nothing was coming to mind.

'White?'

'Yes.'

'British?'

'No. He had an accent.'

'Not English then?'

'Definitely not. Not Home Counties anyway...'

Albert smiled to himself. Not many people used the term Home Counties anymore. It was typical of George, living in his small, old-fashioned world full of printed newspapers and crossword puzzles. No wonder he went to the Isle of Wight for his holidays. He was born out of his time.

'...East European, I think. Polish or Romanian maybe.'

'Or Russian?'

'Possibly. The only thing I remember about him was a ring.'

'A ring?'

'He put his hands on the table before he left. He was wearing a gold signet ring on his right hand. I thought that was odd, wearing it on his right hand rather than the left. And it was unusual. It had a red stone. Onyx I think.'

'Well, it's something I suppose,' said Albert, secretly wondering whether the mysterious guy was either Ross or Buchanan. But it was a long shot. There was no reason why it should be. 'I like this clue,' he said, suddenly changing the subject and pointing back towards the newspaper. '16. Down. "*Drug runners in backless shoes*." Nice and easy. Even I could get that.'

George smiled as he looked at the answer MULES. It was probably the easiest one in the whole crossword.

'So what's the best clue you've ever written then George?'

George drank another mouthful of tea as he gave it some thought, not that it was a particularly difficult question. 'For a long time it was the anagram I did about Margaret Thatcher, "*A politician, that great charmer*." But now it's probably one of the more recent ones, "*They're in the new stadium*." It was published in the *Chronicle* not that long ago.'

'Go on.'

'West Ham United.'

Albert frowned. He wasn't much of a football fan but even he knew that West Ham had recently moved from their ground at Upton Park to the new Olympic Stadium. That didn't sound like much of a cryptic clue at all.

'It's also an anagram,' said George, catching Albert's expression. "*The new stadium*" is an anagram of West Ham United. I got a lot of plaudits for that.'

Albert raised his eyebrows in appreciation as he checked off the two words, mentally matching the letters in each one. That was certainly impressive. Old George was a lot brighter than he looked sometimes.

'...although I have to say, some of the ones I wrote last night were pretty good.'

'Last night?'

'I did another crossword last night. Laura Taylor or whatever her name is has disappeared and that bloke in the café has probably done the same. I thought I'd give them a surprise and try and flush them out.'

'Jesus George, are you serious?'

'Absolutely. I put everything in it that had happened. Every detail I could think of. They told me to keep my head down for a few days but I decided to do the opposite.'

'Bloody hell George, that's a bit risky. When does it come out?'

George picked up his cup again and gave Albert a wicked grin. 'Tomorrow morning. That's why I'm hiding up here with you!'

Eighteen

THE ANCIENT CITY OF WINCHESTER, LOCATED ALONG the course of the river Itchen in rural Hampshire was once England's capital, preceding London by some two hundred years. The city was steeped in historical interest, the present structure dating back to its reconstruction in the late 9th century when King Alfred the Great obliterated the Roman street plan in favour of a new layout to provide better defence against the Vikings. Today the city provided visitors with an unrivalled opportunity to experience Britain's past, its major attractions including Winchester Castle, Wolvesey Castle and Palace, and of course Winchester Cathedral, originally built in 1079 and with the longest medieval nave in Europe. Containing fine architecture from the 11th to the 16th century it attracted thousands of tourists every year, many coming to see the shrine of Saint Swithun, or the final resting place of Anglo-Saxon monarchs such as Egbert of Wessex, later monarchs such as King Canute and William II, as well as the novelist Jane Austen.

The city was also home to Winchester College, founded by William of Wykeham in 1387 and reputedly the oldest public school in the United Kingdom. When Henry VI founded Eton College in 1440 he took Winchester as his model, visiting it on many occasions and removing its Headmaster and some of the Scholars to start his new venture. Today, the College educated around 700 boys of which 70 Wykeham Scholars still lived in its medieval buildings; eating supper in College Hall, the original Scholars' dining room and attending services in the 14th century Gothic Chapel.

Wykeham Antiques was a small but busy antique shop, nestled in the narrow row of privately owned shops in Peel Lane, midway between the Cathedral and the College and not far from the Wykeham Arms, one of Winchester's most famous pubs. Its owner, Jonathan Lander, was something of an amateur enthusiast, having converted his lifelong interest in collectables into a successful, thriving business. An unremarkable but profitable career in marketing had given him the financial security to take a leap of faith and do something that he was really passionate about and the attraction of Winchester, and in particular the shop's location in the heart of the city's historic centre, was an opportunity too good to miss.

Like many middle-aged professionals who had left the City, Lander had developed a more bohemian approach to life, his days now spent between the shop in Peel Street and the local auction houses, browsing through catalogues and rooms full of clutter, hoping to find that elusive old master or classic piece of furniture just waiting to be snapped up from an unsuspecting seller. His only concession to his previous life were the pink shirts that he wore, a legacy of a career spent in Covent Garden studios, these days worn with the ubiquitous blue jeans and various coloured waistcoats, a style which gave him a certain flamboyance with his customers and a certain cachet with the ladies. In fact, to say that Jonathan was something of ladies' man was an understatement, although in truth it was more in his head than in real life. His hair worn slightly too long and his waistline now too round (a product of too many hours spent in the Wykeham Arms) meant that he had become something of a caricature in the local community, an amusing, popular raconteur but ultimately someone with more style than substance. Still, despite an expensive divorce and a weakness for fine wine and expensive clocks, Jonathan Lander enjoyed his life and was a happy and contented man. At least he had been until the visit last night.

Craven found the shop without too much difficulty, a combination of an effective sat-nav and a well-honed sense of direction. He was also early, the events of last night meaning that as soon as he'd finished in Winchester he had to hurtle back up the M3 so that he could update Buchanan on the situation with Ross. That was the trouble with freelance. One minute things were really quiet and then the next minute you had more work than you could shake a stick at. *London buses.* Still, better to be busy than no work at all. Craven checked his watch. Nine-thirty. It was a glorious, bright, sunny morning but already the temperature was in the low twenties, the forecasters predicting the hottest day of the year. He could see one customer in the bookshop next door but the antique shop was definitely empty, other than the assistant of course, standing behind the counter. He pushed the door open and stepped inside.

The girl at the end of the shop looked up in surprise, not expecting to see anyone that early in the morning. Craven gave her a friendly smile as he gently closed the door behind him. The shop itself was larger than it looked from the outside, a reasonable footprint filled with what looked like quality, high-end stock. Craven didn't know a lot about antiques but he knew enough to know that these days a lot of so-called antique shops were mostly full of junk. Many a time he had browsed through the contents of a local dealer, amused to see stuff being sold as rare and valuable items which not that long ago he had thrown away as rubbish and completely worthless. All credit to Jonathan Lander then. He obviously had some standards and had decided to stay at the top end of the market.

'Are you looking for anything in particular,' asked the girl, displaying a confidence which belied her age, 'or are you happy to browse?'

'Actually,' replied Craven, walking up to the counter, 'I'm looking for Mr. Lander. Is he in?'

'He's not I'm afraid. Can I help?'

'I'm not sure. Are you expecting him later?'

The girl gave him a knowing look. 'I was expecting him at 9.00 o'clock. He hasn't shown up yet.'

Craven smiled, quickly reading her demeanour. 'I get the impression that's not an unusual occurrence.'

The girl smiled back. 'You could say that again. I'd give you his mobile number but I've already tried it. He's not answering.'

'And no idea where he might be?'

The girl shook her head and then nodded towards the pub in the distance. 'Too early for the Wykeham.'

Craven nodded to himself slowly as the penny started to drop. He was getting a very insightful picture of the elusive Mr. Lander. 'Not to worry, maybe you can help me,' he said and in the same breath took out a small, black leather wallet which he opened and quickly flashed in front of her. 'I need to speak to him about an investigation into some items that he sold.'

The girl raised her eyebrows as she glanced at the photo of Craven and the official-looking identity card. Craven put it back in his pocket as quickly as it had come out. Impersonating a police officer was a serious criminal offence which risked a custodial sentence. He was always careful not to imply that he was actually a copper but quickly showing the ID card was usually enough to convince most people. Not that it was genuine of course but that didn't matter. It looked the part from a distance and hardly anyone bothered to inspect it properly.

The girl didn't looked phased at the thought of suddenly having to answer questions about a police investigation. In fact she seemed mildly interested. Maybe it was a bit of excitement in an otherwise dull and boring day. Or maybe she knew Lander well enough to know that there was nothing to worry about. He was a wheeler-dealer of course and a bit of a maverick but there was never any suggestion of him doing something dishonest.

'He's not in any trouble,' reassured Craven, 'I'm just trying to identify the origin of something that he sold about a month ago.' He took out the piece of paper that he'd written on at Mrs. Wallis's house and passed the details over.

The girl quickly scanned it and then frowned. 'Photographs? He doesn't deal in photographs.'

'What, never?'

'Well, hardly ever. It's not really his thing.' She turned and looked around the room, indicating to Craven to do the same. It was true. The shop was full of antiques but there was nothing really later than the 1950s. There were a few pieces of furniture, mostly smaller items like an occasional chair or a small chest of drawers but otherwise the stock was mostly clocks, silverware and a miscellaneous array of objets d'art; mostly Victorian or early 20th century. Contemporary photographs didn't fit in at all with the style and period of everything else.

'Well, that's really odd,' said Craven, standing his ground. 'I was sure they came from here. That's what it says in the buyer's record.'

The girl frowned as she handed the piece of paper back. 'The only time he gets any photographs is when he does a house clearance. But only because they're part of all the rubbish that he has to take. He normally chucks them straight away. He's only interested in keeping anything that he can sell on.'

Craven folded the piece of paper and put it back in his pocket. He had no doubt that the girl was telling the truth, he could see that with his own eyes from the antiques in front of him. But he was also certain that the entry in Wallis's file was genuine. Wallis had been a very organised businessman and his record keeping was meticulous.

'Do you know what sort of photographs they are?' asked the girl, trying to be helpful. 'If they were very old it's a possibility I suppose.'

'Not really,' replied Craven. 'The buyer's record simply says "14 x PH. M. D&D." From the other records it looks as though M. stands for monochrome. Black and White.'

'And PH definitely stand for photographs?'

Craven nodded. There was no doubt about that. He'd been through Wallis's filing system with a fine tooth-comb. PH was for photographs, PR for prints and PA for paintings.

'And D&D?'

Craven shrugged. He had no idea what D&D meant. A quick internet search last night had revealed nothing other than Dungeons and Dragons which was obviously meaningless, a chain of restaurants called D&D in London and a whole number of unrelated acronyms such Deaf and Dumb, Drag and Drop and Drunk and Disorderly, none of which looked as though they had anything to do with rare and valuable photographs. The girl went silent for a moment and then squatted down below the counter, obviously looking for something in the drawers or shelves below. Craven leant forward and peered down at her, staring at the top of her head as she rummaged through a collection of books and files.

'Here we go,' she said, suddenly standing up with a dark green ledger in her hand and giving Craven a mischievous grin. 'I'd offer to look it up on our system but we haven't got one. This is it.'

Craven smiled back. She was being more help that he could have ever imagined.

'Do you know the name of the buyer?' she asked, quickly turning the pages to find the latest entry. The ledger was A4 in size and each page had about twenty lined rows, each one filled with the same, florid handwriting written in blue fountain pen ink.

'The Abacus Gallery, London.'

The girl was now running her finger down each page, working backwards from the most recent entry and quickly checking the name of the buyer under each row. 'And the date it was sold?'

'About a month ago. 20th June probably.'

The girl continued the line by line, page by page search but after about six pages she looked up and shook her head. 'Sorry. I've gone back as far as April. Nothing in the name of Abacus.'

'What about David Wallis then?' asked Craven, suddenly thinking that Wallis might have for some reason bought the photos under his own name.

The girl scanned each line again, this time starting from April and working forwards towards the last entry in July, quickly turning the pages as she checked for the name Wallis. As before, she shook her head when she reached the end. 'Sorry, nothing.'

'Oh, well, thanks for trying,' said Craven. 'Looks like I've drawn a blank.'

'I'll give you Jonathan's number, just in case you want to call him,' said the girl, scribbling the number on a scrap of paper and passing it over. 'Or you could try popping back later. He's bound to show up at some point.'

'Thanks. I might do that.' Craven made his way to the door but he had no intention of coming back. As much as he wanted to help Mrs. Wallis he knew a dead end when he saw one and besides, Buchanan's assignment was much more important. It was time to get back up to London and find out what was going on in the aftermath of finding Ross's body last night. Plus he had to try and find George Wiggins, wherever he had disappeared to. He opened the door but then paused for a moment, a thought suddenly running through his brain.

'You mentioned house clearances. Has he done any of those recently?'

The girl shook her head. 'He doesn't really like them. Says they're not worth it...'

Craven smiled to himself. That made a lot of sense. When his own father died they got a local firm to clear out the property but all the decent stuff had already been taken, individually selected by friends and relatives beforehand. The poor guy was just a glorified dustman really.

'...although come to think of it, he did do one about a month ago. It was a big house on Christchurch Road. Jonathan thought there might be some money in that one.'

'Have you got the address?' asked Craven, trying to work out whether it was worth following up or not. It was a complete punt of course, hardly a lead at all but sometimes, in the absence of any other options he had to follow his intuition and suddenly, for some unexplained reason, all of his instincts were telling him this might be important.

'I'll have it somewhere,' replied the girl, squatting down behind the counter again while she looked for a different file, 'but I'm sure there weren't any photographs. I would have remembered if there were...'

Craven's shoulders dropped. Maybe this was a waste of time after all.

'...although somebody there must have been a keen photographer. We got a few cameras from that one. Some of them were quite old and collectable.' She nodded towards a round table near the window, a 19th century burr walnut centre table with a canted edge, cross-banded frieze and four ring turned legs with shaped feet on castors. Craven wandered over and looked at the collection of items displayed on the top, mostly an assortment of paper knives, magnifying glasses and candle snuffers but in the middle were two cameras, both very old but both in fabulous condition. Whoever they belonged to had taken great care to look after them.

'We've already sold a couple,' continued the girl 'but those two came from the same lot. Nice, aren't they?'

Craven nodded as he picked one of them up and turned it over, a 1936 Zeiss Super Ikonta complete with leather carrying case. He didn't know anything about cameras or photography but he guessed that these were probably quite rare, particularly in such good condition. Certainly the price tag of £195 gave that impression.

'Here's the address,' said the girl, walking over with another piece of paper, 'but the house is probably empty now, or sold to someone else. So I've also given you the contact details of the seller. It's the daughter I think.'

'Great. Thanks for your help,' said Craven, looking at the two addresses, both of which were in Winchester so not far away. Certainly worth spending half an hour to follow up. 'And if you see Mr Lander tell him I'd like to speak to him.'

'Will do,' replied the girl as she held the door open to let Craven out and then watched him for a moment as he crossed the road and walked towards St Swithun Street and the Cathedral. Then she closed the door and took out her phone and called Lander's mobile, wondering momentarily whether he was going to answer. It rang for about thirty seconds but then stopped and went into voicemail, her boss's relaxed and friendly greeting inviting her to leave a message. She shrugged and put the phone back in her pocket, certain that he would turn up sooner or later, probably a bit dishevelled and worse for wear but grinning from ear to ear with some cock and bull story about why he was late. She smiled to herself, suddenly remembering why she liked working for him so much, not realising for one second that she would never see him or hear from him again. *"Life's but a walking shadow, a poor player that struts and frets his hour upon the stage, and then is heard no more..."*

Nineteen

'COFFEE?'
Buchanan nodded and eased himself into the armchair as the waiter picked up the silver pot and poured some finest Arabica blend into an empty cup, not bothering to enquire whether Carlisle wanted a refill. The Cabinet Secretary had already drunk a couple this morning and Jenkins knew that two was his daily limit, at least until after dinner before he moved onto the cigars and brandy. Carlisle looked up momentarily and gave Buchanan an efficient smile, their relationship a complex mix of both colleague and adversary; a lifelong game of political chess played beneath a veneer of trust and cooperation.

'Just give me a moment Charles to finish this.'

Buchanan waved his hand dismissively as Carlisle returned to his paperwork, engrossed in the itinerary of the PM's visit to Scotland; a schedule of journeys and visits timetabled down to the last minute. He was going through it in painstaking detail, having learnt from bitter experience not to rely on arrangements made by anyone else, especially those muppets in the DPG or the drones over at Thames House. *If you want something doing properly, do it yourself...*

Buchanan picked up his cup and saucer and took a sip of coffee as he looked around the members' lounge, familiarising himself with the surroundings. He had been in White's before of course but it always struck him as rather condescending and pretentious compared to Boodles, his own club just a few doors down the road. White's did however enjoy the distinction of being the oldest gentlemen's club in the world. Established in 1693 it soon became notorious as a high-stakes gambling house, a place where Regency gentlemen once bet on which drop of rain would reach the bottom of the window pane first or which bluebottle would be the first to fly off. Those who frequented it were known as "the gamesters of White's," Jonathan Swift once referring to it as the *"bane of half the English nobility."* That was in its heyday of course when the club was the unofficial headquarters of the Tory party and where fortunes were won or lost at the card table; a place of capacious leather armchairs and obsequious servants, of hushed conversations in smoked-filled dining rooms and above all, a gentlemen's sanctuary where women were not allowed to enter.

Buchanan picked up a menu and smiled to himself. Not much had changed in over 300 years. The cuisine was still based on the best of British game; grouse, partridge, wild salmon, gull's eggs, potted shrimps, smoked eel and smoked trout. And although there was a vegetarian option it was universally unpopular, much to the delight of its traditionalist membership. Prince Charles had held his stag night there before his wedding to Lady Diana Spencer in 1981 and it remained the languorous resting place of many a Prime Minister until this day.

Its location at 37-38 St James's Street was just a stone's throw from Boodles at number 28, which as far as Buchanan was concerned was a much more prestigious and refined establishment. Boodles was founded in 1762 by the Earl of Shelburne, later the Marquess of Lansdowne and future Prime Minister of the United Kingdom, and was named after its original head waiter, the austere Edward Boodle. Buchanan had been a member since his twenty-third birthday when his father, delighted at his son's academic achievements at Oxford, nominated his membership which was duly approved without objection. Like White's and Brook's, the latter also formed in the same year, Boodle's heritage was as an aristocratic, pleasure-seeking club, providing its raffish members with a discreet and civilised refuge, the sort of place where Bertie Wooster could disappear to, away from the demands of his family and the ever-decreasing circles of PG Wodehouse's plots. To this day, club members could still recline in an haven of tranquillity and munch on Orange Fool, its famous traditional dish. It was also very different from the culture of the great Victorian clubs which followed – The Carlton Club, The Reform Club, The Athenaeum – many of them founded with serious-minded ideals and with more learned objectives than the clubs that had gone before. Still, Boodle's counted many British aristocrats and notable politicians among its members, the more famous of which over the years included Field Marshall Arthur Wellesley, 1st Duke of Wellington, Adam Smith, Sir Winston Churchill and the novelist Ian Fleming. Buchanan had always felt hugely privileged to be a member in such distinguished company. And of course the other advantage of Boodles was that he didn't have to be a member of a club which accepted people like Sir James Carlisle.

Buchanan stared at him across the table, Carlisle's head still buried in his paperwork and oblivious to the scrutiny that was taking place. Buchanan had known him for years, watching each promotion and career move with a detached curiosity. Going to Winchester and Oxford had given him significant advantages in life but the simple truth was that the only reason Carlisle had risen to the dizzy heights of Cabinet Secretary was because he played the political game better than anyone else. He worked hard of course and had a brilliant, razor sharp mind but admirable as those qualities were, they were not the defining qualities for ultimate success. It was the guile and the cunning and the sheer ruthlessness that had got him to where he was. That and the fact that he was a cocksucker. A vile, obsequious parasite who spent his whole life sucking up to his paymasters, outmanoeuvring his opponents and stabbing everyone else in the back. *"I have no spur to prick the sides of my intent, but only vaulting ambition, which o'erleaps itself and falls on th'other."*

'You're staring at me Charles.'

Buchanan raised his eyebrows, conscious that Carlisle was still head down, engrossed in the itinerary but somehow sensing the unwanted attention.

'Just admiring the dedication.'

Carlisle looked up and gave him a thin smile, not fooled for one second by the compliment. Buchanan was someone he had learnt a lifetime ago never to trust. In fact he was one of the few people that Carlisle had failed to get the better of, despite numerous attempts over the years. He wasn't exactly a peer of course, they were hardly competing for the same patronage but they moved in similar circles and Buchanan had an influence and authority which was always a threat. In fact it was second to none. Independent, incorruptible and invariably dangerous. And of course he lived in a world which Carlisle didn't understand at all. Carlisle had spent his whole life in the Civil Service which meant that he had led a safe, cocooned existence for more years than he cared to remember, slightly detached and protected from the real world. And having been a Private Secretary and now the Cabinet Secretary, he was used to getting his own way. Accustomed to controlling events, rather than waiting for things to happen. Buchanan's world was completely the opposite. Machiavellian, dark and extremely treacherous. Not something that could be controlled at all.

Carlisle pushed the paperwork to one side before returning his fountain pen to the inside pocket of his jacket with a flourish. 'Sorry about that Charles. Tedious admin. You know what it's like.'

Buchanan gave him a thin smile back, the veiled insult only too clear. 'No, not particularly.'

'Really? You surprise me.'

'I don't have any time for bureaucracy...'

Carlisle yawned slightly and glanced at his watch. That normally irritated most people.

'...still, I suppose matters of State require a different level of oversight...'

'Indeed.'

Buchanan nodded towards the file. '...and it's reassuring to know that you've found your level.'

Carlisle stared at him across the table, their eyes locked in a cold, silent Mexican standoff. After what seemed like an eternity he picked up the coffee pot and poured himself a third cup. *Bugger the blood pressure.* Then he glanced at his watch again and leant back into the armchair, the soft, ageing leather settling under his weight. 'So, how can I help you Charles? As good as it is to see you of course...'

'Likewise.' Still the thin smile.

'...I am rather busy...'

'Naturally.'

'...so can we get on with it?'

'Of course. I just need to update you on something.'

'Something?'

Buchanan lowered his voice and leant forward slightly. There was hardly anyone else in the club so unlikely that they could be overheard but it all added to the subterfuge. 'Ross.'

Carlisle raised his eyebrows but resisted the temptation to also lean forward. The last thing he wanted to do was give Buchanan the satisfaction of adopting the same body language. It was like acquiescing to his little role play. That was the trouble with spooks. They were all the same. They enjoyed the theatre of it too much. 'Is it done?'

'Yes.'

'Good.'

'Well that's the problem. I'm not sure it is.'

Carlisle frowned, understandably confused by the last comment.

'It's done. But not by us.'

Carlisle frowned even more, trying to work out the implications of what he was hearing. He picked up the cup and saucer and took a gulp of coffee, grimacing at the fact that it was now luke-warm. 'Our cousins?'

Buchanan shook his head. 'They had him under surveillance. They were about to pick him up so they clearly thought he was still alive.'

'Who then?'

'Hard to say. But it looks horribly familiar.'

'Familiar?'

'Body in a holdall. Zipped up and padlocked.'

Carlisle nodded slowly, recalling the case of Gareth Williams, an MI6 code-breaker who was found dead in suspicious circumstances at his SIS safe house apartment in central London. An incident which generated much speculation at the time with all sorts of conspiracy theories appearing on the internet. The fact that Williams was a maths genius with an alleged predilection for cross-dressing also fuelled the more lurid headlines in the red tops, with much speculation about it being an elaborate sex game that had gone disastrously wrong. Williams was an employee of GCHQ but had been seconded to MI6 having recently qualified for operational deployment to work with the US National Security Agency and the FBI on covert surveillance. His naked, decomposing body was found inside a large, red holdall, padlocked from the outside, in the bathtub of the main bedroom's en-suite bathroom. There were no injuries to his body and no signs that he had been involved in a struggle, in fact the whole crime scene was free of any forensic evidence as if it had been deep cleaned. His family were convinced that DNA had been interfered with as part of a cover-up by security services and crucially no fingerprints, including Williams's own fingerprints, were found around the bath or on the padlock. There was also the suggestion that in the days immediately following the discovery of his body his flat was broken into via a skylight, probably by the security services to remove incriminating evidence. There was no sign of forced entry but voicemail messages left for his family and friends were deleted several days after his death. Inevitably the US State Department asked that no details of Williams's work should emerge at the inquest and the Foreign Secretary at the time, William Hague, signed a public-interest immunity certificate authorising the withholding of details of Williams's work and US joint operations. The Coroner concluded that Mr Williams's death was *"unnatural and likely to have been criminally mediated"* but to this day the incident remained an unresolved mystery.

Buchanan picked up his cup and took another sip of coffee. 'It looks identical. Summer time with the heating turned full on. His iPhone was completely wiped, the bathroom door was closed and the keys to the padlock were underneath his body. Even the bag was the same. A red North Face holdall.'

Carlisle frowned for the third time in as many minutes. 'Any idea who might be responsible?'

Buchanan shrugged. The possibilities were endless.

'So what happens next? Has the problem gone away or not?'

Buchanan leant over to his brief case and pulled out a copy of yesterday's edition of the *Chronicle*. 'Have you seen this?'

Carlisle took the paper and immediately scanned the crossword on the back page. He'd heard about it but hadn't actually seen a copy. It took him only seconds to find what he was looking for, his own name written halfway down the grid with a simple, anagram clue for 18. Across. *"The caller is from a northern town."* He quickly looked through the rest, recognising most of the words and more importantly their meaning. The implications were unimaginable. It was obviously connected to Ross. No one else had access to that level of information. Carlisle took a final glug of coffee and slumped back into his chair. 'Who the hell is Xerxes?'

'It's their usual compiler. We're trying to trace him.'

'Trace him?'

'He's disappeared. Last minute holiday.'

Carlisle raised his eyebrows. That obviously meant the guy was implicated. A large envelope full of cash probably in exchange for doing the crossword. He passed the newspaper back to Buchanan. 'And do we know why?'

Buchanan shook his head. 'Not really, other than someone obviously wants us to know that they know all about Artemis.'

'Which presumably means they want something.'

'Exactly. The question is, what?'

Carlisle fell silent for a moment. It was clearly a bargaining ploy. Publish some highly sensitive words in a national newspaper as an opening bid, prior to a much bigger negotiation. It was like laying down a pair of Aces in a game of poker. Persuade the other players to fold before the bidding even started. But what game were they actually playing? And what the hell did they want?

Buchanan folded the paper and put it carefully back into his briefcase. 'The other problem is that we don't know who we are dealing with. It looks Russian but that could be deliberate. If the information got into the wrong hands it could be anybody.'

Carlisle's face darkened. That thought was the most worrying of all. 'You think Ross passed the information to someone else?'

'It's possible. He made a brush pass in London a couple of weeks ago. Other than the compiler, it's our only lead.'

'Maybe we should have talked to Ross first?'

'It's a bit late for that.'

'And Xerxes?'

'I've got my best man on it. If he's out there we'll find him.'

'Best man?'

'Craven.'

Carlisle shivered, the memory of crossing paths with Craven several years ago. Not an encounter that he ever wanted to repeat again. At the same moment the phone in Buchanan's pocket started to ring, the opening bars of Bach's *Passepied* from Orchestral Suite No. 1 in C Major. 'Hello?'

'It's me.'

Buchanan glanced at his watch. As always, Maurice's voice was unmistakeable. 'Obviously.'

'Can you talk?'

'Can I call you back?'

'Okay – but it's urgent.'

'Go on then. Make it snappy.'

'Two things. We've got another crossword. Published this morning...'

'Really?' Buchanan's mind was racing. What on earth was there left to reveal. Surely the first crossword had disclosed just about everything there was to know about Artemis.

'...different content,' continued Maurice, 'but definitely the same compiler. It's got his signature all over it.'

Buchanan glanced at Carlisle. This wasn't going to go down well. 'And the other thing?'

'Our man in a suitcase. It's not Ross...'

Twenty

THE CHRISTCHURCH ROAD IN WINCHESTER WAS A long, straight, tree-lined avenue on the south side of the city; an expensive and desirable location full of large Edwardian houses with substantial, mature gardens. Craven found the address without too much difficulty but it was obvious that the house was empty, the estate agent's board outside confirming that it had already been sold. He pulled over and got out of the car, just to make sure that there was no one in but everything seemed still and quiet, as if the whole place had gone to sleep and was waiting for a new family to bring it back to life again. He looked up at the large bay windows, shielding his eyes from the sun which was burning down from a cloudless, blue sky; the garden still and silent in the intense, oppressive heat. Then he stared at the neat box hedging, the carefully tended borders and the smart gravel drive. No wonder Lander had been keen to do a house clearance here. Even with friends and family getting first pickings there must have been a good chance of finding something valuable in a property like this. Craven got back in the car and checked the piece of paper that the girl at Wykeham Antiques had given him. He didn't know the name of the previous owners at Christchurch Road so had no idea whether Ms. P. Marshall was a daughter or daughter-in-law but either way it looked like an ageing relative had passed away, mother or father probably, and that she had arranged the house clearance. He tapped the second address into the sat-nav and then drove off towards the other side of the city, a ten minute drive probably given the mid-morning traffic.

Kiln Close was a small, crescent-shaped road with a mixture of Victorian and Georgian houses, a few of which were detached but most of them terraced with low front walls and short front gardens. The road was fairly narrow with cars parked on either side so it took him some time to find a space. Eventually he parked a few hundred yards up the road and then walked back to number 17, a traditional Georgian town house with tall, symmetrical windows and a solid black door. Even from a distance he could tell that the police were at the same address. In truth, the patrol car would have also struggled to find a space so they could have been visiting any of the houses along the road but there was something about the way it was parked, angled towards the pavement and towards the front of number 17 that made him think that they were inside. That and the fact that he didn't believe in coincidences. Something very odd was going on in Winchester and all roads suddenly led to Jonathan Lander and to a house clearance that he did several weeks ago.

Craven walked slowly up the road, checking out the lie of the land and making a mental note of any escape routes, just in case he needed to make a sudden exit. A slow, lumbering woodentop was no match for a quick sprint up one of the side alleys and then an impressive leap over a garden fence. As he approached number 17 he took out a packet of cigarettes and then paused outside as he lit one up, taking the opportunity to look at the front of the house. He was hoping that he might see or hear something but the door was firmly shut and there was no way of telling whether the police were there or not. In fact there was no way of telling whether there was anyone home at all. He put the lighter back in his pocket and continued walking down the road, all the way to the end where there was a t-junction, one way leading to the town centre and the other heading out towards Kings Worthy. He crossed over the road and walked back up Kiln Close, now on the other side with the even numbers on his left. He could still see the police car parked outside number

17, still looking as though it was visiting that address but no signs of life and no indication of how long it was going to be there. In the end he decided to walk back to the car and sit down while he waited. There was no point in being impatient. Years of experience had taught him that effective surveillance was all about three things; preparation, concentration and above all, endless, unwavering patience. He'd lost count of how many hours he had spent waiting in cold, uncomfortable conditions, often in foreign and dangerous environments, just to make sure that a covert operation was successful. It was an essential part of any intelligence assignment but it was invariably an uneventful, mind-numbing activity and he'd learnt long ago that impatience was its greatest enemy. At least sitting in the car he was comfortable and he had a radio to keep him company. In fact compared to his previous life this was an absolute doddle.

Craven got back in the car and glanced at his watch, deciding to check on the target every five minutes. Standard surveillance procedure. In the end it was twenty minutes before the coast was clear which meant that it was nearly 11.00 o'clock by the time he made a move. *So much for a quick, early visit and a swift drive back up to London.* He walked back towards the house, hoping that his instincts would be proved right but also mindful that this could be a complete waste of time. There was still the possibility that there was no one at home or even if there was, there was no certainty that Lander's house clearance had anything to do with David Wallis. The whole thing was just a complete hunch.

There was no doorbell so he rapped the knocker three times, a large, heavy brass handle with a solid, round striking plate. The door opened within a matter of seconds and Craven stared in disbelief at the rather plain, middle-aged woman, initially looking stressed and exasperated at the interruption but then looking back at him in abject horror.

He glanced at the piece of paper again, just to make sure that he had the right name. A myriad of connections and permutations were suddenly racing through his mind. What the hell was going on? 'Mrs. Marshall?'

She regained her composure and gave him a faint smile, knowing that he had already recognised her. 'Yes. I'm sorry, I've forgotten your name. Mr...?'

'Craven. We met yesterday at your sister's house. Fiona Wallis.'

'Yes, of course. Come in Mr. Craven.'

Penny Marshall turned and walked up the hall, leaving Craven to shut the door and follow her into a reception room on the left. If her sister's house was contemporary and minimalist this was exactly the opposite; a classic, Georgian drawing room furnished entirely in keeping with the character of the property. Solid oak floors, period walnut furniture, exquisite gilt mirrors, heavy draped curtains and elegant chandelier lighting. In all respects it was perfect, other than the fact that it was a complete mess. A couple of small tables had been knocked over and the drawers of several cabinets and a bureau were wide open with their contents strewn across the floor. Either she was having a clear out or she had just been burgled. Given the police car outside it had to be the latter. Craven stared at her in concern. 'I'm sorry, have I called at the wrong time?'

She gave him a tired smile, running her fingers through her hair as she looked around the room at the mess, wondering where to start. 'No, it's okay Mr. Craven. It will be nice to have the company to be honest. Can I get you a coffee?'

He nodded. 'A coffee would be great, thank you.'

'How do you take it?'

'Black, one sugar please.'

She disappeared into the kitchen and Craven stood motionless for a moment, partly still in shock at seeing her again and also while his brain went into overdrive, trying to work out what was going on. Suddenly it looked as though she might be the connection between David Wallis and Jonathan Lander but exactly how or why he wasn't sure. In fact he didn't have a clue.

She was going to take several minutes in the kitchen so he decided to nose around, taking care not to touch or move anything that had been disturbed. In the centre of the far wall was a fireplace with a large, marble mantelpiece on top of which were a few photographs, a collection of family snaps in silver and pewter frames. He picked up what appeared to be the earliest one, an old black and white photo of a man and woman, in their mid-20s probably, presumably her parents but taken many years ago when they were young and carefree and full of life. He studied their faces, looking older than their counterparts would today, a product of time and different generations but revealing an innocence and ambition which were much the same. A young couple, probably recently married or engaged, looking forward to a life full of hope and adventure. Unsure about where their future lay but confident that they would always face it together. A smiling, determined partnership standing side-by-side, hand-in-hand on an English seaside promenade. Undoubting, optimistic and above all, unashamedly in love.

'Coffee will be five minutes.'

'Thanks.' Craven hadn't heard her walk back into the room. He turned round and looked at her and then put the photograph back onto the mantelpiece, making sure that he put it in exactly the same position. Suddenly he felt as though he was intruding on something very personal.

'My parents. Taken on their honeymoon.'

Craven nodded in acknowledgement. 'They look very happy. Where was it taken?'

'Southwold. They had a long weekend I think. It was all they could afford.'

Craven smiled to himself. That was a familiar story all right. His parents were exactly the same. Not Southwold of course, that was much too posh for his Mum and Dad but it was definitely a long weekend by the coast somewhere. He racked his brains. Margate. Or maybe it was Ramsgate. Either way it was what

187

everyone did back then, or at least everyone from the East End. It was the only thing most people could afford. A simple church service with the bride wearing a tailored suit and carrying a posy, followed by a reception above a local pub, the catering provided by friends and family; tinned salmon sandwiches, sausage rolls, home-made wedding cake and an urn full of builder's tea. The men swilling pints of bitter and smoking Players cigarettes, sharing jokes and chatting up the bridesmaids, the top buttons and ties undone at the earliest opportunity. And then a few days away by the seaside, sometimes in a borrowed car. Battered, old leather suitcases, a bed and breakfast on the seafront, cockles, eels and fish and chips. Another time, another place. It seemed like a million years ago. These days people spent tens of thousands of pounds just on the wedding day itself, let alone the honeymoon. It was as if for some people the ceremony was more important than the marriage, what with the designer wedding dresses, the expensive venues, and the live music and professional videos. And whatever happened to the good old stag night when the bridegroom went out the night before and got legless with his best mates? Now they were flying to Amsterdam or Prague or some other exotic location for several days at time. And the girls were no better. Aeroplanes full of common, vulgar women wearing pink tutus and L plates with fake boobs and huge blow-up penises. It was appalling. The world had gone absolutely stark raving bloody mad.

'It's my favourite photo of them...'

Craven turned round and looked at her, her eyes welling up with tears.

'...Dad was always an incurable romantic. Every anniversary he took Mum away and always somewhere special for the bigger ones. Rome on their 25th. Paris for their 40th. But they both said they had never been happier than when they were at Southwold.'

Craven gave her a sympathetic smile, not sure what to say.

'I was going to ring you...'

'Really?'

'...but you beat me to it. You don't miss much Mr. Craven, do you?'

Craven shrugged. He had no idea what she was talking about but the last thing he wanted to do was let her know.

'And I assume you're a man of the world?'

'Of course.'

She paused a second and gently bit her bottom lip, as if deciding whether to say something or not. 'Thank you for telling Fiona that David wasn't having an affair. That was very good of you...'

Craven held his hand up to wave away the gratitude. Suddenly the penny had dropped. Literally.

'...it's not something I'm proud of. My sister's husband...'

'Of course not.'

'..but it's hard. Losing a partner is devastating but at least you're allowed to grieve.' She turned and stared around the room again, partly to stop Craven seeing her fill up with tears. 'All I want to do is tell everyone how much I loved him and how much I miss him. But I can't. It's not allowed.'

Craven shuffled on the spot a couple of times, not sure where to look.

She gave him a weak smile, 'I'll go and get that coffee.'

She disappeared into the kitchen and Craven blew out his cheeks, still processing the news that David Wallis was having an affair with his wife's sister. No wonder she looked embarrassed to see him. Even more reason to continue nosing around the room. In the corner was a bureau with most of its contents spilled out onto the floor, a collection of papers, documents and stationery including some cheque books and a small leather wallet containing several credit cards. He knelt down and looked at one of the documents, an ageing, yellowing marriage certificate, written in faded, flowing ink and folded neatly into four. He picked it up and looked at it, just as Penny Marshall walked back into the room carrying a tray with two cups of coffee. He stood up as she put one cup on top of the mantelpiece for him. There was too much mess to put it anywhere else.

'Do you know what's been taken?' he asked, putting the marriage certificate carefully on the bureau.

Penny shrugged, cupping the coffee with both hands as if the warmth was giving her comfort. 'I haven't had time to look properly. I stayed at Fiona's last night to keep her company. I only got back a couple of hours ago.'

'They've left some valuable stuff here,' said Craven, nodding towards the pile of papers on the floor. 'Cheque book, credit cards... '

'I know. I checked my jewellery as soon as I got in. I keep it upstairs. It's all still there.'

Craven put his hands on his hips as he looked around the room again, his expert eye taking in every detail, every piece of information from what was still an undisturbed crime scene. This wasn't a burglary, at least not a burglary where they nicked anything of value that they could lay their hands on. It was someone looking for something very specific. Something they were desperate to find. Something they were prepared to kill for. It was probably a godsend that she wasn't at home last night. He walked over to the mantelpiece and picked up his cup of coffee. 'Can I ask you a question?'

She nodded, still cupping the mug in both hands. 'Of course. Anything.'

'Can I ask what perfume you wear?'

'I wear two or three different types. Cartier, mostly at the moment.

'But not Serendipity?'

'No. I don't know where Fiona got that from. It's not one of mine and David definitely wasn't seeing anyone else. I would have known...'

Craven nodded slowly as he processed the information, trying to make sense of it all. If Wallis was having an affair with his sister-in-law it obviously had nothing to do with Serendipity. It looked like his wife had spotted all the secretive behaviours of a cheating husband but connected it to the wrong perfume, a perfume that was worn by somebody else. Not someone he was having an affair with but someone he was doing business with. Business which ultimately got him killed.

'...besides, I made sure not to wear any perfume when I was seeing David. It's one of the first things you learn Mr. Craven if you're cheating on someone. How not to get caught.'

Craven raised his eyebrows in surprise. Penny Marshall was tougher than she looked. She wasn't showing any regret or remorse for what she had done. Only sadness and grief that Wallis had died and a sense of bitterness that she couldn't tell the world how she felt. He took another mouthful of coffee and then walked back over to the bureau and picked up the marriage certificate again. 'Can I ask you about your parents?'

She nodded and reversed slowly into one of the armchairs. 'What would you like to know?'

'They lived at Christchurch Road?'

She nodded again and smiled, a fond recollection of a happy childhood washing over her. Long hot summers, dark, foggy bonfire nights, white, magical Christmases. *"There is a time of year, a brief and seductive moment when the last warm days of spring spill gently into the first, early days of summer which fills your very heart with a renewed and impulsive yearning for love and laughter and life. An idyllic spell of sun kissed days and warm light evenings, when scented breezes drift through twilight windows and with closed eyes, intoxicate your mind and senses, recalling long, forgotten childhood games. A time of dreams and unyielding optimism which melts the shadows of winters cold and then, as quickly as it came, is lost beneath the soft, incessant rain which brings the English summer in."*

Craven coughed gently, trying not to intrude on her memories. She gave him an apologetic smile. 'Sorry. Miles away.'

'Not a problem. Christchurch Road?'

'Yes. They lived there most of their lives. Fiona and I grew up there. It's always been our family home.'

'It looks like a lovely house.'

'Thank you. It was wonderful. We were very lucky.'

'And your parents. Are they still alive?' Craven was choosing his words carefully. He was pretty certain that they were both dead but he didn't want to assume anything.

She shook her head. 'Dad died about ten years ago and Mum passed away last month. She was 82. She was incredibly independent after Dad went. Very stoical in that British sort of way. Determined to cope and not be a burden to anyone. In the end the house and garden got too big for her but she refused to move. She wanted to stay until the end.'

Craven smiled at her. She was having a tough time but she was coping admirably. Most people would have crumbled having lost a parent and their lover in a matter of weeks. 'And the house clearance. Wykeham Antiques?'

She shrugged. 'I just picked them out of the phone book. Or the local paper actually. Fiona and I kept a few personal things but otherwise they took everything else.'

'Including photographs?'

She gave him a knowing smile. 'Thousands. Tens of thousands. Dad had been a keen photographer all his life. It was his passion. He even had a dark room at one point. There were boxes and boxes full of photographs. I assumed they would just throw them away.'

Craven looked at the marriage certificate again. Something was bothering him but he couldn't work out what it was. 'So the fact that they sold some on to David was nothing to do with you?'

She shook her head. 'I didn't know anything about it. Not until I saw the name on David's computer yesterday. They could have been Dad's photos I suppose but they could have come from anywhere.'

Craven stared at her, unconvinced. The girl in the shop had been emphatic that they didn't normally deal in photographs. They had to be part of the house clearance. He looked at the marriage certificate and studied it carefully. *John Graham Marshall, bachelor, aged 25, married Elizabeth Susan Pope, spinster, aged 23 on 31 August 1957 at All Saints Church, Winchester.* He gazed across at Penny Marshall, still cupping her mug of tea and staring into the middle distance, not looking at anything in particular. A plain, middle-aged woman, now completely on her own, struggling to cope with the loss of the two closest people in her life. He wondered how long she had been in love with her brother-in-law. It could have been years. It might even be the reason why she never married. She was probably thinking about him right now. He tried one last question.

'If they were photos from your father's collection, do you have any idea what they might be?'

She snapped out of her trance and looked back at him, giving him an apologetic smile. 'Dad took thousands of photographs. Millions probably. It could be anything. He loved churches. And he had a passion for chimneys. But he took photos of just about everything. And I haven't lived at home for over twenty years. I'm sorry Mr. Craven, I haven't a clue. Mr. Lander will know, presumably?'

Craven checked his watch. Lander had disappeared into thin air. Anyway, it was time to go. Buchanan would be wondering where he was. This was looking like a dead end and besides, he had the little matter of Damien Ross to follow up on. Plus the elusive George Wiggins of course. He thanked Penny Marshall for her time and for the coffee and then made his excuses and left, leaving her to tidy up the mess and pick up the pieces of her life. He walked back to the car, wondering how long it would take him to drive back to London. He slid into the driver's seat and tapped a postcode for central London into the sat-nav. He didn't need it to find his way around London of course but he wasn't sure of the quickest way out of Winchester. The date and time on the screen stared back at him, also confirming how many miles it was and how long the journey would take. And then it hit him. *The marriage certificate*. Suddenly it was jumping off the page. That and something she had said earlier. He didn't know exactly what the photos contained but suddenly he knew what this might be about. It was breath-taking. No wonder they were prepared to kill for it. He turned the key in the ignition and pulled out onto the road. He needed to warn Buchanan. In fact, he needed to warn everybody before it was too late…

Twenty-One

MAUREEN GREEN HAD SPENT HER LIFE IN ESSEX. BORN and bred in Brentwood she went to school at the local comprehensive, married in the local church and then moved out to Shenfield, a small conurbation situated one mile to the north-east of Brentwood serving predominantly as a dormitory town for commuters into London. Historically an old village on the original Roman road linking London to Colchester it was now a typical small suburb, many of its residents suffering the daily battle in and out of Liverpool Street, the fast and regular train service guaranteeing a busy and crowded journey. Maureen had spent her working life commuting into London, initially for a short spell in the City but then moving onto Fleet Street which was more to her liking and where she spent the rest of her career. The newspaper industry was often accused of being full of mavericks, fuelled by too much alcohol and questionable morals but compared to EC3 it was a positive paragon of virtue, at least it was to Maureen. Apart from a couple of short breaks to have her children (both now grown up and gone) she'd spent almost 40 years working somewhere between The Strand and Ludgate Hill, initially for one of the broadsheets but for most of the time at the *Chronicle*, her loyalty and commitment to the paper, and to Vinny Goldman personally, being second to none.

In fact there was a rumour that when they were a lot younger, Maureen and Vinny had once had a fling but it was something they both denied and their refusal to comment on it over the years meant that the gossip eventually fizzled out until it became no more than a faint and unreliable anecdote in the history of the firm. Maureen's loyalty to the *Chronicle* however was unquestionable. She was never a journalist of course, she didn't have the investigative or literary skills to be a reporter but what she lacked in creativity she made up for in organisation and common sense. Starting in administration she quickly made a name for herself as someone who could instil order and discipline in an otherwise chaotic newsroom and within a few years had been promoted to Office Manager, a role which she embraced with relish and one which suited her perfectly. Inevitably, being a woman in Fleet Street meant that she had to develop a resilient attitude to the rabble of young reporters and the locker room mentality but that was not a problem for Maureen. There was no banter that she couldn't keep up with, no admonishment that she couldn't deliver and no bullshit that she couldn't see through.

As the years went by she became the lynchpin of the organisation, the person at the centre of the firm who knew everything that was going on and more importantly, the one person who knew how everything worked and how to get anything done. She was also the heart and soul of the company, managing the conflicting roles of Sergeant Major and Agony Aunt without difficulty. Some said she had a heart of gold and a rod of iron, dishing out bollockings or putting a consoling arm around a young, naive reporter with equal measure and with equal aplomb. And in all that time, while Maureen managed the engine room with a well-honed efficiency Vinny was carving out a career for himself, crawling his way up to the bridge. When he finally got promoted to Editor, Maureen's status at the *Chronicle* was cemented and unchallengeable. Everyone knew that she was Vinny's most loyal supporter and also his eyes and ears of the organisation. People were always wary about crossing Vinny but nobody dared get on the wrong side of Maureen. She had a heart of gold all right but once you crossed the line with Maureen, that was that.

Lots of staff couldn't imagine the firm running without her and many thought that she would never retire, the *Chronicle*, Fleet Street and the newspaper industry having become her whole life. She had a husband and children of course but her commitment and dedication to her work had been absolute for almost 40 years. If the company needed someone to work through the night, work all weekend or cancel their holiday for a special assignment, Maureen was always there, leading from the front with her sleeves rolled up, never asking her staff to do anything that she wasn't prepared to do herself. But in typical Maureen style, once she made her mind up to do something she always did it properly. As she approached her 60th birthday she planned her retirement with the same ruthless efficiency that she managed her job and when the day came to leave, she walked out of Empire House and instantly drew a line under the past. No fuss, no regrets and no turning back.

She'd known George and Albert for years of course but once she retired she never thought that she would ever see them again, so the call she took that morning took her by surprise. By the time they turned up on her doorstep it was late morning and their arrival was greeted with lots of noise and excitement. Maureen put the kettle on and for the next half hour they caught up on each other's news, Albert and Maureen swapping stories about retirement and George updating both of them on the latest gossip and news at the *Chronicle*. Eventually they reached a natural pause so Maureen brewed a fresh pot of tea and then they settled down to business, her sitting in her favourite armchair whilst George and Albert sat at either end of a large, comfortable sofa.

'So, what's this all about?' she asked, picking up her cup and taking a sip of finest breakfast tea. 'Sounds like you two are up to no good. What's going on?'

Albert and George exchanged a knowing look. They'd talked about what they were going to say on the drive down from Burford and had both agreed that the situation was far too dangerous to let

Maureen get involved. They needed her help but somehow they had to try not to tell her too much. 'We need a favour Maureen,' said Albert. 'I'm sorry to bother you but we don't know who else to ask.'

Maureen looked at the pair of them, wondering what on earth they could possibly be mixed up in. Albert had always been a bit of an old rogue but she was surprised to see George there as well. She'd always remembered him as being far too sensible to get involved in anything underhand. Not that she knew what was going on yet but they both had a guilty look about them, like a couple of naughty schoolboys. 'Well, I'll try if I can,' she said, easing herself into the back of the armchair. 'How can I help?'

George shifted uneasily in his seat, hoping that they wouldn't have to get into too much detail. Maureen had finished work a few years ago now but she'd lost none of her natural authority and he still felt a bit intimidated by her, even though they were sitting in her living room. 'We need to get hold of a file,' he said, deciding to get straight to the point. 'It's one of Albert's old files which we think is probably still archived off-site. We just don't know the name of the firm or how to get hold of it.'

Maureen frowned. 'But anyone at work can tell you how to do that George. All you have to do is ask someone?'

George squirmed again, feeling even more uncomfortable. They were already straying into more detail than he wanted to. 'That's a bit difficult,' he replied. 'I'm on holiday at the moment and it's all a bit...well...you know...sort of...'

'Complicated,' interrupted Albert.

'Complicated?'

'Unofficial. Plus it's a bit risky...'

Maureen's eyes lit up, her interest suddenly sparked by the thought of some exciting new scoop or exclusive story.

'...but before you ask, we can't tell you what it's about. It's better that you don't know.'

Maureen sighed, her curiosity deflated as quickly as it had been raised. 'So what file are you after?'

Albert gave her an apologetic look. 'Sorry Maureen. Like I said, it's probably better that we don't say too much. Trust me, it's for your own good.'

'Well, have you got the reference number then?'

George and Albert exchanged a confused look. 'Reference number?' asked George, as if he'd just been asked a complicated question about quantum physics or applied mathematics.

Maureen raised her eyebrows in exasperation. 'Yes, you know, the reference number. That's how it works. How do you think they find anything once it's been filed?'

George shrugged. 'I don't know Maureen. I've never really thought about it.'

'Well think about it now. They can hardly run an archive without a coding system can they? Everything is given a reference number when it's first registered.'

George and Albert exchanged another sheepish look and then shrugged. Obviously they didn't have a reference number. They didn't even know where the files were kept.

Maureen shook her head in disbelief as she got up and walked over to a wall cabinet on the other side of the room; a cheap, flat-pack piece of imitation teak which had held her family photos, a few books and an assortment of china ornaments for more years than she cared to remember. At the bottom of the unit was a sliding door which she bent down to open, revealing a pile of old diaries, ledgers and a few ring binders. She picked up a diary from the top of the pile and returned to her seat. 'Do you know what year you are looking for?' she asked as she flicked through the pages.

'The year it relates to?' asked Albert, 'or the year it was filed?'

'The year it was filed.'

'1998'

'Sure?'

Albert nodded. 'Positive.'

Maureen continued flicking through the diary until she suddenly found what she was looking for. 'Here it is,' she said, pointing to a name on the page, 'Don Harrison. C.A.S...'

George looked at Albert and shook his head. The name meant nothing to him.

'...Corporate Archive Services. They're over at Wapping. At least that's where they used to be. Although I suppose it could be another supplier by now...'

George picked up his cup and took a large gulp of tea. This was starting to feel like a wild goose chase.

'...or even if it is the same firm, Don might not work there anymore.'

'Worth a shout though,' said Albert, trying to remain optimistic.

'I suppose so,' said Maureen, leaning over to pick up the phone. 'Only one way to find out.'

She carefully dialled the number and then they all waited patiently for the call to be answered. Prompt customer service was clearly not one of C.A.S.'s core values. After what seemed like an eternity the phone was finally answered by a male voice; middle-aged, working-class with a rough East End accent. It sounded like the call had been put straight through to the storage depot and one of the warehousemen or fork-lift truck drivers had picked it up, clearly not that pleased by the interruption. 'Yes?'

'Hello,' said Maureen not flustered for one moment by the brusque and unhelpful response at the other end. 'Could I speak to Don Harrison please?'

'Don't know if he's in luv.'

Maureen bristled slightly, the authority in her voice quickly putting the guy in his place. 'Well press star followed by 154 darling and we'll find out, won't we?'

The guy paused for a second, his instinct to give her an equally blunt reply but then thought better of it. Don Harrison was the Warehouse Manager and not someone you got into an argument with. Whoever this stroppy woman was she knew his extension number and sounded like she knew him really well. Maybe it was his missus. The last thing he needed was to get on the wrong side of the boss just before the weekend. 'Who wants him?'

Maureen winked across at George and Albert. It looked like they were getting somewhere. 'Tell him it's Maureen at the *Chronicle* and before you ask, no, I can't ring him back.'

'Hang on.'

The phone went dead and again, all three of them waited patiently for the call to be answered at the other end. The silence went on for several minutes and then just as they were at the point of contemplating giving up it was suddenly broken by a very loud, surprised voice. 'Bloody hell Maureen, I thought you'd retired?'

Maureen grinned. It was just like old times. 'Hello Don. How are you?'

'I'm fine Maureen. How are you luv? Still dancing?'

'Always Don, always. Off to Blackpool tomorrow. How about you? Still playing darts?'

'Twice a week Maureen. I was going to give it up but the Doctor says I need the exercise.'

Maureen chuckled. She didn't miss the work but she missed the people and most of all she missed the banter.

'Anyway, what are you up to Maureen? Seriously, I thought you'd retired?'

'I had. They couldn't manage without me. First sign of trouble and they asked me to come back.'

'Really?'

'Well, sort of. Just temporary to help them out. Anyway, I need a favour Don.'

'Go on.'

'I need to get a file back and the silly buggers this end have lost the reference number.'

Don Harrison gave a sharp intake of breath, like a builder being asked how much a job was going to cost. 'Not much I can do without a number Maureen. Needle in a haystack otherwise.'

'I know, I know. But they know which year it was filed.'

'Still not much use without the number,' interrupted Don. 'Don't see how I can find anything without a number. Year or no year.'

'I know, I know,' replied Maureen, trying to appease him. 'But I thought if I sent someone over they could have a quick look for it. They know which year and they know what file they're looking for.'

Again, there was a sharp intake a breath, this time followed by a long pause. Don was clearly uncomfortable with the suggestion that he let someone he didn't know inside his warehouse. 'I'm not sure about that Maureen. We're meant to deliver the file to you, not you come and search for it. This is a secure storage area.'

Maureen glanced over at George and Albert and raised her eyebrows. This was going to take longer than she thought. George smiled back. He was only listening to one end of the conversation but it was clear that Maureen was having to use all her old charm to try and persuade the guy. In the end it took her about ten minutes to eventually get Don's agreement and only then, providing that whoever she sent over had some proper ID with them. 'He'll have a driver with him,' she said checking that George had got his security pass, 'but his name's George Wiggins and I'll make sure that he's got his Company ID with him. He'll be right over.'

As soon as Maureen put the phone down George and Albert were on their feet, ready to go. Suddenly it felt as if they were making progress. A trawl through Albert's old file after all these years might just shed some light on what had now become a new enquiry. They thanked Maureen for all her help and then said their goodbyes and left, closing the front gate behind them as they walked over to Albert's car. Wapping was only about 25 miles from Shenfield which meant they'd be there in 45 minutes.

Maureen stood on the front step and waved at them for a moment before closing the door. Then she walked across the room and picked up the phone again, this time not needing to look up the number. She knew this one off by heart.

Less than 30 miles away Vinny Goldman was sitting in his office when the phone rang. He stared at it in exasperation for several seconds before picking it up. Why did the bloody thing always ring when Maxine was out to lunch? 'Hello?'

'Hello Vinny. It's Maureen.'

Vinny leant back in his chair and then swivelled round to look out the window, the sun bouncing off the office blocks in the distance as the view of the West End shimmered in the midday heat. A faint memory from over thirty years ago of him and Maureen staggering out of a Covent Garden wine bar on a warm, summer evening before tumbling into a hotel room for a night of secret, illicit passion. *"Lust is the headstrong beast which forgetful of future suffering hurries us along the forbidden path, until we are lost and trampled underfoot."* Hello Maureen. Long time no speak. What can I do for you?'

Maureen smiled to herself. 'It's the other way round Vinny. It's more a case of what I can do for you. I think I've got a story for you…'

Twenty-Two

CHARLES BUCHANAN HOVERED IN FRONT OF JEAN Pettipher's desk as he waited for her to finish the phone call. She glanced up at him, conscious that he wanted to speak to her and that time was of the essence. She nodded her head a couple of times indicating that she was trying to hurry up, the telephone in her left hand and the pen scribbling furiously in her right. Whoever was at the other end was doing all the talking and Jean was taking copious notes. Eventually the call finished and she put the phone down, throwing Buchanan a frustrated look as she turned the page over on her notepad and quickly wrote a number on the blank page. She tore it off with a flourish, the top of the paper ripping neatly along its perforated edge. 'Grosvenor Square. Christine Michaels wants you to call her back.'

Buchanan raised his eyebrows. He knew what that was all about. A botched CIA job on British soil and a pair of birdwatchers with fractured ribs claiming foul play. Part apology, part complaint. Or maybe they weren't up to speed yet. Perhaps they still thought it was Ross's body in the hold-all and wanted it back. The prodigal son finally coming home. He took the note paper and folded it over before putting it in his pocket. Either way it would have to wait. He had more important things to do than trying to appease Christine Michaels. 'Anything from Craven?'

Jean nodded. 'He called about twenty minutes ago. He's on his way in but he might be a couple of hours.'

'A couple of hours? Where is he?'

'Winchester, apparently.'

'Winchester? What the hell is he doing in Winchester?'

Jean shrugged. She had no idea what Craven was up to but that was situation normal. Even when he worked there, there was no chance of keeping track of him. He was always a law unto himself.

'What about Maurice? Is he around?'

'He's been here all night. He said he's ready when you are.'

Buchanan took a deep breath. That was something at least. You could always rely on Maurice. 'Good. Tell him to come through.'

Jean picked up the phone to call Maurice as Buchanan went into his office and shut the door. He walked over to the large veranda windows that looked out over the garden and stood there for a moment, the familiar view of The Mall and St James's Park in the distance. Things were starting to unravel and he needed to get them under control as soon as possible. Ross knew more about Artemis than almost anyone else and suddenly it looked like he had broken cover. God knows what had happened in that flat but wherever Ross was now, they needed to find him and they needed to find him quick. He took the piece of paper out of his pocket and looked at the telephone number that Jean had written down; a secure, direct line into the US Embassy in central London. Something didn't feel right. Michaels wasn't a member of the diplomatic staff so what the hell was she doing over at Grosvenor Square? The CIA occupied a separate, anonymous office block near Lambeth Bridge, handy for the drones over at Thames House and Vauxhall Bridge, so something was definitely going on. And there was something else that didn't make sense. Why were the Americans watching Ross in the first place? What on earth were they waiting for? Why didn't they simply terminate him, or at least lift him right away and put him through the ringer? What on earth were they waiting for? He glanced at the telephone number again, wondering if he should call Michaels after all. He walked over to the desk and picked up the phone, just as the door opened and Maurice walked in, looking hot and flustered as he struggled to juggle a pile of papers and separate files. 'Sorry, Jean told me to come straight in.'

'Not a problem,' replied Buchanan, putting the phone back down. 'Take a seat Maurice.'

Maurice eased himself into one of the two leather chairs opposite Buchanan and balanced the papers carefully on his lap. Buchanan's desk was always clean and tidy and he never felt comfortable putting anything on it, at least not uninvited.

'So, where are we?' asked Buchanan, sitting down in his chair. 'What have you got for me?'

'Where do you want to start?'

'How about our man in a suitcase.'

'Well, definitely not Ross,' replied Maurice. 'I managed to get a DNA profile for him and this one doesn't match. It looks like someone called Roman Limonov.'

'Soviet?'

'Russian.' Maurice put the stack of files onto the empty chair next to him and then took a beige, manila folder off the top and passed it across the desk. Buchanan opened it and quickly scanned the front sheet, a brief bio summary of a forty year-old FSB agent including a coloured photo in the top right-hand corner. Then he turned the page and looked at a more detailed history; education, training, operational assignments, plus a series of official appointments and overseas postings. Maurice was keen to keep talking but resisted the temptation, knowing that nothing irritated Buchanan more than being asked to read something and then being talked to at the same time. Eventually Buchanan closed the file and handed it back. 'There's nothing more recent than about seven years ago. Why the gap?'

'His last posting was Helsinki. Cultural Attaché. After that he went covert. Black Operations. We have limited intel after that...'

Buchanan raised his eyebrows. That meant Limonov was essentially a trained assassin. A lone wolf deployed by the FSB to terminate specific targets.

'...although we suspect he was responsible for Litvinenko and Nemtsov. And possibly Mollier.'

'Mollier?'

'Sylvan Mollier. He was the cyclist murdered in the French Alps.'

Buchanan nodded. He remembered the case but didn't recognise the name. Someone had worked hard to make sure that everyone thought that Mollier was just an unfortunate witness to the murder of the British al-Hilli family who were holidaying in France; an innocent bystander who happened to be in the wrong place at the wrong time, whereas in fact it was the other way round. The British al-Hilli family slaughtered on a French hillside for witnessing something that no one was meant to see. Which meant no one ever remembered Mollier's name. Unlike Litvinenko and Nemtsov of course. Everyone knew about Alexander Litvinenko; a fugitive officer of the Russian FSB who fled to London with his wife and family and was later granted asylum in the UK. He became a journalist and author, publically accusing the Russian secret service of staging apartment bombings and other terrorism acts in order to bring Vladimir Putin to power. Several years ago Litvinenko was assassinated, poisoned by a lethal dose of polonium-210 served in a teapot in the Millennium Hotel in Mayfair, inducing acute radiation syndrome. A murder which remained unsolved to this day. And the case of Boris Nemtsov was almost as famous. An influential politician and one of the most important figures in the introduction of capitalism into the post-Soviet Russian economy who was assassinated on the Bolshoy Moskvoretsky bridge near the Red Square in Moscow. Like Litvinenko he was a powerful, outspoken critic of the current government, regularly publishing in-depth reports detailing the corruption under Vladimir Putin and rallying against the war in Ukraine. All of which looked horribly familiar. Increasingly there was reliable intelligence that opponents of Putin were being systematically neutralised and it looked like Roman Limonov was his chief executioner. Although not any more.

'And Salisbury? Anything to do with that?'

Maurice shook his head. If Limonov had had anything to do with Salisbury, Sergei Skripal and his daughter would both be dead.

'But we're sure it's him?'

Maurice nodded. 'Pretty much. He'd only been in the bag about 12 hours so the body composition was good. We're waiting for lab results but the visual ID suggests it's him. The mug shot is spot on and he was wearing some distinguishing jewellery; a red, onyx signet ring on his right hand.'

Buchanan swivelled his chair and looked out the window for a second. Limonov's role as a FSB agent was pretty clear but what it didn't explain was what the hell was he doing in Ross's apartment? Ross had defected to the Soviets years ago so they were on the same side. Was it a meeting of comrades that unexpectedly turned into an argument and then got out of hand? Or was it something more sinister than that? Whatever the explanation it would have been an interesting confrontation. Ross was one of the most formidable agents Buchanan had ever met but Limonov was a hardened, professional assassin.

Maurice put the file on the floor and took the next one off the top of the pile. 'I brought the file on Gareth Williams with me. I thought you might want to see it?'

Buchanan leant forward and took the folder, again quickly scanning the front sheet before turning the page and looking at a more detailed history. Williams was a brilliant mathematician who began studying part-time at Bangor University while still at school, graduating with a first class degree at the age of seventeen. Perfect recruitment fodder for the security services. After gaining a PhD at the University of Manchester he was spotted by MI5 when he was a post-graduate at St Catherine's College, Cambridge, dropping out to join GCHQ part-way through his course. The police visited his top floor flat in Alderney Street, Pimlico after colleagues noted he had been out of contact for several days and found his naked, decomposing body padlocked inside a large North Face holdall, exactly the same as Limonov last night.

Buchanan looked up and glanced across at Maurice. 'The details look identical.'

'They are.'

'Copycat?'

Maurice nodded. 'The padlock key was underneath his body. We never went public with that. It's absolutely identical.'

'Which means Ross might be responsible for Williams's murder?'

Maurice shuffled uneasily in his seat. He was never that comfortable contradicting his boss. 'Possible. But I doubt it. Ross hasn't been active for over ten years. And besides, it looks more like Limonov's tradecraft.'

Buchanan frowned, not keeping up with Maurice's line of thinking. Limonov had shot Boris Nemtsov four times in the back at close range. This was nothing like that.

'Limonov used as many different methods as he could. No two hits were the same, as if he was doing it on purpose. Making a statement. "Look at me, the professional head-hunter." This is the guy who even laced a teapot with polonium-210 in the middle of a London hotel. It's like something out of a James Bond film. A body zipped up inside a padlocked bag has got Limonov's signature all over it. Ross never used anything other than a pistol or a garrotte.'

'So what are you saying?'

'I think Limonov went to Ross's flat to kill him and met his match.'

Buchanan raised his eyebrows. 'Why would the Russians want to murder Ross?'

Maurice shrugged. 'I don't know. But I reckon Ross used Limonov's holdall to make a statement of his own. *"He who kills by the sword, dies by the sword."*'

Buchanan said nothing and opened the file again, flicking through the pages as he imagined Limonov confronting Williams. There was a whole section on the possibility that Williams may have been accidentally killed by a lover during a bizarre sex game that had gone disastrously wrong. An absurd, clumsy sideshow fabricated by the drones over at MI6 to try and deflect the press, which turned out to be a complete waste of time. None of it really stuck and anyway, it wasn't long before the real facts hit the headlines; Williams's illegal hacking into Bill Clinton's personal data files. A security breach which caused a diplomatic incident at a time when Williams was working on a joint operation with the American National Security Agency to monitor cash flows from Russian terrorists and crime gangs.

Buchanan closed the file and handed it back to Maurice. The link to Clinton was curious, particularly given Ross's involvement in Artemis. But none of that explained why the Americans wanted him alive and the Russians wanted him dead. Given he had defected from the CIA to the Soviets surely it should have been the other way round?

'I've brought the paper,' said Maurice, picking up a copy of the *Chronicle*.

'Paper?'

'The crossword.'

Buchanan leant forward and took the newspaper, turning it over and quickly scanning the crossword on the back page, the answers neatly filled in by Maurice's team and the first three words across; COMPILER, INNOCENT and BLACKMAILED not needing any explanation.

'It's an impressive job,' continued Maurice. 'It looks like he compiled the first crossword under duress and is now trying to tell us as much as he can. He's even managed to put everything in the right order...'

Buchanan quickly scanned the answers, the next six words; LAURA, TAYLOR, FOURTEEN, BEDFORD, CLOSE, and TENTERDEN underlining what Maurice had just said.

'...although he's had to make some of the clues general knowledge rather than cryptic. That must be the first time that's ever happened. The readers must be wondering what the hell is going on.'

'Although some of these are cryptic,' said Buchanan, pointing to the clue for 14. Across, *"Entrapper fumes in redolence,"* the answer PERFUME hidden in the middle of the sentence.

'I know. And like I said, he's trying to give us as much information as he can.'

Buchanan looked up and frowned, not sure what Maurice was talking about.

'He could have picked any number of different words ending in "per" to make the beginning of PERFUME. Goalkeeper, Landscaper, Redeveloper...'

'Paratrooper?'

'...Exactly. Why use Entrapper? It's an unusual choice. It must be deliberate. I reckon it's connected to the word BLACKMAILED.'

Buchanan raised his eyebrows in appreciation. The guy was good. In fact he was better than good. It was ingenious. George Wiggins was leaving clues left, right and centre. No wonder he had disappeared.

'...and it's linked to the next answer, SERENDIPITY. I've asked someone to go out and buy some. It's made by Janvier.'

'Worn by Laura Taylor presumably, whoever she is. Our mystery blonde in the park perhaps?'

'Possibly.' Maurice reached over to the stack of folders and quickly found another file near the top. 'Not her real name though. Nadia Lukashenko.'

Buchanan leant forward and took the file. Another Soviet from the sound of it.

'This one is British,' said Maurice as if reading his mind. 'Mixed parentage. Her father was a lecturer in Russian Studies at the LSE but her mother was British. They were part of the North London intelligentsia. Their children were born and bred in Islington.'

Buchanan opened the file and scanned it quickly. Lukashenko had read politics at Sussex and then joined the University in a research role, where she stayed for several years before joining a tour operator as a travel courier, the perfect cover for a FSB sleeper. The rest of the information was patchy. Most of her time seemed to be stationed in Moscow with only one short, two year assignment in Vienna. No known associates and current whereabouts unknown. He closed the file and handed it back. 'Doesn't tell us much, other than a name.'

Maurice pulled a face, not entirely in agreement. Anyone who read politics at Sussex was bound to be a socialist in his opinion. Besides, her presence in the park at the same time as Ross wasn't a coincidence. She must have been the contact who collected the drop.

Buchanan said nothing, still not convinced that it made much difference. They were still looking for three people; Damien Ross, George Wiggins and Laura Taylor, aka Nadia Lukashenko but they weren't making much progress in finding any of them. They just knew Lukashenko's real name now, that's all.

'You should finish looking at the crossword,' continued Maurice. 'Look at the answers going down. At least it confirms that everything is connected.'

Buchanan picked up the paper again and looked at the first four words running vertically down the grid; RED, ONYX, SIGNET and RING. Maurice was right. Everything that had happened in the last few days was all connected, which meant that it all linked back to Artemis; Ross's reappearance, the brush pass in the park and now Limonov's murder in Ross's flat. The only problem was, none of it made any sense. Why had Ross suddenly turned up in London after all these years and why had he killed Limonov? And how on earth did George Wiggins, a crossword compiler for a daily newspaper, know a trained FSB assassin?

'I wonder where Ross is now?' said Maurice, voicing exactly what Buchanan was thinking.

Buchanan smiled ruefully to himself. Ross had a major problem. If he had really defected to the Soviets there was no way he could go back to the States. And now it looked like he'd fallen out with Moscow. If it hadn't before, the confrontation with Limonov had sealed his fate. Limonov was Putin's man and there was no way back from that. Suddenly Ross was on the run with nowhere to hide and nowhere to go. Which made him all the more dangerous. A renegade agent, armed and dangerous, backed into a corner with just about everybody out to get him. There was no telling what he might do. Buchanan checked his watch. Where the hell was Craven? It was a race against time and Ross could be at other end of the country by now. Or even worse, he could be round the corner, waiting to strike… *"Send danger from the east unto the west, so honour cross it from the north to south, and let them grapple: O, the blood more stirs to rouse a lion than to start a hare!"*

Twenty-Three

S HEPHERD MARKET WAS A QUAINT, LITTLE ENCLAVE
tucked away between Piccadilly and Curzon Street in the heart
of London's exclusive Mayfair; a small, charming square with a
village-like atmosphere and a variety of chic boutiques, intimate
cafés and impressive Victorian pubs. Developed by Edward
Shepherd in 1735 it was something of a hidden gem, evocative
of a secret rendezvous with its private doorways, narrow alleyways
and curvy, cobbled streets. It had always been a bohemian quarter,
popular with artists, musicians and writers as well as a haunt
for punters looking for upmarket prostitutes. Famous residents
included Cass Elliot, better known as Mama Cass who died at Flat
12, No. 9 Curzon Place in 1974 and Keith Moon of The Who,
who died at the same flat in 1978.

Damien Ross sat in the window of The Market Tavern,
a pub where every drink was poured with a generous serving
of quirky personality. Upstairs, the boudoir-inspired décor of
the Chesterfield Room gave a nostalgic nod to a bygone era of
reckless gamblers, famous brothels and bawdy tales. It wasn't quite
Montmartre but it was as close as he could get in the centre of
London. Once upon a time the doorways to the apartments above
the shops and restaurants had little postcards discreetly advertising
the promise of "Madame Fifi" or something similar, usually a
fading, middle-aged seductress wearing a silk dressing gown and
too much lipstick, kept warm by the bar of an electric fire eating
Turkish Delight and drinking Noilly Prat.

Ross took a large swig of red wine and instinctively put his
hand in his jacket pocket and took out his cigarettes. He looked

at the packet of Gitanes, the familiar blue and white design nestled perfectly in his palm. He turned it over a couple of times, contemplating whether to have one or not. It meant going outside which meant taking a risk. Not something that he wanted to do. In fact not something that he dared even think about. Not today. Not after the encounter with Limonov. Easy decision then. He put the cigarettes back in his pocket and checked his watch. Half past one. They should be arriving any minute now, although separately of course and probably from opposite directions. Making sure that they minimised the risk of being followed. He stared out of the window at the Turkish restaurant which was directly opposite, the place already buzzing with locals and tourists enjoying the lunchtime atmosphere. That was the other problem with going outside for a smoke. He'd lose his seat which meant losing an almost perfect view of the front door and the windows either side.

Ross took another sip of wine and then looked up and down the road again, the sun seemingly trapped in the narrow lanes; a breathless, sweltering heat which lingered even in the doorways and shadows. The street was packed with people standing outside the bars and cafes but he still had a clear view of anyone coming in either direction. Besides, he wouldn't have any difficulty spotting Parovsky. He'd recognise that fat bastard anywhere, what with his large, portly frame and the ubiquitous check waistcoats that he always wore. It gave him a slightly comical appearance which he used to his advantage, belying the dangerous, cold-blooded character that was lurking just below the surface. A tough, seasoned campaigner who started life as a lowly KGB officer, working alongside Vladimir Putin and tracking his promotion to lieutenant colonel; close colleagues with a shared reputation for ruthless ambition and gratuitous violence. Parovsky's career had since flourished under the Putin regime and his reputation was now notorious, both throughout the FSB and beyond. Ross had met some dangerous, evil bastards in his time but Parovsky was up there as one of the worst. Lukashenko on the other hand was exactly the opposite, a FSB agent with a conscience; someone with a moral compass who put friendship and loyalty before ideology. But he was still surprised when he saw her in the park. All he knew was that a mule was going to pick up the empty envelope and then after that, someone else was going to pick up the newspaper from the rubbish bin. It could have been anybody of course, pretending to be just strolling by but as soon as he spotted her from a distance he knew that it was her, still the same after all these years. He tried to catch her eye as they walked past each other on the way out but her refusal to give him even the briefest glance was a real giveaway. It was almost impossible not to look at someone if they were staring at you hard enough, especially if you were walking towards them with no one else around. Her reluctance to acknowledge him was definitely avoidance rather than indifference; the behaviour of an experienced agent trying to look normal but sometimes achieving exactly the opposite. Or maybe it was just guilt.

Another five minutes went by with not much happening, other than a procession of tourists going backwards and forwards while Ross took periodic sips of wine, trying to make it last as long as possible. Eventually he spotted Parovsky approaching from the north end of Shepherd Street, walking purposefully towards the restaurant but all the time checking the buildings and people around him. He walked straight past initially, pretending to look at a menu in a cafe window about twenty yards up the road, obviously cautious about being invited to a location that he hadn't checked out beforehand. Ross smiled to himself, a brief flash of memory from the night before; Limonov on his knees begging for mercy, his hands tied behind his back and the plastic cable-tie secured firmly around his neck. Tight enough to dig into his throat but not enough to actually suffocate him. Well, not immediately. Like wearing a shirt collar two sizes too small. Eyes bulging and gasping for breath, like a fish, slowly choking to death. No wonder he had talked. In fact he was hard to shut up. Names, dates, locations. Typical head-hunter. They could dish it out but none of them could really take it. Not like a genuine agent.

Parovsky on the other hand was the real deal. The guy would never talk, not even with a syringe full of babble-juice in his veins or a pistol shoved in his mouth. He was still standing outside the cafe, still pretending to read the menu but periodically looking up and down the street. Eventually he checked his watch and walked back towards the restaurant. He stood outside for a couple of seconds, making one last precautionary sweep and then pushed the door open and went inside. A waiter looked up and gave him an efficient smile. 'Table for one?'

Parovsky held up the middle three fingers on his right hand. 'Three. Name of Voronin.'

The waiter checked the diary and then ushered him to a table at the back of the restaurant. Parovsky scanned the room and then chose the chair on the opposite side of the table, unfolding the napkin and laying it neatly across his lap. Then he took out his Serdyukov SPS and placed it discretely under the napkin. FSB protocols. *"Always work in cells of three. Always book hotels and restaurants using an alias. Always sit with your back to the wall with a view of the room in front of you."*

Across the road Ross was still nursing his glass of wine, hoping that one of the staff would offer to get him a refill so that he wouldn't have to leave his seat. He took out his wallet, contemplating whether to buy another drink or not and then checked the contents. Two hundred and ten pounds. That wasn't going to last long, particularly now that he didn't have anywhere to stay. A couple of days at the most. The credit cards weren't of any use either. As soon as he used one they would be onto him like a shot. The wine would have to wait but that wasn't a problem. A little bit of alcohol to loosen you up before a wet job was fine. In fact it was almost obligatory. But too much would definitely be a mistake. He needed his reactions to be razor sharp and another glass might have the opposite effect. Taking someone out in the middle of a crowded restaurant was going to be a challenge. It meant firing the shots in quick succession before anyone had time to react. He put the wallet back in his pocket, all the time keeping one eye on the street outside. Parovsky was probably sitting at a table by now, checking his watch, wondering when Lukashenko was going to turn up and more importantly, wondering where the hell Limonov had got to. He was probably also trying to decipher the menu. Ross smiled to himself. That was typical of Limonov, arranging to meet them somewhere which he knew Parovsky would hate. *Turkish for God's sake.* The only time the fat bastard went that far south was to execute a load of Muslims.

Ross picked up the glass and drained the last dregs of wine. Lukashenko would be here any minute which meant it would be time to go. He put his hand in his jacket pocket and pulled out a small, white envelope, folded over to protect its contents. Then he took out his phone and slid off the back cover, carefully removing the SIM card which he snapped in half. He unfolded the envelope and tipped the contents onto the table, a collection of half a dozen or so SIM cards covering all the UK networks. He picked one at random and put it in the phone, taking care not to switch it on. Then he put the remaining cards back in the envelope and folded it over again. If he was going to make a call it needed to be untraceable which meant he was allowed one call per card. Two hundred and ten pounds and six or seven phone calls before he ran out of time and ran out of luck. *May as well go out with a bang.* He glanced out the window again, just in time to spot the familiar figure of an attractive, blonde, middle-aged woman approaching the restaurant. Medium height, medium build and definitely the same person that he had seen in St James's Park.

Lukashenko walked straight up to the front door and went inside. Again, a waiter greeted her arrival before ushering her to the table at the back of the dining room. Parovsky looked up from his mobile phone and gave her the briefest of nods as she sat down in the chair opposite, her back to the door. The waiter left a menu in front of her and then disappeared, assuming that they wouldn't be ordering until the third guest arrived. Lukashenko looked around the room, much like Parovsky had done to check the layout and escape routes. Then she folded the napkin across her lap and picked up the menu, idly scanning the contents.

'Roman not here yet?'

Parovsky shook his head and said nothing. He had always been a man of few words.

'And no message?'

'Nothing.'

Lukashenko continued staring at the menu, processing the information for a second. 'It's not like him to be late.'

Parovsky ignored her and continued looking at his phone. She talked too much but she was right. Limonov was always on time but perhaps there was a reason today. Maybe he got there early and was outside, watching them go in first. That was the trouble with head-hunters. The job turned them into a bunch of voyeurs. Cat and mouse. Hunter and hunted.

'So what are we going to do?'

'We'll give him ten minutes.'

Lukashenko glanced at her watch. 'And then what?'

Parovsky picked up the menu and gave her a sarcastic smile. 'And then we have something to eat.'

Ross stood up and systematically checked that he'd got everything, patting his pockets in sequence as he went through an established routine: *phone, wallet, keys, passport, pistol.* The SIG Sauer was nestled in a shoulder holster, halfway down his left ribcage, discreet enough to be out of sight but close enough to rely on in a split-second. It was like having a best friend by your side. Close, familiar and very reliable. Then he picked up the large, paper carrier bag and checked the contents, making sure that everything was still okay. Finally he picked up his rucksack, slung it over his shoulder and made his way to the door, the brightness of the sunlight hitting him as he stepped out into the street. He put on the baseball cap and a pair of sunglasses, partly to protect him from the blistering heat but also to disguise his appearance as he walked across the road. He looked towards the restaurant, trying to imagine where they were sitting. Back of the room probably. Parovsky with a view of the door if he had any sense, which meant going in through the front was virtually impossible. In fact it was out of the question. Not unless you wanted to get your head blown off.

The back of the restaurant was just around the corner via Trebeck Street, a narrow alley leading to a small cobbled courtyard and then to a back door to the kitchen. The courtyard was full of empty vegetable crates and food cartons, plus a large, metal garbage bin on wheels, brimming to the top with general rubbish. An overflowing ashtray on the window ledge confirmed that this was where the kitchen staff popped out for a crafty cigarette break. Ross walked up to the door and knocked on it firmly, three times in quick succession. It opened within a couple of seconds, the guy dressed in checked trousers and chef's whites, probably thinking it was a delivery. He looked at Ross with some suspicion. 'Yes?'

Ross shuffled nervously on the spot, all part of the careful portrayal. 'Sorry to bother you, I've got a reservation today at one-thirty.'

The guy nodded dismissively to the other side of the courtyard. 'Entrance is round the front.'

'I know, I need a favour.' Ross stepped forward slightly and opened the carrier bag, inviting the chef to look inside.

The guy frowned as he leant forward and peered down at the large, round birthday cake finished in crisp, white icing with the words "Happy Birthday" written in flowing, silver letters.

'It's a surprise. I can't walk through the front door with it. Besides, I need to light these first.' Ross put his hand in his jacket pocket and pulled out a packet of twelve candles, six blue and six pink. He rattled the packet, as if to accentuate the point. Like a box of matches. 'I haven't seen him in years. It would be great if you could help.'

The guy stepped back a pace and nodded. It wasn't the first time they'd been asked to serve a birthday cake. 'You want us to bring it out with the coffee?'

Ross shuffled again. 'I was hoping I could light it now and make a surprise arrival through the kitchen. A sort of grand entrance singing "Happy Birthday."'

The guy looked at him and frowned again. That was a lot more unorthodox. Letting customers into the kitchen was generally a no-no. God knows what they might see. 'Wait there a second.'

The chef disappeared and Ross waited patiently by the door, wondering whether to have a cigarette or not. It always helped calm his nerves before a job but today he thought better of it. He didn't want to give them an excuse not to let him in and a punter reeking of French tobacco might be just enough to put them off. Eventually another guy turned up at the doorstep, this time dressed in a black suit with an open neck shirt. Probably the head waiter, or maybe the manager. 'You got a birthday cake you want to deliver?'

Ross stepped forward and opened the carrier bag again, as he had before.

The guy looked at the contents and then stared at Ross, as if trying to make his mind up. Then he opened the door wider and gave him a brief nod. 'Okay. Come in.'

—◁◁◁—

Inside the restaurant, Lukashenko glanced at her watch for the umpteenth time. 'He's twenty minutes late. Something doesn't feel right.'

Parovsky looked at her across the table but said nothing. She was probably right but he needed to be sure. Limonov was meant to be giving them all the information that he'd extracted from Ross last night. If they left too soon and missed him all hell would break loose. Better to give him another ten minutes. Maybe he got the times mixed up.

Lukashenko picked up the menu and read it again, if only for something to do. It was bad enough having to sit and wait for someone who obviously wasn't going to turn up, let alone having to do that with someone who was virtually monosyllabic. She fanned the menu to keep herself cool while she thought of something to say, something else to break the interminable silence.

'How was Winchester?'

'Fine.'

'No issues then?'

Parovsky shook his head. 'Not really.'

'Did you find anything?'

'No. All clean.'

'And no trace back to us?'

Parovsky shook his head again. 'The house was empty. She wasn't around to see me.'

'And the Antique Dealer?'

Parovsky smiled to himself. That was a different situation altogether. Jonathan Lander was probably still trussed up in the boot of his car, parked at the furthest end of a supermarket car park. Even if the police found it today Lander wouldn't be talking to anybody, not with a plastic bag over his head and a rope around his neck. He was probably stone cold and as stiff as a board by now. Parovsky also checked his watch, just to make sure how much longer they should wait when suddenly his phone burst into life. He picked it up and answered it immediately, expecting to hear the familiar tone of Limonov's voice, apologetic about being late. He couldn't have been more wrong, the British accent instantly recognisable.

'Hello?'

'Where are you?'

'The rendezvous. Waiting for Roman.'

'He's not coming.'

'Problem?'

'He didn't make it.'

Parovsky paused, trying to work out exactly what was being said. 'Do you know where he is now?'

'Not exactly. Zipped up in a body bag somewhere probably.'

'And Ross?'

'Don't know. Either miles away running as fast as he can...'

Parovsky shivered. He knew what was coming next.

'...or round the corner, looking for you.'

'Time to abort then.'

'That would be my advice.'

'Plan B?'

'Plan B.'

Parovsky ended the call and put the phone in his pocket. Lukashenko looked at him enquiringly across the table. 'What's happened?'

'He's not coming.'

'Why not?'

Parovsky shrugged. He didn't have time for lengthy explanations. Besides, there was no point now.

'So, are we leaving?'

'I am.' In the same breath Parovsky pulled out the Serdyukov from beneath his napkin and fired two shots in quick succession, directly across the table. The first bullet hit Lukashenko squarely in the middle of the forehead, jolting her sideways as the back of her skull exploded behind her. The second hit her in the neck, a spray of deep, crimson blood arcing through the air and landing on the crisp, white tablecloth, like a bright, red waterfall cascading from above. In an instant the quiet, subdued hubbub of lunchtime conversation descended into screaming, hysterical customers and crashing furniture. Lukashenko's chair toppled over as if it was in slow motion, her body limp and lifeless before it hit the floor. In the same millisecond, the double swing doors to Parovsky's right opened and two people walked into the room, a waiter, carrying a large birthday cake with lighted candles, singing the first bars of "Happy Birthday" and someone walking behind him, out of sight as though he was taking cover behind the guy in front. Instinctively Parovsky spun round and fired three more shots in quick succession. The first hit the centre of the cake which the waiter was holding chest-high in front of him, the bullet splattering pieces of gateaux and icing in all directions before hitting him straight in the heart. Ross instantly dived to his right and threw himself behind a table as the second and third bullets zinged over his shoulder and thudded into the wall behind.

Parovsky was now standing up, adrenalin pumping through his veins and his heart pounding ten to the dozen. Five seconds of mayhem. Still the screaming of hysterical customers and the noise of crashing furniture. Lukashenko was on the floor to his left, her brains blown out across the floor and blood still pumping out of her throat. The waiter was to his right, collapsed forwards with his face down in the centre of the cake, like some sort of macabre, comical, slapstick assassination. But where was the other guy? Hiding behind the table in the corner. It had to be Ross. There for the kill but dangerous when cornered. Decision time. Hunt or be hunted…

Ross crouched close to the floor. Suddenly he was pinned in the corner with no means of escape. Parovsky was only yards away. Five rounds fired. Ten rounds left. He needed to act quickly. He couldn't see Parovsky or the back of the dining room but he could just about see down one side of the restaurant. Lots of upturned tables and chairs plus a large glass chiller, six-feet tall stacked full of white wine, bottles of beer and soft drinks. *Perfect.* He waited a second, listening as hard as he could for any signs of movement. Nothing. He crouched onto one knee and took a couple of deep breaths to regulate his timing. *Fire on the exhale.* Then he took one more deep breath and fired a single shot into the chiller which exploded like a thousand chandeliers shattering onto marble. In the same breath, as the sound of breaking glass burst into the room he stood up, pistol in both hands and fired four rounds in succession in the direction where Parovsky had been standing. *Centre, nine o'clock, three o'clock, centre again.*

Ross stood his ground, half waiting for shots to be fired the other way but nothing happened. He paused for a second, waiting for the dust to settle and for the after-sound to subside. More screams from the corner of the restaurant, two women out to lunch who were never, ever, coming back. And then the sound of a police siren. Distant at first but slowly getting louder. He looked at where Parovsky had been standing which was now empty and the front door which was wide open, as though someone had just walked out. And then he saw the body of Lukashenko lying on the floor, prostrate and lifeless, slaughtered like a butchered animal. *"These violent delights have violent ends and in their triumph die, like fire and powder which, as they kiss, consume."* Ross stuffed the SIG Sauer back into his holster and stared at her, a life less ordinary, now cut short by betrayal. Parovsky was no fool. *"He who fights and runs away, lives to fight another day."* It was time to do the same.

Twenty-Four

THE DRIVE BACK FROM WINCHESTER LOOKED RELATIVELY straightforward. Ten minutes to get onto the motorway and then a quick drive up the M3 before cutting through Richmond and then picking up the Cromwell Road into Kensington and Knightsbridge. No more than a couple of hours with a bit of luck. And any journey, even a car drive, was an opportunity for some uninterrupted thinking time; a chance to work through all the previously unconnected details and get a probable explanation sorted before he saw Buchanan. Already a pattern of events was starting to form in his mind but he needed time to think everything through before deciding whether to still trust his initial instinct; the key, underlying issue which explained what was going on and which underpinned everything else.

Craven usually put his foot down when he was driving but was happy to pootle in the inside lane today, his arm resting on the open window to compensate for the lack of air conditioning. It was too hot to go belting up the motorway with the windows closed and anyway, it gave him the opportunity to have a cigarette and enjoy the warm, summer weather. He put the radio on for a few minutes but found that it distracted him too much so turned it off, letting his mind wander back to his first meeting with Fiona Wallis. There was no doubt that her intuition had been correct, her antenna fine-tuned to detect even the slightest shift in behaviour after years of living with the same person. But not even she could have guessed that her husband was having an affair with her own sister. And Craven certainly wasn't going to enlighten her on that particular point. Firstly, it was none of his business and secondly both Fiona Wallis and Penny Marshall had already suffered enough. Revealing that piece of information would be like unleashing a tsunami. Besides, if he could work out why David Wallis had really been killed, any conjecture about him being unfaithful would quickly be forgotten.

He pulled out into the middle lane for a moment to overtake a particularly slow van and then settled back into the inside lane again, happy to keep pootling along at 70 miles per hour. He smiled to himself at the absurdity of him doing the maximum speed limit yet still being overtaken by virtually everyone else on the road. *What's the point of having speed limits if no one takes any notice of them?* Then he turned his mind back to the matter in hand. Fiona Wallis was right about her husband's secretive behaviour but it had nothing to do with the perfume that she had smelt on his clothes. And it certainly wasn't the affair or some cooked-up story about drug dealing that had got him killed. It was obviously something to do with the photographs that he had bought from Jonathan Lander in Winchester; photographs which Lander had in turn acquired as part of the house clearance from Penny Marshall's parents. The thing that Craven couldn't work out was how did the photos get from Jonathan Lander to David Wallis?

What was interesting was that the antique shop had no record of the transaction. Not surprising perhaps given the propensity for antique dealers to deal in cash but the girl in the shop hadn't remembered the photos at all, and she seemed pretty familiar with everything else. All of which suggested that Lander had decided to unload them to a specialist dealer straight away, no doubt because he recognised that they were rare and collectable and it gave him the best chance of getting the best possible price. Plus it enabled him to shift them as quickly as possible. Either way, not something he was likely to achieve by selling them from a provincial antique shop in deepest Hampshire. But whatever the reason, it meant that either he knew of David Wallis because Penny Marshall had mentioned her brother-in-law in conversation, or the whole thing was just a complete coincidence.

He drove on for a couple more miles, churning the facts over in his mind. Coincidence or not, the key issue was what did the photos contain and who had Wallis sold them to? He wasn't sure about the latter but he had a couple of good mug shots of Billy Bunter and his blonde companion which might be able to help. As soon as he got back to London he would ask Buchanan to check them out. A long shot possibly but worth a try. And he was absolutely certain that whoever had bought the photos had gone back to murder Wallis to remove all trace of the transaction. And now it looked as though Lander had disappeared, possibly for the same reason. That meant that the photographs portrayed something so incriminating that someone was prepared to go to any lengths to prevent anyone else from knowing about them.

All of which brought Craven back to his original conclusion. It was the marriage certificate that had unlocked it for him, in particular the date of the wedding. 31st August 1957. That and the comment made by Penny Marshall that her father always took her mother somewhere special to celebrate the bigger anniversaries. Rome for their 25th and Paris for their 40th. That meant that they were in Rome in August 1982. All very romantic but neither here nor there. But it also meant that they must have been in Paris on 31st August 1997, which was much more interesting. In fact it was incredible. Craven blew out his cheeks at the enormity of what he had just concluded. Penny Marshall's parents had been in the same place at exactly the same time as one of the most famous, unsolved incidents of the 20th century. And for someone who didn't believe in coincidences that was absolutely breath-taking. It meant that everything to do with this case; the mysterious photographs, Wallis's subsequent murder and probably Lander's disappearance, were all linked to that one, historic event.

Craven put his foot down, suddenly mindful that he needed to get back to London and see Buchanan as soon as possible. It was probably worth calling ahead to agree a time, which meant stopping for five minutes somewhere. The motorway services were only ten minutes away so he could pull in and make a call from there. Plus he needed to get some petrol. The fuel gauge was showing a quarter full, enough to get him into central London but not enough to get him all the way home. *Might as well fill up now and ring Buchanan at the same time.* He drove on for another ten miles or so and then turned off towards the services, pulling up at the furthest end of the car park so that he could telephone in peace. Despite the open window the car was baking hot so he got out and leant on the front wing while he made the call, watching the endless stream of vehicles driving in behind him. As always, Buchanan's phone was answered within seconds.

'Jean Pettipher.'

'Hello Petty, it's me. How are you?'

Jean smiled and blushed slightly, her usual reaction when speaking to Craven. She'd worked with dozens of agents throughout her career but Craven had always been her favourite. No one else called her Petty. 'I'm fine thank you. How are you doing?'

'Much better now I'm speaking to you. Have you missed me?'

Jean smiled again. She wasn't taken in by Craven's flattery for one moment. He was incorrigible but harmless. 'Like toothache. I meant how are you doing in terms of getting back. Where are you?'

'Fleet.'

'Fleet?'

'Services on the M3. I should be back in about an hour and a half. Is he around?'

Jean quickly checked the diary on her screen. 'He's got meetings but I can shuffle things. Shall we say two o'clock? Or two-thirty, just to be on the safe side?'

'Perfect.'

'Here?'

Craven hesitated. He hadn't been back inside the Greenhouse since he resigned and went freelance several years ago. And he wasn't keen to start now. 'No. In the Garden is best. Usual spot.'

'Okay, I'll let him know.'

'Thanks.'

'He's only got half an hour though. Don't be late.'

'Don't worry. Have I ever let you down?'

'How long have you got?'

Craven grinned. 'Thanks Petty. Look after yourself.'

'And you.'

He switched the phone off and put it back in his pocket. Good old Jean. The day she left Vector would be a sad day for everyone. An end of an era. Then he got back in the car and drove round to the petrol station to fill up. While he was in the shop he bought a sandwich and a bottle of water, plus twenty cigarettes. Difficult to have lunch whilst driving but he could always eat when he got to the Garden. Or maybe stop somewhere en route if he was early. He put the sandwich and water on the back seat and then drove down the slip road towards the motorway. A few hundred yards ahead he could see someone standing at the side of the road, holding a large cardboard sign in one hand and their thumb thrust out with the other, trying to hitchhike a lift. Craven couldn't read the sign from that distance but that wasn't what he was really looking at. It was the girl that was holding his attention. A couple of cars ahead braked slightly but then carried on, the drivers probably cursing their luck as they drove past with their wives or girlfriends sitting next to them. Craven had no such problem.

He indicated that he was pulling over and then started to slow down, all the time keeping his eyes on the figure ahead. She looked about eighteen or nineteen and was tall and slim with long, straight, dark hair parted down the middle. She was also incredibly suntanned, as if she had just returned from a couple of weeks in the South of France or the Costa del Sol, her slender, bare limbs glistening in the sun. But it was what she was wearing that was really turning heads. Or rather what she wasn't. She was dressed in a pair of frayed, denim shorts, probably a pair of old jeans cut as high as possible and then above her waist, a loose, white, sleeveless vest, like an athlete's running top but without the markings and very baggy. Other than a pair of grey trainers on her feet and a pair of sunglasses perched on her head, that was it. Just a pair of tiny, blue shorts and a loose white top. And a large, cardboard sign which said "London."

Craven came to a stop and leant over the passenger seat, the window already open. As he did so the girl bent forward to speak to him and the loose white top also dropped forward, confirming that she was wearing nothing underneath. He gulped slightly as he caught a glimpse of her suntanned body, the deep, bronze colour offset by an engaging smile and perfect white teeth.

'Hi, are you going to London?'

'I am,' he replied, holding her gaze as he tried not to stare down the front of her top. 'Where are you after?'

'Hyde Park. But anywhere in the centre will be fine.'

He smiled back. 'You're in luck, I'm going right past. Hop in.'

'Ooh, thank you,' replied the girl as she opened the door and slid into the passenger seat. Craven watched her as she put a black rucksack by her feet and then crossed one leg over the other, the effect of which accentuated how short the shorts really were, the frayed edge cutting deep into her thigh. The smell of suntan lotion and a light, citrus perfume wafted over like an aphrodisiac.

'Gosh, it's hot in here,' she said, suddenly taking hold of the front of her top and jerking it in and out vigorously, as though she was fanning herself. Again, Craven caught a glimpse of her body underneath, appearing and then disappearing in fractions of a second, like a voyeur glued to a flickering "What the Butler Saw" machine. He gave her an apologetic shrug. 'Sorry, no air-con. It's broken.'

'Oh well. Not to worry. Do you mind if I take my shoes off?'

'No, go ahead,' replied Craven, smiling to himself at how direct and confident she was. She'd only been in the car a few seconds and she was already making herself comfortable. Still, anyone prepared to hitchhike on their own, particularly dressed like that, had to have a bucket load of confidence. He watched her as she tried to take off her trainers without undoing them, levering the heel of her left foot with the toe of her right but they were too tight. Eventually she gave up and bent over to undo the laces. For the second time the front of her top fell forward, this time revealing a small, perfectly-formed, teenage breast; a tiny, silver stud pierced through a soft, pink nipple. Craven turned his head and looked out of the driver's window, the distraction of her sitting next to him almost too much to bear. Maybe it was a mistake giving her a lift after all. Driving up the M3 in this heat was painful enough but trying to do it with a full scale erection was going to be excruciating.

'There you are,' said the girl triumphantly, wriggling her toes as though she was on the beach. 'Ready!'

'You need to belt up,' said Craven, nodding towards the buckle above her head.

'Oops. Sorry, forgot about that.' She twisted around and pulled the belt over her shoulder, the strap running diagonally across her body. Craven watched her as she struggled to click the buckle into place, not sure whether to help her or not. Again, a waft of perfume and suntan oil caught his senses as she bent closer to him, their bodies only inches apart. The seatbelt had the effect of at least holding in her top. Unfortunately it also pinned the material to her body, emphasising the outline of her breasts; a pair of small, round apples pressed up tight against the fabric. Craven let out a long, slow sigh and then started the car.

'Thanks for stopping,' said the girl, the engaging smile and perfect white teeth still ever present.

Craven turned his head to look at her and smiled back. 'Not a problem. Happy to help.'

They drove on for a few miles, Craven more than comfortable to stay in the inside line and take his time. There was no way that he was going to bomb up the motorway with the windows closed, the heat would be absolutely stifling. Besides, there was no rush now that he wasn't seeing Buchanan until two-thirty and the girl certainly wasn't in any hurry. Hitchhikers took all day trying to cadge lifts so she was bound to be ahead of schedule. He was practically taking her door-to-door for God's sake. Except of course he didn't know where she had started from, or how long she had been on the road. Still it wouldn't be long before he found out. He half expected to be driving in silence while she spent the journey on her mobile phone, listening to music or browsing on social media, or whatever it was they did these days. Either that or long periods of awkward silence punctuated by him trying to make polite conversation. But he couldn't have been more wrong. There was no sign of a smartphone or the ubiquitous white earphones and she seemed happy enough to just sit and talk. In fact she was very natural and chatty. Craven was actually enjoying her company.

'So, where did you start thumbing from?' he asked, intrigued to prove his assumption about her being ahead of schedule.

'Southampton. I'm at Uni there I got a lift straight up to Fleet so I'm going to get to London in two rides. I've been really lucky.'

Craven looked at her, one arm relaxed on the open window and the other stroking her long, bare legs as she checked the state of her suntan. Luck had nothing to do with it.

'So where are you going?' she asked. 'London as well?'

Craven nodded, not wanting to say too much. He could sense that there was a follow up question coming so quickly changed the subject. 'That's an impressive suntan you've got there.'

The girl grinned. 'I know. I've just come back from Portugal...'

'Lucky you.'

'...two weeks in the Algarve. It was amazing.'

'Sounds great. So much for being a poor student then?'

She grinned again, the gentle teasing landing exactly as intended. 'Family holiday with my parents. Bank of Mum and Dad...'

Craven smiled to himself, the financing of modern teenagers suddenly coming back to him. How the world had changed. He could just imagine what his father would have said if he'd asked him to pay for a holiday at that age. "Foxtrot Oscar" probably.

'...but they don't mind, they wouldn't see much of me otherwise.'

'Well, it looks like you had fantastic weather.'

'It was fabulous. Thirty degrees every day. Now I just need to try and keep it topped up.' This time she stroked her left arm as she rotated it clockwise and anti-clockwise, looking at the evenness of her tan. 'That's why I'm going to Hyde Park.'

Craven frowned. 'What, you're going all the way up to London just to sit in Hyde Park?'

The girl giggled at the absurdity of the Craven's question. 'No, I'm meeting some friends in the West End later. I'm just really early so I thought I'd stop and get some sunshine. And I need to eat somewhere. I bought some sandwiches at the services.'

'Me too. So why Hyde Park?'

The girl shrugged. 'It's the biggest. More chance of finding a secluded spot.'

Craven raised his eyebrows and then glanced across at her to see if she was joking or not. Secluded sunbathing meant only one thing to him and that was an image which wasn't helping him concentrate on the road. 'So, what sandwiches have you got?' he asked, changing the subject again and nodding towards the black rucksack which was still lying by her feet.

'Chicken and avocado with mayo.'

'Nice.'

'And you?'

'Brie and grape.'

'Ooh, I love brie and grape. We should swap. Half each.'

Craven smiled. 'That sounds kind of messy.'

'Not if we stopped and had lunch at the same time. We could sit in the park.'

'Nice thought but I'm on a schedule.'

'Don't you have to stop? After so many hours driving?'

'That's lorry drivers. It's doesn't apply to cars.'

'But you've got to eat at some point. Hyde Park is lovely...'

He looked at her again, trying to work out whether she was serious or not. He'd never been any good at reading women and he certainly couldn't read her. Was it just silly banter or was she actually flirting with him? Or maybe she wasn't flirting at all. Perhaps she just was just being friendly. Or maybe she really did fancy his choice of sandwich filling.

'...and anyway, you could put some lotion on my back. I can't do it myself.'

'Me?' Craven's response practically spluttered in disbelief.

'Well I can't just walk up to someone in the park can I? Not a complete stranger that I've never spoken to before. That would be weird. Like, totally random.'

Craven smiled to himself, the language of each generation distinctive from the last. This time he kept his eyes on the road, suddenly needing to concentrate on something other than the what she had just said. Luckily Jean's caution about not being late was still nagging at the back of his brain, otherwise the temptation might have proved too much. 'I'll think about it,' he said, trying to avoid the conversation going any further. 'Let's see what time we get there.'

In the end it took about an hour to get into central London, Craven sticking to the speed limits and the girl idly chatting about this and that but about nothing in particular. Eventually they reached the Cromwell Road and then cut up through Exhibition Road, passing the Victoria and Albert Museum on their right and Imperial College on the left. At the junction with Kensington Road they drove straight across and entered Hyde Park via West

Carriage Drive. Craven could have dropped her off by the main road but there was parking ahead, just before the Serpentine and it wasn't far out of his way. Besides, given what he'd been thinking earlier the location felt more than appropriate, almost as if it was meant to be. He pulled into the car park and drove into a space at the far end where it was quiet. 'There you go,' he said, turning off the engine, 'door to door.'

'Thank you so much,' said the girl, undoing her seat belt. 'I still can't believe I've got here so quickly. You've made my day.'

Craven looked at her, bending down to put her shoes back on, the front of her top falling forward as it had before. If anyone was making somebody's day it was definitely the other way round.

'Are you sure you don't want to stop and eat something? she asked, suddenly sitting back up and holding his gaze. Her head was tilted slightly at an angle and there was a look in her eye, as if the invitation was being delivered with subtle innuendo.

Craven stared back, not sure whether the signals were real or just a figment of his imagination. He paused for a second, uncertain about what he should do and again, Jean's words about not being late nagged at the back of his mind. Eventually he gave her an apologetic shrug and tapped his watch. 'I wish I could but I'd better be going.'

She continued staring at him, still the same fixed gaze as if trying to communicate something else. 'I can't tempt you then?' she asked, a strand of hair pushed coquettishly behind her ear.

Craven gulped and looked at his watch again as if to emphasise the point. He was more tempted than he had ever been in his whole life but he knew he didn't have any choice. Buchanan would kill him. 'Sorry, I really do have to go.'

She held the gaze for a few more seconds and then her body relaxed, her face breaking into a broad, genuine smile. 'That's a real shame. But thank you for the lift.'

'My pleasure.'

'You didn't mind me asking though?'

'No, of course not.'

'No hard feelings then?'

Craven glanced down at his groin. 'I wouldn't say that.'

She laughed, the electricity between them unmistakeable. 'Could I ask one small favour?'

'Of course.'

She bent forward again and this time rummaged through the top of the rucksack, pulling out a bright orange plastic bottle which she thrust towards Craven. 'Would you mind putting some of this on my back?'

Craven took the bottle, his mouth open in gobsmacked silence as she twisted round to turn her back on him, crossing her arms under her waist and then pealing the loose, white top over her head. He stared at her in disbelief, her long, dark hair cascading down a bare, sun-bronzed back. Then she suddenly twisted round to look at him, a broad grin on her face and her hands cupped over her breasts. 'If you could put it on your hands first, otherwise it might make me jump…'

Twenty-Five

ALBERT LEANT ON THE SIDE OF HIS CAR AND TOOK another puff on the roll-up, blowing a thin cloud of smoke into the air. George had been gone almost fifteen minutes which meant he was having trouble finding the file. Not that it was any surprise of course. Without a reference number it was indeed like looking for a needle in a haystack. Poor old George was probably on his hands and knees sifting through piles of boxes, checking each file one by one without any idea what he was actually looking for. Albert took another drag on the cigarette and then flicked the butt across the car park. This was going to take longer than he thought. Not that he would have been of much help, even if they had allowed in him. He couldn't remember what the file looked like either and although he knew when it was archived he had no idea whether that was at the beginning of the year or towards the end. It was all too long ago. Still, there was no desperate hurry. It was much too hot to do anything quickly and other than the fact that he was getting hungry they had all afternoon. It wasn't as if anything was going to happen.

He got back into the car, switched the radio on and then leant back into the driver's seat and closed his eyes, letting the music wash over him. 1997 was a long time ago. In some respects it felt like only yesterday but in others it seemed like a lifetime ago. Britpop was ruling the waves, blockbusters like *Titanic* and *Jurassic Park* were dominating the silver screen and J. K. Rowling's first novel, *Harry Potter and The Philosopher's Stone* was being published to an unsuspecting public. Bill Clinton had been re-elected as US President and Tony Blair was in Number 10, overseeing the return of Hong Kong to Chinese rule for the first time since it had become a British colony in 1842. Closer to home Scotland had voted to create its own Parliament after 290 years of union with England, and in the Middle East, seventy tourists were gunned down by Islamist terrorists in Egypt's Valley of the Kings. A different era but it could have been only yesterday. But of all the events that happened that year there was one which stood out amongst all the others; one which shook the world and which made news headlines in every country across the globe. Albert could feel himself drifting off, drifting back to that fateful summer's day in 1997, a day which he would never forget. The telephone call from Paris at 03.00 in the morning, the sheer disbelief that she could be dead and then the desperate, manic rush to cover the story...

It was about ten minutes later when he was woken up by the sound of the passenger door opening and George sliding into the seat next to him.

'Keeping you up, Albert?' said George, grinning from ear to ear.

'Must have dropped off,' replied Albert, pulling himself up and blinking several times to get his focus. 'You found it then?' he added, nodding to the large, blue file which was now resting on George's lap, the bulging contents kept in place by two large elastic bands.

'Hope it's the right one,' said George, passing it over. 'Took me ages to find it.'

Albert took the file and stroked the front cover, the title and archive date written in his own handwriting over twenty years ago, a flood of memories suddenly rushing back. He blew out his checks for a second, the emotion of holding something that he thought he would never see again and then the enormity of what they were dealing with also hitting home.

'So, where next?' asked George, sensing that Albert was tempted to open the file there and then. 'We can't go through it here.'

'Can you remember where you were when it happened?' asked Albert, ignoring George's question.

George nodded. Everyone could remember where they were when they heard the news. It was like the assassination of JFK a generation before. 'I was on holiday in Cornwall. We put the TV on in the morning and couldn't believe it. Nobody could.'

Albert nodded. That was the same the world over. Sheer, absolute disbelief.

'So where next?' repeated George, nodding towards the file still on Albert's lap. We ought to go through it properly. Back home?'

Albert shook his head. 'No, it's too far. Take too long. Besides, it's half past one. I need to eat something.'

'Me too,' replied George, putting on his seatbelt. 'I know just the place. Let's get going.'

Albert frowned. 'Really? Round here?'

'Not far,' said George, glancing at his watch. 'It should be nice and empty by the time we get there. Give us some time to go through it properly.'

Albert started up the engine and George directed him back to the main road and then on towards the city, the skyline dominated by the buildings clustered around Lloyd's of London. They drove through Aldgate, down Leadenhall Street and Cornhill and then onwards to St. Paul's, Ludgate Hill and eventually Fleet Street. It took about twenty-five minutes to get there and just as George had predicted, by the time they had parked the car most of the lunchtime crowd had gone back to work and the place was relatively quiet.

'Afternoon Dino,' said George, staring at the specials board as he always did. Not that it ever changed. 'How's business?'

'Not bad,' replied Dino, twisting round to look at the large, plastic clock on the wall behind him. 'You're late today?'

George nodded. It was half-past two and he was starving. 'This is Albert by the way,' he said, thumbing towards Albert who was standing beside him. Dino and Albert nodded a polite exchange while George picked up a menu, still trying to decide what to have.

'You boys hungry then?' asked Dino, 'or do you just want drinks?'

'Hungry,' said George, still staring at the menu. He didn't normally eat much at lunchtime but it was mid-afternoon now and anyway, it would save having to cook something later on. 'What have you got?'

Dino shrugged. 'Sausage and mash. Egg and chips...'

'Ham, egg and chips?' interrupted George.

'Sure.'

'Make that twice,' said Albert. 'And two cups of tea.' Like George, he didn't normally eat that much in the middle of the day but ham, egg and chips was too good an opportunity to pass up.

Dino disappeared into the kitchen while George and Albert picked a table for four at the back of the café. 'Plenty of leg room for me and plenty of room to spread out,' said George as he sat down and moved the menu and salt and pepper pots to one end.

Albert pulled out a chair opposite and put the file on the table. 'Right, let's see what we've got then,' he said as he took off the rubber bands and opened the front cover. On top was a clear plastic wallet full of photographs, a dozen or so pictures taken at the scene of the accident. Albert opened it up and took out the first one, a shot of a black Mercedes limousine taken only minutes after it happened, the front of the car completely destroyed with the occupants still trapped inside, the two on the driver's side both dead on impact and the two on the passenger side barely alive. No-one wearing seat-belts. He passed it over to George as he took out a couple more, a close-up of Henri Paul slumped over the steering wheel and then a shot of the back of the car, the S280 badge and the registration number, 688 LTV 75, clearly visible.

'How long did it take you to work it out? asked Albert, passing the next two photos across the table.

'Straight away, more or less,' replied George, grimacing as he looked at the carnage in front of him. 'I had all the answers given to me so it wasn't that difficult really. Once I'd looked up Artemis it was pretty obvious.' He put the photos down and fished out the copy of the crossword from his rucksack, the paper folded firmly

241

into four quarters. He opened it up and flattened it out on the table, turning it 90 degrees so that they could both look at it.

'What did it say about Artemis then?' said Albert, searching for the clue that George had written; *"Greek deity in a la carte mistake."*

'It just said that she was a Greek goddess and that her Roman equivalent was Diana. Suddenly all the other answers made sense. Well, most of them anyway.'

'That one is different though,' replied Albert, still staring at the newspaper. 'All the other answers are straightforward. Paris, Assassination, Pregnant, Embalmed. No interpretation needed. But why use the word Artemis? Why not simply use the word Diana?'

George shrugged. He had no idea but Albert was right. Unlike the clues that he had written earlier in the week there was nothing cryptic about the answers. Whoever had drawn up the crossword was trying to tell them something and had chosen words which were clear and unambiguous. Even if you didn't know what they all meant, anyone seeing them together on the same page would be able to work out the connection.

'Which must means the word Artemis is significant,' continued Albert. 'It has to mean something else.'

George shrugged again. 'Makes sense I suppose. You've not heard it before?'

Albert shook his head as he started leafing through the file. 'No, I don't think so, although it was a long time ago. Maybe there's something in here.'

George looked back at the crossword, searching for the other answers that they didn't recognise. If Albert was going to trawl through everything he might as well look for those at the same time. He took out a piece of paper and wrote down the words BUCHANAN, CARLISLE, MULES, ROSS and VECTOR.

'MULES we know,' said Albert, glancing at the list. 'Jean-Claude Mules was the Paris police commander in charge of the investigation. He was assigned as soon as it happened. He was also the person who signed Diana's death certificate.'

'Wow, you've got a good memory,' grinned George, impressed at Albert's recall. 'Are you sure we need the file?'

Albert pushed the papers to one side and leant back into his chair, letting his mind drift back to August 1997. It was a long time ago but George was right; his memory of it, or at least most of it, was razor sharp. It was the biggest thing that he ever worked on so not something he was likely to forget. He paused for a second as Dino plonked two mugs of tea on the table and then disappeared into the kitchen again. Albert closed his eyes, letting the images from over 20 years ago come back to life. George picked up his mug and cupped it with both hands while he waited for Albert to start talking.

'The world's press were in a state of frenzy. It had been building up for several weeks but by the time they arrived in Paris it was at absolute fever pitch. Virtually every member of the paparazzi was there, everyone waiting for them to make an announcement and every photographer hoping to land that once-in-a-lifetime shot. It was complete bedlam. The crowd outside the Ritz was apparently the worst anyone had ever seen, even for people like Diana who were really hardened to it.'

'And did everyone know what the announcement was about?'

'More or less. Diana was an absolute master at manipulating the press and she hadn't made any secret about the relationship. In fact she practically flaunted it as soon as it started. She and Dodi had been inseparable from the moment they first met and her behaviour had become less and less discreet, as if she wanted the whole world to know that she had finally found the man of her dreams. They'd only been together about six weeks but everyone was expecting them to announce their engagement that weekend.'

George raised his eyebrows in surprise. 'Six weeks? I didn't realise it was that quick.'

Albert nodded. 'It was really quick. There's a chronology in the file somewhere. I remember writing it to keep track of everything.'

He started rummaging through the papers again and after a bit of searching suddenly produced it with a flourish, a detailed history of events all carefully listed in chronological order.

'Here it is,' he said, pointing to the first date at the top of the page. 14th July. Diana had apparently sat next to Mohamed Al Fayed at a charity dinner earlier in the year and he'd invited her to join his family on their summer holiday in the south of France. Fayed had a private villa in St Tropez and a £20 million yacht moored in the harbour at Cannes. He even arranged for his private jet to fly Diana and the two princes from Gatwick down to Nice.

'And that's where she met Dodi?'

Albert nodded again. 'Not that it was pre-arranged. He was in Paris about to celebrate Bastille day with a bunch of friends when he suddenly got a call from his old man, telling him to fly down and join them. Apparently Fayed thought Diana would appreciate the company.'

George took a mouthful of tea and also leant back into his chair. Six weeks was no time at all. It must have been a real whirlwind romance.

'It sounds corny,' continued Albert 'but it was love at first sight. Ever since her divorce Diana had become increasingly lonely and she'd been through a host of failed relationships with frankly some fairly inappropriate people. She was surrounded by lots of hangers-on and she was also constantly being humiliated by Charles's relationship with Camilla. For once in her life she was being accepted into a family on her own merits, and by people who weren't overawed by her background or royal connections. And of course it was a world full of luxury and refinement which was second to none. As well as the family estate in St Tropez Fayed had properties in the UK and Gstaad, he owned a castle in Scotland and he'd also acquired the Duke of Windsor's former house at the Bois de Boulogne, in Paris. If you add to that the flotilla of super yachts, a Gulfstream jet, a helicopter and a fleet of Ferraris, it was an opulent lifestyle that even Diana wasn't used to.'

'And Dodi?'

'Dodi was by all accounts a really nice guy. Equally loaded of course. He was in the middle of building a dream mansion in Malibu and he had expensive apartments all over the world; London, New York, Paris, Dubai. But apparently he wasn't your typical, privileged, spoilt playboy. Everyone said that he was very laid-back and that there was nothing arrogant or macho about him. It seems that he generally strolled through life and was very charming and attentive. That was probably part of the attraction to Diana who was always celebrity wary. They got on from the moment they met and were pretty much inseparable after that.'

Albert passed the chronology across the table as if to accentuate the point. George scanned it quickly, several pages of dates, times, locations and names. The itinerary was also staggering. Albert was right. From the moment they met on 14th July up until their deaths at the end of August Diana and Dodi seemed to have spent as much time together as they could. Varying their bases between Kensington Palace and Dodi's apartments in Park Lane and in Paris, they managed to fit in a cruise around the Mediterranean and then another holiday on the Cote D'Azur, visiting Portofino, Elba, the tiny island of Molara and then finally Sardinia, mostly on *Jonikal,* Fayed's luxurious private yacht.

'I've got some photos here somewhere,' said Albert, sifting through the file again. 'Here we are. This was taken on the 17th July, just a couple of days after they met.'

'They look very happy,' said George, staring at the photo, a picture of Diana in a purple swimsuit looking radiant and relaxed, playing with her sons and with Dodi's arm around her waist.

Albert gave him a knowing smile. 'No-one could remember seeing her so happy. But like I said, Diana was the consummate professional at manipulating the world's media. A few weeks earlier Charles had made an announcement that he was going to throw a massive ball at Highgrove to celebrate Camilla's fiftieth birthday.

Diana was furious. It was something he had never done for her in all the time they were married.'

George frowned, not exactly clear what Albert meant.

'Camilla's birthday was on the same day, the 17th July. The cynics believe Diana made quite sure which photographs would dominate the front pages the following day. Ever since they divorced, this was war...'

George handed the photo back. The animosity between Charles and Diana was legendry but he was still surprised at the lengths to which they went to undermine each other.

'...and you have to remember, whatever Diana thought of Dodi, the royal family were horrified. They thought she was a neurotic paranoid whose behaviour was becoming more and more erratic. To them Dodi was just a flamboyant, Egyptian playboy who spent his life indulging in casual relationships with a string of famous actresses and models. But worse than that, he was the son of someone who had been a thorn in the side of the British Establishment for more years than they cared to remember. But the final straw was the realisation that she might actually be considering getting married to him. That had all sorts of unthinkable connotations.'

George raised his eyebrows. He could think of a couple immediately. Like Diana converting to Islam for instance. Or the birth of a brown-skinned, Muslim half-brother to the future King of England. It was unimaginable.

'Anyway, the week before they arrived in Paris they were anchored off St Jean Cap Ferat. The paparazzi had been following them for weeks and were becoming increasingly aggressive. They even brought in helicopters to buzz the yacht in the hope of getting exclusive pictures. Dodi took Diana shopping in nearby Monaco one day and they popped into Alberto Repossi, Dodi's favourite jewellery store in the prestigious Hermitage Hotel. The rumours about an engagement were rife and when they decided to fly to Paris a few days later it was pretty much confirmed that they were going to pick up the ring from the jeweller's Paris branch. By the time they arrived the world's media were already there and it was an absolute circus.'

'Ham, egg and chips,' announced Dino, suddenly appearing out of nowhere carrying two plates of food. 'You want any mustard, sauces?'

'Brown sauce please,' replied Albert, moving the file out of the way.

'And some vinegar please,' added George, picking up his knife and fork in anticipation. He was absolutely ravenous.

The pair of them tucked into the food, heads down and oblivious to anything going on around them. Neither of them noticed the last few customers getting up and leaving and neither of them noticed the large, imposing figure enter the café and walk straight up behind them.

'Hello Albert,' said Vinny, picking up a long, golden chip off Albert's plate. 'Long time no see.'

Albert looked up, his mouth open in surprise while his fork, dripping with bits of ham and egg froze midway between his plate and his gob.

'And how are you George?' asked Vinny turning his attention the other side of the table, 'I've been looking for you everywhere. How's the holiday going?'

Twenty-Six

ROSS STOOD STILL FOR A MOMENT AND SURVEYED THE wreckage, the sound of screaming customers now reduced to a terrified, pitiful whimpering and the dust literally settling in front of his eyes. *Time to go.* He picked up the baseball cap and put on his sunglasses again. Then he turned and went through the double doors back into the kitchen. He was tempted to leave by the front door and try and follow Parovsky but he knew it was too late for that. The narrow, cobbled streets and numerous alleyways provided a perfect escape route and the old campaigner would be long gone by now, mingling anonymously in the crowds of tourists. Besides, walking out the front was far too risky. Too many people congregating to see what had happened plus the sound of police sirens getting louder by the second.

The kitchen looked deserted at first but then he noticed a couple of staff huddled in the far corner, staring at him intently while clutching long, stainless steel knives. The others had obviously escaped out the back door, or maybe they were hiding somewhere. It looked like there was a walk-in freezer or some sort of food store at the back of the room. Perhaps they had locked themselves in and the two guys outside had drawn the short straw; someone needed to let them out again when it was all over. Ross stared back and gave them a nod, as if to say that he was done and there was nothing to worry about. Then he walked towards the exit, picking up a shiny, red apple from one of the worktops as he left.

Three things hit him as soon as soon as he got outside. Firstly the sunlight, which was dazzling; secondly the heat which was like walking into an oven; and lastly the wail of sirens which sounded like they were literally on top of him. He headed north towards Curzon Street and then turned right, walking east for a couple of minutes before cutting through Lansdowne Row and then doubling back down Berkeley Street towards Piccadilly. He could still hear the sirens, several more heading in convoy towards the scene but it didn't matter now. He was only a few streets away but he was as invisible as all the other thousands of people enjoying the mid-summer afternoon. He crossed the road in front of the Ritz Hotel and then made his way into Green Park, managing to find an empty seat about half way down towards The Mall. He needed time to collect his thoughts and try and work out what he was going to do next.

He sat on the bench and took out his phone. Then he opened the address book and paged through the list of names, searching for the FSB safe house where Parovsky and Lukashenko had been staying. It took him a few seconds to find it but the details meant nothing to him. It was years since he'd been in London and his memory of the capital, or particularly the boroughs and postcodes wasn't good. There were a couple of KGB safe houses that he recollected from years ago but they were west of London somewhere. Chiswick or Hammersmith rang a bell. This looked like it was closer to the centre. Westminster perhaps, or Victoria more likely. Probably a grey, run-down terraced property with large, soulless rooms and dark, second-hand furniture. Drab, bleak and lifeless but out of sight from prying eyes.

He continued paging through the addresses, a collection of names and contacts that he had acquired over the years; a shadowy, eclectic list of faceless people but all of them meticulously stored and kept up to date. Insurance in the event of a final emergency. And it didn't get any more final than this. He hovered over the last number, tempted for a second to call it but then changed his mind. Better to deal with Parovsky first. If Moscow had authorised Limonov's operation last night then Parovsky was the person most likely to pick up the pieces. He was already on the ground and anyway, after the exchange in the restaurant it was going to get personal.

He closed the address list and opened the map application, quickly locating the safe house and then looking at a picture of the outside of the property. He smiled to himself as he switched the phone off, partly because it was an anonymous, grey terraced house in Victoria, just as he thought, but also because the pace of technology never ceased to amaze him. Once upon a time it would have taken him ages to do that sort of research but now it took only a matter of seconds. Millions of people were walking around with more surveillance capability in their pockets than he would ever have thought possible.

He picked up his rucksack and continued his way through Green Park, crossing the road in front of Buckingham Palace and then turning right towards The Royal Mews and on towards Victoria. Ross was American by birth but had spent a lot of time in Europe so he was familiar with neighbouring districts having very different characteristics. The Arrondissements in Paris for example; Bastille, Montparnasse, Pigalle... London was no different and it always intrigued him how some of the most expensive and exclusive areas sat cheek by jowl with some of the poorest and most run down. The odd juxtaposition of Dulwich, squeezed between Brixton and Peckham. And Victoria, tired and scruffy with Belgravia on one side and Westminster on the other.

It took him about ten minutes to find the right house, one of twelve identical properties in a narrow side street off the main road. At one end of the street was a white-fronted Georgian pub with black and gold signage and large, colourful hanging baskets. At the other end was a corner shop with a faded yellow awning and a red letter box on the pavement outside. And parked in front of house number 12 was a distinctive, small white van; old, dilapidated and with no markings. The safe house was at number 8 but it was a typical FSB cleaning operation. Park the vehicle two or three doors down the road and then wipe the property until all traces of occupancy had been removed. Which meant Parovsky had already flown. Moved to another safe house probably, or on to the Russian Embassy if they needed to buy some time. Ross decided to walk down the street while he tried to work out what to do next. There was nowhere that he could sit and wait and standing outside the safe house wasn't an option. He started on the right-hand side and walked slowly towards the pub at the other end of the road. As he passed number 8 he stopped and lit up a cigarette. There was no way of telling whether there was anyone at home but the Citroen van, a couple of doors down had all the tell-tale signs of a FSB service vehicle. In fact not unlike the one Ross had used all those years ago, parked in the woodland near Nant before he fired a bullet through Andanson's skull and then torched the car with him still inside.

He continued down the street and then crossed over the road by the pub and walked back up the other side. He was running out of options. Limonov was Putin's man so the message from Moscow was unequivocal. And after Parovsky there was no going back. Plus he'd burnt his bridges with the Americans years ago. They were probably out there looking for him right now. Suddenly he had nowhere to hide and nowhere to go. There was only one option left but he needed to be sure about Parovsky first.

He walked up to the corner shop and went inside, taking a few minutes to look around. In the end he bought a newspaper, only because he felt obliged to buy something before taking half a dozen free magazines out of the wire basket by the till. They were thin, flimsy flyers, full of local ads printed on recycled, coarse paper. Perfect for what he had in mind. He put the baseball cap and newspaper in his rucksack and then pushed the sunglasses on top of his head as he crossed the road. Then he went over to the first house and knocked on the door. It was answered within a few seconds by a smart, elderly woman, probably in her mid-sixties.

'Hello,' said Ross, giving her his best smile and still clutching the freebie magazines to his chest. 'Can I ask you if you think the world would be a better place if there was only one religion and no more wars?'

The woman's face changed. Part exasperation at being disturbed, part pity at the naive evangelist standing in front of her. 'Actually, I think the world would be a better place if there wasn't any religion at all.'

Ross continued smiling at her, unphased by the response. Inside, he agreed with every word she had just said but he kept the pretence going, as if he'd just shoved a coat hanger in his mouth. 'Would you be interested in finding out more about...'

'No thank you,' interrupted the woman, the door closing politely but firmly in his face. He raised his eyebrows and relaxed the smile. *Thank God for that.* The last thing he needed was someone who wanted a long conversation about the meaning of life, or even worse, someone inviting him in. As he turned and walked towards the house next door he took a sideways glance at number 8 but there was no sign of life, no nosey neighbour peering out behind the curtains. He rang the bell at number 4 and waited for what seemed like ages before the door opened, a guy about fifty years of age wearing torn jeans and a cheap, crumpled t-shirt seemingly less than pleased at being interrupted. He looked Ross up and down as though he was a piece of shit under his shoe.

'Hello,' said Ross, repeating his quickly rehearsed line. 'Can I ask you if you think the world would be a better place if there was only one religion and no more wars?'

'Piss off.' The door was slammed with impact, hitting the frame in perfect timing with the words. Ross smiled to himself as he turned away and walked towards number 6. *Two down, two more to go.* And as he did so he caught a glance of someone in the window of the safe house, no doubt wondering what all the noise was about. Number 6 had a door bell and also a door-knocker; a heavy, ornate, black handle with a large, round striking-plate. He pressed the bell and waited about thirty seconds before realising that there was no one at home. *Perfect.* Then he raised the door-knocker and slammed it as hard as he could, three times in succession but slowly, with a deliberate pause in between each one. The door literally shook with the force of it and the noise bounced off the striking plate. *The whole street must have heard that.* Ross stood his ground. Still no signs of life in front of him but in his peripheral vision he detected some movement in the window next door again. He waited another thirty seconds and then stooped down and looked through the letterbox. Then he rapped the knocker again, another three purposeful strikes, making sure that the person in number 8 was getting the message. *The quickest way to get rid of me is to open the door.* He waited another thirty seconds and then stooped down and looked through the letterbox one more time. Eventually he gave up and turned away and walked up to the safe house. He had barely rung the bell when the door was opened by a middle-aged guy with bad skin and lank grey hair, wearing blue overalls and latex gloves.

'Yes?' Both the voice and the look conveyed an impatience that he wanted to get rid of Ross as soon as possible.

'Ne dvigayutsya,' said Ross, his Russian accent honed to perfection after years behind the iron curtain. In the same breath he pulled out the SIG Sauer and pointed it straight at the guy's chest.

The guy looked taken aback but didn't move. He wasn't expecting Ross to speak Russian and he certainly wasn't expecting him to pull out a gun.

'Put your hands on your head and walk backwards. Slowly.'

'I thought you were selling religion.'

'God moves in mysterious ways.'

Ross raised the pistol slightly, as if he were about to fire and the guy instantly put his hands on his head and stepped back two or three paces. He was only a cleaner for God's sake. This wasn't what he was getting paid for. Ross stepped over the threshold and closed the door behind him, all the time keeping his eyes and the gun trained on the target in front of him. 'Keep moving.'

This time the guy did as he was told, walking backwards down the hall and then reversing into the living room on the right. Ross followed him step for step, making sure that he kept his distance but staying close enough not to miss.

'What do you want?' asked the guy, standing in the middle of the room, his hands still on his head. His face was getting redder and sweat was beginning to trickle down his forehead. Plus his arms were starting to ache. Ross looked around the room, just to get his bearings. He wasn't planning on staying long but he needed to make sure that there were no surprises. No colleague lurking in the corner. No electronics switched on and transmitting every word. But everything looked safe. The room was fairly tidy, other than there was a large holdall and a plastic crate full of cleaning materials on the dining table. It looked like the guy had only just turned up and had barely started.

'Where's Parovsky?'

The cleaner shrugged and then shook his head. 'Never heard of him.'

'The person that was living here. Where's he's gone?'

The guy shook his head again. 'I'm just the cleaner. They don't tell me anything.'

Ross looked at him, trying to work out whether he was telling the truth or not. It was probably true. Why would a cleaner know anything, other than how to clean-sweep a house? Mind you, even if he didn't know Parovsky's name or where he'd gone, he probably knew where all the other safe houses were.

'What other houses do you clean?'

The guy shook his head and glared back. He was only a cleaner but he was still FSB. He was saying nothing.

Ross glared back at him, irritated that now he had to make a decision. The guy wasn't a risk, in fact he wasn't material at all. He was just a low-paid operator who did what he was told. The sensible decision was to walk away. But there was another issue. Something else to consider. It was about making a statement. Damien Ross leaving his mark. Hunt or be hunted. The FSB thought they were looking for him. Time to turn the tables. Let them know it was the other way round.

'Get on your knees.'

The cleaner looked at him, his face suddenly filled with terror.

Ross jabbed the pistol forward, indicating that he meant it. The guy dropped to his knees, his hands still firmly on his head.

'Now, put your head on the floor.'

The guy hesitated for a moment but then leant forwards, his arms and forehead resting on the carpet, like a Muslim on a prayer mat.

Ross tried one last time. 'What other houses do you clean?'

Still the guy said nothing, the blood rushing to his head making him feel dizzy. Then he started muttering something. Russian, jumbled, unintelligible...

Ross looked at him, still trying to decide what to do. A fleeting thought went through his mind, wondering whether there was a wife at home somewhere, or a couple of children maybe. Then he remembered Limonov last night, breaking into his apartment with only one thing on his mind. Orders from Moscow. He stepped forward and nestled the end of the SIG Sauer behind the cleaner's ear. 'Do you know what happens next?'

The cleaner stopped muttering for a second and froze, the tension and the silence suddenly overwhelming.

'Molit'sya.'

The guy moaned and then started muttering again.

Then Ross pulled the trigger and the guy's brains exploded in front of him, most of it splattering onto the carpet; a sickening mess of blood and membrane and tissue. *"Now cracks a noble heart. Good-night, sweet prince; and flights of angels sing thee to thy rest."* He waited a moment for the noise and chaos to subside, the body twitching for a second before it slumped over into a foetal position. Ross kicked it gently, just to make sure. Then he took out his phone and opened the address book, scrolling down to the last entry as he had done earlier in the park. He looked at the name Vector, wondering whether the telephone number next to it was still current. *Only one way to find out.* He pressed the dial button and then put the phone to his ear. Less than two miles away the phone was answered almost instantly.

'Jean Pettipher.'

Ross smiled to himself. A familiar voice, still there after all this time. 'Charles Buchanan please.'

'I'm sorry, he's in a meeting. Can I take a message?'

Ross hesitated. He needed to speak to Buchanan personally. 'Can you interrupt him? It's urgent.'

'I'm sorry, not at the moment. He should be free in about fifteen minutes. Can I can get him to call you?'

Ross hesitated again. 'Not really, no. I'll call him back. Tell him it's Damien Ross. And tell him I want to come in...'

Twenty-Seven

S T. James's Park in the City of Westminster was the oldest Royal Park in London and without doubt, Buchanan's favourite. Originally a marshy water meadow through which the Tyburn flowed from Eton College the site was acquired in 1532 by Henry VIII as ideal land for deer hunting, the passion of kings and queens at the time. The royal court was based at the Palace of Westminster and Henry decided to create a deer park conveniently nearby, putting a fence around it and building a hunting lodge that later became St. James's Palace. The deer park stayed largely unchanged until 1603 when James I became King and decided to drain and landscape the park, introducing several ponds, channels and islands which were used to lure birds that were shot for the royal table. James kept a collection of animals there, including camels and crocodiles, as well as aviaries of exotic birds along what is now Birdcage Walk.

The park became more formal under the reign of Charles II who became King in 1660. During his exile in France after the English Civil War Charles had been impressed by the elaborate gardens belonging to the French royal family, so when he returned home the park was redesigned by the French landscaper, Andre Mollet, who introduced traditional lawns, flower beds and tree-lined avenues. The King entertained guests there and also courted his favourite mistress, Nell Gwyn, the diarist, John Evelyn, a contemporary of Samuel Pepys writing on 4th March 1671: *"I had a faire opportunity of talking to his Majestie and thence walked with him thro St. James's Parke to the Garden, where I both saw and heard a very familiar discourse between the King & Mrs. Nellie."*

In the 1820s the park got its final, great makeover, commissioned by the Prince Regent, later George IV and overseen by the architect and landscaper, John Nash. Today, the modern 57 acre park was still very much as Nash designed it, the canal transformed into a large, natural-looking lake surrounded by fashionable shrubberies, elegant lawns and romantic, winding pathways. Surrounded by some of the country's most famous landmarks including Buckingham Palace, Clarence House, St. James's Palace and Westminster, it was a green and tranquil space where Buchanan could sit and think in private; a place for quiet, uninterrupted reflection away from all the politics and mindless games of the Whitehall circus. His favourite seat was on the diagonal path that ran from the Artillery Memorial towards the Blue Bridge, facing south-east with a view of the Foreign & Commonwealth Office and the Cabinet War Rooms in the distance. Given its proximity to the lake and to the bandstand it wasn't the most secluded spot but that wasn't a problem. It was close to the Greenhouse and perfect for a discreet, private conversation.

He sat on the bench and checked his watch for the third time in as many minutes. Where the hell was Craven? It wasn't like him to be late but there was still no sign of him. And no message that he was held up but on his way. He stood up for a moment, hoping to spot someone amongst the crowd of people in the distance, many of them walking in his direction. The park was always busy and full of people. That was part of its attraction. No better place to go unnoticed than in the middle of a crowd. But for whatever reason, at the moment Craven wasn't one of them. Buchanan sat down again and wiped his forehead, the sun beating down with an unrelenting ferocity and the humidity now sticky and uncomfortable. Then he pulled out his phone, pressing the speed dial to make a call. As always it was answered in a matter of seconds.

'Jean Pettipher.'

'Jean, it's me. Have you heard from Craven?'

'No, nothing. Is he not with you?'

'No. I've been here ten minutes. No sign.'

'That's not like him.'

'I know. Are you sure he said the Garden?'

Jean nodded. 'Positive. I suggested here but he said "no".'

'Okay, I'll give him five more minutes. Has our cousin called back?'

Jean knew what that meant. Ross. 'Not yet. Christine Michaels called again...'

Buchanan threw his eyes up in the air. The last thing he needed at the moment was a conversation with the Ice Queen.

'...she said it was urgent.'

'Okay, I'll call her later.'

Jean put the phone down and smiled to herself. She knew he wouldn't. Not without an incentive.

Buchanan put the phone back in his pocket and checked the path in both directions again. Still nothing. What the hell was going on? Then he took out his newspaper and started to read, oblivious to the throng of tourists around him, some strolling by the lakeside to see the ducks and pelicans, others just relaxing in deckchairs and watching the world go by. It was two or three minutes later that he became aware of someone at the other end of the bench. He looked up to see Craven sitting there, taking out a packet of cigarettes and about to light up.

'Where did you come from?'

'Winchester.'

'I meant just now.'

Craven twisted around and nodded towards the distance behind him. 'The Mall. I came through the Marlborough Gate.'

'You're late.'

'Sorry. Heavy traffic.'

'Couldn't you have rung?'

'I was driving. It's illegal.'

Buchanan gave him a scathing look. When did Craven ever worry about whether something was legal or not? He spent his whole life on the wrong side of the law. That was what made him such a good agent. 'Don't you have hands-free or something?'

Craven took a drag on the cigarette and smiled to himself, unable to get the picture of him rubbing sun-tan lotion into the girl's naked body out of his mind. The one thing he didn't have was hands-free.

'Anyway, I've got fifteen minutes. What were you doing in Winchester?'

'Just a job I'm finishing off. Suspected adultery.'

'Tasteful.'

'It's turned into a murder case.'

'Domestic?' Buchanan suddenly had a vision of a jealous wife, uncontrollable with rage, inflicting the ultimate revenge on a cheating husband. *"Hell hath no fury like a woman scorned."*

Craven shook his head as he fished his phone out of his pocket, paging through a few photos until he found the one he was looking for. 'No. But I think it might be connected to something else. Do you recognise her by any chance?'

He passed the phone over and Buchanan took it, expecting to see a picture of a poor, grieving widow. Instead it was a photo of an attractive, middle-aged blonde, staring straight into the camera lens, a shot clearly taken from across the other side of a busy road. He looked at Craven in disbelief. 'Where did you get this?'

'Bloomsbury. A couple of nights ago. Why, do you recognise her?'

Buchanan stared at the photo again, unmistakably the same woman on the surveillance footage, the same person that had passed Ross on the way out of the park and who had almost certainly picked up the discarded newspaper. How on earth did Craven get a photo of her? And more importantly, why? He passed the mobile back, still trying to work out the connection. 'Her name is Nadia Lukashenko. Also known as Laura Taylor. FSB.'

Craven raised his eyebrows in surprise. He wasn't expecting that. A known dealer perhaps, or someone with a criminal record. But not FSB. 'Is she active?'

Buchanan nodded. 'Or at least, she was. She's lying on a marble slab at the moment waiting for a PM.'

'Jesus. What happened?'

'Professional hit. A lunchtime altercation in Mayfair.'

'One of ours?'

Buchanan shook his head. 'No. Damien Ross, probably.'

Craven took another long drag on the cigarette and stared at Buchanan in confusion. The last time he saw Damien Ross he was zipped up inside a large, red holdall in the bathroom of his apartment. That didn't make any sense at all.

'Things have moved on a bit. That wasn't Ross's body inside the flat last night. It looks like he had an uninvited visitor and took exception to the interruption.'

'So who was in the bag?'

'A Russian head-hunter. Roman Limonov.'

Craven shook his head. It wasn't a name he had ever heard of. 'So where is Ross now?'

Buchanan shrugged. 'Not sure exactly. But apparently he wants to come in...'

Craven raised his eyebrows as he took a final puff on the cigarette and then stubbed out the butt on the path in front of him. Suddenly everything to do with David Wallis had a different perspective. What had started out as an ordinary domestic case now looked like it involved the Russian security service. And someone coming in from the cold was just extraordinary. There hadn't been one of those for years.

'...but in the meantime he seems to be working his way through a FSB cell. First Limonov, then Lukashenko. Two down, one to go.'

'So who's next?'

'A FSB Colonel. Probably the case handler.'

'This guy perhaps?' asked Craven, swiping the screen on his mobile until he found the photo that he was looking for. Again, he passed the phone over and just as before, Buchanan stared at the picture in disbelief, a perfect shot of Ilia Parovsky standing on a pavement outside a row of shops. 'Where the hell did you get this?'

'I was watching an Art Gallery near the British Museum. The fat guy turned up with the blonde. He stayed on lookout while she went inside. Three minutes later my client's husband is dead and the gallery is minus one file full of photographs.'

'Photographs?' Suddenly Buchanan was leaning forward, hanging onto every word. He'd spent the last week trying to work out what Ross might have passed onto Lukashenko via the dead drop and now here was Craven, working on a completely unrelated case who might have the answer.

Craven nodded. 'Photos which the gallery bought from an antiques dealer in Winchester.'

'And do you know what was on them.'

'Not exactly. They came from a local house clearance. But I think I know where and when they were taken.'

'Go on.'

'Paris. The weekend of the 30th and 31st August 1997.'

Buchanan stared at Craven in silence, his mind racing ten to the dozen. How on earth could some sordid, parochial, domestic case possibly be connected to Artemis?

'I think fatty and blondie bought the photographs and then went back to cover their tracks. The file they took would have had copies of all the photos plus a record of their provenance, including both the purchase from the dealer in Winchester and then the sale to them.'

Buchanan stared into the middle distance, not bothering to correct Craven's assumption. Lukashenko didn't buy the photographs and neither did Parovsky. Suddenly everything was becoming clear and starting to make sense. Ross must have bought the photos. It was the only logical explanation. That's why he was in London. Flown in from Moscow after all these years. Despite all the risks he was probably one of the few people alive who would know whether they were significant or not, or even genuine. And then of course, assuming that they were, he bought them from the gallery and then passed them onto Lukashenko in the park, the very same park in which they were sitting now. The coincidences were staggering. But the key question was what did they contain and what were the Russians going to do with them?

'It looks like they're removing all trace of the transaction,' continued Craven. 'Unfortunately including the gallery owner.'

'We need to find out what's on those photos,' said Buchanan, suddenly snapping back into the conversation. The fate of some tin-pot gallery owner was neither here nor there. Finding the photographs and making sure they didn't get published was absolutely critical.

'I kind of assumed that.'

'Maybe the dealer in Winchester knows. Or perhaps he kept copies for himself.'

Craven shook his head. 'I tried that. The guy's disappeared.'

'Disappeared?'

'Not out of character apparently but it doesn't look good.'

'The house clearance then. Someone there must know.'

Craven shook his head again. 'That's where I was this morning. She hasn't got a clue. And definitely no copies. And even if there were, it looks like our FSB friends are ahead of us.'

Buchanan frowned, confused by the last comment.

'She was burgled last night. All the hallmarks of a black ops.'

Buchanan fell silent again, thinking through his options. He had no idea what was on the photos but whatever it was, it had to be toxic. Why else would Ross break cover after all these years? And it also explained the crossword. Exactly as Carlisle had predicted. A precursor to another conversation; a bigger negotiation yet to take place. The Russians holding all the cards and threatening to publish. *Give us what we want otherwise we'll tell the world about Artemis.* Except of course they weren't involved in Artemis. They wouldn't even recognise the name. They must have got that from

Ross. One of the few people who knew what it meant. One of the few people who was actually there and still alive. The CIA traitor. Finding the photos was now the priority which meant finding Ross was even more important than before. He didn't have them any more of course but he was the one person who knew what was on them. And there was always a chance that he might know where they were.

'So do you know where this Parovsky guy is likely to be?' asked Craven. 'I assume he's still got the photographs?'

Buchanan shrugged. That was always possible of course but much more likely that he'd handed them over to someone else. They were probably back in Moscow by now, or at least stowed away somewhere safe; an anonymous safety deposit box in an underground vault. Or under lock and key in the Russian Embassy. And anyway, finding Parovsky wasn't going to be easy. That would be like looking for a needle in a haystack.

'So what do we do next?'

'Not sure. Wait for Ross, probably.'

'You want me to do anything?'

Buchanan was just about to answer when his mobile burst into life, as usual the familiar opening of Bach's *Passepied* from Orchestral Suite No. 1 in C Major. He pulled it out of his pocket and answered it immediately.

'Hello?'

'It's Jean. I've got our cousin on the line. Can I put him through?'

Buchanan hesitated. If they were going to arrange a place to meet, talking on the mobile wasn't safe. Anybody could be listening in.

'I've also got a message from Maurice. He's been monitoring phone traffic. George Wiggins has just made a call.'

'Where is he?'

'Central London. They couldn't get an exact fix, the call was too quick but it's somewhere around Fleet Street. He rang his wife and said he was with someone called Albert...'

Buchanan frowned. The name Albert meant nothing to him.

'...Maurice said there was a bit of background noise. It sounded like a restaurant or maybe a café. Perhaps he's back at work.'

Buchanan stopped for a moment, suddenly remembering something that was in the crossword that morning. The paper was still on his lap. He put Jean on hold for a second and unfolded it quickly, scanning the back page where the words CAFÉ, MINT and LANE were written across the middle of the grid in sequence, still in Maurice's distinctive handwriting. He hadn't heard of Mint Lane before, which is why he'd looked it up on the internet earlier in the day and discovered it was just around the corner from Fleet Street. And more importantly, there were only two cafés in the area, a sandwich and coffee shop called Cantina and an Italian place called Francorelli's. It was just a hunch but worth a try. 'Jean, tell Maurice he might be in Mint Lane, possibly in a café called Cantina or one called Francorelli's.'

'Okay. Mint Lane. Where's that?'

'Just off Fleet Street.'

'Do you want me to get you the postcode?'

'No, we'll find it.' Buchanan looked across at Craven who was poised for action, trying to interpret a conversation from one end of a phone call, assuming that it was news on either Ross or Parovsky.

'Mint Lane, near Fleet Street. Our crossword compiler's just made a call. From a café called Cantina probably. Or maybe Francorelli's. Go and pick him up.'

Craven frowned, slightly disappointed at the instruction. 'Is he important anymore?'

Buchanan shrugged. 'I don't know. But there's nothing else you can do at the moment. I need to meet Ross on my own.'

Craven nodded and stood up and left while Buchanan asked Jean to put the call through. The phone clicked and then went silent for a moment, both parties waiting for each other to speak. After about five seconds Buchanan decided to go first.

'Hello?'

There was a pause at the other end before Ross eventually spoke, a voice that Buchanan hadn't heard in over fifteen years. Unmistakably American but with a heavier European accent now. 'Long time no speak.'

'Likewise. How are you?'

'Busy...'

'I heard.'

'...and in demand.'

'Nice to be popular.'

'Definitely not popular. Just in demand.'

'I thought you'd retired.'

'I had.'

'So what happened?'

'I got bored.'

'All that state television and free vodka.'

'Something like that.'

Buchanan twisted round and caught a glimpse of Craven, leaving the park through the Marlborough Gate, exactly the same way that he had come. 'I hear you want to come in.'

'Maybe. Do you know where Ilia is?'

'Ilia?'

'No games. Yes or no.'

'No.'

'And would you tell me if you did?'

'Probably not.'

'That's a pity.'

'What do you want him for?'

'Just a friendly chat.'

Buchanan paused. It was time to stop the cat and mouse games and cut straight to the chase. 'We ought to meet.'

'Agreed. Where are you?'

'The Garden. Usual place.'

'Just like old times.'

'Something like that. You?'

'Not far away.'

'Okay. How about here?'

'No thanks. Too public.'

'The Greenhouse then.'

'Don't be ridiculous. Somewhere neutral. Just you and me.'

'Any preference?'

Ross paused while he took a long drag on a French cigarette. 'No, you suggest somewhere.'

'Not on the phone. Can I call you back from a landline?'

'No. One number, one call.'

Buchanan paused again. Ross was obviously using different SIM cards to make sure he couldn't be traced. There was no way he was going to take a second call on the same number. Which meant calling back wasn't an option. There was an obvious alternative. 'You could ring me back at the Greenhouse. I can be back there in no time...'

Ross thought for a moment. That was a possibility but the Greenhouse was full of surveillance equipment. He'd be standing on a pavement somewhere, talking on the phone like a sitting duck and they'd be tracking his exact location. And then the Drones would turn up, all pumped up and trigger happy. The tables would be completely turned. And besides, he'd already phoned twice. He just wanted to get on with it.

'...How about I leave now,' continued Buchanan, 'and you call me in fifteen minutes?'

'No. I'd rather agree something now.'

'That's risky.'

'Life is risky. Get over it.'

Buchanan thought for a moment, racking his brains for somewhere that they could meet. Suddenly he had an inspiration. 'Can you get to Soho?'

'Sure. Whereabouts?'

'Waldron Court. Number 9. Ask for a copy of *The Conquistador*.'

'A book shop?'

'Don't ask.'

'Okay, what time?'

Buchanan checked his watch. He had a meeting with Carlisle that he couldn't move. 'Four-thirty?'

'Done. See you then.'

—◊—

Less than a mile away Ilia Parovsky was sitting in a Soho coffee bar, drinking a black tea and checking his phone every thirty seconds. He was tempted to simply get a taxi over to the Russian Embassy in Kensington Palace Gardens but he knew that wasn't allowed. He had to wait for instructions. Besides, they might not send him there. It might be the Defence Attaché's Office at Highgate, or possibly another safe house. Or even a flight back to Moscow, straight into a debriefing at the Lubyanka. He took another sip of tea and checked his watch. It was over an hour since he'd left the restaurant and he was getting impatient. Where the hell were they? He drained the last dregs from the cup and was just contemplating whether to order another when his phone, lying on the table top started to vibrate. He picked it up and answered it, expecting to hear a familiar Russian voice. 'Hello?'

Just as in the restaurant, he couldn't have been more wrong. A perfect British accent. 'Where are you?'

'Dean Street. A coffee bar.'

'Alone?'

'Of course.'

'Plan B executed?'

'All done.'

'Any problems?'

'Not really.'

'Have you heard anything?'

'Nothing. Still waiting.'

'I've got something for you.'

'What?'

'Someone's just made a phone call. You could pay them a visit and say hello.'

Parovsky smiled to himself. That sounded more like it. Better than sitting on his backside doing nothing. Time for a bit of old fashioned retribution. *"If you prick us do we not bleed? If you tickle us do we not laugh? If you poison us do we not die? And if you wrong us, shall we not revenge?"*

Twenty-Eight

'WHAT DID YOU WANT TO GO AND DO THAT FOR?' ASKED Albert, staring across the table at George in disbelief.

George looked slightly guilty as he turned the phone off and put it back in his pocket. He knew that it was risky but at the moment he didn't really care. The important thing was that he'd spoken to Margaret to check that she was all right. And to reassure her that he was okay. Suddenly it felt important for him to do that, whatever the consequences. He had no idea where this was all going to end but he wanted Margaret to know that he was thinking of her. Just in case. Besides, he owed her that at least. If he'd thought a bit more about her last week they wouldn't be in this position in the first place.

Albert shook his head in frustration. After everything that had happened that was just reckless. In fact it was sheer, bloody stupidity. 'You could have used my phone,' he said, trying to sound sympathetic, 'or Vinny's.'

George glanced across at Vinny who was still standing at the counter, ordering a cup of coffee. 'I told her not to answer any calls unless they were from me. On my number. I just needed to speak to her.'

Albert shook his head again. George clearly didn't understand how dangerous the situation was. 'Well you'd better not use it again,' he said, adopting the tone of a scolding parent. 'And take the SIM card out. Let's just hope no one is monitoring your calls, otherwise you're going to get us both killed.'

'I don't think that's very likely,' grumbled George, pulling the phone out of his pocket again. 'I can't imagine anyone is really trying to find me.'

'I wouldn't bank on it,' said Vinny, carefully balancing a cup and saucer in his left hand as he wandered over. 'I've just met someone looking for you.'

Albert shuffled over so that Vinny could sit next to him, directly opposite George. He also moved the file out of the way so that Vinny could put his coffee down and spread out a bit.

'Someone by the name of Craven. Mean anything to you?'

George shook his head and said nothing. He was racking his brains but the name meant nothing to him.

'Well he's very determined to speak to you George,' continued Vinny, nodding towards his right arm in a sling and his wrist heavily bandaged. 'Where do you think I got this from? Playing snooker?'

Albert and George looked at each other and frowned, the threat of violence suddenly a reality and much too close to home.

'Well, me neither. I've no idea what's going on so you'd better start talking. Particularly if there's a story in it. According to Maureen it could be a front pager.'

Albert and George exchanged another glance. That at least explained one thing. No wonder Vinny had suddenly turned up. One sniff of an exclusive and he was like a rat up a drainpipe.

'So what happened then?' asked Albert, also nodding towards the sling and Vinny's heavily bandaged wrist.

Vinny shrugged, as if the injury was nothing really. He'd had a lot worse in his time and his pride was still hurting more than his wrist. 'He wanted to know all about you George. And where he could find you. Luckily you were on holiday so I didn't know where you were.'

'So how did you know we were here?' asked Albert. 'Maureen didn't know where we were going.'

Vinny tapped the side of his nose. 'Journalism Albert. Good old fashioned research. Remember that?'

Albert smiled. He did remember that. In fact he had never forgotten. He was the best journalist that had ever worked for Vinny and they both knew it.

'So, what have you two been up to?' asked Vinny, picking up his cup and taking a slurp of coffee. 'And what's all this about you trying to get hold of an old file?'

'It's a long story,' replied George, starting to look a bit sheepish again. 'But I think Maureen might be right. It could be the biggest story we've had in years.'

Vinny leant forward as George and Albert brought him up to speed, starting at the beginning when George first met Laura Taylor at the Red Lion and then the mysterious meeting in Francorelli's, discovering the empty house in Tenterden, the two crosswords published on consecutive days, their visit to see Maureen this morning and then finally retrieving the file from the storage firm at Wapping. 'We were just going through it now,' added George, nodding towards the stack of documents at the end of the table.

'How was Maureen then?' asked Vinny, going off subject for a moment, a fleeting memory of her working at the *Chronicle* suddenly coming back to him.

'She was fine,' replied Albert. 'Enjoying retirement I would say.'

'Good.' Vinny leant over and slid the file towards him, the brief moment of sentiment passing as quickly as it came. 'Let's get down to business then. What do we know?'

'We were just going through the background,' said George. 'How Diana and Dodi ended up in Paris that weekend. Do you remember all of that?'

Vinny gave him an old fashioned look. 'Does Dolly Parton sleep on her back?'

George smiled. He'd forgotten how politically incorrect Vinny could be at times. In fact it was hard to say who was worse, him or Albert. In truth they were as bad as each other; both outrageous but both very, very funny. They spent the next thirty minutes or so going through the pile of papers, continuing to sort everything into order so that they had a clear sequence of events, cross-checking the formal police documentation with the various witness statements and all the time looking for the last few words from the original crossword. Vinny also showed them the telephone number that he'd rung earlier but there was nothing in the file that helped identify Jean Pettipher or who she worked for. Similarly, nothing on the names Dampier or Craven. For Albert it was something of a cathartic experience, seeing his hand-written file notes and his typed submissions for the first time in over twenty years. He'd always had a good memory for everything that he worked on but now certain words or phrases were jumping off the page as if it was only yesterday.

'Let's start at the beginning,' said Vinny, moving the file to one side again to make some room. 'Let's see if we can at least get the facts straight before we start looking at all the conspiracy theories. What time did they arrive?'

'3.22 pm,' replied George, scanning the document in front of him. 'They flew into Le Bourget airport from Sardinia in Fayed's private plane, a green and gold Gulfstream IV jet. The Ritz Hotel sent two cars to pick them up, a black Mercedes 600 limousine driven by Philippe Dourneau, who was Dodi's chauffeur, and a black Range Rover driven by Henri Paul, who was the acting Head of Security at the Ritz.'

'Henry Paul was the one driving the car when they crashed.' interrupted Albert, just to make sure that Vinny knew who was who.

'Exactly,' continued George. 'But at this point they were in separate vehicles. Dodi and Diana travelled in the Mercedes with Trevor Rees-Jones, one of Fayed's bodyguards, while Henri Paul took the other bodyguard, Kez Wingfield, plus René the butler, two female members of the *Jonikal* crew and all the luggage to Dodi's apartment.'

'Which was where?' asked Vinny.

'In the rue Arsène Houssaye,' replied Vinny, not needing to look it up. Some of the details were imprinted permanently on his brain. 'It's just off the Champs-Élysées, near the junction with the Arc de Triomphe.'

Vinny nodded although not really any the wiser. He had never been that well-travelled and the districts and locations of Paris were generally a mystery to him.

'Le Bourget is in the northern suburbs of Paris,' continued George. 'On the way into the centre Dodi and Diana stopped off to look at Villa Windsor, the house where the Duke of Windsor lived in exile with Wallis Simpson. Fayed had acquired a long-term lease on the property from the French Government and had spent a small fortune refurbishing it. There's some speculation that Dodi was trying to persuade Diana to consider making it their home but apparently she thought it was too gloomy. They spent about thirty minutes there before driving the short journey to the Ritz Hotel in the Place Vendôme.'

'I've got all the stuff on the Ritz,' said Albert, picking up several pages of typed summary, all stapled together. 'There were quite a few paparazzi waiting outside for them but nothing like the number that would be there later on. The transfer from the car to the hotel went smoothly and they checked into the Imperial Suite just after 4.30 pm. Diana then went to the hairdressing salon to freshen up while Dodi went to collect the engagement ring from Repossi's. The jeweller's local branch was less than a hundred yards away across the Place Vendôme but for some reason Dodi decided to drive there in the Mercedes. He took Trevor Rees-Jones with him while Kez Wingfield followed on foot with Claude Roulette, the hotel acting manager. After that they stayed in the hotel until about 7.00 pm. when they drove over to Dodi's apartment to get ready for dinner.'

'So where were they going?' asked Vinny, starting to get confused by the sequence of events.

'*Chez Benoit*,' replied Albert. 'It's a restaurant on the edge of Les Halles. It was one of Diana's favourites. They had a reservation and probably wanted to change before dinner. All their luggage was at the flat. Plus René would have been on hand, waiting for them with chilled champagne.'

'So what was the point of going to the Ritz then?'

Albert shrugged. 'It was just a drop-off really. They probably stopped there because Dodi needed to pick up the ring and it was just around the corner. But they always intended to eat out and stay at Dodi's apartment.'

Vinny pulled a face, still not convinced but it probably wasn't important. 'Okay, so what happened next?'

'That's when it all started to go wrong,' said George. 'For some reason they persuaded the two bodyguards that they needed some time to themselves, so were going to drive to the apartment without them. There must have been some disagreement about that because in the end Philippe Dourneau drove them in the Mercedes but Trevor Rees-Jones and Kez Wingfield followed immediately behind in the Range Rover, this time driven by Jean-Francis Musa, the owner of the Etoile Limousines company which rented the cars to the Ritz.'

'So what happened to the other driver?' asked Vinny. 'Henry Paul. Where's he gone?'

'No one really knows,' replied Albert. 'He'd finished his shift so had left for the day but there's lots of speculation about where he went.'

Vinny raised his hand, indicating that he wanted Albert to stop there. This was a story full of speculation and he wanted to concentrate on the facts first.

'The journey to Dodi's apartment was straightforward,' continued George 'but when they got there it was absolute bedlam. Someone must have tipped off the press because there was a huge crowd of paparazzi swarming outside and the mood was very aggressive. Even for someone battled-hardened like Diana this was at a level which she had never seen before. Apparently it was a real feeding frenzy and very menacing. Lots of photographers intimidating them to try and get that exclusive picture. By the time they managed to get inside the flat both Dodi and Diana were really shaken up.'

'And do we know who tipped off the press?' asked Vinny, his journalistic instinct kicking in.

Albert shook his head. It could have been anyone. The Ritz employed a lot of people and most of them were low paid. A quick tip off to the press would have been easy money. And the prize of course was astronomical. When Dodi and Diana had been holidaying on the *Jonikal* one of the photographers had managed to get a shot of them kissing on deck, a picture which was splashed all over the front page of the *Daily Mirror*, it's editor Piers Morgan having bought it on a one-day exclusive from the Italian paparazzi who had staked out the yacht. The following day the photo was bought by other national newspapers and given similar treatment, making the photographer in excess of £1 million. It was little wonder that the situation outside the apartment was so hostile.

'They stayed at the flat for a couple of hours,' said George, turning over the sheet of paper and scanning the other side. 'There's a whole section here about them changing for dinner and what they were wearing when they left. Versace mostly, in the case of Diana. It says Dodi took some cigars with him, plus a cigar cutter and a mobile phone, none of which were found after the crash.'

Vinny frowned. He wasn't sure whether that was relevant or not so looked at Albert to get his reaction. Albert shrugged. It was more speculation. Maybe one of the photographers or rescue workers took them as a souvenir but none of the items had come to light since, which was surprising. So there was also a more sinister explanation. One that was directly connected to the assassination theory.

'They left the apartment at 9.30 pm,' continued George, 'seemingly with the intention of going to Chez Benoit but the crowd of photographers outside was so bad that Dodi decided that it was too dangerous to eat out in public. He cancelled the reservation en route and then called Trevor Rees-Jones in the back up Range Rover and told him that they were going back to the

Ritz and would have dinner there. That's about it. I haven't got anything else on their visit to the apartment and they never saw it again after that.'

Vinny leant back in his chair and reflected for a moment, trying to visualise the events in Paris over twenty years ago. Everyone knew that Dodi and Diana had been killed in a car crash in the Alma Tunnel but whether it was really an accident remained a mystery to this day. There were countless conspiracy theories of course, most of them implicating the Royal Family and the security services but no one really knew what had actually happened, or at least no one who was prepared to talk. Until now that is. The crossword that George had shown him had clearly been written by someone who knew more than most and it felt like they were almost there, almost at the point of uncovering the truth. Maybe, just maybe, understanding the background and particularly the sequence of events leading up to the crash would help them get there.

'The problem they had now,' continued Albert 'is that the Ritz wasn't ready for them to come back. Claude Roulet was still standing outside Chez Benoit waiting to orchestrate their arrival and there was no one left at the hotel to respond to their last-minute call for extra security. When they turned into Place Vendôme there was a huge crowd waiting for them, over one hundred photographers and tourists, all jostling to get a better vantage point and get that exclusive picture. This time the transfer from the car to the hotel didn't go well. If the situation outside the apartment was bad, this was even worse. And it was deteriorating rapidly. We've got some pictures of it somewhere.'

Albert rummaged through the pile of documents in front of him and pulled out a couple of black and white photos, obviously taken in the middle of the maelstrom that had unfolded outside the hotel. He passed one over to Vinny and the other one across to George. They both showed Diana looking terrified, jumping over people's legs and running, swaying from side to side, as if she were dodging attacks from all angles. By all accounts it was only her fitness and athleticism that enabled her to get to the hotel foyer in one piece. In the corner of each picture were two small, yellow circles, highlighting the faces of two people at the edge of the crowd, both of them watching the ensuing mêlée with a detached interested rather than being actively involved.

'Who are these two?' asked Vinny, pointing to the grainy figures on the right-hand side of the photo.

'Richard Spearman and Nicholas Langman. MI6.'

'What the hell were MI6 doing there?' asked Vinny.

Albert gave him a knowing look. 'Lots of speculation about that as well. But as you said, probably better that we get through the hard facts first.'

Vinny nodded, acknowledging the reminder. Good investigative journalism was all about disciplined research and the last thing they needed now was to go off track.

'Dodi guided Diana to the hotel's L'Espadon restaurant,' continued Albert, 'but she was far too agitated to cope with the staring gaze of dozens of gawping diners, so they decided to eat in private in the Imperial Suite. If only they had decided to stay there they would probably still be alive today but it was always their intention to return to Dodi's flat afterwards, once things had quietened down a bit outside.'

'Why did they want to do that?' asked George. 'Surely with everything going on outside it was safer to stay where they were.'

Albert shrugged again. 'Not sure really. The Imperial Suite is about as romantic and luxurious as you can get but maybe they just wanted to be at home, in their own private space. It's pretty much accepted that Dodi had proposed to her that evening so they probably wanted to consummate it somewhere where they felt comfortable and at ease, away from all the attention of the hotel staff and the world's media.'

'That looks like a decision that cost them their lives,' said Vinny ruefully.

'Possibly,' replied Albert, 'and if they thought things were going to quieten down outside they couldn't have been more wrong. They were hotting up. A sort of madness had descended on the paparazzi which was spreading through them like an infectious disease. Everyone knew about the engagement so they were all expecting some sort of announcement but the rumours about Diana being pregnant were also rife. She'd been photographed the previous week in a swimsuit that revealed a slight bulge in her belly. She'd dismissed it as just tummy fat which she said she was planning to get rid of by liposuction but the newspapers weren't convinced. Anyway, it was the size and the mood of the mob outside that gave Dodi the idea about using a couple of decoy vehicles and then driving to his apartment in a third, unmarked car. That was the decision that probably got them killed.'

'You boys want some more drinks?' asked Dino, suddenly appearing out of nowhere. 'Or anything else to eat?'

'A cup of coffee would be nice,' said Vinny, leaning back in his chair again. 'All this research is making my brain hurt.'

'Are you sure Dino?' asked George, conscious that they were the only customers left and it looked like he was closing up. 'Aren't you waiting to lock up?'

'No, you're fine,' replied Dino. 'I've closed now but I've got a bit of cleaning to do. As long as you don't mind me tidying up around you.'

'Thanks,' said George. 'Another tea then please.'

'Make that two,' added Albert, standing up and stretching his legs. 'I'm just popping outside for a smoke.'

'Put the door on the latch,' said Dino, walking back to the kitchen, 'otherwise you won't get back in.'

Albert wandered outside and rolled up a cigarette, dropping a few strands of tobacco into a cigarette paper and then expertly rolling the contents before licking the gummed edge and lighting up. He took a long drag and blew a thin stream of smoke into the air, the nicotine hitting his central nervous system in a matter of seconds. The process of going through the file was fascinating but he wasn't sure whether they were actually making any progress. Nothing particularly new had come out although it was early days. They hadn't finished going through the chronology yet and there was lots of speculative stuff to consider after that. It was probably going to take the rest of the day before they finished. He took another drag on the roll-up and wandered up the lane a bit, looking absent-mindedly in a couple of shop windows; a small florist with brightly coloured displays and an upmarket wine shop, selling what looked like high-end, expensive stock. How these small, independent traders managed to make a living, let alone cover the cost of their rent was beyond him but then again, people in London always had been prepared to pay silly prices for everything.

He turned around to look back down the lane and noticed a man walking towards him. Not someone he had ever seen before but there was something about the guy's appearance which jogged his memory. Something that George had said earlier. A large, portly guy with an over-elaborate moustache, a loud and flamboyant bow-tie and a large-checked waistcoat. *Mr. Toad.* Albert watched intently as Parovsky walked up the lane, carefully checking all the shops and premises before stopping outside Francorelli's. He walked up to the bay window and looked through it, spotting that there were only two people inside, both of them sitting at a table at the far end of the cafe. One was a large fat guy with his back to the door, wearing a blue and white striped shirt and a pair of red braces, his suit jacket hanging on the back of his chair. It also looked like his right arm was in a sling. The other guy, sitting opposite him and facing the door was older; a tall, lanky guy with a bald head and large, round glasses. *Bingo.* Definitely the crossword compiler that Lukashenko had chatted up in the Red Lion. The crossword compiler that was now trying to make trouble for them. Parovsky looked at them for a second and then moved to the door. The sign said closed but it looked like it was slightly ajar. Perfect...

Albert watched him from a distance. There was no way that he could confront the guy but he couldn't just stand there and do nothing. He took out his phone to ring George but then remembered that was pointless. George had switched his mobile off and anyway, he'd taken the SIM card out so it wasn't working at all. Albert looked at his phone in frustration, a handful of names programmed into it but none of them of any use. Vinny probably had a mobile on him but Albert didn't know the number. He looked back down the lane for a second, desperately trying to think what he could do. Mr. Toad was still hovering outside the cafe, looking like he was contemplating going in. He could call the *Chronicle* of course and ask for Vinny's number but it didn't look like he had time for that. And anyway, they might not give it to him.

Parovsky peered through the glass door, making a mental note of the layout of the cafe. It was perfect. Just the two of them inside and no one else around. He didn't know the fat guy with his back to him but that didn't matter. Whoever he was he was expendable. The only risk was the compiler and he looked too old and useless to be any sort of threat. All he had to do was walk straight up to them, "pop-pop" the compiler and then "pop-pop" the fat guy and walk straight out. Thirty seconds max. He'd be back at the embassy within the hour, drinking Russian tea and enjoying diplomatic immunity. He put his hand inside his jacket and felt the grip of the Serdyukov nestling next to his ribcage. Familiar, reassuring, reliable. Like an old friend. Then he glanced at his watch. No time like the present.

Albert watched in horror, somehow interpreting the body language. He was running out of options and he was running out of time. Suddenly a breath of wind caught his senses, the faint promise of a cooler breeze to break the oppressive, stifling heat. He looked up above, the clear blue sky slowly disappearing under a blanket of grey, sprawling clouds billowing in from the west, the scent of rain dark and heavy in the air. Then he looked up at the sign above the cafe, the word Francorelli's painted in stylish, yellow letters on a lime-green background. Underneath it said "Proprietor, D. Molinari" and then a phone number, a London phone number beginning with 0207. Last chance. Albert tapped the number into his mobile and hit the send button, praying it would be answered immediately. It rang a couple of times and then stopped, the familiar voice of a male Italian picking up the call.

'Hello?'

'Dino?'

'Yes?'

'It's Albert. I was with George just now.'

Dino grinned. 'Don't tell me. You forget to put the door on the latch. You're locked out.'

'It's not that. I'm outside. Someone's about to come in.'

'Someone?'

'Someone looking for George. It looks bad.'

'Bad?'

'Really bad. We need to do something. Quick.'

'What do you mean we need to do some...'

'Jesus, he's got a gun! He's coming now!'

The phone at the other end went dead.

Parovsky took one last look through the glass, all the time caressing the pistol in his right hand. Then he pushed the door open and walked inside...

Twenty-Nine

'IT LOOKS LIKE THERE'S A STORM COMING.' CARLISLE looked out of his office window and peered up at the sky, the dense, unbroken cloud darkening to a gun-metal grey, bathing everything in an eerie, greenish hue. Outside, the treetops which had been parched and motionless for days were starting to sway in a freshening breeze, a precursor to the main event that was just around the corner.

Buchanan said nothing. There was a storm coming alright but it had nothing to do with the weather.

Carlisle walked over to the door and pressed the light switch, a small crystal chandelier above their heads producing a dull, amber light, barely competing with the mid-afternoon gloom. Then he sat down and stared across the desk at Buchanan, a colleague and adversary for more years than he cared to remember. Buchanan stared back and gave him a thin smile. Carlisle had called the meeting so it was up to him to speak first. In the distance a low rumble of thunder rolled across the sky, echoing across the city rooftops.

Carlisle shuffled a few papers and then opened and closed a couple of drawers, more for effect than out of necessity. It never hurt to keep people waiting a bit, especially someone like Buchanan. A gentle reminder about seniority and who was more important. Eventually he pulled out a file from the right-hand pedestal and laid it on the desk in front of him. 'Coffee?'

Buchanan shook his head. He'd had enough coffee for today and besides, he had an appointment to keep. Whatever they were discussing he needed this to be quick.

'Or water perhaps?' continued Carlisle, sensing that Buchanan was in a hurry and getting impatient. There was nothing more entertaining than slowing things up when the other party wanted to do exactly the opposite. He stood up again and walked over to a small side table behind him. 'Still or sparkling?'

'I'm fine thank you. Nothing for me.'

'Or something stronger perhaps?' Carlisle glanced at the antique bracket clock at the other side of the office and then frowned. 'Although it is a little early I suppose...'

Buchanan palmed away the offer and glanced at his watch, mindful that he also needed to keep an eye on the time.

'...unless you work in the Foreign Office of course.' Carlisle allowed himself a little smile as he unscrewed the top off a bottle and poured himself a glassful of sparkling water, every movement slow and deliberate as he screwed the top back on and then walked back to his desk. 'Anyway, how are you Charles?'

Buchanan leant back in the chair, crossing one leg over the other, ready for the sparring that was about to begin. 'I'm fine thank you James, if a little busy. How can I help?'

Carlisle stared at him and played with the corner of the file. 'We need a little chat...'

Oh good. I love our little chats.

'...I need to update you on something.'

'Go on.'

Carlisle smiled, still playing his waiting game. 'First things first. I hear we had an incident today.'

'Incident?'

'A diplomatic incident. Red on red...'

Buchanan nodded, suddenly realising what Carlisle was referring to. The shooting in Mayfair. The drones over at Thames House would be all over it by now.

'...I understand Ross was involved.'

'It looks like it.'

'Do we know where he is?

Buchanan shook his head. 'Not exactly. But he can't be far away. I've got a meeting with him at 4.30.'

'A meeting?' Carlisle stared at Buchanan in disbelief. Ross had walked out over ten years ago and then disappeared off the face of the earth. Buchanan was making it sound like a regular catch-up or some sort of routine management meeting.

Buchanan brushed the nap on his trouser leg, still feigning indifference to perfection. 'I spoke to him earlier. He says he wants to come in...'

'Interesting.'

'...so I need to know what our position is.'

'Position?'.

'On Ross. Dead or alive?'

Carlisle said nothing but stared at Buchanan across the desk, processing the information and the impact of Ross suddenly wanting to trade. A situation that they would have welcomed a couple of days ago. But now the situation was much more complex. The last twenty-four hours had changed everything. Now it was hard to know exactly what they wanted.

'Preferably before I see him this afternoon,' added Buchanan, giving Carlisle a sarcastic smile.

Carlisle held his gaze for a second but then turned away, resisting the temptation to get into political point scoring. 'All in good time Charles. I need to update you on something first.'

'You said that.'

'The Russian's have broken cover. Finally, all this noise about Artemis is beginning to make sense.'

'So, what is it they want?'

'Well that's the problem. They want more or less everything.' Carlisle patted the file in front of him. 'I assume you're familiar with UNCLOS?'

Buchanan nodded. It was a while since he'd read any detail on the subject but the headlines were still fresh in his mind. The UN Convention on the Law of the Sea (UNCLOS) was an agreement first established in 1982 to resolve jurisdiction claims in the Arctic; the last great unprotected wilderness. A vast polar region of ocean and ice-covered seas surrounded by treeless permafrost; a harsh, inhospitable landscape that was the true, final frontier on an otherwise conquered planet. It had been a safe haven for endangered wildlife and home to its indigenous people for thousands of years but all that was changing; it was now an area increasingly under threat. Whilst nations and empires had fought for centuries over land and sovereignty claims across every other part of the globe, the territorial race for the Arctic had taken place via negotiation and diplomacy under the governance of the United Nations. Canada had been the first country to declare possession of a region early in the 20th century, quickly followed by successive claims from the United States, the USSR, Denmark (via its government of Greenland) and then Norway. UNCLOS had finally been agreed on the basis that a nation could only claim an exclusive economic zone up to 200 miles from its recognised borders unless it could prove that the continental shelf on which it sat extended beyond that, in which case the zone could be extended to 350 miles. Otherwise, international law declared that all other land, together with the high seas including the Arctic Ocean itself were not owned by any one country. Buchanan couldn't remember many details beyond that, other than one further point which was absolutely crucial; the region contained the largest untapped reserves of oil, gas and valuable minerals in the world. It was no surprise then that everyone was scrambling to stake a claim. The territorial boundaries were unclear but the prize was astronomical.

'There's been a development,' said Carlisle, opening the file and taking out the first sheet of paper.

'Development?'

'One which threatens to change the balance of world power beyond all recognition.'

Buchanan raised his eyebrows. Carlisle was normally the master of understatement. This had to be something significant.

'The Russians and Canadians have been sabre-rattling over disputed territory claims for as long as anyone can remember. Russia has recently re-submitted its petition to the UN claiming exclusive control over one million square miles of Arctic sea shelf, including an area known as the Lomonosov Ridge, which Canada and Denmark also claim. The Russians assert that this, and the area up to and including the North Pole, are part of the Eurasian continent.'

Buchanan frowned. 'They've been claiming that for years haven't they?'

Carlisle nodded. 'They have. Putin made a speech on a nuclear icebreaker in 2007, urging greater efforts to secure what he called Russia's "strategic, economic, scientific and defence interests" in the Arctic. Over the last decade they've conducted countless expeditions to map the ocean floor, covering tens of thousands of miles to substantiate that claim. They've also started militarising the region by restoring military bases on some of the islands and outposts under the guise of protecting crucial shipping routes.'

Buchanan shrugged. None of that sounded particularly new.

'What's changed,' continued Carlisle, as if reading his mind, 'is that the Americans have struck gold.'

'Literally?'

Carlisle delved back into the file and pulled out another sheet of paper. 'As good as. Black gold. It's a series of oil and gas fields but with the prospect of yields that we've never seen before. Production volumes that will make the output of Saudi Arabia look minuscule by comparison. They're forecasting untapped reserves of around 25% of global production. And based on latest seismic data that forecast looks conservative.'

'Jesus.'

'Exactly. Whichever nation controls that region of the Arctic is probably guaranteed economic prosperity and political supremacy for the next hundred years.'

Buchanan blew out his cheeks and stared out the window, trying to work out the implications of what Carlisle had just said.

The ramifications were massive. An oil strike of that scale would almost certainly pit superpower against superpower. And the spoils were so vast that the likelihood of a diplomatic solution had to be close to zero. Which meant the prospect of military action was probably very real. If events spiralled into military conflict it was going to bring a whole new meaning to the phrase "Cold War."

'Plus of course,' continued Carlisle, 'the reliance on the Middle-East to provide fossil fuels disappears overnight. Imagine that. No more kowtowing to semi-educated Arabs wearing tea-towels on their heads. And no more need to invade third-world countries in order to prop up US sympathetic regimes. We can leave the dictators and rebel factions to carry on killing their own people and not have to get involved. The world map is going to change for ever.'

Buchanan smiled to himself. Carlisle's language never failed to reveal his true xenophobia. 'So which region is it in?'

'Well that's the issue. It's an area of ocean seabed immediately under the North Pole. A region which is beyond any of the economic zones, so it's regarded as international waters.'

'So not owned by anyone.'

'Exactly. Except it's part of the territory which the Russians are claiming belongs to them.'

'And do the Russians know?'

'They didn't. But they do now. The Americans had a complete lockdown on the information but somehow it's leaked. They think they've got a mole.'

Buchanan looked out the window again, wondering for a moment whether the comment about a mole was something to worry about or not. Outside, a jagged, silver streak of lightning suddenly split the sky and then a few seconds later a boom of thunder rumbled overhead, the first few droplets of rain falling out of a damp-smelling air and pattering the windowpane. An ominous, timely reminder of nature's raw power over man. 'What about the environment?' asked Buchanan, subconsciously making the connection. 'What's the impact going to be on that?'

Carlisle stared across the desk and gave him a grim smile. 'Catastrophic. It'll be like detonating a carbon bomb and releasing billions of tonnes of carbon dioxide into the atmosphere.'

'That's scandalous.'

'I agree. But no one is going to care about global warming in the future. In fact the faster it happens, the easier and cheaper it will be to extract everything. And the irony of course is that it's only possible because man-made climate change has caused the region to grow warmer in the first place. Twice as fast as the rest of the planet apparently. In 2007 the European Space Agency reported that excessive ice loss had opened up the Northwest Passage, rendering it fully navigable for the first time since records began. Global warming is making the huge reserves of oil now accessible. The whole continent is going to get plundered and ravaged, if not by war then by the politicians and the oil corporations.'

Buchanan put his head in his hands. The analysis was terrifying. It already looked like events were irreversible and the outcome was nothing short of apocalyptic.

Carlisle searched through the file again and pulled out a series of photographs, half a dozen black and white shots which he passed across the desk. 'Satellite reconnaissance of the area taken a couple of months ago. Russian military manoeuvres on a massive scale. 40,000 troops, 50 ships and over 100 aircraft. Demonstrating their capability to rapidly establish military presence on the Novaya Zemlya and Franz Josef archipelagos...'

Buchanan stared at the photos, not sure what to say. He didn't recognise the locations but the prognosis was clear enough. Tensions with Russia were already high following their expansionist ambitions in the Ukraine and the intervention in Syria. Those were going to pale into insignificance compared to the Arctic.

'...they're not actually preparing for war of course, it's just a show of strength to give them more leverage at the negotiating table.'

'And do they have a case?'

Carlisle nodded. 'Possibly. They've been asserting ownership of that area for years, long before the Americans started any geological exploration. They first filed a claim in 2001. They even planted a Russian flag on the ocean seabed, immediately under the North Pole. There's an article on it somewhere.' He rummaged back through the file, quickly locating another document, a copy of various intelligence reports including a blurred image of the Russian flag ceremoniously staked into the ocean floor. 'Here it is. 2007. A Russian expedition called *Artika* employed MIR submersibles to collect water and sediment samples in order to substantiate their claim to the Lomonosov Ridge. For the first time they managed to descend 14,000 feet to the seabed and planted a titanium deep-sea flag to assert it now belonged to Russia.'

'That must have gone down well.'

Carlisle smiled. 'As ever, there were some interesting exchanges between the Canadians and the Russians. There's a quote here from Canada's Foreign Affairs Minister at the time. He said; "This is posturing. This is the true north, strong and free, and they're fooling themselves if they think dropping a flag on the ocean floor is going to change anything. This isn't the 14th or 15th century."' Carlisle passed the article over to Buchanan to look at. 'As you can imagine, the Russians gave a robust response to that, something about the heritage of pioneers leaving flags when they reached previously unexplored territory. And also reminding the Canadians that they and Denmark have been planting flags in the disputed Arctic territory of Hans Island for years. Plus of course the Americans planted a flag on the moon and no-one objected to that.'

Buchanan passed the document back and then glanced at his watch again. He needed to leave soon if he was going to get over to Soho in time. 'So what happens next?'

Carlisle put the papers in the file and then put it back in the desk drawer. 'There's a summit in Stockholm next month. The UN are preparing the agenda but it's a side show really. The real negotiations have already started. Which brings us back to Ross.'

'Ross?'

'We've had an approach from the Russians. They want a pre-meeting with us and the Americans, to agree what they call "negotiating protocols."'

Buchanan gave a wry smile. He could see where that was going.

'Given that we don't have any territorial claims in the Arctic and we're not a major player at the summit, that can only mean one thing.'

'Artemis?'

'Exactly. We need to find out what the hell Ross is up to. And more importantly what information he passed to the Soviets.'

Buchanan stood up and buttoned up his jacket. 'Well, we're about to find out. I need to leave.'

Carlisle remained seated but looked up at him for several seconds, a fixed, unwavering stare emphasising the seriousness of the situation. 'There are lot of things riding on this Charles. We can't afford to get this wrong.'

'I'm aware of that.'

'I hope so. This is much bigger than some squalid murder of a second-rate, minor royal. What happens next could determine the future of the planet.'

Buchanan looked across the room at the bracket clock, its slow and purposeful tick a chilling reminder that they were running out of time. *Tempus Fugit.* Outside, a second flash of lightning, brilliant and buzzing with electricity forked across the sky, like a serpent sent to bite the earth. The wind held its breath and a split second later a massive crack of thunder reverberated overhead, practically shaking the building with its ferocity. And like a portent, the downpour began, unleashing relentless, torrential rain from dark, growling clouds; like an ocean thrown from the sky.

Thirty

PAROVSKY PUSHED THE DOOR WITH HIS LEFT HAND AND stepped inside, his eyes locked on the two people on the table at the far end, straight ahead of him. Both of them looked deep in conversation, oblivious to the fact that someone had just walked in. And there was no one else around. A straightforward hit then. The big fat guy with the loud, striped shirt and red braces had his back to the door and was going to be slow to move. No risk whatsoever. Which meant hitting the compiler first, just in case he looked up and tried to react before the first round was fired. But that wasn't likely. It was only fifteen paces from the front door to the back of the café. Ten seconds max. Three rounds for the compiler and then three rounds for the fat guy. Maybe four, given his size. Then reverse out. In and out in thirty seconds. Probably less. No need to shut the door then. Focus on the first target and walk straight up to him. Not fast but not slow. Pistol in the right hand pointing down towards the floor. Aimed and fired in the final three strides. Two to the chest and one to the head. Two shots in rapid succession. Then a third, aimed separately. Then swivel and ditto the fat guy. One extra maybe to the chest. Just to make sure. Efficient. Professional. Clinical.

Parovsky had only moved a couple of paces when a massive bolt of lightning cracked overhead, lighting the room like a thousand flash bulbs suddenly going off. In the same instant a huge clap of thunder exploded above him, as if an incendiary device had struck the building. He flinched momentarily, a fleeting thought about terrorist attacks flashing through his mind before realising that it was just a storm, albeit one of biblical proportions. In front of him both George and Vinny looked up, equally startled by the noise and the power of the storm. The first thing that George saw was Parovsky at the other end of the café, walking towards them, staring at them in a strange, obsessive way, the door still open behind him. It looked odd, threatening, dangerous. And it was a face that he'd seen before. *Mr Toad from the Red Lion in Tenterden.* His brain was processing as fast as it could but was too confused to work out what was going on. *What the hell is he doing here?* He shouted something and tried to stand up, Vinny also twisting round to see what George was looking at.

Parovsky had stepped forward a couple of paces, still focused on the table ahead. The compiler was starting to move and the fat guy, slow and lumbering was also staring at him, looking like he was going to get up as well. Which meant he might have to shoot now. But that risked not hitting the target. Or not hitting it properly. So maybe take out the fat guy first. Easier to hit from a distance. Out of the corner of his left eye, in the furthest part of his peripheral vision he suddenly sensed something else; a blurred, shadow of someone else in the room heading towards him. A millisecond decision required. Focus on the target or swivel left? He kept walking forward, his right arm now raised with the Serdyukov aimed straight ahead. Only seconds away. The compiler already on his feet and the fat guy half-way out of his chair. Which one to hit first? *Decisions…*

Dino was not a big man but that meant he was quick on his feet. He was in the kitchen when he took the call from Albert, cleaning everything down and preparing a few things for the following day. He didn't understand what was happening but he slammed the phone down as soon as he heard the word "gun." The kitchen was full of all sorts of stuff that he could have grabbed; knives, meat cleavers, even a bone saw but Dino didn't have time to think about what he was doing. Instinctively he picked up a pan of boiling water that was next to him; a large, wooden-handled saucepan which was three-quarters full, bubbling and steaming on top of the stove. He held it out in front of him and practically ran into the café, just as the thunder and lightning exploded overhead, illuminating a large, portly guy moving towards the table at the back of the room. A second later the guy's arm raised up, pointing a pistol straight at George and Vinny, his left arm moving up towards the gun to fire double-handed. Dino would have preferred to have been closer but he knew that he had no more than a second to act. He pulled the saucepan back slightly to get some momentum and then swung it forward as fast as he could, aiming the contents directly at the guy's face.

Parovsky was just at the point of pulling the trigger when the water hit him, some of it on his left shoulder but most of it on the side and front of his face. The impact was instant, a combination of absolute shock and sheer, excruciating pain as the scalding hot water melted his skin and then ran down his neck and the inside of his shirt. He screamed and stumbled to the right for a second, putting his arm up to defend himself and shouting something unintelligible in Russian. Dino kept moving forward, this time swinging the saucepan through the air, trying to hit Parovsky with it on the side of his head.

The saucepan hit Parovsky on his raised left arm, hard enough to hurt but not hard enough to break anything. Dino hesitated, not sure what to do next, the empty pot still gripped firmly in his right hand. He had tried his hardest but the guy was still standing. Parovsky turned and looked at him for a moment and then raised the Serduykov and fired three rounds, two in quick succession and then a third. Dino tried to put his hands up, like a prisoner of war about to be captured on the battlefield; brave but beaten, praying for mercy, pleading for his life. But he had barely moved before the bullets hit him. The first one struck him in the shoulder. Not a fatal shot but enough to knock him backwards. The second bullet slammed into his chest, just above the heart and then the final one hit him squarely in the forehead, a small trickle of blood instantly running from a perfectly formed, small, round hole. Another streak of silver crackled and fizzled across the sky, the room again momentarily lit by a thousand spotlights. By the time the glare had subsided Dino had hit the floor, the saucepan spilling out of his hands and clattering across the hard, polished tiles.

George and Vinny froze in absolute terror, transfixed by the sight of Dino's body which was lying prostrate on the floor, twitching for several seconds before it eventually died, the only movement a foam of blood and air bubbling around his lips as his lungs expelled a last, final breath. Parovsky twisted round and raised the gun again, aiming straight at George who was standing to his left. *One down, two to go.* Then he squeezed the trigger and fired.

Like Dino, Albert was not a big man but he knew all about torque and momentum. He'd played cricket when he was a lot younger plus a few games of golf in his later years. He wasn't particularly good at either but the one thing that he always remembered was that making the perfect shot wasn't about hitting the ball hard, it was about swinging through it; letting the weight of the bat or the club do the work. Like using a sledgehammer or a scythe. Swinging the weight in the right way to get maximum power with minimum effort. Albert had watched Parovsky enter the café and had simply followed him in through the open door, walking about ten paces behind, close enough to react quickly but far enough away not to be seen. He'd watched in disbelief at Dino being shot and then in absolute horror as Parovsky turned on George and Vinny. The chairs in Francorelli's were not particularly heavy but that meant they were easy to pick up and even easier to swing. And being made of tubular steel they were very rigid and very strong. Albert picked up the one nearest to him and then swung it in a huge, sweeping arc, like a windmill turning in a gale. The chair smashed into Parovsky's upper arm in the same split second as he squeezed the trigger, the impact of which jerked his hand downwards and to the right, pulling the shot into the café wall. Again, the attack had hit him hard enough to hurt but not hard enough to break anything. Parovsky was a big man. Overweight and not particularly fit but he had enough fat and muscle to absorb the weight of a metal chair, even one that was being wielded with maximum force. He shouted out in pain and then twisted round to see who was behind him. And that was when Vinny hit him.

Vinny had only just got to his feet and had been watching the unfolding nightmare in complete and utter shock. He'd never seen anyone killed before and he'd certainly never seen anyone murdered with a gun. For a couple of seconds he was frozen to the spot, terrified by what was happening and certain that he was also going to die. He had no idea who Parovsky was but it was clear that the guy was a professional and knew exactly what he was doing. Vinny's whole life flashed before him for a moment but then for some reason the finality and hopelessness of it all kicked in. Suddenly it felt like a release, as if now he didn't have anything to lose. No point dying like a quivering coward if you could go down fighting, dying like a man. And besides, he was Vinny Goldman, the streetwise kid from Bermondsey who didn't take shit from anyone. He hadn't done that in over 50 years and he wasn't about to start now. It was like he'd suddenly got a whole new burst of life, as if the adrenaline was literally pumping through his veins.

Vinny had been something of a tearaway when he was younger and like a lot of east end kids the only thing that had kept him on the right side of the law was the local boxing club, a run-down, working class gym which instilled a sense of discipline, pride and a code of conduct into a group of otherwise wayward teenagers. It was years since he'd put on a pair of gloves or stepped inside a ring but it wasn't something you forgot. It was in his blood and besides, in his heyday Vinny could mix it with the best of them. Thirty years ago he was a useful middleweight; light on his feet and even faster with his hands, with a reputation for a winning one-two combination. As Parovsky twisted round to look at Albert, Vinny stepped forward on his toes and unleashed an almighty left hook, aimed perfectly at Parovsky's jutting jaw line and followed through with as much bodyweight as he could manage. It was a massive punch, a real haymaker of a blow which smashed into Parovsky's chin like a sledgehammer.

Parovsky stood there for a second, his eyes glazed over and his ears starting to rush and fill up. His legs wobbled slightly as he tried to keep his balance, fighting against the sensation to simply collapse onto his backside and close his eyes. Vinny had seen that reaction before. Many times in fact. An opponent, desperately trying to stay on their feet, hoping that the bell would sound any second and save them from hitting the canvas. In his previous life he would have followed that up with a right uppercut, a fierce, bludgeoning punch smacked firmly into the underside of the jaw. That would have put the guy's lights out for sure but today it wasn't an option; Vinny's right arm was still bandaged up and in a sling. Completely useless in a punch-up. And now his left hand wasn't much use either. He shook his clenched fish vigorously to try and get rid of the pain but it was hurting like hell. He had hit Parovsky so hard that it felt like he had broken something else, a couple of fingers probably. He certainly couldn't use it again to hit anything. Parovsky wobbled again, stumbling slightly forward as he struggled to stay upright, the pistol still clenched firmly in his right hand. He looked like he was on the point of either falling over or suddenly regaining his composure, but it was hard to say which. There was only one thing for it. Vinny also stepped forward and without warning slammed his forehead down onto the bridge of Parovsky's nose, the impact of which was like a wrecking ball smashing into an over-ripe tomato. The bridge of Parovsky's nose broke on impact and his body hit the deck like a sack of potatoes, his head cracking against the hard, tiled floor. *Out for the count.*

Vinny looked at him for a second and then collapsed back into his chair, the adrenaline rush now gone and the realisation of how close he had come to death suddenly kicking in. His hand trembled as he felt the centre of his forehead, wondering whether he had broken something else. That sort of move wasn't part of the rules, certainly not the sort of thing you could get away with inside a boxing ring, not even larking about in training. But it was definitely something he had resorted to once or twice before, getting into a scrap behind the local boozer on a Saturday night; a toe-to-toe fight with some vicious hard-nut from the other side of the river. George was also shaking from the shock of what had happened but managed to walk over to Dino to check if there was anything he could do. He knelt down but it was no use. There was no pulse and no sign of breathing. Dino had definitely gone. He went back to his chair and sat down, all of a sudden overwhelmed by a sense of loss and guilt. If it hadn't been for his stupid actions in the first place none of this would have happened and Dino would still be alive. 'We should call an ambulance,' he said, still staring forlornly at Dino's body.

'A bit late for that,' replied Albert, stooping down to pick up the pistol which had fallen out of Parovsky's hand. 'Not much use to him now.'

'The police then,' said George. 'This has gone far enough now. We need to call the police and tell them everything we know.'

On the opposite side of the table Vinny twitched slightly. Thirty seconds ago he could barely stand up, let alone think about work. But now he was starting to recover and his journalistic brain was already back in gear. The last thing he wanted to do was call the police. There was a front page exclusive here and those didn't fall in your lap very often, certainly not when you could give a first-hand account from inside the story. The events of the last couple of minutes were front page news in their own right, let alone any connection to a bigger scoop about the death of Princess Diana. If they could prove that, this was going to be the biggest event of his whole career. 'I don't think we should be too hasty,' he said, trying not to sound too insensitive. 'The police aren't going to be able to do anything for poor Dino. All they will do is turn up in their size twelves and trample over everything. And then the government will put a D-notice on everything and we'll never find out the truth. I think we should think carefully before calling them.'

'In case you risk losing your exclusive?' asked Albert, unable to disguise the cynicism in his voice. He was a lifelong, hard-nosed journalist himself but even he was surprised at Vinny's mercenary attitude.

Vinny shrugged. He didn't see any conflict at all. Business was business. And besides, this was about telling the public the truth about what was actually going on. Ground-breaking journalism as far as he was concerned.

'So, what are going to do then?' asked George, putting his head into his hands.

The three of them looked at each other in silence for a moment, none of them quite sure what to say. Then, just like a team of synchronised swimmers they turned their heads in unison to look at the front of the café, suddenly aware that someone had just appeared in the doorway; a tall, mysterious looking figure outlined against the storm-lit sky. *"Brief as the lightning in the collied night, that, in a spleen, unfolds both heaven and earth; And ere a man can say--Behold! The jaws of darkness devour it up."*

'I'll tell you what we're going to do,' said Craven, nodding towards Parovsky's body which was still lying unconscious on the floor. 'We're going to wake him up and then we're going to make sure he starts talking.'

Thirty-One

BUCHANAN STOOD IN THE DOORWAY OF 70 WHITEHALL, the extensive offices and briefing rooms of the Cabinet Office behind him. The storm was already passing, the torrential downpour now reduced to a light drizzle and the first slivers of clear, blue sky appearing in the distance. If he waited five minutes it would be completely gone and then he could walk over to Soho. There was no point trying to get a taxi in central London in the middle of the afternoon, particular in this weather. All the cabs were full and the traffic was gridlocked anyway. Across the road tourists were appearing from doorways or whatever shelter they could find, a noisy, excitable gaggle of umbrellas and makeshift rainwear making a dash for it towards their next destination, no doubt another historic building or important landmark from the city's essential visitor guide. Buchanan glanced at his watch and then pulled out his mobile. Time to call Craven and see how things were going. He pressed the speed-dial button and waited a couple of seconds before it was answered.

'Hello?'

'It's me.'

'Obviously.'

'Where are you?'

'Mint Lane. In a cafe called...' Craven looked up and scanned around the room, trying to spot something to remind him of the name. '...Francorelli's. I'm guessing it's Italian.'

'And is he there?'

Craven smiled to himself as he looked at George still sitting at the table at the far end, nursing a cup of hot sweet tea and looking very sorry for himself. Definitely more Wiggins than Xerxes at the moment. 'Yes, he's here.'

'Good. Does he know anything?'

'Don't know yet. I'm dealing with something else first.'

'What's that?'

'Our fat friend that we were discussing earlier.'

Buchanan raised his eyebrows in surprise. *Parovsky*. 'What the hell is he doing there?'

'Not a lot at the moment.'

'Can he talk?'

'Not yet. But he will. What do you want?'

'The photos from the Art Gallery. We need them back.'

'Okay, leave it with me.'

'Good. And just to be clear. Do whatever it takes. There's no Geneva convention here. Understood?'

'Understood.' Craven put the phone back in his pocket and stared at Parovsky's body, still lying prostrate on the floor. It was time to wake him up...

Buchanan gazed up at the sky again. The rain had stopped and the sun was starting to break through on the horizon, a glimmer of bright, radiant gold shining through white, fluffier clouds. He walked down the steps and then hesitated for a moment, trying to work out the quickest route to Soho and Rupert Street. The trouble with Whitehall was that there was no decent cut-through to the Mall; it was either turn right towards the Cenotaph and Westminster or turn left and head towards Nelson's Column and Trafalgar Square, a decision that he took on an almost daily basis as he made his way back and forth to the Greenhouse. Neither option was ideal but in the end he decided to head north, passing Horseguards Parade and the Household Cavalry Museum on his left and gazing across at the Banqueting House and the Old War

Office Buildings on the other side of the road. The traffic was always busy but today it was particularly bad; three lanes of taxis, cars and buses, a solid queue of idling engines and blue exhaust fumes, everyone trying to be patient as the traffic lights changed to green and quickly back to red again but nothing moving ahead. It took him a couple of minutes to walk up to Trafalgar Square, the pavements clogged with foreign tourists and numerous street vendors, mostly selling postcards and cheap London memorabilia. A vast sea of red, white and blue. He thought about turning left along Cockspur and then going up the Haymarket but in the end decided to cut through to Whitcombe Street, navigating the numerous traffic lights and pedestrian crossings to get from one side of the square to the other. That gave him a much quieter route into Soho and then it was just a brisk walk up Wardour Street and a few minutes more to get over to Walker Court.

Soho was a district of the City of Westminster, an area of about one square mile bordered by Fitzrovia to the north, Covent Garden to the east, St James's to the south and Mayfair to the west. Its name first appeared in the 17th century and was believed to have derived from the former hunting cry of James Scott, 1st Duke of Monmouth who used it as a rallying cry at the Battle of Sedgemoor in 1685. Despite the intentions of landowners to develop Soho on the grand scale of neighbouring Bloomsbury, Marylebone and Mayfair it never really became fashionable with the rich and increasingly immigrants began to settle there, especially French Huguenots who poured into the area in 1688, after which it became known as London's French quarter. By the mid-19th century most respectable families had moved out, replaced by prostitutes, public houses, music halls and small theatres and by the early 20th century the place had become a magnet for artists, musicians and intellectuals. Today the area continued to be synonymous with the arts, although many of the music clubs and famous coffee bars had now disappeared. Club Eleven, which opened in 1948 at 41 Windmill Street was generally revered as the fountainhead of modern jazz in the UK while the Harmony Inn in nearby Archer Street was a notorious, unsavoury cafe and hang-out for musicians during the 1950s. Over the years famous venues such as the Whisky a Go Go, The Flamingo Club, The Roundhouse, The Marquee Club and Ronnie Scott's had all nurtured the birth of musicians, bands, writers and poets, hosting thousands of gigs and launching the careers of hundreds of now famous acts.

Soho was also the heart of London's theatre land, home to many well known venues although again many of the more famous establishments had long closed. The Windmill Theatre for example was notorious for its risqué nude tableaux vivants in which the models had to remain motionless to avoid censorship. It opened in 1931 and was the only theatre in London which never closed, except for twelve compulsory days between the 4th and 16th September 1939. It stood on the site of a windmill that dated back to the reign of Charles II and remained a famous landmark in Soho's history until its closure in 1964. Before the introduction of the Street Offences act in 1959 Soho was also the centre of London's sex industry, the streets and alleys packed with prostitutes and clip joints, the latter intimidating customers into buying extortionately priced drinks in return for the promise of illicit entertainment. But by the 1980s tougher enforcement by the Metropolitan Police together with tighter licensing controls by the City of Westminster led to a crackdown on illegal premises and by the late 90s, a substantial relaxation of general censorship had reduced the red-light district to just a small area around Brewer Street and Berwick Street.

Buchanan wasn't really interested in Soho's sleazy past but he found some of the other historical facts and connections fascinating. The fact that Karl Marx lived at numbers 28 and 54 Dean Street for example, or that John Logie Baird first demonstrated television in his laboratory in Frith Street, now the location of Bar Italia. And further up the road in Frith Street one could still see a plaque above the stage door of the Prince Edward Theatre, identifying the site where Mozart lived for a few years as a child. Not many people knew that. But of all the historical facts about the area the one which intrigued him most was the outbreak of cholera in 1854. A local doctor, John Snow, mapped the addresses of the sick and identified the cause of the outbreak as water from a public water pump located at the junction of Broad Street (now Broadwick Street) and Cambridge Street (now Lexington Street) close to the rear wall of a public house. He persuaded the authorities to remove the handle of the pump, thus preventing any more of the infected water from being collected. The spring below the pump was later found to be contaminated with sewage, Snow's intervention being one of the earliest examples of epidemiology and public health medicine in a real life crisis. Almost every structure that stood on Broad Street in that late summer of 1854 had now been replaced by something new, thanks in part to the *Luftwaffe* and in part to the creative destruction of booming real estate development. The original pump had long gone of course but a replica with a small memorial plaque and without a handle to signify John Snow's action was erected not far from the original site. And you could still buy a pint of beer at the pub on the corner of Lexington Street, not fifteen steps from the site of the pump that once nearly destroyed the neighbourhood. Only the name of the pub had changed. It was now called the John Snow.

For a moment Buchanan thought about walking up to Broadwick Street but then changed his mind. He had plenty of time but there was always a risk that Ross might be early, a lifelong discipline of carrying out reconnaissance in advance of using new locations. About halfway up Shaftesbury Avenue he passed the junction with Old Compton Street and then turned left into Brewer Street, the cars heading towards him on the one-way system although the traffic much lighter now. On the left, about ten yards up the road was a pillar box, a large, round post box finished in bright red with a sloping, domed top. Buchanan didn't think anything of the black, anonymous saloon which pulled up beside it, no more than two or three yards in front of him, a guy jumping out of the passenger seat to no doubt quickly post a letter. Except that he didn't. As he walked towards Buchanan the car moved forward a few yards, pulling up immediately beside them. The exchange took only a few seconds but was executed with practised efficiency, the off-side rear door suddenly opened and Buchanan swiftly bundled into the back seat, a guiding palm pushing his head down to stop it hitting the top of the doorframe. A split second later the door slammed shut and then the guy was getting back in the front, the engine still running and the driver slowly pulling away. The whole manoeuvre was over in a matter of seconds, Buchanan hardly having time to shout, let alone react or offer any resistance. Instinctively he tried the door handle, a desperate but futile attempt to get out, the child locks already securely activated. Then he turned his head to look at the person sitting next to him, the languid pose and cold, indifferent smile all too familiar...

Even as a child Ilia Parovsky had not really been afraid of anything. A brutal, alcoholic father, two older brothers and a tough, working class upbringing in one of the roughest suburbs of Moscow had taught him how to look after himself from an early age. At the age of nine or ten he was regularly absconding from school and by the time he was thirteen he was running his own street gang, terrorising the local neighbourhood and offering self-styled protection with equal measure. Most people were wary of Ilia but his defining moment came towards the end of a long, hard winter, shortly before his fifteenth birthday. His two brothers, Mikhail and Nikolai had been drinking in a local bar and fuelled by too much beer and vodka had got into an altercation with a couple of women, two random females who objected to the unwelcome attention and said so in no uncertain terms. Mikhail, never a guy to take "no" for an answer was egged on by his younger brother and the situation soon spiralled out of control, the ensuing mêlée deteriorating into lots of pushing and shoving, the women shouting that they were being molested by a couple of perverts and Nikolai, recognising when a situation was well and truly lost, retaliating by calling them a pair of *"fat, ugly, lesbian bitches."* Inevitably the brothers were thrown out of the bar but they simply moved on to the next one up the road. Unfortunately, unbeknown to them the two women were sisters of Dmitri Bortsov, a vicious, intimidating psychopath who controlled the local drugs market and who had a reputation for retaliation and uncompromising violence. And that was in relation to business. This was personal.

Ilia had been in his bedroom that evening when he heard the car screech to a halt outside the house, the sound accompanied by lots of shouting and car doors slamming. He looked out of the window just in time to see his two brothers being hauled semi-conscious up the garden path, Dmitri Bortsov yanking Mikhail by his shirt collar while his henchman, an evil, sadistic thug known as "Mad Andrei" was pulling Nikolai by his head, two nicotined stained fingers shoved up his nostrils and his heels dragging along behind him. Rather than just dump them on the doorstep Bortsov hammered on the front door with his fist, several rapid loud bangs in succession, a calling which had become his trademark and a portent for anyone unlucky enough to live in his jurisdiction. Ilia's father was slumped in his armchair, unconscious in a drunken stupor like he always was by 7.00 o'clock every evening so Ilia's mother answered the door, praying under her breath and wiping her hands nervously on her apron. As she opened the door she saw Dmitri Bortsov staring back at her, his piercing, blue eyes fixed onto hers and his jaw, slack and menacing as it chewed constantly on a piece of grey, discoloured gum. Then she saw her two sons, curled up on the ground, their faces barely recognisable given the beating they had just taken, a couple of likely lads full of vodka and high spirits suddenly jumped on as they cut through the estate, no match for the frenzied attack with baseball bats, iron bars and steel-toed boots. She looked back at Bortsov, desperately wanting to say something but knowing that she daren't. He moved forward a step and then leant his head forward, as if he was about to whisper something in her ear. She turned her head slightly and then he growled his throat, rolled his tongue and spat at her, a huge globule of thick, yellow spit hitting her in the face, just below the eye. She stood there for a moment, not sure what to do, the sudden shock of what had happened making her flinch and then her hands tremble. Bortsov continued staring at her and then leant forward again, this time delivering the warning with a solitary finger swiped horizontally across his throat. 'Next time I will kill them.' Ilia's mother stared down at her feet, knowing that he meant it and then Bortsov and his mate burst out laughing, kicking Mikhail and Nikolai several times in the ribs before walking back down the path.

Ilia had watched the whole episode from the landing, hidden out of sight behind the banister but able to see and hear everything. His brothers were the only people in the world that he looked up to and his mother was the only person that he had ever loved. Inside he was seething, desperate to do something in retaliation but knowing that it was better to wait and that revenge was best served cold. But this wasn't just about avenging the shame and humiliation that had been brought upon his family. It was about sending a message to the outside world. And a message about Ilia Parovsky as much as about anything else. There was an anger building up inside him, like a volcano, burning the inside of his stomach lining away. He needed to do something and he needed to do something now. That night Ilia didn't go to bed. He sat for hours, staring out of the bedroom window, rocking backwards and forward as the anger continued to rage inside him, imagining the retribution that he was going to unleash. He left the house at 3.00 am and under cover of darkness crossed the estate to where

Dmitri Bortsov lived, a grey, soulless, ground-floor apartment on the southern edge of the Glinka housing block. Breaking into the flat was easy. Ilia had learned how to force open windows when he was a child, one of the many products of a misspent youth. The only issue was making sure that he didn't wake anyone. He crept through the kitchen and then into the bedroom where Dmitri was fast asleep with his girlfriend, him lying on his back wearing a white T-shirt and snoring his head off and her, lying on her side, a bare shoulder poking out from under the duvet. Ilia didn't bother to wake him up. He took out the long-bladed knife, leant over Bortsov's sleeping body and simply cut his throat in one deep, swift, movement, the blade slicing his neck from ear to ear and severing everything in its path. Bortsov barely woke up, uttering no more than a few gurgling sounds as his life literally flowed out of him, his throat spraying bright, crimson blood onto white Egyptian cotton. The girlfriend however woke up with a start and screamed hysterically, instantly retreating into the headboard and pulling up the duvet to protect her modesty. Ilia put a finger to his lips as he walked round to her side of the bed, the knife still in his right hand and a look of absolute terror etched on her face. First he took hold of the duvet and yanked it away, revealing a cowering, naked body, her hands clasped over two large breasts and her knees stuck firmly together. He leant over her, as though he was about to touch or kiss her and she shrank even further backwards, convinced that he was about to rape or murder her. Then he growled his throat, rolled his tongue and spat at her, a large globule of thick, white spit hitting her in the face. And then he leant even closer, this time swiping a finger horizontally across his throat. 'Next time I will kill you.'

Within half an hour he was emerging from Mad Andrei's apartment, hauling his naked, semi-conscious body out into the front courtyard and towards the street, two fingers shoved up his nose and his heels dragging along the path behind him. Andrei had been in bed on his own and was sleeping on his front, which made a single cut to the throat impossible. He was also a light sleeper and had started to stir as soon as Ilia had entered the room. Without time to do anything else Ilia stabbed him several times in the back, just beneath the left shoulder blade hoping that he would puncture a lung, or maybe his heart. The effect however wasn't instant and Andrei had rolled over and tried to resist, the pair of them getting into a brief tussle before Ilia stabbed him several more times in the stomach. By the time they got outside Andrei was barely breathing, his body losing massive amounts of blood and his mind already drifting into darkness. As Ilia dragged him towards the pavement he made as much noise as he could, shouting at the top of his voice so that everyone in the neighbourhood would hear what was going on. He pulled the body into the road and then hauled it around, so that it was now facing back towards the apartments. Then he grabbed a handful of hair and lifted the head onto the pavement, the neck now raised off the ground and at 45 degrees to the body, almost as if it was eating the edge of the kerb. As he looked up Ilia could see lights being turned on in the flats above, people pulling back curtains or opening windows to see what was happening. He paused for a second, waiting for his audience to get into position. Savouring the moment. Like an actor, waiting to deliver his line. Or a magician, about to reveal a dazzling finale. Then he raised his right foot and stamped down as hard as he could, Andrei's neck snapping instantly under the weight of his boot, the sound ricocheting off the buildings into the still, night air. Almost immediately, windows were being shut and curtains were being closed again. Nobody was going to shed a tear for Andrei Vygotsky and nobody was going to call the police. From that moment Ilia's reputation and future was assured. No one ever crossed the Parovsky family again and nobody ever dared stand up to Ilia himself. There was a new order in place and he was going to spend the rest of his life totally in command, unafraid of anything or anyone else. Well, other than one thing perhaps. Just one. Something that went back to his childhood. Something so deep rooted in his psyche that it would never leave him. A fear so absolute that he had to file it away and never think about it again, otherwise it would gnaw away at his soul. Or at least that was the plan...

Ilia was about seven when his mother took him and his two brothers to the seaside, an unexpected and impromptu holiday to see a distant relative who lived in St. Petersburg, something which had never happened before and which because of the events of that week would never happen again. Ilia was told that his father was working away so wasn't able to join them but in truth his parents had had a series of increasingly violent arguments and his mother had decided to take the children away, partly to protect them from the situation and also to give herself some respite from the endless, interminable rows. Either way, it was mid-summer and St. Petersburg was close to Repino, one of the finest seaside resorts in the whole of Russia. While his mother sat happily in a deck chair reading the paper and watching the world go by, Ilia and his brothers spent endless hours on the beach, playing in the sand and enjoying the freedom of their first ever holiday. Ilia was fascinated by the sea, particularly the constant, rhythmic swell of the ocean and the endless, hypnotic motion of wave after wave, crashing onto the shore. And then there was the noise; a cacophony of sounds the like of which he had never heard before. He spent hours paddling at the water's edge, feeling the surf splash over his ankles and then listening to the tide, sucking the shingle back towards the sea, the force of which ran across his feet and in between his toes, the beach literally moving beneath his feet.

Ilia knew that the sea was dangerous and that he wasn't allowed to venture much beyond the shore. He had never learnt to swim, mainly because no one had ever bothered to teach him. Plus of course Moscow was miles away from the coast so there was no reason to learn and besides, most of the time it was too cold for swimming, even in the local swimming pool. "Knee deep," his mother had said and for a couple of days Ilia had obeyed her assiduously, making sure that he didn't stray too far out or get the bottom of his trunks wet. But as the week went on he got more and more adventurous. Mikhail and Nikolai couldn't swim either but they were wading up to their waists, in fact up to their shoulders sometimes and they didn't seem to be in any trouble. Ilia had seen people drowning before. Not real people of course but people in films and on the television. And the drama was always the same. It was always very loud and splashy, the person yelling and thrashing about in the water, waving their arms and shouting for help before disappearing under the waves and then reappearing again in dramatic fashion. Which is what surprised him. Because it was nothing like that in real life. One minute he was standing on the seabed, his body bobbing up and down with the rise and fall of the water and then all of a sudden it had gone, the current pulling him a few yards to the right. As he put his feet down there was nothing underneath him and his body dropped for a second, the water lapping around his chin and only the faintest touch of shingle at the tip of his toes. He rotated his arms a couple of times, trying to keep himself afloat but as the current pulled him further out the seabed completely disappeared. This time he sank beneath the surface, a stream of cold, briny water rushing up his nose. With super human effort he managed to break the surface again, his mouth gulping at the warm, summer air and the sun, glistening on the water, beating down from a clear, blue sky. Another world, so near yet so far away. And then, with barely a splash it all disappeared again, his body sinking lower this time, his hair rising upwards like seaward rippling in the currents and his limbs, tired and struggling. Suddenly he couldn't hear the noise and chatter of the beach any more, the water closing in around him, still and silent, enveloping him in its darkness. A strange sensation of panic, his eyes wide open in fear and his mouth clamped shut, every cell in his body screaming for oxygen but unable to move. Desperately holding his breath, his head dizzy and pounding and his heart, hammering against his ribs as he sank slowly to the bottom, the sea swallowing him whole.

Ilia didn't remember much beyond that, certainly not Nikolai wrapping his arms around his chest and pulling him to the surface, or being dragged up the beach, another holidaymaker, a local Doctor, turning him on his side and basically saving his life. But the memory of that day never left him. No matter how hard he tried the nightmares always returned, waking him up thrashing and screaming as he tried to hold his breath, his heart pumping nineteen to the dozen and the sweat literally pouring down his face. But now it was happening for real, not just in a dream. The wave was crashing over him, the ice-cold water hitting him in the face and running down his neck. Freezing, wet and very, very real...

Craven looked at him and frowned, wondering what on earth was going on. Normally throwing a bucket of cold water over someone just woke them up. This guy looked absolutely terrified, as if he was having a complete meltdown. Craven took a drag on his cigarette and continued staring at him, happy to wait a few seconds. After all, this wasn't going to be quick. Much better to take his time. Let the reality of events sink in first before turning the screw. Parovsky stared back at him, slowly regaining his composure, trying to work out where he was. He looked around the room, a kitchen full of large, stainless steel units, too much stuff crammed into too small a space. It was obviously the kitchen at the back of the café, his memory of the exchange with Vinny suddenly flooding back to him. Then he looked down, his arms tied to the arms of a chair, two cable-ties on each side, one around his elbow and one around his wrist, both pulled tight enough to stop him moving. And similarly, his ankles, each one secured to the front chair legs, his whole body tied-up so that he couldn't move.

Craven took another drag on the cigarette. Time to start the interrogation. 'Name?'

Parovsky stared back at him but said nothing, a faint recollection of someone he had seen before but couldn't remember where.

'Rank?'

Parovsky still said nothing, his face expressionless, determined not to give even the slightest response.

Craven moved forward and bent over him, looking at where the boiling hot water had hit him in the face. His skin was covered in sores and blisters, some of them white and puffy and ready to burst. And most of them were still damp from the bucket of cold water which had just been thrown over him. Perfect for stubbing out a fag end. That ought to kick off proceedings nicely. Something gentle to get things going. Craven took a final, long drag on the cigarette and then blew the smoke out, smiling to himself as he paused and savoured the moment. Like an actor, waiting to deliver his line. Or a magician, about to reveal a dazzling finale...

Thirty-Two

'CHARLES. HOW UNEXPECTED. WHERE CAN WE DROP YOU?'
Buchanan looked at Christine Michaels sitting next to him on the back seat, a perfectly manicured pose, her arm resting on the central console and one leg crossed casually over the other. He gave her a thin smile and then turned away to look out the window, the car already back in Wardour Street and now heading south. Back towards Shaftesbury Avenue and away from Rupert Street and Walker Court. Slow moving traffic and crowds of pedestrians. Inside he was seething but the last thing he needed was to make matters worse. Ross would be at the sex shop in ten minutes and whatever Michaels wanted he needed to get this over and done with as quickly as possible.

'Is there anywhere in particular Charles or are you happy for us to just drive around while we talk?'

'Anywhere in Soho is fine.' He twisted round to look at her, their eyes fixed in a cold, dispassionate stare, the body language conveying more than words could ever say. Then he took out his phone and started swiping the screen, casually scanning the pages as if he was bored. 'So, what are we talking about?'

Michaels ignored him and leant forward to give instructions to the driver. Then she relaxed back into her seat and also stared out of the window, watching the ebb and flow on the pavement opposite, a constantly moving throng of people in both directions. 'It's funny isn't it, how London has become so cosmopolitan.'

'Funny?'

'Surprising. An island race with so much heritage. Centuries of glorious history. You'd think that you would try and preserve it better...'

Buchanan frowned at her. What the hell was she talking about?

'...all those scruffy little people with their scruffy clothes and scruffy kids and scruffy pushchairs. Look at them. Every colour under the sun. Half of them probably don't even speak English.'

Buchanan looked at her with contempt. 'We prefer it that way.'

'Really?'

'It's called liberalism. Having a social conscience.'

'Which means what exactly?'

'Which means having a culture of tolerance.'

Michaels practically snorted with derision. 'Tolerance? Tolerance for what? Letting every terrorist that wants to come here simply walk through the front door...'

'Not at all.'

'...and paying them welfare for the privilege of being here. All at the expense of the tax payer.'

'That's not how it works.'

'You Brits don't have a clue what's going on...'

Buchanan raised an eyebrow but said nothing. There was a lecture coming. So much for the special relationship.

'...UK nationals being trained in Syria and then allowed to come back home, Jihadists travelling around Europe like innocent tourists. So-called economic migrants being allowed in without so much of a challenge. Europe is making the global security crisis worse and you Brits are the main culprits. The whole country is like a fucking training camp.'

Buchanan winced, the swearword from a cultured, middle-aged female somehow sounding worse and landing with maximum impact. Michaels continued staring out of the window, her foot tapping impatiently while she fiddled with the platinum bracelet on her wrist. A coiled spring ready to fire. 'You've been ignoring me Charles.'

'Not at all. I've been rather busy.'

'Really?' A long, quiet sigh underlined the disbelief.

'I was just about to call you.'

Michaels gave him a withering look, not fooled for one second. The response was pitiful. 'Two of my people are in hospital.'

Buchanan said nothing. There was no point getting into an argument about what happened last night. The Americans chose to mount a covert operation on UK soil so they took their own risks. If they didn't have clearance they could hardly complain. Besides, anyone that picked a fight with Craven got exactly what they asked for.

'Your man. What's his name?'

Buchanan shrugged, still saying nothing.

'You should keep him on a leash.'

Yes, we probably should.

'So, who was in the holdall?'

'Roman Limonov. FSB head-hunter.'

Michaels pulled a face. She'd never heard of him. 'And Ross?'

'What about him?'

'Have you seen him?'

'No. You?'

Michaels glared at him. 'Don't be ridiculous. If I knew where he was I wouldn't be sitting here talking to you.'

Buchanan allowed himself a faint smile. It was time to turn the tables. He looked out of the window again, the car now travelling east along Old Compton Street. Hundreds of people clogging up the pavements and spilling into the road. 'I didn't say I didn't know where he was. I said I hadn't seen him.'

Michaels stared at him, her mouth stuck open in astonishment. 'What, have you spoken to him?

'Of course, haven't you?' Buchanan's response was accompanied by a nonchalant shrug, just to rub it in.

Michaels fell silent for a moment, processing the information. On reflection maybe it wasn't that surprising. Ross had defected years ago. He was hardly likely to walk into the American Embassy after all this time. He wasn't exactly the prodigal son. And if the

Russians had sent a head-hunter to pay him a visit there was no way back from that. The guy was running out of options. The Brits were probably his only chance of finding a safe harbour.

Buchanan glanced at his watch. He was going to be late. Time to soften the tone and move the conversation on. 'We assumed he was dead.'

Michaels eased back into the seat, her body relaxed at Buchanan's admission. It was the first honest exchange between them. 'So did we.'

'In fact, we couldn't find any evidence of him being active after he defected. Absolutely nothing.'

'No, neither could we.'

'It was as if he'd retired...'

'A bit young for that.'

'...or just walked out.'

'I know. It never made any sense.'

'So where's he been? And more importantly, what's he been doing?'

Michaels shook her head. 'We don't know. He definitely went to Moscow but after that there was nothing. He just disappeared into thin air. Completely off the grid. We spent years trying to find him but in the end we gave up. Like you, we assumed he was dead.'

Buchanan glanced at his watch again. 'I need to go. Are we done?'

Michaels eyed him suspiciously. 'Meeting someone?'

'Something like that.' He peered out the window. 'Where are we?'

Michaels also peered out of the window. 'Soho Square. We can drop you somewhere if that helps.'

'No, quicker to walk. Here will do.'

Michaels nodded at the driver who pulled over at the top of Frith Street. For Buchanan it would have been quicker to accept the lift but that wasn't an option. The last thing he needed was anyone following him. Much better to disappear into the crowd and then leg it over to Rupert Street. He opened the door and gave

Michaels one last glance before he got out. 'If I hear anything I'll let you know.'

'Thanks. And if you speak to him before we do, give him a message from me.'

'Go on.'

'He has something we want.'

'Something?'

'A name.'

'Anyone in particular?'

'He'll understand.'

Buchanan smiled to himself. So that's what this was all about. Suddenly everything was starting to make sense. The Americans were about to enter the most critical negotiations in a lifetime and everything was in their favour. Except for one thing of course. They had a mole. Which meant that every piece of confidential information, including every detail about the Arctic oil fields and probably even their negotiating tactics was being leaked to Moscow. Which in turn meant that the Russians would have the upper hand. No wonder the Americans wanted Ross alive and under 24 hour surveillance. Hoping to flush out the identity of a traitor rather than storm in and risk a bodged operation. And it also explained why the Russians suddenly wanted him dead. One minute he was living a peaceful, anonymous existence in Moscow and the next minute he was the most wanted man on the planet. Not because he had done anything wrong but simply because he knew too much. A piece of information so valuable that they daren't risk it getting into the wrong hands. Compromising a double-agent was neither here nor there but losing their advantage at the negotiating table would be absolutely catastrophic. The key question was who was the mole? Plus of course why did Ross know their identity? If he had really been inactive for all these years how on earth did he know something so secret? Still, Buchanan was about to find out. Or at least he was going to try.

He stepped out of the car and started heading down Frith Street. Then he could cut across to Dean Street and make his way over to Walker Court. Five minutes max if he was really quick and then he'd only be a couple of minutes late. Michaels watched him from the car, the tiny GPS tracker barely visible on the back of his jacket, just below the shoulder-blade where it had been placed when he was manhandled into the car. The brief scuffle and the heavy handed push more than enough distraction for him not to notice. She took out her mobile phone and opened the tracking app, the software taking a couple of seconds to pick up the signal and then plot his location onto a map of the surrounding streets. She smiled to herself as she watched the round, green, flashing blob move slowing down Frith Street, making its way back into the heart of Soho. *Touché Mr Buchanan. Touché...*

It took Craven about ten minutes to persuade the others to leave. George wanted to stay with Dino, more out of respect than because he could actually do anything but he thought he should at least wait until the police or the ambulance arrived. Albert of course was determined to stay with George but it was Vinny who decided that they should leave. The altercation with Parovsky had shaken him up and he just wanted to get out of there, back to somewhere safe and familiar. And no disrespect to Dino but he didn't know him from a bar of soap and besides, there was still a story to be published. In fact, more than a story. A front page exclusive with the *Chronicle* having a unique, inside track. If they took the files with them and could unearth the mystery of Diana's death it would be the greatest scoop of his whole career.

Craven locked the front door behind them and then went back into the kitchen. Parovsky was still sitting there, tied to the chair, his body motionless and his head bowed forward as he closed his eyes and tried to block out the pain. Craven sat down in the empty chair opposite and stared at him, thinking about where to start. The kitchen was full of all sorts of possibilities, the trick was trying to find a method that got the quickest results. Unless you were being sadistic of course. Then it would be a case of finding something that took as long as possible. The history of torture was littered with some of the most disturbing and brutal interrogation techniques ever invented, devised by people who must have had very twisted but creative minds. During the Middle Ages torture was considered a legitimate way to extract confessions or punish offenders and some of them were positively barbaric. Skilled torturers would use a variety of methods and instruments designed to take as long as possible while inflicting the most excruciating pain on their victims; in many cases the process of torture being part of the actual execution.

Like the Tub method for instance, where the convicted person would be restrained inside a large wooden tub with only their head sticking out. The executioner would paint their faces with milk and honey and before long flies would begin to feed on them. The victim was also fed regularly and would end up swimming in their own excrement. After a few days, maggots and worms would devour their body as they decayed alive; an agonising and gruesome death. Or the Rat method, a technique where the prisoner was tied to the ground and then a live rat was placed on their stomach covered by a metallic container, which was gradually heated. As the metal cage got hotter and hotter the rat would frantically look for a way out, which inevitably meant gnawing its way into the stomach and then burrowing through the intestines, a sadistic and gruelling death which lasted several hours. And some of the most inventive methods were much older than those. The Sicilian Bull for example originated in Ancient Greece. A hollow piece of brass in the shape of a life-size bull was cast with a door on the side that could be opened and latched. The victim would be placed inside the bull and a fire set underneath it until the metal became literally yellow as it was heated. The victim would then be slowly roasted to death while screaming in excruciating pain. The bull was purposely designed to amplify the screams and make them sound like the bellowing of a live animal. Alongside the Judas Cradle, the Rack and Crucifixion of course, man's inhumanity to man seemed to know no bounds.

Parovsky lifted his head and stared at Craven, trying but failing to remember where he had seen him before. His whole head and face was covered in blood and hurt like hell, and his broken nose, courtesy of Vinny meant that he could only breathe through his mouth. But he knew that there was a lot worse to come. And he also knew how this was going to end. No amount of KGB or FSB training really prepared you for what was about to happen but at least he was under no illusion about the end-game. And anyway, even if he did hold out, the key was in his pocket. They were going to find it anyway. It was about the only thing he was carrying because it was the only thing of value that he had left. He tried to move his arms and legs but it was no use, they were all tied firmly to the chair. Whoever the guy was he knew what he was doing. Which wasn't a good omen...

Craven stood up and walked over to the other side of the room, looking for ideas about where to start. He opened a few drawers and cupboards, carefully selecting a range of items which looked as though they might be useful. After a couple of minutes he had an assortment of knives and forks, a selection of spices, plus some bottles of cleaning fluids, all laid out on one of the worktops, the combination of which would do the trick. There was also a small blowtorch used for browning food, like searing steaks or crème brûlée. Not that he could imagine this sort of place serving crème brûlée but the kitchen obviously used it for something. Either way, it was probably going to come in handy later on. He picked up a large, serrated knife, perfect for opening a few wounds. Something nice and straightforward to kick off with. Or maybe the potato peeler, the thin bladed strip perfect for scraping off the top layers of skin. Something a bit slower and more subtle to set the tone.

Followed maybe by a handful of chilli powder rubbed into each eye, or perhaps some white pepper, a tea-towel stuffed in the guy's mouth to stop the screams, an unbearable, searing pain like nothing he had ever felt before. And then there was the bleach of course. Sodium Hypochlorite. Probably the most dangerous, corrosive liquid found in every household but readily available from any supermarket. Perfect for giving the guy an eye wash to get rid of all that pepper. After that he'd be begging Craven to finish him off. Which meant that he'd tell him everything he wanted to know.

Craven looked across at Parovsky whose head had slumped forward into a semi-conscious position once more. Time to wake him up again. He picked up a frying pan, a heavy, cast-iron beast of a thing with a large wooden handle and a hardened, blackened base from years of use. He walked over and planted his feet at 45 degrees to the chair and then torqued his body and swung his arms as hard as he could, bludgeoning it into the side of Parovsky's head, the blow delivered with maximum momentum and follow through. Despite the weight of Parovsky's body the force of the attack shunted the chair a few inches and the sound of metal on bone literally cracked and bounced off the walls. Parovsky's head rocked to one side as he screamed in pain and then he opened his eyes and stared at Craven with absolute hatred and defiance.

Craven stared back at him. Cold, dispassionate, ruthless. 'Ready?'

Parovsky said nothing. He was born ready but he wasn't going to give anyone the satisfaction of co-operating. Whatever happened, he would go down like a foot-soldier. Battle-hardened and loyal to the end.

'Where are the photos?'

Parovksy maintained his silence, still staring at Craven with defiance.

'Tell me where they are and I'll make this quick.'

Still Parovsky said nothing. No sound. No movement. No discernible response.

Craven shrugged. *Your funeral pal.* Then he walked over to the worktop and picked up a tea-towel and a tin full of white pepper. Suddenly he couldn't be bothered with the entrée or the hors d'oeuvre. It was time to get straight to the main event. He walked back and grabbed Parovsky by the hair, pulling his head backwards with a vicious jerk. Parovsky yelled and in the same moment Craven stuffed the tea-towel in his mouth, the effect of which instantly made it hard for him to breathe. His nose was broken and congealed with dried blood so breathing through his mouth was the only option. Suddenly there was a lack of oxygen getting in and he was panting for his life, desperately trying to suck fresh air through a crumpled, linen tea-towel.

Craven looked at him. He didn't care less what sort of pain Parovsky was in, the guy was going to end up stiff anyway but the last thing he needed was him passing out. Or even worse, dying on the spot. Suffocating on a tea-towel before he had a chance to tell Craven where the photos were. Which meant that it had to come out. But that didn't work either, because then he'd be screaming his head off. The sort of pain that Craven was about to inflict was going to induce the loudest possible response. Louder than Parovsky had ever shouted in his life. Craven looked at him, a large, overweight specimen struggling to catch his breath, his diaphragm heaving up and down in fast, rapid movements, all the time practically choking on the coarse, dry material that was shoved in his mouth. And that was the problem. The tea-towel was bone dry. If it had been wet Parovsky could have breathed through it much better. No wonder he was struggling.

Craven thought about taking it out and wringing it under the tap but then changed his mind. There was no point giving him an opportunity to start shouting the house down. Much better to leave him where he was for the moment. A bit of pain and fear never did the process any harm. He walked over to the sink and turned on the tap, filling the bucket again with cold water. Parovsky watched him from a distance, not sure what was going on, his body already starting to twitch. After about thirty seconds Craven turned the tap off and walked back, holding the bucket in his left hand, ready to throw it straight into Parovsky's face. A face which had suddenly changed, the resolute stare full of defiance and hatred now replaced by what looked like involuntary spasms and wide-eyed terror. Craven frowned. What the hell was going on? Maybe the guy was close to keeling over. Time to open up his airways then. He swung the bucket backwards and then in one swift movement threw the whole lot into Parovsky's face. Full frontal, ice cold and with maximum force. If that didn't sort the problem out, nothing would.

And that was when it happened, just as it had before. Parovsky wasn't in a position to scream and shout or frantically wave his arms and legs about but that's what his body was trying to do, despite being tied down. Inside he was thrashing about like a madman, the chair moving backwards and forwards from the energy that was being unleashed but all the time restraining Parovsky's body in its firm, vice-like grip. Craven watched him in disbelief, another full-scale meltdown just like the one before. Same trigger and same response. Except this time it was even worse. Complete, uncontrollable hysteria. He smiled to himself. Maybe, just maybe, he had found a shortcut to get the information that Buchanan wanted. He put the bucket down and walked back to the sink. Then he put the plug in and turned the tap on, wondering how long it would take to fill it up. Quite a while by the looks of it, given how large and deep it was. Then he walked back to Parovsky and started to drag the chair across the room, towards the sink and towards the running water. Parovsky started struggling again, trying but failing to scream and shout but then he stopped. Suddenly he knew that it was no use. There was no point trying to fight. And there was no way that he could undergo any sort of water torture. Anything but that. It was all over. He was a dead man anyway. Now he just wanted it to be over. He looked up at Craven, his eyes pleading for mercy. Craven bent down and pulled the tea-towel out of his mouth.

'Something you want to tell me?'

Parovsky swallowed huge lungsful of air, the first proper oxygen he had breathed in ages. And about to be his last. He nodded down towards his right leg. 'There's a key. In my pocket.'

Craven put his hand in Parovsky's pocket and fished it out; a long, thin, silver key on a small ring, with a bright red fob with white lettering, just like the old-fashioned type that hotels used in the days before electronic door locks and magnetic swipe cards. He looked at the writing on the fob, half expecting it to say *Hotel California, Room 36.* It didn't of course. It said *Argento* on one side and had two sets of numbers on the other, including 4716 written across the bottom edge. 'Anything else?'

Parovsky shook his head. 'No, that's it. That's everything.'

'Good.' Craven shoved the tea-towel back in his mouth and started dragging the chair towards the sink again, smiling to himself as he could feel Parovsky kicking and screaming again behind him. Well, not actually kicking and screaming but trying his best. Not pleading for his life but pleading for the opposite. *"It seems to me most strange that men should fear; seeing that death, a necessary end, will come when it will come..."*

Thirty-Three

IT TOOK THEM NO MORE THAN FIVE MINUTES TO WALK back to Fleet Street. George was still feeling guilty about leaving Dino behind but Albert and Vinny had already moved on, their minds already turning towards the job in hand and to tomorrow's front page. Neither of them had met Dino before and besides, there was nothing that they could do for him now. It was just a mark of respect really but one which George knew would have to wait. The priority now was to try and unravel the mystery of what happened during that fateful weekend in Paris in 1997 and then see if they could work out how it all related to the events of the last week. And in particular to what they had just witnessed in Francorelli's. That alone was going to be front page news. Vinny ordered some coffee and then the three of them spread out around the large meeting table in his office. Maxine also brought in some bottles of water and some biscuits and snacks, just in case they were hungry. Plus it looked like it was going to be a long night. Nothing unusual about that of course if you worked in the newspaper industry but there was something about the way they settled down that made her think that they were there for the long haul.

'So, where were we?' asked Vinny, gingerly picking up a mug of coffee, his left hand now almost as useless as his right.

Albert opened the file and shuffled through the papers, passing some over to George to also look at. 'Diana and Dodi were at the Ritz, having dinner in their room rather than in the restaurant. It would have been easy for them to stay there but for some reason they decided to go back to Dodi's apartment again. We're not sure why.'

Vinny nodded, the sequence of events coming back to him. But it still didn't make any sense. It must have been nearly midnight by the time they decided to leave the hotel and as Albert had said, it would had been far safer to stay where they were. Especially with a crowd of baying photographers outside.

'The driver, Henri Paul, was back at work by then,' added George, reading through a thick pile of statements pinned together by a large bulldog clip. 'He'd gone off shift at 7.00 pm but was apparently called back at Dodi's request. He turned up just after 10.00 o'clock.'

'Do we know where he'd been?' asked Vinny.

George shook his head as he scanned the pages, turning each one over in quick succession. 'No. It looks like no one has ever found out. There's lots of speculation that he'd been drinking somewhere but there's no proof of that. Plus of course it's a convenient explanation for those who maintain that it was just an accident. A car full of innocent passengers killed or seriously injured by a reckless, drunken driver.'

'Could still be true though I suppose?' said Vinny.

'I don't think so,' replied Albert, taking the bundle of papers from George for a moment and flicking through the pages. 'The issue about whether Henri Paul was responsible or not has been the main point of conjecture for years. We spent months investigating that and it was pretty clear that was exactly as George had said, he was the convenient scapegoat to explain that it was a genuine accident. But none of the evidence stood up to scrutiny. And of course he wasn't alive to defend himself.'

Vinny nodded, acknowledging the argument. 'Okay. But let's park that for the moment. Let's stick to the sequence of events. What happened next?'

Albert took off the bulldog clip and then slid a bundle of papers across to Vinny, nodding towards them as he spoke. 'These are the statements from the two bodyguards, Trevor Rees-Jones and Kez Wingfield. And also from Thierry Rocher who was the hotel night manager. They all confirm that Dodi asked Henri Paul to come back in and that about an hour later Dodi announced he and Diana would be going back to the apartment. And specifically that they would be leaving from the back entrance in rue Cambon.

Vinny picked up the first document and quickly scanned it. It was a statement from Kez Wingfield who together with Trevor Rees-Jones had been seated outside the Imperial Suite, waiting for instructions. According to Wingfield, Henri Paul approached them at 11.30 pm and told the stunned bodyguards they would not be travelling with Diana and Dodi and that he, Henri Paul, would be responsible for driving them and for their safety. And crucially, no second back-up vehicle or bodyguard would be needed. The plan apparently was that Dodi had organised an extra car which would be taken to the rear entrance and that they would all leave in about half an hour. Henri Paul was going to drive to the apartment and Wingfield and Rees-Jones would be in the two vehicles which they had used earlier, which would remain outside the front to act as decoys.

Vinny finished reading Wingfield's statement and then picked up the second document, a similar statement from Trevor Rees-Jones confirming exactly the same sequence of events, other than there was a lot more detail about the standard security arrangements deployed by the Ritz. It was pretty clear that Dodi and Henri Paul had agreed the plan between themselves and that it was totally contrary to the long-standing security regulations specifically approved by Al Fayed. According to Rees-Jones these were written down in a manual and known to the bodyguards off by heart. One instruction, covering the movement of VIPs, stated that the personal bodyguard and up to seven other bodyguards had to operate within the immediate vicinity of the VIP and be directly responsible for the VIP's safety at all times. Whenever Al Fayed moved he used an armoured limousine, a back-up car and eight bodyguards. Dodi was now proposing to take the world's most famous woman across Paris in a single car with no one else in attendance, on the recommendation of his friend and acting security chief. Not that Rees-Jones took this lying down. He provided a detailed account of a heated argument between himself and Dodi, the latter eventually conceding to let the bodyguard travel in the front of the car with them but for whatever reason, refusing point blank to use a second, back-up vehicle.

'Do we actually know whose idea this was?' asked Vinny, looking up from the papers.

'Not entirely,' replied Albert 'but it's generally accepted that it must have been Henri Paul. And that he must have used some very persuasive arguments to convince Dodi to disregard all the protocols that his father had used for over twenty years.'

Vinny pulled a face. That was the second thing that didn't make any sense. Why on earth would Dodi agree to drive across Paris without proper security? He scanned the rest of the document and then picked up the third statement which was from Thierry Rocher, his testimony concentrating on the events leading up to the moment when everyone left. Shortly after midnight, Frederic Lucard who worked as a chauffeur at Etoile Limousines was told to drive a Mercedes S280 to the back of the hotel in rue Cambon. It was a standard limousine which meant that it didn't have bulletproof armour or even tinted windows. Henri Paul meanwhile had appeared at the front entrance several times, telling the crowd of paparazzi that Dodi and Diana would be leaving soon, obviously trying to convince them that they would travelling in the cars parked outside. Rocher's testimony then referenced CCTV footage which had been subsequently viewed and independently verified. At 12.14 am Dodi and Diana emerged from the Imperial Suite looking relaxed and happy and went straight down a flight of stairs which led to the rear entrance. There they waited in a narrow service corridor, the camera capturing them chatting to Henri Paul while Trevor Rees-Jones kept watch for the limousine. At 12.19 am the Mercedes, registration number 688 LTV 75 arrived and Frederick Lucard handed over the keys to Henri Paul while Trevor

Rees-Jones shepherded his charges into the back seat. Dodi sat on the left-hand side, immediately behind Henri Paul and Diana sat next to him, behind Rees-Jones. At the same time, Kez Wingfield who was sitting in the Mercedes in front of the hotel was told that they were about to leave and moments later the original Mercedes and the Land Rover sped off. The crowd of photographers however had guessed the ruse and most of them were already in, or making their way towards, rue Cambon. At exactly 12.20 am Henri Paul pulled away from the Ritz and drove off at speed, leaving a trail of popping flashbulbs behind him.

Vinny finished reading Rocher's testimony and then went back to the statement of Trevor Rees Jones. There was a paragraph at the end which likewise covered the final moments before they left. While he was waiting for the limousine to arrive Rees-Jones remembered spotting a small, white, hatchback, parked outside with its boot open, alongside a scooter or small motorbike and two or three people. As they pulled away from the hotel one of the last things he recalled was the white car following them. That and the fact that Henri Paul seemed absolutely normal and in control. Beyond that he remembered virtually nothing, his recollection of any subsequent events largely erased by the accident and the horrendous injuries which nearly killed him. In fact he was later quoted as saying that his one fear was that his memory would one day return, because in that event he was almost certainly a dead man.

Vinny slid the papers back across the table. 'So, remind me, how did they crash? Didn't they drive the wrong way or something?'

Albert nodded as he unfolded a large street map of Paris and spread it out on the table, the three of them then standing up to pore over it. 'This is the Ritz Hotel,' he said, pointing to the Place Vendôme in the 1st arrondissement, 'and this is where Dodi's apartment was in rue Arsène-Houssaye. All they had to do was drive down rue Cambon towards the Place de la Concorde and then turn right into the Champs Elysées. Rue Arsène is at the end,

330

just before the Arc de Triomphe. It's about a mile and a half, so five minutes in a car.'

'So what happened?' asked Vinny, tracing the route with his finger. At that time of night the roads must have been fairly empty so the worst that could have happened was that they were forced to stop at traffic lights, which would have given the paparazzi the opportunity to take a few more shots through the car window. But that was hardly an issue, given how short the journey was. All Henri Paul had to do was drive straight there at a sensible speed.

'From this point we're reliant on witness statements and police reports,' replied Albert. 'George has got those.'

George picked up the pile of papers in front of him and started reading from the top, trying to paraphrase as best he could for the other two. 'It looks like they drove down rue Cambon and then turned right into rue de Rivoli, heading towards the Place de la Concorde. At the same time a lot of the journalists who had been outside the front of the hotel were mounting motorcycles to give chase and were streaming down rue de Castiglione, about 150 yards behind...' George leant over and pointed to rue de Castiglione on the map, the road running north to south, parallel with rue Cambon towards the centre of Paris. '...but at the traffic lights outside the Crillion Hotel, instead of turning right into the Champs Elysées, Henri Paul carried on south, heading towards the river Seine.

'Why would he do that?' asked Vinny, still looking at the map. It was the third thing that didn't make any sense. Driving up the Champs Elysées was the shortest, safest and most direct route. If they were going to Dodi's apartment they were now driving in the wrong direction.

'We don't know,' replied Albert. 'Nobody knows. Some people think that he might have decided to take a long way round to shake off the press but that doesn't seem very likely.'

'It says here,' interrupted George, scanning the statement in front of him, 'that most of the press had already given up the chase and had decided to head straight to rue Arsène. The consensus was that there was a much better chance of getting a good picture when Dodi and Diana arrived at the flat, rather than trying to take one en-route.'

Vinny frowned, still trying to work out what had happened 'So where were they going?'

Albert smiled. 'Like I said, nobody knows. One theory is that they never intended to go to Dodi's apartment but had planned all along to go somewhere else, possibly a secret location that Henri Paul had arranged. That's why they didn't want any bodyguards to go with them, because they wanted to keep it a secret. And of course if no one knew where they were going, there wouldn't be any crowds of photographers when they arrived, so they wouldn't actually need any security.'

Vinny looked at the map again, trying to see if there was an obvious destination on their route. The logic made sense but of course it was pointless. The possibilities were endless.

'Once they had crossed Place de la Concorde,' continued George, 'they turned right onto Cours la Reine, which runs parallel with the river.' Again he pointed to the road on the map so that Vinny and Albert could see where it was. 'It's a fast-track dual-carriageway so they were now driving at speed, heading east to west.'

'At this point,' added Albert, 'there was another vehicle heading in the same direction, which was a white Fiat Uno driven by one of the paparazzi.'

'The same car that had been parked outside the back of the hotel?'

Albert nodded. 'Almost certainly. The driver was James Andanson who crucially was also an occasional employee of MI6. The Fiat was some distance in front of the Mercedes.'

'How could it be in front?' asked Vinny.

'It's a good question.' replied Albert. 'The assumption is that Andanson had no need to follow Dodi and Diana because he knew where they were going.'

'We've got police records here,' said George, 'confirming that as he approached the last turn-off on the Cours Albert 1er, about 350 yards before the Alma tunnel, Henri Paul was driving at 64 miles per hour. He could have turned off there and taken the slip road leading to Avenue George V, which would have taken him back towards Dodi's apartment but he decided to keep going. At this point camera footage shows him pulling into the left-hand lane of the outside carriageway in order to overtake the Fiat Uno which had been crawling in the right-hand lane. But as he did so, two things happened; first, the Fiat Uno started to pick up speed, as if it didn't want to be overtaken and secondly, at the same time a motorcyclist with a pillion rider overtook both of the cars, just before they entered the tunnel.'

Vinny raised his eyebrows. That sounded like an accident waiting to happen. It had to be more than just a coincidence.

'The next thing that happened was that the Fiat Uno, which was still gaining speed, eased left in front of the path of the Mercedes. Apparently there's a notorious ramp at the entrance of the tunnel and as he crossed it, Henri Paul had to swerve violently to the left to avoid a major collision, which meant that the Mercedes was now angled towards the centre of the carriageway. It looks like he clipped the back of the Fiat with his right wing but on its own that wouldn't have been fatal. But what happened next was. At exactly the same moment that the two cars touched, the pillion rider on the motorcycle turned round and directed the full glare of an immensely powerful hand-held flashlight into the face of Henri Paul, effectively blinding him for several seconds.'

'Could it have been a photographer,' asked Albert, 'with just a powerful camera?'

Albert shook his head. 'It was much too bright. And besides, it's an established disabling technique used by the security services and by special forces. The SAS have been using flashlights to blind and disorientate targets in surprise raids for years. The effect on

Henri Paul would have been catastrophic. He would have been totally blind and incapable of steering a car.'

'The Mercedes was still travelling at 64 miles an hour,' continued George, 'and drove headlong into the thirteenth concrete pillar in the central dividing reservation. In the split second that he had to react Henri Paul pushed the gear lever into neutral, presumably frantically trying to find a lower gear but it doesn't look like he had time to brake. There were no tyre marks or evidence of breaking on the tarmac. The airbags all functioned on impact but as nobody was wearing a seatbelt they gave only minimal protection. Dodi Fayed and Henri Paul died almost instantly and Trevor Rees-Jones was knocked unconscious. He literally had the front of his face ripped off.'

'And Diana?' asked Vinny.

'Still alive,' replied Albert, giving him a knowing look, 'which we presume wasn't part of the plan. That's when it gets really interesting…'

Thirty-Four

B Y THE TIME BUCHANAN GOT TO THE SEX SHOP IN WALKER Court he was seven minutes late. He checked his watch as he pushed the beaded curtain to one side and stepped into the gloom, wondering whether Ross had already arrived. As before the place was practically empty, just a couple of customers browsing through a collection of DVDs plus the same guy behind the counter at the far end, head down reading a magazine and oblivious to the film playing behind him on the monitor. This time it was a full-scale Roman orgy complete with marble sculptures, togas and laurel leaves; a room full of frenzied, copulating bodies, everyone seemingly intoxicated by the sheer hedonism of it all. Buchanan stared at it for a moment, the men significantly outnumbered, each one being pleasured by three or four women; a mass of naked, writhing, flesh. He shook his head in disbelief and then walked up to the counter, waiting a second for the guy to pull his head out of the magazine, a series of glossy photos from the latest motor show somewhere. Geneva probably. Fast, expensive cars shining brightly under spotlights. Henry or whatever his name was was obviously a petrol-head.

Buchanan gave him an efficient smile. 'Do you have a copy of *The Conquistador?*'

The guy turned and nodded towards the door on his right. 'Upstairs. Room on the left.' Same drill as before. Still the same, cultured accent. Southern, educated, middle-class.

'Anyone else arrived?'

This time Henry shook his head but said nothing.

Buchanan nodded in acknowledgment and then went through the door and climbed the stairs. The fact that Ross was late wasn't a surprise. In fact he probably wasn't late at all. He was almost certainly early but waiting outside somewhere, letting Buchanan arrive first, making sure that there was no one following behind. No back-up drones from Thames House or even worse, no trigger-happy surveillance team from a third party. And Ross had more third parties to worry about than most. Buchanan pushed the door open and looked around the room, the memory of meeting Craven a few days ago suddenly coming back to him. As before it was sparsely furnished, just a table and four chairs in the centre and a small cabinet by the far wall, next to three or four cardboard boxes stacked on top of each other. On top of the cabinet was an old-fashioned telephone, a small notepad and pen plus a faded, plastic air-freshener, the contents of which looked as though it had dried up and stopped working years ago. The only other thing of note was the TV monitor fixed into the corner of the room, angled and pointing down slightly so that it could be viewed from the table. Buchanan glanced at it for a moment, the excerpt now moved on to a close-up of a Roman Centurion lying on his back, one girl sitting astride his face, grinding in ecstasy, while two others were draped either side of his body, a slow-motion montage of them stroking each other while bringing him expertly to a crescendo. A huge, throbbing penis filled the screen, rock-solid and thickly-veined, its large, purple head glistening with saliva and about to explode at any minute. Buchanan watched fixated as the guy groaned and arched his back, resisting the moment for as long as possible before Vesuvius finally erupted, the girl on his face coming at the same time; a shuddering, crashing wave of squirming bodies and spent body fluids.

Buchanan shook his head again and then turned away, lifting the flap on the cardboard box that was in front of him, wondering what was inside. He half-expected to see more pornography, magazines perhaps or maybe some sex toys. He raised his eyebrows in surprise as he stared at the contents, a box full of stationery; piles of lined A4 writing pads, brown and white envelopes, headed note paper and an assortment of brightly coloured memo pads. He smiled to himself as he closed the flap, the sudden realisation that owning a sex shop was no different from any other enterprise. The actual product was irrelevant, or at least coincidental. It was all about running a business; attracting customers, generating revenue, managing expenses and of course making a profit.

'Nice place you've got here.'

Buchanan wheeled around. Ross had walked into the room without making a sound, a trick perfected years ago and one which few people could emulate. Buchanan stared at him, a familiar figure albeit much older now, his characteristic dark, tousled hair and dishevelled appearance belying a razor-sharp mind and a shrewd, calculating disposition. And the broad, lopsided grin was still the same; infectious, childlike and disarming. A sort of ageing Syd Barrett. Buchanan smiled back. 'Hello Damien. Long time no see.'

Ross nodded in return but continued scanning the room, getting a feel for the layout and trying to work out the dimensions. Then he closed the door behind him and paced up and down a few times, checking the contents and making sure that he felt comfortable with the space. Like a cat, marking out its territory. He paused by the window on the far wall and looked down at the street below, the pavement still bustling with tourists and local traders. A typical Friday afternoon. Then he looked around the room again and frowned, three bare, solid walls and no other means of escape. 'No fire exit then?' he asked, the question clearly rhetorical.

Buchanan scanned the room and shrugged. 'Just the door and one window.'

'No way of getting out then, if we were in a hurry?'

Buchanan shrugged again. 'No, I suppose not.'

'What's in the other room?' asked Ross, walking back towards the door. He turned the handle and opened it, crossing the landing to the room opposite in just two or three strides. He tried that handle but nothing moved, the door obviously locked and the room out of bounds. Buchanan stood behind him, saying nothing. He had no idea what was in there. He'd only been to the place once before.

'Maybe it's a storeroom,' said Ross, trying the handle one more time but to no avail.

'The guy downstairs should know,' suggested Buchanan.

Ross shook his head. There was no point spending any more time trying to find out. Far better to get the meeting over and done with and then get out of there. Besides, there was every chance that the second room was identical to the first; the same layout with just one door and window and no other means of escape. They both turned around and made their way back, Buchanan ahead with Ross a couple of steps behind.

'I assume this place is safe?' asked Ross as they both sat down at the table, Ross on the left and Buchanan immediately opposite, facing the monitor.

'Of course.'

'Maybe a safe house would have been better,' continued Ross, staring around the room again, still taking in its dimensions, 'something with more options in terms of getting out.'

'You said you wanted somewhere neutral. No one knows we're here...'

Ross put his hand in his pocket and pulled out a packet of cigarettes, a blue and white packet of Gitanes. He held it up enquiringly, the silent request conveyed with the merest movement of his hand. *Do you mind if I smoke?*

Buchanan waved his palm in approval. '....besides, more options in terms of getting out means more options in terms of someone else getting in.' He nodded towards the door. 'At least here we control what happens.'

Ross lit his cigarette and took a long, deep drag before blowing the smoke out across the room. That much was true. The only way in was up the stairs. They had complete command in terms of access. Like a childhood game, chanted with sneering authority, a fleeting memory of him running around in short trousers wearing a home-made paper crown and carrying a wooden sword. *"I'm the King of the castle and you're the dirty rascal..."*

Buchanan stared at the packet of cigarettes and particularly the lighter which was lying on top. Ross had obviously kept it after all these years. Taken from Dodi's body only seconds after the crash, together with his mobile phone and a cigar cutter; the mobile phone standard procedure but the others taken on a whim. Or out of necessity probably. Quicker to hang onto rather than put back into a dead man's pockets. Or perhaps it was something darker, like stretcher-bearers rifling through the uniforms of dead comrades, fallen in the field of battle at Passchendaele or the Somme. Either way it was now a CIA keepsake; a sort of macabre memento from a fatal car crash. One of the most famous car crashes in history. Everyone thought that a local Frenchman, Eric Petel, had been first on the scene but they were wrong. Ross had been waiting at the tunnel entrance waiting for events to unfold exactly as planned; a pre-arranged location with orders to carry out immediate surveillance. A thirty second window to quickly assess the damage and then get out of there. Strict instructions not to take any action but to report back immediately. Two dead but two still alive. One of them Diana. Not what they wanted to hear. Immediate panic at the Paris Station in Avenue Gabriel. And even greater panic back home in Langley, not to mention Giliot Junction two thousand miles away. Mission Artemis only partly accomplished. Plan B suddenly being rolled out.

Ross took another drag on the cigarette and stared across at Buchanan, waiting for the interrogation to begin.

Buchanan stared back and held his gaze, conveying that it was time to start. 'So, do you still want to come in?'

Ross shrugged, a casual, nonchalant gesture as if he couldn't care less. It wasn't as if he really had any choice. Another long, slow drag on the cigarette. He knew what was coming next.

'The debrief will be intensive,' continued Buchanan, 'you've been away a long time...'

Ross gave him a weak smile, unnerved but resigned to the understatement. It was more than just a long time. It was another world away. Paris was a distant memory now, like an old sepia photograph. And his life in the US before that was ancient history, as if it was something that had happened to someone else.

'...but we need to talk now. There are some things that can't wait.'

Ross nodded in agreement but said nothing. He took a final lungful of nicotine and then stood up and walked across the room. He needed to stub out the cigarette and the only option was the air-freshener which was sitting on the top of the cabinet. He screwed the filter into the plastic base, taking care not to set it alight and then walked back to the table and sat down again.

Buchanan leant forward, both elbows on the table, impatient to get things moving. 'So, where are the photographs?' he asked. On his back the GPS tracker, silent and unseen, continued to transmit his exact location.

'No idea. I handed them over a couple of weeks ago.'

'I know that. We saw the footage...'

Ross allowed himself a wry smile, the thought of his classic newspaper drop being captured on film and watched by dozens of spooks appealing to his sense of posterity.

'...but do you know where they are now?'

'I guess Ilia might still have them. But more likely that he's passed them on. They could be anywhere.'

'Is that why you wanted to know where he was?'

Ross smiled grimly to himself. 'No, that was something else.'

Buchanan stared at him across the table, trying to work out what was going through his mind. 'Something else?'

'Something personal. Just between him and me.'

'Go on.'

Ross shuffled uneasily in his seat. He knew it was something that had to come out but that didn't make it any easier to talk about.

He hesitated for a moment, took a deep breath and then eventually spoke. 'There was a shooting earlier today. In Mayfair. It wasn't me.'

Buchanan frowned. 'What do you mean it wasn't you? We know you were there.'

'I was. But it wasn't me who shot Nadia. That was Parovsky.'

'Why would he do that?'

'To get back at me. And because he worked out that it must have been her that tipped me off.'

'Tipped you off?'

'About Limonov. I knew he was coming. I wouldn't have stood a chance otherwise.'

Buchanan eased back into his chair, one leg crossed over the other, like a patient, sitting in a doctor's waiting room. Suddenly it made sense. Limonov was a trained assassin, a professional head-hunter who killed people for a living. An expert in his field. Ross was a formidable agent but he was right; there was no way he should have survived a covert assassination attempt. He was no match for Limonov. Not unless he knew he was coming.

Ross took out the packet of Gitanes again and lit another cigarette, using the pause to buy some time and gather his thoughts. Again, he used Dodi's lighter, this time holding onto it, turning it over in his hand like a set of worry beads, 'I assume you want to know why I left Paris?'

'Of course.'

'And I guess you thought I defected?'

'Obviously.'

Ross took a long drag on the cigarette and blew a thick cloud of smoke into the middle of the room. 'Well it was nothing like that. No crisis of conscience. No conversion to another ideology. I'm still American, born and bred. Always was, always will be...'

Buchanan frowned again. None of that was making any sense. One minute Ross was living in Moscow, the next minute he was extolling the American Dream; principles of democracy, equal opportunity and free expression. *What on earth is he talking about?*

'...but I met someone. Simple as that. I fell in love with someone that I wasn't supposed to. And after that, everything unravelled.'

Buchanan nodded slowly to himself, the penny starting to drop. 'Nadia Lukashenko?'

Ross nodded in return. 'We met on an assignment. A simple exchange of information. I was the high-flying CIA officer and she was a FSB sleeper. She'd only been in Paris a few weeks. It was obvious that they'd only just made her active and that it was her first operation. The first time I saw her she was sitting on a bench in Luxembourg Gardens. It was meant to be a simple brush pass. Someone that I would barely notice. And definitely someone I was never meant to see again.'

'So what happened?'

Ross turned his head and stared into the middle of the room, not looking at anything in particular, his memory turning back to those early days in Paris. The relationship with Nadia had been instant. He knew that he was in trouble as soon as he saw her and sensed that she felt the same. The chemistry was unbelievable, like nothing he had ever experienced before. Or since. He turned back and looked at Buchanan, waiting patiently for an answer, at least having the good grace not to push too hard. 'The situation was crazy but we arranged to meet. After that there was no going back.'

Buchanan leant forward again and looked at him in disbelief. 'What, you mean you actually had an affair? With someone from the FSB?'

Ross sighed and shook his head. As far as he was concerned it was never an affair, it had always been much more than that. They had spent almost a year together, living a double lie; a secret, illicit relationship on top of the clandestine life of being security agents. They both knew it was dangerous but it was still the happiest period of his life.

'What on earth were you thinking of? You could have both been killed.'

'I know. And we weren't stupid. We knew it couldn't last. But some people spend a lifetime trying to find their perfect partner. Their soul mate. I found mine sitting on a bench in the centre of Paris. The problem was she was working for the other side...'

Ross paused and took another drag on the cigarette. Buchanan stared at him across the table but said nothing. There was no point interrupting. It felt like a confession and Ross was suddenly talking more than he had ever talked before.

'...so something had to give. We talked a lot about both of us quitting and disappearing somewhere. Or maybe staying in France. But we knew that was impossible. Neither side was going to let that happen. So we also talked about one of us quitting but somehow keeping the protection of one of the agencies. And then Nadia got posted to Moscow. Suddenly it was an opportunity for us to get what we wanted. To be together and to come out of hiding. So I took a decision. One day I simply walked out and never came back.'

'Seriously? You gave up your career, just to be with a girl?'

Ross smiled to himself. He knew Buchanan wouldn't understand. 'We moved to Frunzenskaya and rented an apartment. Nadia went to work every day and I stayed at home. It was tough at first but after a while I got a job in a local market and then I did some language teaching. Everything off the grid of course. After a couple of years it felt like normal life. We bought groceries, went to the park, ate in restaurants, went to the cinema. Eventually it was as if my previous life had never existed...'

Buchanan eased back into the chair again, slowly processing what he had just heard. No wonder everyone thought that Ross was dead. The guy hadn't defected at all. He had literally walked out and disappeared off the radar. Hidden away in a grey, anonymous Moscow suburb and in the Russian black economy. But more than that, he had given up everything, his whole life as he knew it, in order to be with Nadia Lukashenko. The power of love.

'...but eventually the inevitable happened. Nadia got posted to Vienna and I couldn't go with her. The Russians wouldn't give me a visa. We spent two years living apart and when she came back to Moscow something had changed. Maybe she had met someone else, or maybe she had moved on. Either way, she moved out and we separated.'

'So why didn't you come home?'

Ross turned his head and stared across the room, his eyes suddenly going red and welling up. 'I didn't really have a home. I'd given that up a long time ago. Besides, I wanted to stick around. In case she changed her mind...'

Buchanan looked at him in sympathy. It was clear that Ross still hadn't got over her. God knows how he was feeling after the confrontation with Parovsky and the shooting in Mayfair.

'...but it was stupid really. She never did. I hadn't seen her for years when she contacted me a couple of months ago. I thought maybe she was willing to try again but I was wrong. She just wanted a favour.'

'Artemis?'

Ross nodded. 'An art dealer in the UK had bought some previously unseen photographs of Princess Diana, taken during the weekend that she died in Paris. He was selling them on the Internet. Apparently they were taken by a couple of tourists who were staying at the Ritz, celebrating their anniversary. Nadia knew that I had worked on Artemis and wanted someone to come to London to check their authenticity.'

'Why would you do that? After everything that happened.'

'I thought maybe if I helped her out she would change her mind. About us I mean. And if not, well, then it was an opportunity to get out of Russia. Time to move on. I flew over, bought the photos and then did the exchange.'

'So what's on them?'

'Well, that's the problem. Do you remember where we went for something to eat that evening?'

Buchanan shook his head, unable to recall the name of the place. An anonymous Brassiere not far from *Chez Benoit*. But that wasn't what was worrying him. Something much more important was suddenly on his mind, which was now racing ahead.

'*La Salle Blanche.*' It seems our anniversary couple were in the same place. So not only did they take some of the last pictures of Diana before she died, they also took some holiday snaps of themselves enjoying Parisian nightlife, including some shots inside the restaurant. And there is one in particular of his wife, seated at a table, toasting a glass of wine. And guess who's sitting at the table behind her? In the background but as clear as picture.'

Buchanan looked at him in horror. 'Please tell me it was taken before they turned up.'

Ross shook his head. 'Unfortunately not. You, me, Henri Paul and James Andanson. The four of us having a cosy meal together.'

Buchanan turned his head and stared towards the window. He couldn't think of anything to say. It was worse than he thought. In fact it was worse than he had ever imagined. No-one had discovered where Henri Paul had disappeared to between the hours of 7.00 and 10.00 that evening and suddenly here was irrefutable proof that he was sitting in a local restaurant with James Andanson, the driver of the white Fiat. Not to mention the CIA's head of Paris station and Buchanan himself. It was absolute, bloody dynamite. No wonder the Russians were trying to use it to leverage advantage in Stockholm next month.

'Anyway, I handed the photos over,' continued Ross, 'and went back to the apartment. They wanted someone to compile the crossword so I agreed to do that. I quite enjoyed it to be honest, it was an interesting challenge. After that I...' He stopped mid-sentence, interrupted by the sound of Buchanan's mobile suddenly ringing.'

'Hello?'

'It's me.'

'Obviously.'

'I've got some good news for you.'

'Good. I could do with some of that.'

'I'm with our fat friend. He was very talkative.'

'Was?'

Craven looked down at Parovsky's body, prone and lifeless on the floor, the head and torso still soaking wet. Definitely past tense. 'Correct. He won't be talking anymore.'

'Is that the good news?'

'Partly.'

'Go on.'

'I've also located the merchandise.'

'Is it safe?'

'Very...'

Buchanan let out a long, slow, sigh of relief. Maybe there was still a chance of limiting any damage.

'...the items are in a safe deposit box. A private bank in the City.'

'And do you know where?'

Craven smiled to himself as he stared at the large, silver key in his right hand. 'Absolutely. Do you want me to go and get them?'

Buchanan thought for a moment, tempted to get hold of the photos as soon as possible but also wary about anyone else seeing them. Even Craven. Perhaps it was better if he did that himself. 'Do you have an address?'

'Yes. And a code number and a key.'

'Can you drop them off?'

'Sure. Where are you?'

'Soho. Same place as before.'

'On my way.'

Buchanan put the phone back in his pocket and looked across at Ross. Time to complete the de-brief. 'So, what happened with Limonov?'

Ross gave him a rueful smile. He wondered when they would get to that. 'I thought that once I'd done what they wanted they would lose interest in me. Either let me go or at least fly me back to Moscow. But I was wrong. They knew that I was under surveillance and that I could be picked up at any moment. That wasn't something they were prepared to let happen.'

'So what were they so worried about? You hadn't worked for the CIA for years?'

Ross shuffled uneasily in his seat. 'I knew the name of someone. Someone that I could contact if things went wrong.'

'A mole?'

'I think so. Nadia briefed me before we left. It was clear that she shouldn't have done but I was on my own. She was in a cell with Parovsky and Limonov, I was working without any cover. No safety net at all. She gave me the name in case anything happened. Plus she told me...' Again, Ross stopped mid-sentence, this time interrupted by the ringing of the old-fashioned telephone on the other side of the room. He and Buchanan looked at each other for a second, wondering whether to answer it or not. Then Buchanan walked over and picked up the receiver. 'Hello?'

'It's Henry. Downstairs.'

'What's up?'

'We've got visitors.'

'Visitors?' Buchanan threw a glance across the room to Ross, indicating that they had a problem.

'Uninvited guests.'

'How many?'

'One in the shop pretending to browse. And at least two outside, maybe three.'

'And provenance?'

'Can't tell. But they're not surveillance. It's definitely a hunting party...'

Thirty-Five

VINNY LEANT BACK IN HIS CHAIR AND PUSHED HIS ARMS high above his head, his whole body stretched as far as it would reach as he let out a long, growling yawn, like a lion, sated and dozing in the African shade, or a big old, grizzly bear, slow and lumbering but irritable and dangerous. He looked across at George and Albert, both of them heads down and still ploughing through the papers. 'I need some fresh air,' he said, standing up and stretching his arms again. 'I'll get Max to get us some more coffee.'

'Good idea,' replied Albert, pushing the papers to one side and also standing up. 'I'll have a smoke. You coming George? Stretch your legs?'

George shook his head, too engrossed in finishing the document that he'd only just started reading. Besides, there wasn't much fresh air to be had when Albert was puffing on his rollups. Albert stared at him for a moment, wondering whether there was any further reply and then shrugged and left, his hand already reaching for his baccy tin as he wandered off towards the lift. Vinny meanwhile had already collared Maxine on the other side of the office and was organising some more refreshments. George glanced up at them and then went back to the document, a detailed chronology of activity immediately after the accident, compiled over 20 years ago by Albert.

The Mercedes S280 had crashed head-on into the thirteenth concrete pillar of the Alma tunnel's central reservation at 12.24 a.m. The motorcycle with its two unidentified occupants and the white Fiat driven by James Andanson had both failed to stop, remarkable given the seriousness of the incident and the fact that Andanson was a photojournalist. The first person on the scene was a local motorcyclist called Eric Petel who had been riding along Cours Albert 1er and had been overtaken by the car. Petel arrived shortly after the collision and described the crumpled wreckage with its horn blaring and the engine still racing at very high revs, an indication that Henri Paul had moved the gear stick into neutral. Petel recognised Diana and tried briefly to help her but then quickly realised that he needed to call the emergency services. As he didn't own a mobile phone he went to the nearest public telephone located off the Place de l'Alma and called from there. Not convinced that they really understood the seriousness of the situation, or the importance of the passengers, he then decided to go to the nearest police station and report the incident in person. The next people to approach the vehicle were paparazzo. Romauld Rat and his driver Stephane Darmon who earlier that evening had been stationed outside Dodi's apartment. They drove past and then parked their motorcycle, a Honda 650, some way ahead and walked back. Within seconds several more photographers arrived including Christian Martinez and Serge Anal, who also dialled 112 to request emergency assistance. A Dr. Frederic Mailliez who had been driving in the opposite direction on the way home from a party also stopped to provide assistance, reporting in his statement that by then the paparazzi were already in full flow, swirling round the wreckage like a wake of hungry vultures, shooting its occupants from all angles. Mailliez confirmed that the driver and the rear seat passenger immediately behind were both dead but that the two passengers on the other side of the car were both alive. The front passenger had been hurled against the dashboard and windscreen, the impact of which had literally ripped off the left side of his face which was now hanging loose. However, the woman in the back, who Mailliez incredibly said he did not recognise, seemed to be in better shape. He immediately made two telephone calls, one to confirm that two ambulances were on their way and the other to request heavy cutting gear that would be needed to free Trevor Rees-Jones. By then, two off-duty volunteer firemen who had been driving in the opposite direction had also stopped to help.

At 12.30 a.m. the first police officers arrived and found the scene in absolute chaos with photographers practically fighting each other in their attempts to take pictures of the crash. Most of them were more concerned about getting the perfect shot of Diana rather than trying to help and some were poking their lenses through the shattered windows and buckled doors. One of the officers, Lino Gagliardone tried to hold back the paparazzi while his colleague, Sebastian Dorzee checked the condition of the car's occupants and reported back to the local station. Dr Mailliez had managed to tilt Diana's head back slightly and put an oxygen mask over her nose and mouth. At this point she was semi-conscious and talking, although Mailliez said that he could not make out what she was saying. At 12.32 a.m. two teams of firemen arrived under the direction of the officer in charge, Sergeant Xavier Gourmelon. He immediately decided to cut the roof off the Mercedes so that they could extract Trevor Rees-Jones, who appeared to be the most seriously injured of the two casualties. He also assigned one of his team, Philippe Boyer, to take over from Dr. Mailliez and look after Diana until the emergency service, Service d'Aide Médicale Urgente (SAMU) arrived. Boyer attached a surgical collar around her neck while two other firemen attended to Trevor Rees-Jones. Goulmelon confirmed that at this point Diana was conscious, stating that he heard her say 'My God, what's happened?' and that he saw her move her left arm and legs.

From 12.35, numerous French officials started to arrive including Madame Maude Coujard, the duty prosecutor who would oversee the investigation into the crash. She immediately placed the case in the hands of the Criminal Brigade, the French judicial police who investigated criminal and terrorist cases as well as sudden, unexplained deaths. Its chief, Commander Jean-Claude Mules decided to put his most trusted senior officer, Martine Montiel, in command and she arrived at the crash site shortly afterwards. Almost immediately, Montiel in consultation with Coujard decided that the paparazzi were probably to blame and that they had almost certainly harassed the Mercedes and its occupants to the extent that they were forced off the road. As a result, seven photographers including Romauld Rat and Christian Martinez were promptly arrested and taken into custody.

At 12.44 a.m. the camion de désincarcération or can-opener arrived and within minutes spotlights had been set up to assist the process of removing the roof. By now Dr. Jean-Marc Martino, a resuscitation specialist with the SAMU team had taken over attending to Diana while a completely different team, led by Dr. Le Hote were looking after Trevor Rees-Jones. Once the roof had been cut off, the bodies of Henri Paul and Dodi Fayed were removed and laid out on the road. Medics worked for over thirty minutes on Dodi, giving external heart massage in an attempt to resuscitate him but to no avail. Meanwhile Dr Martino had attached a drip to Diana's arm to sedate her as she was still agitated and crying out. He personally supervised the firemen and medics who hoisted her from the rear of the car, taking great care when lifting her out as she was partly wedged on the floor, in between the back seat and the passenger seat in front. Dr. Martino described Diana's state as "severe but not critical" and noted that she was still speaking, although not clearly. But as she was being transferred onto the stretcher she went into cardiac arrest and immediately the full seriousness of her condition became apparent. Dr. Martino gave her respiratory ventilation by inserting a narrow tracheal tube down her throat and administering heart massage, the treatment also taking place on a stretcher by the roadside. Eventually he managed to revive her and immediately instructed ambulance driver Michel Massbeuf to transfer her to one of the waiting ambulances, where he continued to treat her.

The transfer was timed at 1.28 am and the ambulance, together with its escort of two police cars and two motorcycles pulled away from the Alma tunnel at 1.30 am, over an hour after the accident first happened. The Pitié-Salpêtrière hospital was not the nearest but was considered to have the best facilities to treat Diana's injuries. However, the ambulance was not driving flat out with its sirens blazing, in fact it was driving so slowly to prevent the journey aggravating her condition that it took thirty-six minutes to complete the distance of *just over four miles, an average speed of seven miles per hour. As they were crossing the Austerlitz bridge Diana's blood pressure became dangerously low and Dr. Martino, requiring complete immobility to give urgent treatment, ordered the convoy to stop. At that point they had already passed two major hospitals and were less than half a mile from their destination, a thirty-second dash if driven at high speed. Dr Martino however determined that Diana's condition required immediate attention and he applied external heart massage and injected a large dose of adrenalin directly into the heart, ensuring that his patient was well enough to continue before instructing Massebeuf to drive on. The stop added another ten minutes to the journey, much to the concern of the senior politicians, police and British Ambassador, Sir Michael Jay, who were waiting impatiently at Pitié-Salpêtrière for their arrival, at one point wondering whether the ambulance had actually got lost.*

At 2.06 am the ambulance finally arrived and Diana, unconscious and receiving artificial respiration was transferred into the care of the hospital's head of intensive care unit, Professor Bruno Riou. At 2.20 am she suffered a further cardiac arrest and duty surgeon Maniel Daloman opened her chest and applied external heart massage. Shortly afterwards, Professor Alain Pavie, a specialist heart surgeon who had been called in took over and quickly established that massive internal bleeding was coming from a ruptured pulmonary vein, a major link between the heart and lungs. Pavie sutured the 2.5 centimetre split while heart massage and constant injections of adrenaline were administered to keep her heart going. A staggering total of 150 5ml doses were injected but no cardiac activity could be re-established. At 3.00 am Professor Pavie extended the original incision and began massaging the heart by hand and at 3.30 am Sir Michael Jay was warned that the prognosis was pessimistic. After all other attempts to produce a spontaneous heart rhythm failed, Pavie ordered electric shock therapy in a last-ditch effort to restart the princess's heart. Time after time massive electrical charges were arced between the hand-held terminals pressed on her chest but her heart failed to respond.

Finally, and by mutual consent, all attempts at resuscitation were
abandoned and the princess was declared dead at 4.00 am.

George put the document down and blew out his cheeks. Albert's notes written all those years ago had brought events back to life as if it were only yesterday. The facts were captured in remarkable detail, a testimony to Albert's journalistic rigour but none of them really answered the one, overriding question; the great unsolved mystery. Or at least not conclusively. Did Diana die in what was simply a tragic accident or was she actually murdered?

'You want some more coffee George?' asked Vinny, holding an empty mug in his hand.

George looked up and blinked at Vinny in surprise. He'd been so engrossed in reading that he hadn't heard him come back in.

'Or some tea maybe?'

'No, coffee's fine,' replied George, leaning back in his chair and rubbing his eyes. 'Albert not back yet?'

'Not yet,' replied Vinny, pumping some coffee out of the flask with his one good hand. 'Still smoking probably. What are you reading?'

'A timeline of the accident,' replied George, sliding the papers across the desk. 'From the moment they crashed up until the point that she died. You should read it.'

Vinny popped a biscuit in his mouth and then leant forward and picked up the papers. It looked like Albert was going to be a few more minutes so he had time to catch up on some of the background. George took a slurp of coffee and then shuffled through the stack of documents in the file, looking for something else to read while they were waiting. Several pages from the top was another chronology, this one compiled in a different format by a different journalist and this time detailing the events immediately after Diana's death. George glanced at his watch and then leant back in his chair and started reading again.

Immediately following Diana's death the last rites were
administered by Roman Catholic priest Father Clochard-Boussuet

who anointed Diana with holy oil. An official bulletin, signed by Professors Riou and Pavie was also agreed which stated;

"The Princess of Wales was the victim of a high-speed car crash tonight in Paris. She was immediately taken by the Paris SAMU emergency services which carried out initial resuscitation.

On her arrival at Pitié-Salpêtrière hospital, she had massive chest injuries and haemorrhaging, followed rapidly by cardiac arrest.

An emergency thoracotomy revealed a major wound to the left pulmonary vein.

Despite closing this wound and two hours of external and internal cardiac massage, circulation could not be re-established and death occurred at 4 o'clock this morning."

The public announcement of Diana's death was not made until at 5.45am but Mohammed Al Fayed was aware long before then. Earlier that evening the decoy Range Rover driven by Philippe Dorneau and carrying Kez Wingfield had driven straight to Dodi's apartment, as previously arranged. Concerned at the non-arrival of the Mercedes Wingfield went up to the apartment and called Trevor Rees-Jones to see where they were. He got no reply but assumed that perhaps Dodi and Diana had decided to go onto a nightclub, something that they had done before. Dorneau however had stayed outside and was chatting with some of the journalists when one of them received a call about the accident. Dorneau drove down towards the Alma tunnel to try and get more details and then telephoned Wingfield to confirm their worst fears. Wingfield in turn passed the news directly to Mohamed Al Fayed's chief of personal security, Paul Handley-Greaves, in London and at 1.30 am Fayed was informed that his beloved, eldest son was dead and that Princess Diana could be dying. Within the hour bodyguards drove him to Gatwick Airport, ready to board a private helicopter to Paris. At the same time, the switchboard at Buckingham Palace, alerted by the Foreign Office, awakened Prince Charles who was holidaying with his sons at Balmoral and was also told the news. Like Fayed, Charles also made plans to board a flight as soon as possible. In Paris meanwhile, two controversial decisions were taken in the early hours of the morning. Firstly, a decision to partly embalm Diana's body from the pelvis up, the order apparently passed on to the French authorities by Sir Michael Jay on behalf of Prince Charles's office at St James's Palace. The procedure took place at 4.45 am, in direct contravention of French law which prohibited embalming if a post-mortem was to be carried out, the formaldehyde corrupting crucial toxicology tests.

At 4.55 am Fayed's helicopter landed at Le Bourget airport and the grief-stricken tycoon was driven straight to the Pitié-Salpêtrière hospital to claim Dodi's body. The Queen's flight carrying Prince Charles, Diana's two sisters – Lady Jane Fellowes and Lady Sarah McCorquodale – and a small group of aides and servants landed in Paris shortly after 5.00 am. They too drove straight to the hospital, Charles travelling with Sir Michael Jay in a silver Jaguar bearing the royal standard. Fayed had only stayed at the hospital for ten minutes and had already left when Charles and his entourage arrived at 6.00 am. They were taken to the second floor room where Diana's body was laid out and where Paul Burrell, who had flown out by a scheduled flight early that morning, was already waiting. He, Prince Charles and Diana's sisters stood quietly around the body for several minutes before it was placed in a double coffin, a grey casket with a window inside an oak coffin, in accordance with French customs regulations.

By the time they left the hospital the second controversial decision, taken by the Criminal Brigade, had been carried out; namely that a mechanical street cleaner using huge, mechanical scouring brushes and a mixture of disinfectant, strong detergent and water had been sent through the Alma tunnel to remove all evidence of the crash. Normally an accident of that scale involving VIPs would have closed the road for 24 hours but less than six hours after it happened the tunnel was fully reopened to traffic, the only clue to a major incident having taking place being the large chunk of concrete missing from the base of the thirteenth, concrete pillar.

Diana's body was flown back on Queen's flight BAE 146 to RAF Northolt, where eight men removed the coffin from the aircraft's hold,

covered it with the royal standard and then transferred it into a
waiting hearse. Charles flew on to Balmoral to be with his sons while
Lady Jane Fellowes, Lady Sarah McCorquodale and Paul Burrell
followed the hearse to a London undertaker, where the princess's
personal doctor, Doctor Meyer Wheeler, was waiting. He later carried
out an autopsy, as required under British law, at the Hammersmith
and Fulham mortuary in west London, prior to Diana's body being
taken to lie in state in the Chapel Royal at St James's Palace.

Again, George blew out his cheeks as he put the document down, just as Albert sauntered back into the room, all relaxed and languid from his dose of nicotine.

'So, are we ready to start again?' asked Albert, also pouring himself a cup of coffee.

'We were ready five minutes ago,' said Vinny, winking at George across the table. 'What do you want to cover next?'

'Well, we've spent enough time going through all the facts,' replied Albert, with a mischievous grin, 'so I think it's about time we discussed what really happened...'

Thirty-Six

'PROBLEM?'

Buchanan switched off his phone and nodded. That was something of an understatement. He looked across the room towards the door, half-expecting to see someone come bursting through it at any moment. Then he looked at Ross again, still waiting for an answer, sensing that it was something serious. 'Hunting Party. Downstairs.'

'Jesus!' Ross immediately pulled out his pistol and darted across the room, poking his head around the door frame to see if he could hear any activity below. 'Company?'

'Not sure.'

'How many?'

'Three or four. One in the shop, two or three outside.'

Ross stood in the doorway, listening for a few more seconds but there was nothing discernible, just the low hubbub of the shop beneath them. Then he crossed the room and looked out of the window, trying to see if he could spot anything in the street below. There were still lots of people milling back and forth but no signs of any surveillance, nothing to tell him whether it was a Company operation or not. And that was crucial because if it wasn't CIA then they had to be Russian, which was going to be even worse. The Americans wanted to syphon his brain and then throw him into gaol for the next hundred years, whereas the Russians just wanted to kill him. Not that either option was part of his plan. 'Who do we have downstairs?'

'Just the kid.'

'Jesus, what sort of place is this?'

Buchanan stared back at him but said nothing. He was beginning to wonder the same thing himself. On reflection a safe house would have been better. Or a hotel lounge somewhere, bland and anonymous in the centre of London. Even a bench in St James's Park would have been safer than this. And how the hell did they know where to find them? It wasn't as if the sex shop was even on the radar.

'You must have been followed,' said Ross, as if reading his mind.

'Impossible,' replied Buchanan, his nose tilted upwards, offended by the accusation. 'It must have been you.'

Ross glared back at him. 'Don't be ridiculous.'

Buchanan shrugged his shoulders and stared at the door again, still expecting someone to come through it at any second. Working out how anyone knew where they were was hardly the priority at the moment. Besides, he knew that he hadn't been tailed, he'd been fastidious in his movements, doubling back and covering his tracks several times, constantly checking for any signs of someone behind him. He was 100% certain that he hadn't been followed. But likewise he couldn't imagine anyone tailing Ross. He was far too experienced and streetwise for that.

'Let's try the other room,' said Ross, suddenly deciding that they had to do something. Staying where they were, frozen on the spot like sitting ducks was no strategy at all. He walked over to the doorway and then crossed the landing to the room opposite, trying the handle again but to no avail. Then he stepped back a pace, lifted his right leg and smashed his boot firmly into the door, just at the point where the lock met the door frame. The lock mechanism was an old-fashioned mortice, probably thirty or forty years old and built to withstand a lot more than just a heavy kick from an unwelcome intruder. The door and frame however were made of cheaper, low grade timber and splintered immediately under the weight of his boot. The whole assembly moved an inch or so, a gap of daylight from the room behind suddenly appearing in front of them. Ross lifted his foot again and smashed it into the same spot while Buchanan kept watch at the top of the stairs, conscious that the noise would be travelling down to the shop below. The lock shifted another inch but still didn't yield so Ross gave it a third kick, following through with as much momentum and bodyweight as he could manage. This time the frame gave way and the door swung wide open.

Ross walked into the room and quickly surveyed its contents, the size and layout identical to the one on the other side. The interior however was completely different, this time no table and chairs in the centre but a large, modern desk pushed up against the right-hand wall; a standard set-up with laptop computer, separate monitor and an old, battered, swivel chair on five plastic castors, the desk surface virtually hidden beneath a pile of papers and invoices. On the opposite side of the room were a number of filing cabinets and then the rest of the floor was taken up by stacks of cartons and cardboard boxes, so much so that it was difficult to walk from one side to the other; a typical small, cramped office cum stockroom. At the far end in the middle of the wall opposite the door was a sash window, in exactly the same position as in the other room. Ross squeezed through the stack of boxes and looked out, expecting to see another sheer drop to the street below but this time the window looked out over the rear of the property which backed onto Wardour Street and then Dean Street beyond that. He was staring at a view of rooftops and chimneys; a myriad of flat and gabled roofs and a jumble of dormer windows, air conditioning units, rain gutters, aerials, skylight windows and metal fire-escapes, the whole landscape stretching as far as the eye could see, all the way into deepest Soho. And more importantly, suddenly a means of escape.

Immediately he started to unscrew the window lock which secured the upper and lower frames, checking as he did so whether the sash cords were still in place and whether the window had been painted shut. That was the problem with old sash windows, often they were impossible to open after years of neglect and not being used. But fortunately this one was in good condition and not too difficult to open. The lower frame juddered and jammed slightly but after a couple of shoves Ross managed to push it as high as it would go, certainly high enough for him to get his body through and make a quick exit. Buchanan stood behind him as Ross poked his head out and stared at the ledge below, a six foot drop which was probably harder than it looked, and then a simple jump across to one of the flat roofs heading north towards Peter Street.

'How far is it?' asked Buchanan, resisting the temptation to also stick his head out.

'Five, six feet,' replied Ross, still scanning the rooftops and planning his escape route. 'Do-able.'

'We've got movement downstairs. You'd better be quick.'

'Rucksack. It's in the other room.'

Buchanan darted into the room next door and by time he returned, Ross was sitting astride the window ledge ready to make his move, one leg resting on the office floorboards and the other dangling outside. Buchanan could also hear raised voices from downstairs. Henry was doing his best to keep them at bay but it was only a matter of time now. Seconds probably.

'You stay here and hold the fort,' said Ross, taking the ruck sack and stuffing the SIG Sauer back into his holster. 'Keep them here as long as possible...'

Buchanan nodded. He had no intention of jumping out of a window and then clambering across a load of rooftops. Those days had long gone. Besides, whoever was downstairs wasn't looking for him. It was Ross that they were after.

'...you go back in the other room.'

'You didn't tell me the name.'

'Name?'

'The mole.'

'Janus. I don't know his real name.'

'Definitely a him?'

'That's what she said. I've got a number but haven't called it.'

'What's the number?'

Suddenly the noise of people shouting wafted up the stairs, an altercation in the shop below which meant they were on the move. Persuasion and diplomacy finally giving way to threats and ultimatums, Henry probably standing his ground but with his hands now on his head, trying not to get shot. Ross swivelled his other leg over so that he was now sitting on the window ledge, ready to jump. He twisted round and looked at Buchanan. 'Time to go. I'll text it to you.'

Buchanan nodded and then turned and left, closing the door behind him, or as much as he could given that the lock was broken. Then he went back into the first room and pulled out his phone. His pressed one of the speed dials and waited for Craven to answer.

'Hello?'

'It's me.'

'Obviously.'

'Where are you?'

'The Strand. On my way back to you.'

'Change of plan. Go and pick up the merchandise.'

'Problem?'

'Sort of.'

'Need any help?'

'No, just pick them up. I'll call you.'

'Anything else?'

Buchanan hesitated. He didn't know the address of the safe deposit box and if anything happened to Craven he wouldn't know where the photos were. And if Parovsky had put them there for safe keeping, there was a good chance that someone else knew where they were. Like the FSB for example.

'You'd better give me the address, just in case.'

'Over the phone?' The surprise in Craven's voice was unmistakeable. Passing details on a mobile was against all protocols.

361

Whatever was going on in Soho had to be serious. Downstairs, the shouting suddenly got even louder and then Buchanan heard the door open and the first sound of footsteps on the stairs. Seconds away.

'Yes, over the phone. Make it snappy.'

'It's number 12, Colebrook Street. Argento Bank. You want the post code?'

'No, that's fine. Argento Bank, 12 Colebrook Street. Text me the box number.' Buchanan switched the phone off and put it in his pocket, repeating the address in his head several times to make sure that he remembered it. There was no way that he could risk writing it down. He managed to pull out a chair and sit at the table again, just as two people burst into the room, the first guy wearing a grey suit and white shirt and holding a pistol in both hands which was sweeping 180 degrees left to right as he scanned the room. The guy behind him was wearing blue jeans with a black bomber jacket and a grey baseball cap, similarly holding a Beretta in both hands, part covering his partner and part covering the landing behind him.

'Where is he?' snapped the suit, the accent unmistakably American.

'Where's who?' frowned Buchanan.

The suit looked at him in disbelief and then turned to his colleague. 'Check the other room.'

The guy in the baseball cap nodded and disappeared while the suit reversed into the doorway, covering the landing with his pistol but all the time keeping one eye on Buchanan. Within seconds his partner reappeared and Buchanan watched the two of them huddled together, a whispered conversation confirming that Ross had escaped through an open window and then discussing what to do next. The suit pulled out a phone and made a quick call, checking with the team downstairs whether there was any sign of Ross outside but getting a negative response. Then the guy in the baseball cap disappeared again, back into the second room with instructions to go out onto the rooftops and see if he could follow Ross.

'Where's he gone?' snapped the suit, walking back into the room and still pointing the Beretta firmly in Buchanan's direction.

Buchanan shrugged. 'He didn't say.'

The suit stared at him for several seconds and then took out his phone again and made a second call. This time Buchanan could hear the faint voice of a female at the other end.

'Yes?'

'It's Carter. Target has flown.'

There was a pause at the other end, the information being digested and clearly not to someone's taste.

'The Brit is still here,' continued the suit, feeling the need to fill the silence. This was a conversation that was not going to go well.

'Are we in pursuit?'

'Affirmative. But no line of sight.'

'Jesus Christ!'

This time it was the suit's turn to keep quiet. Losing track of a target didn't happen very often, certainly not during what was meant to be a closed operation. No surprise then at the reaction on the other end of the phone. He could feel the simmering explosion coming down the line. Far better to not say anything.

'Where's Buchanan now. Is he still with you?'

'Right next to me.'

'Put him on.'

The suit offered the phone over, indicating that someone at the other end wanted to talk.

Buchanan took the mobile and relaxed back into the chair. 'Hello?'

'Charles, it's Christine Michaels.'

'Christine. What an unexpected surprise.'

Michaels ignored the sarcasm. No time for playing games. 'Where's Ross?'

'How did you know I was here?'

'Never mind that. Do you know where he is?'

'I assume you had me followed?'

'Just tell me where he's gone.'

'Am I being watched?'

'For the last time, where's Ross?'

'Have you got me under surveillance?'

Michaels paused, irritated by Buchanan's pretend indignation and high moral ground. The last thing she had time for was a conversation about protocols but she knew that she didn't have any choice. Buchanan was as stubborn as a mule and they weren't going to get anywhere until she answered his question. She took a deep breath, more out of exasperation than concern. 'We've had this conversation Charles. Your people keep an eye on me and my people keep an eye on you. It's what we do.'

'Keep your friends close and your enemies closer?'

'Something like that.'

'So which are we?'

'That depends Charles, on whether you're going to help me.'

Buchanan raised an eyebrow. At least she was being honest. The file said direct and forthright and maybe on this occasion it was a positive attribute. He glanced up at the monitor which was fixed into the corner of the room, angled and pointing down at him so that it could be viewed from the table. The film extract was on a loop, the silent montage returning to its climax, the screen filled with graphic images and Vesuvius about to erupt again. He smiled to himself, the odd juxtaposition of watching erotic images while talking to Michaels; a cold, ruthless adversary and one of the most sexless, dispassionate women he had ever met.

'So, are you going to help me?'

'I don't know where he went. He didn't tell me.'

Michaels paused, trying to work out whether Buchanan was telling the truth or not. It was difficult to tell, stuck on the other end of the phone and not able to see the whites of his eyes. 'When did he leave?'

Buchanan glanced at his watch, not that it was going to tell him anything. He had no idea what time Ross jumped out the window. 'Five, ten minutes ago. He wasn't keen on sticking around to meet your welcoming party.'

'Did you pass on the message?'

'Sort of.'

'And?'

'He has a name. And a contact number.'

Michaels paused again, her mind suddenly in overdrive as it raced through the implications of Buchanan's response. 'Then we should talk.'

'Not yet. You frightened him off before I got all the details.'

'We still need to talk.'

'Besides, he wants to come in. To us, not you. We need to debrief him first. I'll let you know.'

'We don't have time for that. He must have told you something?'

Buchanan hesitated, still thinking about Ross's request to hold them up for as long as possible. Agreeing to see Michaels was going to burn at least another half an hour. 'Okay, do you want to meet?'

'Just tell me now.'

'Not on the phone. Face to face or not at all.'

Another sigh of exasperation at the other end of the phone. *Stubborn as a mule.* 'Okay, as long as we do it now.'

'Fine. Do you want to come here?' Buchanan smiled to himself as he glanced up at the screen again, the thought of Michaels walking into the sex shop conjuring up all sorts of bizarre images. Amusing, certainly but almost unthinkable.

'No, you come to me. Put Carter on again.'

Buchanan passed the mobile back and sat patiently as instructions were conveyed. In less than a minute they were ready to leave, his chaperone insisting on checking the second room before they went downstairs. The sash window was still wide open but there was no sign of the guy in the baseball cap. The suit stuck his head out, scanning the horizon and then made a call, telling his partner to make his way down to street level and meet them outside. Then he closed the window frame, carefully screwing the lock back into position before checking that the room was left exactly as they had found it. Other than the door of course which was looking worse for wear, the lock damaged beyond repair and bits of splintered wood all over the floor. Two minutes later Buchanan was being ushered into the back of a black limousine, a baby-sitter either side of him and the car speeding south towards the river.

Back at the shop life subsided back to normal. Henry checked the rooms upstairs and then went back down to the counter, a late flurry of customers providing an unusual distraction as he started to file a report. Upstairs, everything was still and quiet, other than the occasional creaking of timbers, the tell-tale sounds of an old, Victorian building settling into the summer heat. Except in this case it wasn't. After about five minutes one of the ceiling tiles in the second room started to move, immediately above one of the stacks of cardboard boxes. Ross moved the tile to one side and then swung his legs over the joist before dropping down onto the cartons and then onto the floor below. Exactly the reverse of how he had climbed up there as soon as Buchanan had left the room. The dilemma was the window of course. If he had really escaped over the rooftops he would have shut it behind him while he was still sitting on the window ledge, just before he jumped. Hoping that the CIA wouldn't realise where he had gone, or at least taking a while to work it out. Give him more time to get away. But he needed to leave it open. Telegraph to them that he had flown. It was a bit of a giveaway really, much too obvious to be true but they were too pumped up to notice. Or maybe too thick. But Buchanan would have worked it out. He was old school. Sharp as a knife. That's why he repeated it out loud. Or maybe it was just coincidence. Serendipity. Either way, he had what he needed now. That was the beauty of being in a roof-space. Sound rises. Argento Bank. Number 12, Colebrook Street. Time to move. Time to buy some insurance and sort things out. Once and for good...

Thirty-Seven

'So, where do we start?' asked Vinny, standing up again and stretching his legs. He wandered over to the window and looked down at the street below, the traffic as usual solid in both directions and the pavements full of thousands of people, most of them commuters making their way home but hundreds of others standing outside the pubs and bars enjoying an early evening drink. Vinny couldn't hear the noise through the triple glazing but a lifelong career in Fleet Street meant that he knew what a typical Friday evening sounded like; a vibrant, buzzy, cacophony of people unwinding after a hard day at work and everyone getting ready for the weekend.

'Well, let's start with Henri Paul,' replied Albert, shuffling through the pile of papers as he searched for a specific file note, 'particularly as he's been vilified as the main culprit. The drink-sodden French chauffeur careering along at 120 miles per hour who caused the death of the nation's best-loved woman.'

'Not true then?' asked Vinny.

'Not true at all,' replied Albert, finding the piece of paper that he was looking for. 'It's still the official explanation from the establishment but the story about Henri Paul being drunk at the wheel was leaked by the French authorities on 1st September, long before samples of his blood had even been analysed. "As drunk as a pig" is what it said and that he'd guzzled the equivalent of two bottles of wine or a dozen whiskies before he lost control and rammed the car into a concrete wall. When the results were finally released, they indicated that he had more than three times the legal limit of alcohol in his bloodstream but they also showed that it contained 20.7 per cent carbon monoxide.'

'What's the significance of that then?' asked George, also standing up to stretch his legs.

'It means that it couldn't have been his blood sample,' replied Albert. 'Anyone with that level of carbon monoxide in their body would have been vomiting and suffering from crippling headaches, virtually incapable of either walking or driving. And anyway, we've got CCTV footage of Henri Paul waiting at the hotel for the car to arrive looking absolutely stone-cold sober, which is how Trevor Rees Jones described him as well.'

'So whose blood sample was it?' asked Vinny, walking back to the table to pour himself another cup of coffee. 'And more importantly, what happened to Henri Paul's sample?'

'It's all in here,' replied Albert, sliding the piece of paper across the table. 'It looks like a complete cover-up.'

Vinny and George moved closer together and then bent over and started to read; a simple typed paragraph that looked like an extract from a much larger document. *There were twenty-two other investigable deaths in Paris that night and one of them was the suicide of a depressed unnamed male who drank a large quantity of alcohol before attaching a hose from the exhaust pipe of his car to its interior. A desperate, lonely death of someone whose blood sample would have matched exactly the one purported to have come from Henri Paul. The French police refused then, and still refuse until this day, to identify the other people who died that night, or to release the pathology results of their blood tests. The Pathologists involved also refused to allow independent samples to be taken from Henri Paul's body, or to allow independent tests on the blood and urine samples taken during the autopsy. No outside party, including Henri Paul's parents were permitted to have a representative pathologist present when the body was re-examined, or to have further samples taken of tissue or body fluids. French judges also refused to allow DNA tests to be carried out on the blood and urine samples which were claimed to have come from Henri Paul. Incredibly, when his body was finally released to his parents, Judge Hervé Stephan, who was appointed to head up the official inquiry, ordered that it should be buried or cremated immediately and that no test of any kind could be carried out. His parents were assured that the blood samples already taken would be preserved but years later officials admitted that the samples, the only forensic evidence to support the police version of it being a drink-driving accident, had been destroyed.*

'You're right,' said Vinny, standing up straight, 'it looks like a complete cover up.'

'And he wasn't driving at 120 miles per hour either,' replied Albert. 'We know from the crash investigation that the car was doing exactly 64 miles per hour when it hit the pillar. Hardly speeding for a dual carriageway at that time of night.'

'So Henri Paul is completely innocent then?' asked George, beginning to wonder why they were still talking about him.

'Probably,' replied Albert, again searching through the pile of papers for a particular document, 'although it's not as simple as that. There's a renegade former MI6 agent called Richard Tomlinson who worked for the British Secret Intelligence Service between 1991 and 1995. He's gone on record to confirm that Henri Paul was a long-serving, paid informant of MI6, regularly receiving payments in cash for the information he supplied.'

Vinny smiled to himself. That was more like it. Just the mention of MI6 meant that they were getting into the meat of the conspiracy theories which was just what his readers wanted to read about. A bit of mystery and intrigue and some good old-fashioned political subterfuge.

'Immediately after the crash they found over FF12,000 in cash in Henry Paul's pocket and several days later discovered FF1.7m in his personal bank account, an astonishing amount of money for a hotel Security Manager. One view is that MI6 constructed the plot to murder Diana and persuaded Henri Paul to drive through the tunnel that night. He wouldn't have known what was going to happen of course, or even that there was a plan to do anything at all. MI6 probably arranged somewhere discreet and private for

Dodi and Diana to stay that night and Henri Paul arranged to drive them there rather than taking them back to the apartment. That's why they were driving down towards the River Seine rather than along the Champs-Élysée. And it also explains why Dodi was so relaxed about not having any bodyguards with them. They weren't planning on going back to the apartment at all. Henri Paul was taking them to a secret location that only he and Dodi knew about. Or at least that's what he thought.'

'That's a pretty big accusation,' said Vinny, suddenly having a vision of armies of lawyers rubbing their hands in anticipation, probably followed by a long and expensive legal case and numerous trips to Lincoln's Inn and the High Court. 'Do we have any facts to back that up?'

'Plenty,' replied Albert. 'Let's start with Slobodan Milošević.'

'What's he got to do with anything?' frowned George, confused at Albert's comment. He knew Milošević was the President of Serbia before being charged with war crimes in connection with the conflicts in Bosnia, Croatia and Kosovo. But he couldn't see how any of that connected him to the death of Princess Diana.

'Well, nothing directly,' said Albert, 'but Milošević was also subject to an assassination plot by MI6 and the similarities to the accident in Paris are startling...'

Vinny raised his eyebrows. MI6 no doubt deployed lots of different methods to get rid of people but maybe this was more than a coincidence.

'...in fact they're almost identical. Again, Richard Tomlinson has gone on record to confirm that in 1992 he saw a three-page document which was an outline plan to assassinate Milošević. The document was typed and circulated to a number of senior MI6 officers, confirming that it was a serious and formal proposal. The plan was to kill Milošević by causing his car to crash as it entered a motorway tunnel, by using a high-powered strobe light to blind the driver.'

'Doesn't mean that Diana's death was necessarily caused by MI6 though,' said George, conscious that someone needed to play devil's advocate. 'Just because they've done it before doesn't mean it was them.'

Albert nodded in agreement. 'That's true. It's a method used by lots of agencies. Ex MI5 officer David Shayler has publicly stated that car accidents were regularly deployed, simply because they're such common causes of death. It makes it easy for the establishment to claim that anyone crying foul play is simply a conspiracy theorist.

'Like Diana's bodyguard,' said Vinny, unable to recall his name but remembering that he had died in a road traffic accident in 1987, a year after being moved to the Diplomatic Protection Squad following rumours that he and Diana were having an affair.

'Exactly. Barry Mannakee. And there are other facts that link the death of Diana to MI6.'

'Such as?'

'Well these two for example,' replied Albert, sliding a photograph across the table. 'Conclusive proof that the security services were involved.'

Vinny leant forward and picked it up, the black and white photo that they had looked at earlier when they were first sitting in Francorelli's. A picture taken outside the Ritz when Dodi and Diana were battling to get through the crowd as they transferred from the limousine to the hotel foyer. In the corner of the photograph were the two MI6 agents watching the ensuing melee, their faces highlighted by small, yellow circles.

'What are their names again?' asked Vinny, passing it over to George.

'Richard Spearman and Nicholas Langman. Spearman was particularly well connected because prior to being in Paris, he was the personal secretary to David Spedding, the chief of MI6.'

'It's not exactly a covert operation though, is it?' said George, staring at the picture and frowning in confusion. Something didn't add up. If MI6 were really involved in a plot to murder Diana, why on earth would two of their agents be standing outside the

Ritz hotel, as bold as brass, surrounded by the world's press. It didn't make sense.

Albert nodded, acknowledging the challenge. It was a good question and one that he had grappled with unsuccessfully for more years than he cared to remember. George was right, it wasn't covert at all. It didn't make any sense but for the moment, absent of a credible explanation, it was an anomaly that they had to put up with.

'Anything else on MI6?' asked Vinny, contemplating whether to go for a comfort break or not. Too much coffee and mineral water were starting to have the inevitable effect on his system but he didn't want to miss anything.

'Yes, James Andanson,' replied Albert, shuffling through the stack of papers again as he looked for a particular file. 'There's a whole dossier on him and it's one of the strongest links of all.'

Vinny smiled to himself. He remembered all the coverage on James Andanson the first time around. Albert was right, it was probably the most compelling evidence linking Diana's death to MI6. 'I need a piss,' he said, moving towards the door. 'You keep going and I'll catch you up.'

Albert and George exchanged a knowing look at Vinny's choice of language while Albert continued to shuffle through the documents to find what he was looking for, eventually sliding a file across the table. George pulled out a chair and then sat down and opened the front cover. Inside were a bundle of papers and numerous photographs, some of Princess Diana but mostly of a balding, overweight, middle-aged man, usually wearing an open-neck shirt and sporting a decent suntan, the backdrop invariably a beach or ocean and the sky behind him a deep shade of blue. In some of the photos he was holding an expensive looking SLR camera with an improbably large lens; proudly displaying the tools of his trade. George moved the photos to one side and then picked up the top sheet and started to read.

James Andanson, real name Jean-Paul Gonin, was one of the world's top paparazzi who had made a career out of travelling around

Europe taking pictures of celebrities, royalty, and the rich and famous. He had also amassed a million-pound fortune, on one occasion making £100,000 pounds from a single photo of Prince Charles kissing Tiggy Legge-Bourke, the former nanny to William and Harry, in Klosters, the exclusive Swiss ski resort. Andanson had taken pictures of Princess Diana throughout the summer of 1997 and a French Special Branch operation unconnected to her death discovered that on 24 August he had actually spent the day on board the Jonikal with Dodi and Diana, having reached a deal with Diana in St Tropez to take photos of her in a high-cut swimsuit.

Andanson was also a photographer with political connections at the highest level and was rumoured to have links with several intelligence agencies, including the French DST and MI6. Two weeks after the crash, the Criminal Brigade finally admitted that the traces of white paint in scratches found on the Mercedes S280 indicated that a slight collision had taken place in the mouth of the Alma Tunnel. The trace of colour on the front right wing and on the right wing mirror of the Mercedes both originated from the same vehicle; a white Fiat Uno built in Italy between 1983 and 1987. Judge Stephan reported that the driver of the Fiat could not be identified, despite long and detailed investigations made by the enquiry team. This contradicted the statement of Commander Mules who said that his men didn't even search the whole of Paris for the mystery Uno, let alone the whole of France. In 1998, ex-Scotland Yard detective chief superintendent John McNamara, who headed up an investigation on behalf of Mohammed Al Fayed, succeeded in doing what the Criminal Brigade had failed to do. The white Fiat Uno had been sold to a dealer in October 1997, approximately six weeks after the fatal crash, having undergone bodywork repairs on the side and rear light, and having been repainted.

The owner of the car at the time of the crash was James Andanson.

Confidential forensic analysis contained in Judge Stephan's report places Andanson squarely at the centre of events in the Alma Tunnel. One such report states, "They indicate that paintwork and plastics from *a white Fiat Uno, owned by James Andanson, match exactly evidence recovered from Diana's Mercedes, which clipped a Fiat Uno before crashing. The computer analysis of the infrared spectra characterising the vehicle's original paint, Bianco 210, and the trace on the side-view mirror of the Mercedes, shows their absorption bands are identical."*

Andanson himself told the police that he was nowhere near Paris on 31 August, producing a petrol receipt and a motorway toll ticket to prove that he had driven from his home in central France at 3.45 am for a flight to Corsica from Orly airport. They were both receipts which could have been obtained by someone else. In contrast, Andanson's son, James, told police that his father was grape-harvesting in Bordeaux and had telephoned home that morning at 4.30 am, whereas Andanson's wife, Elizabeth, had claimed that her husband was at home that night and had left at 4.00 am the following morning. Andanson had subsequently boasted to close friends that he had been in the tunnel when the Mercedes crashed but French police had declined to follow this up, maintaining that in any event, the Fiat Uno played no more than a passive part in the tragedy.

'Wow, that's some connection,' said George, putting the paper down. 'Where is he now?'

'Dead,' replied Albert. 'Three years after the accident his body was found in the burned-out wreckage of a car parked in remote woodland, near Nant.

'You're joking?'

'Not at all. The car, a black BMW, was locked but there was no sign of the key, either inside the vehicle or outside. Andanson's charred body was in the driver's seat but his head was detached and was resting between the front seats. There was also a hole in his left temple which according to Christophe Pelat, one of the local fireman called to the scene, looked like a bullet hole. Even the location was suspicious. The car had travelled two miles up a pot-holed track, across empty countryside, bumped a further mile uphill across cow pastures, and then forced its way through dense forest to a clearing that few locals even knew existed.'

'That's incredible.'

'I know. What's even more incredible is the verdict of the inquest which concluded that Andanson committed suicide, despite the fact that he was hundreds of miles from where he should have been and that there was no suicide note. The French pathologist decided that the hole in his skull had been caused by the intense heat of the fire, rather than by a bullet wound.'

'Another cover-up by the French authorities?'

'Absolutely. And in June 2000, a month after his death, there was an armed robbery at the SIPA photo agency which is where Andanson worked. Three armed men, wearing ski-masks and balaclavas shot a security guard in the foot and held dozens of employees hostage for several hours while they ransacked the place. Despite phone calls from staff to the police, the Paris gendarmerie failed to respond, convincing everyone that the raiders themselves were members of the French security service. They stole nothing of real value but dismantled all the security equipment and then removed cameras, laptop computers and computer hard drives, which is where Andanson's royal pictures were stored.'

'That's unbelievable,' said George. 'Surely all of that is enough to prove that Diana's death was a conspiracy.'

'Unfortunately not,' replied Vinny, walking back into the room. 'Enough for us to run a story on it but not enough to prove anything.'

'The *Daily Express* have been running stories on it for years,' said Albert, 'long after the rest of us gave up. But they've never been able to prove anything either. And not being able to identify the two guys on the motorcycle hasn't helped.'

'Could they have been paparazzi?' suggested George, wondering whether the guy on the back of the bike was just taking photos with a particularly strong flash.

Albert shook his head. 'All the paparazzi were well known to the police and the whereabouts of all of them were accounted for within hours after the crash...'

'All except Andanson,' interrupted Vinny.

'Absolutely,' replied Albert, acknowledging the correction. 'This is the guy who spent his whole career following Princess Diana around Europe yet claimed not to be in Paris on what was going to be one of the most important days of her life – her engagement to Dodi Al Fayed. Anyway, twenty years on, everyone else connected to the incident that night has been identified. The two on the motorbike are the only exception. Plus the guy riding pillion was using a military grade flashlight. Whoever they were, they weren't journalists.'

'So where does that leave us?' asked George, picking up the newspaper and staring at the crossword again. They still hadn't discovered anything that explained the last few words that they were looking for.

'It leaves us with a simple choice,' replied Albert. 'Either you believe the official verdict that it was a tragic accident caused by a drunken driver who was driving too fast, and that everything else is just coincidence; or you believe that she was murdered and that everything since has been an elaborate cover up.'

'I think she was murdered,' said George emphatically. The last couple of hours going through Albert's old files had totally convinced him. The evidence, albeit circumstantial, was overwhelming.

'So do I,' added Vinny with equal conviction, although in truth he would have opted for that version of events anyway. A conspiracy story was far better for circulation figures than a genuine accident. No one was really interested in reading about that.

'Good,' replied Albert. 'Then the only other thing we need to agree on, is why?'

'Which presumably,' said Vinny with a glint in his eye, 'brings us to the Royal Family?'

Albert nodded. That was exactly where it brought them. There were a couple of other conspiracy theories of course but none that had anything like the same traction or popularity with Fleet Street. They had already discussed the fact that Diana had become an embarrassment and that her proposed engagement to Dodi Fayed was the final straw. The prospect of her marrying into the Al Fayed family was bad enough but the thought of her actually converting to Islam was unthinkable, as was the possibility of her being pregnant and producing a Muslim half-brother or half-sister to the future King of England. The decision to partially embalm her body within hours of the crash had been taken by Prince Charles's office at St James's Palace, despite the fact that he was no longer the next of kin, and passed onto the French authorities by Sir Michael Jay, the British Ambassador in Paris. Plus of course, following his divorce from Diana, Charles desperately wanted to remarry. In the eyes of the church, the only way that he could legitimately do that and still be King was if he became a widower. All the time that Diana was still alive, any plans to marry Camilla Parker Bowles were just wishful thinking. And Diana herself lived in constant fear of assassination, believing that she was under continual surveillance and that Charles was plotting to murder her. In October 1996, less than a year before her death, she wrote; *"This particular phase in my life is the most dangerous. My husband is planning an accident in my car…brakes failure and serious head injury, in order to make the path clear for him to marry"*. There was no doubt in Albert's mind that all roads led back to St James's Palace. If not to Prince Charles personally, then at least to the Royal household.

'I still don't see how that really helps us though,' persisted George, still holding the crossword and waving it in his right hand. 'We might have a better understanding of why she was killed but it doesn't explain how any of that is connected to the events of the last week, or what's just happened in Francorelli's. Nor does it help us with the words in here which we still don't understand.'

'What are the words again?' asked Vinny.

'BUCHANAN, CARLISLE, ROSS and VECTOR,' replied George, quickly scanning the crossword. 'And we're still not sure what ARTEMIS means.'

Albert nodded again. George was right. They all had a better understanding of what happened twenty years ago but they still weren't any closer to what was going on now. 'And there's not much else in the file,' he said, shuffling through the pile of papers again, 'so I think we've reached a dead end.'

The three of them stared at each other in silence for a moment, not sure what to say or do next. Then suddenly Vinny stood up and walked out of the room, leaving Albert and George with the departing instruction, 'Wait here, I'll be back in a minute.' True to his word, he was back in less than sixty seconds, clutching the piece of notepaper that Hayley had given him earlier with the London telephone number that he had called previously, plus the names DAMPIER and CRAVEN added in his own handwriting.

'Time for some good old-fashioned British journalism,' said Vinny, picking up the telephone in the corner of the room. 'We might not know what's going on but they don't know that, do they?'

'Who's "they"?' asked George, not sure what Vinny was going to do next.'

'I don't know,' replied Vinny, starting to punch the telephone number into the keypad, 'but whoever they are, I think they're on the other end of this phone.'

Less than a mile across London the telephone rang unanswered. Maurice stopped and looked at it, unsure whether to pick it up or not. He was just on the point of going home and the last thing he needed was to be held up on a Friday night. Jean had already left and Buchanan had been out all afternoon, so he was practically the last person to leave. He turned towards the door as if he was going to ignore it and then looked back at Jean's desk again, the phone still ringing, the methodical, repetitive sound somehow conveying that it was something important and urgent. Suddenly he turned back and picked it up.

'Hello?'

'Who am I speaking to?' asked Vinny at the other end.

'Who are you after?' replied Maurice, remembering Vector's protocols about answering the phone. He hadn't worked with Jean for all those years for nothing.

'Anyone that can help me,' said Vinny with more confidence this time. 'How about Mr. Craven. Is he around?'

Maurice flinched. How on earth did anyone connect this number to Craven? He hadn't worked at Vector for years.

'Or Buchanan maybe?' continued Vinny, trying his luck and picking one of the names from the crossword at random. Besides he knew where Craven was. Still at Francorelli's probably, still trying to get the fat Russian to talk.

'Perhaps I can help?' asked Maurice, trying to be as non-committal as possible.

'Maybe. And you are?'

'Greaves,' said Maurice, picking the first name that came into his head. Ever the Jewish, North London football supporter.

'Right Mr Greaves,' said Vinny, getting all authoritative and puffing his chest out. 'My name is Goldman and I'm the editor of the *Chronicle*. I'm ringing to inform you that tomorrow we are going to run a special edition with a six page exclusive on the assassination of Princess Diana. A full exposé revealing how she was murdered by MI6 on the instructions of the Royal Family and revealing for the first time new facts relating to Artemis, Vector, Carlisle and Ross...'

Maurice flinched again at the other end of the phone. He knew that those were just names from the crossword but hearing them repeated by somebody else was still unnerving. And had *The Chronicle* really worked out how and why Diana was killed or was the guy on the other end of the phone simply bluffing?

'...so if you want to make a statement or give your side of the story, you need to contact me by 10.00 pm. Otherwise we put it to bed. Clear?'

'Crystal,' said Maurice, just before Vinny put the phone down with a slam.

'So, what do we do now?' asked George, not sure whether Vinny's threat was serious or not.

'We write up the story,' replied Vinny with a grim look on his face, 'and then we wait...'

Thirty-Eight

CRAVEN STOOD OUTSIDE ARGENTO BANK IN COLEBROOK Street and looked up at the building, wondering whether it was still open. Normal banking hours had closed several hours ago but Argento was no normal bank, despite the appearance of its traditional, granite-stone premises located deep in the heart of London's square mile. In fact it was a relatively new enterprise, recently established in response to a decision taken by the major UK banks to withdraw from safe deposit services. The four major clearing banks had stopped offering the facility to new customers and all of them were now in the process of gradually phasing out services to existing customers, other than to high-net-worth private clients. None of the other retail banks of any size provided safe custody storage so it was inevitable that a number of new businesses would emerge, started by opportunist investors who saw a gap in the market for a different model. The outside of the building might have looked like a typical, old-fashioned institution but inside it was anything but, the latest developments in biometric technology, digital CCTV recording and encrypted access cards ensuring that security was of the highest order.

Craven walked up the steps and peered through the large, double-fronted glass doors. Unlike the outside of the building the interior was exactly the opposite, the reception a blend of modern, contemporary styles, everything designed in clean, minimalist lines. He tried pushing the door but it was locked. Unsurprising really, given that it was nearly six-thirty on a Friday evening. To one side, fixed onto one of the stone columns was an intercom; a polished, metallic grill for communicating plus a small keypad of assorted numbers and symbols. He pressed one of the buttons and then stared up at the CCTV camera above his head, wondering who or what was at the other end. It could have been anything from a lone security guard occasionally glancing at a single monitor, to a dedicated, high-tech security centre, located off-site and fully equipped with the latest surveillance technology. The latter probably but there was no way of telling. Nothing happened for a few seconds so he pressed the button again, half expecting to get a curt response from somewhere deep inside the building, or even no response at all. As he stood there, wondering whether anyone was going to answer, the door suddenly went "clunk", the tell-tale sign that someone was unlocking it and letting him in.

He pushed the door open and stepped inside, the spotlights in the ceiling bursting into life as he walked towards the reception desk, illuminating his path like a celebrity coming on stage, or a boxer approaching the ring. As he reached the desk a door to his left swung open and a man came through, presumably the security guard although nothing like the crumpled, ex woodentop that he'd encountered yesterday in Fleet Street. This guy was completely the opposite; younger, slimmer, fitter and more importantly smart, polished and professional, totally in keeping with the aesthetics and interior design. And interestingly, he wasn't wearing a uniform. The dark, coarse fabric of a security officer would have been totally at odds with the modern, contemporary feel of the place; a throwback to a completely different time and culture. Even from a distance Craven could tell that the guy's dark blue suit was handmade, the tailor's cut oozing style and quality, as did the flash of silk lining on the inside of his jacket. No shortage of money in the City, obviously. Even the security staff looked like well-heeled bankers.

'Good evening sir,' said the suit, giving Craven a genuine, professional smile. 'How can I help?' The accent was unequivocally British and distinctly cut-glass, much like Buchanan's.

'I wasn't sure whether you were open,' replied Craven, unsure about where to start.

'We're open from 8.00 am to 8.00 pm every day sir, although on prior arrangement we can provide access at any time, 24/7.'

'That's very impressive,' said Craven, unable to think of anything else to say.

'Are you depositing or taking away?'

'Taking away.'

'And the account number sir?' The suit walked behind the reception and leant over the desk, tapping the keyboard to bring a computer monitor to life.

Craven put his hand in his pocket and fished out the key, the long plastic fob containing two sets of numbers; 4716 written on the bottom of the short edge which he assumed was the box number and then 16 digits written along the centre and split into four sets of four, like the numbers on a credit card. Maybe that was the account number. He handed the key over without saying anything, trying to avoid any conversation about the details. Too much risk of him getting something wrong. He was also starting to wonder whether they were going to ask him for any I.D. which was going to be problematic. Parovsky had told him that the account was registered in the name of Olsen, an ubiquitous European name of multiple origins which was obviously an alias, but none of that was of any use if they wanted to see his passport or a driving licence. If it came to that, the only I.D. that he had was the Glock 23 nestling in the left-hand side of his ribcage. That normally opened most doors.

'And the name sir?' asked the guy, looking up from the screen. Still the cut-glass accent.

'Olsen. Although unfortunately I don't seem to have any ID with me,' added Craven, deciding to get his excuses in first. 'Is that a problem?'

'Not at all Mr Olsen,' replied the suit, handing back the key with an efficient smile. 'We don't need to see any ID. The biometric access controls are 100% secure.'

'Of course,' replied Craven, pocketing the key and wondering what on earth "biometric access controls" meant.

'Would you like to access the box now sir?'

'Yes please.'

'This way then please.'

The guy stood up and lead the way down a corridor to their left, Craven following just a few steps behind. After a short distance they reached a pair of lift doors with a third door further on, which looked like access to the stairwell. The suit pressed the lift button and then waited a few moments for it to arrive and for the doors to open.

'So what happens if the biometrics fail?' asked Craven, stepping into the lift and trying to sound as if he knew what he was talking about.

The guy turned round and gave him a benevolent smile, a fine line between humouring him and condescending. 'They never fail sir. Fingerprint technology and iris recognition are 100% unique. The security is absolutely failsafe.'

'That's very reassuring,' replied Craven, his mind racing ten to the dozen as the lift started to move and he tried to work out what he was going to do next. He'd assumed Parovsky had told him everything about the bank but clearly that wasn't the case. The old fox had omitted to tell him about the security access, although not surprising really given what the repercussions would have been. Still, it wasn't too late to remedy that. He glanced at his watch. Time to make a decision. Pull out the revolver and force the guy to open the strong room or move to Plan B. The lift eventually stopped moving and then the doors parted slowly, opening onto a windowless corridor, somewhere in the basement.

'This way sir,' said the suit, holding the door with his left arm and pointing towards the right with his other.

Craven stepped out of the lift but as he did so, put his hand in his pocket and pulled out his mobile, throwing an apologetic palm to the security guard as though he had just received a call. He put the phone to his ear, pretending to speak to someone at the other end. 'Hello?'

The suit stepped away a few paces, still within earshot but a discreet distance from what he assumed was a private call.

'No, I'm in the middle of something,' said Craven, continuing the charade, then pausing to convey that there was a conversation going on. 'Are you sure it can't wait?' Another long pause. 'Okay, I'm on my way.'

He put the phone back in his pocket and then turned and looked at the security guard. 'Sorry about that but I'll have to come back. Something urgent has come up.'

'Not a problem sir,' replied the suit, seemingly unfazed by the change in plan. 'Do you want to wait for the elevator or take the stairs? It's only one flight?'

'The stairs are fine,' replied Craven, checking his watch as he turned towards the door. If the place closed at eight o'clock he had just over an hour so needed to move quickly. They climbed thirteen stairs to a 180 degree turn and then another thirteen in the opposite direction, emerging through the doorway on the ground floor corridor.

'Much quicker,' said Craven glancing at his watch again. 'I should be back in about an hour.'

'That's fine sir,' replied the suit, leaning over the reception desk and picking up a business card. 'Just give me a call if you get held up.'

Craven pushed the front door open and stepped across the threshold, just as someone else walked up the steps and caught the door before it closed, tailgating into the building in one, effortless move. Craven had never met Damien Ross and barely glanced at the guy as he said "thank you" before disappearing into the reception. Likewise, Ross had never met Craven but felt fairly sure that the person coming out was Buchanan's man. It was too much of a coincidence otherwise. Ross had been standing outside, watching the front of the building for several minutes, expecting

Craven to leave with the photos in hand and planning to jump him as soon as possible. A surprise attack as soon as he left the building; sudden, explosive and brutally effective; a split second of mayhem before disappearing into the crowd. And a much better strategy than trying to break into a bank. But now the guy was leaving empty handed. Maybe he wasn't Buchanan's man after all? Either way, if the photos were still inside, Ross needed to make his move now. Take the advantage before anyone else turned up. Both the Americans and Russians wanted him dead and getting hold of the photos was his insurance policy to staying alive. It was either that or defecting to the Brits, which wasn't an outcome he fancied at all.

Ross walked up to the reception desk and as before, the spotlights in the ceiling burst into life, tracking his path and announcing his arrival.

'Good evening sir,' said the security guard looking up from behind the desk, the manners still impeccable and the accent public school. 'How can I help?'

'I was thinking of opening an account,' replied Ross, his own accent a strange, indeterminate mix of American, French and Russian, 'and I wondered if you had any details on the facilities here?'

'All the details are on the internet sir. But we also have a brochure which you can take. It covers all the service options and prices.'

'I was thinking more about security,' continued Ross, taking the brochure but not bothering to look at it. 'Reassurance that whatever I deposit will be safe.'

'100% safe sir. Both the internet and the brochure cover those in some detail.'

'I'm sure. But is it possible to see the facility? No substitute for seeing it in person...'

The suit checked his watch, as if wondering whether he had time or not.

'...a quick look would be really helpful. Just so that I can see it for myself.'

'Of course sir,' replied the suit, suddenly making a decision and standing up. 'If you would like to follow me.'

As before he led the way down the corridor to the left, this time with Ross following a few steps behind. When they reached the lift he pressed the button and then waited a few moments for the doors to open. Once they reached the basement they turned right out of the lift and then walked a few paces down the corridor towards a heavily reinforced steel door. The suit took out a plastic security card and held it up to an electronic screen which suddenly lit up with a digital display, much like a computer keyboard. Then he tapped in a series of numbers and letters before pressing enter. Eventually, a red light in the top corner of the screen blinked amber several times and then turned green.

'It says here that security access is biometric,' said Ross, reading the inside of the brochure. 'That didn't look very biometric to me.'

'Manual override,' replied the suit, pushing the door open and revealing a large, rectangular strong room behind. 'Too many incidents of bank staff having their fingers chopped off, or losing an eyeball. Biometric access is for customers only.'

Ross raised his eyebrows as he stared at the room. That was definitely a risk that he hadn't considered. No wonder the bank staff had different security clearance. No easier way for a bunch of vicious thugs to get round biometric technology than using the body parts of the people who worked there. 'Does that mean you can open all the deposit boxes?' he asked as he took in the size and layout of the room, a security vault about twice as deep as it was wide and all three walls stacked floor to ceiling with thin metal boxes. In the middle of the room was a long, metal table, presumably for clients to put their valuables on when either depositing or taking away.

'We call them trays sir,' replied the suit. 'But no. We can access the strong room but only the customer can access their tray. That requires both a physical key and biometric security clearance. We can override the biometrics but only the client has the key.'

Outside, Craven was still on foot, the Friday night traffic still solid and moving slowly and therefore just as quick to walk. It was only a short distance from the City to St Paul's and then it was just a quick march down Ludgate Hill towards Fleet Street and then onto Francorelli's. As he cut through Leadenhall Market he passed a series of pubs and wine bars, typical City watering holes full of underwriters and brokers, a lot of them standing outside on the cobbles, pint in one hand, fag or mobile in the other. The noise was deafening, a cacophony of hundreds of people clustered in groups, the sound echoing around the market. In the background, the strains of "Life on Mars" wafted out of a doorway somewhere, triggering a fleeting memory of a distant, long hot summer, years ago. And a classic image of David Bowie gazing into camera, his most iconic feature captured in close-up. One blue eye, one brown. The image caught Craven's senses and he suddenly stopped dead. Complete Heterochromia, where each iris was a distinctly different colour, was a very rare condition. In fact in Bowie's case it wasn't Heterochromia at all, it was due to Anisocoria, a condition characterised by the unequal size of his pupils. Bowie's left eye had been famously injured in a fight with his friend, George Underwood, in the spring of 1962, a schoolboy argument over a girl who they had both hoped to go out with. An impulsive punch from Underwood had scratched Bowie's left pupil and as a result had left it permanently dilated, giving the illusion that it was brown, rather than blue. Either way, meeting someone with different coloured eyes was about as rare as seeing a nun in a bikini. And the guy that had just tailgated into Argento Bank definitely had one blue eye and one brown. Craven played the sequence back in his mind. It was only the briefest glimpse as they passed each other through the doorway but there was no doubt about it. And an earlier conversation with Buchanan was now playing like a soundtrack over the visual recall.

"Damien Ross. An ex Cowboy."

"You got any ID?"

"Nothing recent. Male, five-ten, one brown eye, one blue."

"I wasn't planning on getting that close."

Craven took out a cigarette and then flipped open the Zippo lighter, thumbing the wheel and lighting up in one swift movement. He took a long, satisfying drag of nicotine as he snapped the lid shut and then blew out the smoke, trying to work out what was going on. Ross was meant to be with Buchanan, and it was Buchanan who had asked Craven to pick up the photos. A sudden change in plan which sounded urgent. So what the hell was Ross doing there? That was a stupid question of course. There was only one reason why Ross would be at the bank and there was no way that would have been with Buchanan's consent. Craven glanced at his watch. It was going to take him half an hour to get to Francorelli's and then another half an hour to get back, which left him only about fifteen minutes to cut off Parovsky's hands and gouge out his eyeballs. Not difficult given the range of sharp implements in the kitchen but it was still going to be tight. And more importantly it would give Ross a head start of over an hour. By the time Craven got back it might be too late. If the photos disappeared again Buchanan would go apoplectic. He took another drag on the cigarette. If he turned around there was no way he could get to Parovsky and back in time but leaving Ross at the bank undisturbed wasn't an option. The only decision was whether to turn up unannounced or to ring ahead and let the suit know he was on his way. Make sure that everything was alright. He chose the latter. He took a final drag on the cigarette and then stubbed it out on the cobbles as he took out his mobile and the Argento business card. The phone rang six or seven times before it was answered.

'Argento Bank. How can I help you?'

'Hello. My name is Olsen. I was with you just now.'

'Yes Mr. Olsen. Everything okay?'

'Yes, I was just ringing to let you know that I'm on my way back. I got things sorted quicker than I thought. I should be with you in about five minutes.'

'That's fine sir. See you then.'

The security guard pressed the red button on his phone and put it back on the table. Then he clasped his hands around the back of his neck again, the exact same pose as before his mobile rang.

'What did he say?' asked Ross, still pointing the pistol at the suit's chest.

'He's on his way back.'

'Good. How long?'

'Five minutes.'

Ross smiled to himself. *Perfect.* Buchanan's man was going to turn up with the key and the security guard could override the biometrics. In ten minutes he'd have the photos and then be out of there.

Across the City Buchanan put the mobile back in his pocket but was still rooted to the spot. Something was nagging at the back of his brain. A faint, sliver of something that he couldn't put his finger on. Something that didn't make sense, or at least was making him uneasy. He stood there for a moment, trying his hardest to work out what it was but struggling to catch it, like a will-o'-the-wisp; ethereal, delicate and ghost-like, floating in and out of reach. He waited a few seconds, trying not to concentrate and just let his mind drift and flow but it was no use. There was a conversation somewhere, something that was said earlier. Something that intuitively he knew was important; a fragment of a memory which was triggering his senses but which remained frustratingly elusive. He started to walk, the urgency of getting back to the bank more important but all the time trying to recall what was bothering him. The job was already difficult enough but what appeared to be straightforward had the potential to be much more complex. And as always with Buchanan, there was a risk that some things just weren't what they appeared to be. *"Smooth runs the water where the brook is deep; and in his simple show he harbours treason."*

Thirty-Nine

'**W**OULD YOU LIKE A DRINK CHARLES? IT'S BEEN A LONG day.'

Carlisle was standing in front of an antique, walnut cabinet, the doors wide open revealing a stash of bottles of every conceivable shape and size, most of them donated by the Foreign & Commonwealth Office; unwanted gifts from visiting dignitaries.

Buchanan nodded. That much was true. It had definitely been a long day and it wasn't over yet. It was 7.00 o'clock on a Friday evening and he should have been back in Hampshire by now, looking forward to a quiet, relaxing weekend. Instead he was sitting in Carlisle's office, waiting to give the Cabinet Secretary a debrief on the latest events and hoping to put Artemis to bed before lights out.

'What do you fancy?' asked Carlisle, stooping down to peer at the array of bottles, twisting a few around so that he could read the labels.

Buchanan relaxed as he eased back into the leather armchair. He didn't normally drink during office hours but technically the week was already over and besides, a stiff drink was definitely in order after yet another exchange with Christine Michaels. 'What have you got?'

'Oh, pretty much everything. Ouzo from Greece, Aquavit from Norway, Arguardiente from Colombia, Brennivin from Iceland...'

'Have you got any Gin?'

'Of course. Gin and tonic?'

'Perfect.'

Carlisle smiled to himself as he dropped two lumps of ice into a large tumbler, the unmistakeable sound of frozen cubes clinking on cut glass. You could never accuse Buchanan of being over-adventurous. Then he unscrewed the cap on a bottle of Bombay Sapphire and poured out a slug of gin followed by a decent measure of tonic, the effect of which starting fizzing and cracking all over the ice. 'No slice I'm afraid Charles.'

'Not a problem,' replied Buchanan, reaching up to take the glass. 'You not having one?'

'I'll stick to wine,' replied Carlisle, pouring himself a glass of red before returning to his own leather chair, the seat crumpled and worn from years of use. 'So, how is Christine Michaels?'

'Infuriating.'

'I meant other than that.'

Buchanan took a sip of gin and tonic, the blend of botanicals balanced perfectly with the mixer. The perfect way to start a weekend. 'She's very exercised about identifying their mole.'

'I'm not surprised.'

'Someone by the name of Janus apparently. Ross has a phone number but says he hasn't used it.'

'Says?'

Buchanan shrugged. 'It's hard to tell with Ross. He was always difficult to read and he's been living in secret for years.'

'Speaking of which, where is he?'

'Not sure. Our cousins turned up and spooked him. He could be anywhere at the moment.'

'And Artemis?'

'All under control. The Russian cell has been neutralised. There are some photos that we need to get hold of. Craven is picking them up now.'

Carlisle took a large gulp of finest claret and sank back into the chair, slowly rotating his palm so that the wine swirled and aerated in the glass. Then he held it up to the light, gently turning the contents to see the colour. 'And when you get the photos, what then?

Buchanan shrugged again. 'We either put them under lock and key again, or else we'll destroy them.'

'And have you seen them?'

'No.'

'But you know what's on them.'

'More or less.'

'Go on.'

'A picture of me, Ross, Henri Paul and James Andanson sitting in a restaurant together, a few hours before the crash.'

Carlisle took another large mouthful of wine and then smiled to himself. 'Good. Perfect.'

Buchanan stared at him in disbelief. *Perfect?* What the hell was he talking about? Artemis had been a plot carefully constructed over twenty years ago, the subsequent misdirection and charade meticulously maintained until this day. He'd spent half his working life refuting conspiracy theories about MI6 and the Royal Family, the very process of denial having the required, opposite effect, most of the sceptics and indeed some of the neutrals choosing to believe that there was no smoke without fire. The incompetence of the French emergency services was a bonus of course and not entirely unexpected but nevertheless, a helpful addition to a sequence of events which had otherwise been stage-managed from start to finish. The false claims about Henri Paul being drunk, the deliberate destruction of his blood samples, the 1.5 million French francs paid into his bank account – all actions designed to build a suspicious but credible backstory. But it was the decision to embalm the body and the request for MI6 to provide surveillance outside The Ritz which was really inspired.

He took another sip of gin and tonic and reflected on the absurdity of it all. The Royal Family were many things but suggesting that they were murderers, complicit in the cold-blooded assassination of a member of their own family and mother to the heir of the throne was just ridiculous. Particularly if the reason was their supposed opposition to her marrying a

Muslim. Diana had only two years earlier explored the possibility of marrying Hasnat Khan, a Muslim heart surgeon, and the Royal Family had expressed no opposition to that, in fact Prince Charles had given the proposed union his express blessing. But as usual the gullibility of the media was breath-taking, the spin and counter-spin being swallowed hook, line and sinker. Still, if the objective was to persuade some people that Diana had been killed by the British establishment and to convince the rest of the world that the explanation was so ludicrous that the accident must have been an unfortunate but genuine tragedy, then the carefully constructed conspiracy theory had done its job. Everyone taking a polarised position on whether it was true or not and no one bothering to look for a third, alternative truth. And then, just as the story was starting to wane, the pièce de résistance; the decision to assassinate James Andanson, a crime scene so contrived that it was almost laughable. Ross had excelled himself that day. The remote location, the locked, burned out car, the headless victim, the bullet through the skull; all deliberately created to telegraph that this was a contract killing by the security services, reinforcing the fact that it was part of a much bigger conspiracy. And therefore no one bothering to search for the real truth – that Diana had been murdered by the CIA; a joint mission with the Israeli intelligence service which had nothing to do with the Royal Family or MI6. The Americans orchestrating everything from Avenue Gabriel and the two Mossad agents on the motorbike with the powerful hand-held flashlight. An operation so clandestine that neither the JIC nor the UK security services knew anything about it, Vector's involvement being limited to Buchanan, a couple of his Landscapers and to Sir James Carlisle.

'There's been a development.'

Buchanan shook himself out of his train of thought. 'Development?'

'Change of plan. Our cousins are becoming something of a problem.'

Buchanan smiled to himself. That was nothing new. 'Which means what exactly?'

Carlisle took another large gulp of wine, using the pause to choose his words carefully. 'They're being somewhat inflexible over recent events. No desire to share the spoils, which of course contravenes the established protocol. "Strike oil in third world country, US Corporation moves in and extracts black gold, third world country gets a percentage of the deal." That's how it's meant to work. Everybody gets a cut, everybody's happy.'

'But not in this case?'

Carlisle shook his head. 'Our cousins maintain that the Arctic seabed is free, unclaimed territory, not owned by anyone. They want 100% of whatever they find...'

Buchanan tipped his head back and emptied his glass. He could see where this was heading.

'...and if they're not willing to negotiate, the risk of military conflict is suddenly very real.'

'And nuclear?'

'Almost certainly. Putin won't take it lying down, the prize is game changing. The world needs the Americans to come to the table. But without the photos, the Russians don't have any leverage.'

Buchanan frowned. He understood the logic of what Carlisle was saying but surely he wasn't suggesting that they hand the photos over to the Russians? They'd just spent last week trying to do exactly the opposite. And besides, there was the "special relationship" to consider. If the Americans were about to become an even greater superpower then all the more important to demonstrate which side you were on and to strengthen the alliance. Giving the photos back to the FSB would be political and economic suicide.

'Obviously we can't just hand them over,' continued Carlisle as if reading Buchanan's mind, 'but maybe there's another solution. I haven't worked it out yet but either way, we need to make sure that they stay in one piece. I don't want any risk of them being destroyed.'

'I'd better ring Craven,' replied Buchanan, 'just to make sure.' He took out his phone, just at the same time that across the other side of London, Craven switched off his mobile and put in his pocket. The last thing he wanted was it going off and announcing his arrival. Then he pressed the button on the intercom and waited for someone to answer. *"Though those that are betray'd do feel the treason sharply, yet the traitor stands in worse case of woe."*

Forty

OWNSTAIRS IN THE BASEMENT A SHORT, LOUD, ALARM
sounded, three times in succession, making them both jump.

'What's that?' asked Ross, still holding the pistol and pointing it firmly in the suit's direction.

'It's the front door. Someone pressing the intercom.'

Ross smiled to himself. *Good. Best let them in then.* 'Tell him to come down here.'

The suit nodded and then walked across the strong room to a videophone which was fixed to the far wall, about head height just inside the door. He picked up the handset and pressed a button which illuminated a small screen, showing a blurred, grainy picture of the front steps and Craven waiting patiently to be let in.

'It's Mr Olsen again,' said Craven, leaning into the intercom and speaking into the metal grill.

'I'm just in the basement with another customer,' replied the security guard, pressing another button to unlock the front door. 'If you come downstairs to where we were before, I'll meet you there.' As he pressed the button the alarm went off again, this time a longer, continuous sound indicating that the front door had been opened. Then he put the handset down and walked back to the centre of the room. Ross watched him like a hawk. Ideally he would have dealt with the suit there and then. Reduce the risk of him getting in the way once Buchanan's man turned up, or even worse, trying some foolhardy, public spirited heroics. Much better to resolve things now but unfortunately he still needed him alive for the moment, not least to override the biometrics.

Craven pushed the door open and stepped inside, standing still for a few moments as he familiarised himself with the reception again, trying to work out exactly where the security guard and Ross were waiting. The suit said that they were downstairs but Craven wasn't going to take anything for granted, particularly with someone like Ross around. But wherever they were, they clearly weren't on the ground floor. The reception was empty and absolutely silent, except for the low hum of air conditioning. He walked past the reception desk and when he reached the lift pressed the button and waited for it to arrive. He could hear the winding gear whirring into action and the lift slowly coming up from the floor below, confirmation that they were probably downstairs, exactly where the suit said they were. Then he took out his pistol and stepped to one side, just in case someone was coming up from the basement. Eventually the lift arrived and the doors opened. Craven held his breath, his back pressed into the wall and the Glock pointed towards the open lift doors. He waited several seconds but nothing happened, just long enough to be sure that there was no one there. Then he stepped into the lift, pressed the button for the basement and then stepped out again, just before the doors closed. As the lift started to descend he stuffed the pistol back into its holster and pushed open the door which led to the stairwell. Twenty-six stairs from top to bottom. Thirteen straight down to a 180 degree turn and then another thirteen to the bottom. A matter of seconds if he moved quickly. The lift was slow which meant he'd get there before it arrived but he needed to be quiet. Fast but silent…

Down in the basement Ross had a problem. Craven was about to turn up and he also had the suit to keep an eye on. Too much to cover in one go. Which meant that he had to disable the security guard, or least put him somewhere safe for a moment. And given they were standing in the middle of a bank security vault there was an obvious solution to that. Take the guy's security pass and lock him inside, safe and sound out of harm's way until he'd dealt with Buchanan's henchman. 'Give me your card,' he said, nodding towards the plastic holder hanging around the suit's neck.

The security guard duly lifted the lanyard over his head and handed it over, the blue and grey nylon ribbon advertising Argento's branded colours.

'What's the code to the door?' asked Ross, still pointing the SIG Sauer with intent.

'I'll write it down,' replied the suit, 'you'd never remember it.'

Ross watched him take out a small notepad and write down a series of numbers and letters. It suddenly occurred to him that the guy could write anything down as the security code. He had no way of knowing whether he was telling the truth or not. And once he'd locked the suit inside he had no way of getting back in – not without the right password.

'Here you are.' The suit leant forward and offered Ross the piece of paper.

'This had better be correct.'

'It's correct.'

'It'd better be. Otherwise you're dead.'

'It's correct,' repeated the suit. 'You can try it if you like.'

Ross looked at him and decided that he was telling the truth. Besides he didn't have time to check it out. Buchanan's thug would be there in any second. He walked out of the strong room and closed the door behind him, the lock activating automatically. Then he moved towards the lift, the sound indicating that it was only a matter of seconds before it arrived. He stopped short of the lift doors and like Craven had done only moments earlier, pressed his back into the wall and held his breath, his pistol held in both hands and pointing towards the lift doors. A moment later the lift turned up and the doors started to open, just as Ross realised that he had his back to the stairwell door and sensed something behind him. The faintest blur of something moving on the very edge of his peripheral vision, almost as if he had eyes in the back of his head. Something he hadn't accounted for which was a basic, tactical error and which was now a major problem. He spun around, the pistol tracking the exact, same arc but only for a split second before Craven knocked it out of his hands, a perfectly aimed kick sending it spinning through the air and clattering down the corridor.

Craven knew that surprise was his greatest advantage so in the same instant followed through with a flurry of punches, unleashing as much energy and momentum as he could. Maximum impact in the first few seconds. The first couple smacked Ross on either side of his head but he ducked the third, a burst of adrenalin suddenly surging through his body. He swung his left fist into Craven's ribcage followed by a right and then another left into the stomach, the impact of which knocked him backwards for a second. Ross sensed his moment and stamped down hard on Craven's ankle, hoping to break it with a single, massive, pile-driving stomp. Except Craven saw it coming. Despite being winded and a temporary loss of balance he somehow managed to move his foot at the last second. Ross's leg, knee and ankle slammed into the hard, tiled floor with the whole of his bodyweight behind it and immediately a sharp, jolting pain jarred up and down his right side. He froze momentarily as his leg went numb and started to tingle. It was only a millisecond but Craven spotted his chance and smacked him hard on the side of his jaw followed by a fierce uppercut to the underside of his chin. The perfect boxing combination. Ross stumbled slightly, his head spinning and his vision suddenly blurred. He tried to throw a punch but his arm flailed into fresh air, just as Craven kicked him hard between the legs; a huge, ferocious kick which thundered into his bollocks and practically lifted him off the floor, the pain searing through his stomach and up into his neck and down again. He gasped and dropped onto one knee, the pain literally taking his breath away and disabling him. Craven swung his boot again and kicked him hard in exactly the same place, the impact even more excruciating than before. Then he kicked him a couple more times, the first in between his ribs and then finally into the side of his head. Size ten steel toe caps crunching into human bone. *Just like the kid on the pavement. No Geneva Convention.* Ross let out an agonising howl as he slumped onto the floor, his body curled up into a ball and barely conscious.

Craven looked at him for a moment and then walked down the corridor and picked up the pistol which he stuffed into the small of his back, the SIG Sauer nestled into position by his trouser belt. Then he walked back to Ross, removed the security pass from around his neck and dragged him by the collar to the door of the bank vault. He held the plastic card up to the electronic reader which as before burst into life, displaying a QWERTY keyboard. Then he looked down at Ross again. 'What's the password?'

Ross stayed motionless on the floor, his body silent other than for some heavy, laboured breathing and a low, pitiful groan. Craven thought about kicking him again but then thought better of it. He needed to wake him up, not make him fully unconscious. He took out his own pistol and then knelt down and pushed it into Ross's mouth. Then he repeated the question, this time with much more threat and menace in his voice. Ross mumbled something incoherent and Craven bent in closer, jabbing the end of the Glock further down his throat as he asked him again, almost to the point of making him choke. Ross muttered something else and then gestured towards his pocket. Eventually Craven found the piece of paper and within seconds had tapped in the security code and opened the door. Again, he pulled Ross by the collar, dragging him into the strong room before propping him up against the wall, just inside the door.

The suit looked at him and then nodded towards Ross's crumpled body. 'Thank God for that. I thought he was going to kill me.'

'He probably would have done,' replied Craven, walking over to the suit and handing him the Glock. 'Cover him with this and if he tries anything, shoot him.'

The suit raised his eyebrows and pointed the pistol straight at Ross, holding it firmly in both hands. Craven meanwhile moved over to the safety deposit boxes and starting looking for number

4716, which given they were numbered in sequence took him no time at all. He used the combination of the security pass and the long, silver key to quickly unlock it and then pulled out the metal tray to check its contents. Inside was a plain, brown A4 envelope which was sealed. No address, no other markings. Craven resisted the temptation to open it and put it on the table for a moment while he put the tray back in its slot.

'Actually, you can leave that,' said the suit. 'Just go and stand over there, next to Ross.'

Craven turned around and stared at him, a look of complete surprise on his face. Not because of what the suit had just said but because the voice had completely changed. The perfect, refined, cut-glass accent had suddenly disappeared and had now been now replaced by something completely different; a pure, 100% American drawl, all baseball, apple pie and Kentucky bourbon. Craven had never met Tom Draper before. In fact, he had never even heard of him. Neither had Ross for that matter but as he started to regain consciousness he heard the suit talking and started to put two and two together.

'What happened to your accent?' asked Craven, his eyes fixated on his own pistol pointing directly back at him.

'There's nothing wrong with my accent,' replied Draper with a smirk. After several hours it was good to speak in his own voice again. His English accent was convincing of course, perfected after years of listening to Charles Buchanan, hanging onto every word and every syllable, week after week, copying and then practising every inflection and intonation until he had mastered it completely, until he sounded like Buchanan himself. But it was hard work. Much easier to slip back into his natural, American tone.

'So what happens next?' asked Craven, pretty sure that he knew what the answer was going to be.

'I'm taking the photos,' said Draper, picking up the envelope and waving the Glock from right to left several times. 'Like I said, move over there, next to Ross.'

Craven put his hands up, indicating that he wasn't going to argue and then walked back to where Ross was still sitting on the floor, propped up against the wall. Draper tracked him with the pistol as he crossed the room, not noticing that Ross had taken out his mobile and had pressed one of the buttons to call a pre-programmed number. A second later, the phone in Draper's pocket stated to ring. He stopped momentarily, wondering whether to answer it and then noticed that Ross was holding up his own phone, indicating that it was him who was calling.

'Very clever,' said Draper with a sneer.

'So what does Janus stand for?' asked Ross. 'J for Judas and anus for arsehole?'

Draper smiled but said nothing. Breaking into the bank to get the photos seemed like a daunting task several hours ago. First he had to despatch the real security guard and then he had to rely on someone turning up with the key. A mission far from guaranteed but definitely worth it if he could get the photos back. But Ross turning up was the real, unexpected bonus. Something he hadn't thought possible at all. Now suddenly here was an opportunity for him to deal with Ross himself, the very reason he had given Buchanan the memory stick in the first place, confident that once the Brits knew that Ross was still alive they would also want him out of the way. A piece of extra insurance, just in case Limonov didn't manage to kill him. Draper wasn't exactly sure what had gone wrong but it didn't matter now, Ross was seated in front of him, wounded and broken, like a sitting duck. And suddenly there was still a chance that he could get away without his cover being blown.

He raised the Glock and fired three times, not quite at point blank range but close enough not to miss. Ross's body jerked violently as the pistol fired and recoiled with each shot but a second later he looked down at his chest and realised that there wasn't any blood. Draper stared at him in confusion and then looked at the Glock, trying to work out what was going on. Craven watched him drop it to the ground and then move his hand inside his jacket to grab his own pistol. In the same moment Craven pulled out Ross's pistol, the SIG Sauer which was still nestled in the small of his back and fired four times in succession, two to the chest, one to the head and one more to the chest again, all four shots hitting Draper before his hand had even touched his own pistol grip. The force of the bullets forced Draper backwards and then he hit the floor with a crashing thump, dead on impact. Craven however wasn't taking any chances. He walked over to the body, stuck the pistol into the roof of the mouth and then pulled the trigger. Draper's skull exploded into hundreds of pieces as the contents splattered across the white, tiled floor, like a freshly painted Jackson Pollock.

'What the hell just happened?' asked Ross, still checking his body for entry wounds and trying to work out how he was still alive.

'Blanks,' replied Craven, pulling a handful of 0.40 calibre bullets from his pocket and showing Ross the live ammunition. 'I swapped them before I came in.'

'Jesus, I thought I was dead.'

'You would have been.'

'Thanks. What happens now?'

Craven shrugged. 'I'm taking the photos. What you do is up to you. Do you still want to come in?'

Ross shook his head. 'Not really. Would you, if the situation was the other way around?'

Craven likewise shook his head. He couldn't think of anything worse. No matter how bad things got he could never imagine turning to the Yanks for help. He'd much rather take his chances on his own. He and Ross were pretty much alike really. Except Ross had a problem. He was in no condition to survive on the run. He could barely stand up, let alone walk. And he had probably run out of friends and money by now. 'You should think about going home,' suggested Craven. 'You've just killed a double agent, an American traitor. You'll be a hero. The prodigal son returning to a hero's welcome.'

'I'm not a hero,' replied Ross, trying to stand up for the first time. 'And I haven't killed anyone.'

'That's not the way it's going to look,' said Craven offering him the grip of the SIG Sauer. 'Your pistol, your kill. I'm happy to tell it that way if it helps.'

Ross stuffed the pistol back in his holster. He knew the magazine still contained three rounds of ammunition but Craven had saved his life and he wasn't about to try and turn the tables now. Besides, Craven was also trying to save his career, not that he had much of it left. But going home made a lot of sense. And suddenly it was something that he wanted to do more than anything else. 'How did you know he was Janus?' he asked, looking across at Draper's body.

'I didn't,' replied Craven. 'It was something he said when I was here earlier. He asked me whether I wanted to use the stairs or wait for the elevator. It didn't make sense. We don't use the word "elevator" over here. Not with a cut-glass accent anyway.'

'That was lucky.'

'Coincidence. Someone else made the same mistake earlier this week.'

'Serendipity then.'

Craven smiled to himself. *Yes, something like that....*

Forty-One

MONDAY MORNING WAS BRIGHT AND SUNNY, THE intense heat of the previous week having finally broken and the weather returned to normal; a typical English summer of soft blue skies, white fluffy clouds and a warm, light breeze. Vinny had been to Whitehall before of course but never to the Cabinet Office and certainly not to the office of the Cabinet Secretary himself. George and Albert had likewise never been to the Cabinet Office and the fact that they were there at the specific invitation of Sir James Carlisle made the visit all the more remarkable. The three of them waited expectantly in the outer office, George somewhat apprehensive about meeting someone so important, Vinny mostly suspicious about why they'd been invited in the first place and Albert simply interested to be there and enjoying the experience. Whilst George and Vinny sat on the sofa, nervously straightening their ties or periodically checking their watches he browsed around the office, staring at the expensive looking oil paintings or admiring the antique furniture and objets d'art, occasionally picking up a smaller piece to take a closer look.

Joyce Wilson, Carlisle's long suffering PA, gave George and Vinny a sympathetic smile, trying to convey that they shouldn't have to wait much longer. Then she gazed across at Albert, his casual, slightly maverick demeanour ensuring that she kept an eye on what he was doing. Vinny meanwhile glanced at his watch for the umpteenth time. Their appointment was meant to be at 10.00 am and it was already ten past. He was just on the point of asking what the problem was when the phone on Joyce Wilson's desk started to ring. She picked it up, listened for a couple of seconds and then put the handset down.

'Sir James will see you now,' she announced, standing up to lead the way and ushering them into Carlisle's office, each of them shaking hands with him before being introduced to the only other person in the room.

'And this is my colleague, Charles Buchanan,' said Carlisle, not offering any explanation as to who he was or why he was there. George and Albert exchanged a knowing look. They were both familiar enough with the crossword to recognise Buchanan's surname and the lack of any further information made his presence seem all the more significant.

'Please, take a seat,' offered Carlisle, pointing towards three leather chairs, all positioned on the other side of his desk. The three of them sat down, Vinny opting to take the middle chair as it seemed to imply some sort of seniority while George and Albert sat on his right and left respectively, George more than happy to have the extra leg room. Carlisle eased himself into his own desk chair and Buchanan sat behind him to one side, like an independent observer, slightly detached from the main proceedings.

'For the avoidance of doubt,' continued Carlisle, 'this conversation is off the record. Understood?'

Vinny nodded and George and Albert both mumbled their agreement. None of them were expecting anything else.

'In fact, this meeting never took place. That will be in all of our interests, as will become clear to you shortly.'

Again, George and Albert exchanged a knowing glance while Vinny continued staring at Carlisle, determined not to be intimidated or railroaded by the Cabinet Secretary. The journalistic profession was hardly renowned for having a strong moral code but the independence and freedom of the press was its most precious and fundamental principle and one which Vinny wasn't prepared to compromise at any price.

'I understand you've been chasing a story in relation to the death of Princess Diana,' said Carlisle, moving his gaze to look at each of them in turn.

Vinny shrugged, readily adopting the role of spokesman. 'We're journalists. It's what we do.'

Carlisle gave him a condescending smile. 'Of course. I wasn't questioning your motives. And I didn't invite you here to have an argument.'

'So why did you invite us?' asked George, speaking for the first time.

'Because I have a proposition for you,' replied Carlisle, relaxing back into his chair. 'We want to make you an offer.'

'An offer we can't refuse, presumably?' said Vinny, unable to hide the sarcasm in his voice.

'Yes, something like that.'

Vinny looked at George and Albert for confirmation and then shrugged again. 'Okay. I guess there's no harm in listening to what you've got to say.'

Carlisle raised his eyebrows and then smiled ruefully to himself. 'I only wish that was true.'

'Which means what, exactly?' asked Vinny, narrowing his eyes as he looked at Carlisle with suspicion. He didn't have time for all this cat and mouse stuff and people playing games. It was all political bollocks as far as Vinny was concerned. He was a straightforward, no-nonsense, working class bloke who liked people to say exactly what they meant. A spade was always a spade in Vinny's world.

Carlisle glanced around at Buchanan, double-checking that he was still happy to proceed. Buchanan said nothing but gave him a simple nod in return, his face expressionless, like a poker player holding a royal flush. Or maybe no hand at all.

'The proposition,' continued Carlisle, 'is that we tell you what actually happened in Paris the night Diana was killed.'

'Why would you want to do that?' asked Vinny, becoming more and more suspicious.

'Because you want to know the truth. And unless we tell you, you're never going to find it.'

'Who says so?' replied Vinny, his response a mixture of bluff and defiance.

Carlisle said nothing but gave him a dismissive look. They hadn't got a hope in hell of finding out what really happened. He knew it and they knew it.

'And because you want something in return, presumably?' continued Vinny.

'Of course.'

'Which is what.'

'Your agreement not to publish.'

'Why on earth would we do that?' asked Albert, suddenly irritated by the conversation being directed at Vinny all the time. The Diana exclusive had always been his story. His baby. He'd spent three years of his life working on it and then the rest of his career wondering what had really happened and what he might have missed. The biggest, unsolved mystery of a generation and the one story that he'd failed to crack. The only blemish on an otherwise successful career and the one regret when he finally retired. Unfinished business. If anyone was going to agree not to publish anything, as far as Albert was concerned that ought to be him.

'Because in return for you agreeing not to publish,' replied Carlisle, 'we promise not to tell anyone that you know the truth.'

'Is that a threat?' asked Vinny, puffing out his chest and trying to exert some sort of authority.

Carlisle held his gaze for a second, using the pause to full effect. 'Absolutely. To publish would be an act of high treason. That means public vilification and life imprisonment. Or maybe in your case indefinite detention without trial. Or perhaps a visit from one of Mr. Buchanan's associates – I believe you've met Mr. Craven? But frankly that is all window dressing. One phone call is all it would take. You wouldn't even have time to get back to Fleet Street.'

'One phone call to who?' asked George, equally determined not to be intimidated.

Carlisle gave them another patronising smile. 'If I told you that, we would have already crossed the line.'

'And if we don't agree?' asked Vinny, starting to shift uncomfortably in his chair. He'd seen enough of Craven, both in his own office and in Francorelli's to know that he never wanted to see him again. If the threat from Carlisle was something worse than that, then it didn't bear thinking about.

Carlisle shrugged. 'That's up to you. Carry on publishing your conspiracy theory about MI6 and the Royal Family. In its own way it's not unhelpful.'

Vinny looked at George and Albert in turn, trying to read their body language and work out what they wanted to do. Albert shrugged, indicating that he was happy to go along with whatever the other two thought. George however gave him an emphatic nod. He was in no doubt at all. They were already out of their depth and if Craven worked for Buchanan then they were in dangerous company. Albert had warned him that people had died for getting too close to this story and he was right. Dino was already dead. That was enough for George. They only had two options as far as he was concerned. Forget about the story altogether, or find out the truth and then forget about it. And given they were all journalists, that meant only one thing.

'Okay,' said Vinny, turning back to look at Carlisle. 'We agree.'

'Good, let's get on with it then,' replied Carlisle, relaxing back into his chair, the worn, soft leather moving under his weight. He twisted around and glanced at Buchanan again, checking that it was okay to continue. Buchanan gave him a brief nod but otherwise remained expressionless, his body completely still, save for occasionally turning the signet ring on the little finger of his left hand. Vinny, George and Albert similarly eased back into their chairs, happy to let Carlisle talk. Now, finally, after all this time they were going to find out what really happened.

'Let me start by telling you a story,' continued Carlisle. 'In the summer of 1963 President John F Kennedy submitted a proposal which pledged to withdraw all US troops from Vietnam by the end of 1965. In fact at that point he had already signed National Security Action Memorandum 263 which ordered the first 1,000 troops home by Christmas 1963.'

'What's that got to do with Princess Diana?' interrupted Vinny, suddenly wondering why they were talking about JFK.

'Because in making that decision, Kennedy put himself on a collision path with some of the most powerful people in the US, not to mention the CIA. In essence, in making that declaration he signed his own death warrant...'

Vinny pulled a face, still not sure how any of that connected to the events in Paris in 1997 but either way, decided to shut up. He could tell from Carlisle's reaction that now was not the time to keep asking questions.

'...At this point of course the situation in southeast Asia had not yet escalated into full-blown war. Nevertheless, the promise of military conflict meant the promise of lucrative defence contracts for the US arms and fuel corporations, many of which were effectively run by the CIA. Kennedy's decision to pull out of Vietnam was going to cost some very important people millions of dollars. In fact hundreds of millions of dollars. It was a decision that would cost him his life.'

'Are you seriously suggesting that Kennedy was assassinated because he upset a bunch of American capitalists?' said Albert, 'all because he cost them a lot of money?'

'More than just a lot of money,' replied Carlisle. 'A once in a lifetime fortune. Every bullet, every bomb and every aircraft had to be funded by the US government and every bullet fired, bomb dropped or aircraft lost had to be replaced. The Vietnam war cost the US government 220 billion dollars, which is about 3 trillion in today's terms and every single dollar of expenditure had to be borrowed from the US Federal Reserve. A windfall the like of which the US corporations would never see again. And crucially, the people who ran the defence industry were also major shareholders in the Federal Reserve. Mega rich financiers and industrialists who loaned the money to the government in the first place and like any commercial deal charged interest on the transaction, making themselves a huge return. And then the government promptly gave the money straight back to them in the form of defence contracts, on which they also made a profit. One of the most beautifully constructed scams in corporate history. Kennedy's announcement to pull out of Vietnam was popular with the electorate but it was an absolute disaster for some of the richest and most powerful people in the country. It was going to deny them the opportunity to make an absolute killing.'

'Wow, that must have really pissed them off,' interrupted Vinny, his language as ever straight out of Bermondsey and straight to the point.

'Exactly, although Kennedy had already fallen out with the industrial cartels and the CIA by the time he was elected. The right-wing establishment expected Nixon to succeed Eisenhower in '61 but instead of getting a hard-nosed Republican and CIA conspirator they got an unpredictable, modernising Democrat who threatened to overturn the old guard. As soon as Kennedy was in office he promised to "splinter the CIA into a thousand pieces and scatter it to the winds." And to assert his presidential authority he started by making some pretty drastic changes, including firing the CIA Director, Allen Dulles and also the Deputy Director, Charles Cabell, who happened to be the brother of the Mayor of Dallas...'

Vinny, George and Albert all glanced at each other, the significance of Dallas not lost on any them.

'...but it was the decision on Vietnam which sealed his fate. The people who owned the financial and industrial corporations were the same people who had bankrolled Lyndon B Johnson to the office of Vice President, much against the wishes of JFK. As a result, in the autumn of '63 Johnson struck a deal with his military and industrial sponsors to maintain and increase US involvement in Vietnam in exchange for the presidency. A decision that would change the course of history. A month later, Kennedy was assassinated in Dallas on 22 November.'

George looked at Carlisle in disbelief. 'What, are you actually saying that Johnson was complicit in the assassination of JFK?'

'There's no evidence to support that,' replied Carlisle, choosing his words carefully, 'but on Tuesday 26th November, the day after Kennedy's funeral, President Lyndon B Johnson signed National Security Action Memorandum 273, effectively reversing Kennedy's withdrawal policy and sanctioning full commitment to the war in southeast Asia, including sending a further 500,000 troops to Vietnam. A full-scale conflict which would last another 12 years until 1975.'

Vinny, George and Albert looked at each other again, the enormity of what they had just heard starting to sink in.

'And the connection to Princess Diana?' asked Vinny, bringing the conversation back to his earlier question.

Carlisle raised his eyebrows. Now they were getting to the point. And to the reason why they were there.

Craven pulled up halfway along Raines Terrace outside a row of grey, Victorian houses, a typical residential side street in the smarter part of Vauxhall. He put the handbrake on but kept the engine idling as he leant across to look out of the passenger window.

Ross also stared out of the window, scanning the two or three houses nearest to them, trying to read the numbers from a distance. All the properties looked the same to him; large, imposing terraced villas spread over three or four floors, some including a cellar or basement. Once upon a time fashionable homes for the new Victorian "middling-classes." Inside, the rooms would have been light and spacious with large windows and high ceilings, maybe including a room at the top for a maid but all of them decorated with drab, patterned wallpaper and crammed full of dark, heavy furniture and thick, ornate curtains. Somewhere along the road there could even be one still in its original condition. A perfect example with bay sash windows, stained glass doors, wooden picture rails and a fireplace in every room; cast-iron grates with tiled surrounds, all lovingly preserved by a trendy, professional couple or maybe by the ageing relative of the original owner.

But predictably, the houses that Ross was staring at had all been modernised at some point, a few into multiple flats but most into commercial properties, typically small independent businesses. Number 23 had a polished brass plate by the front door which looked like a Dental Practice, or possibly a firm of Chartered Accountants. Ross couldn't tell which but it was definitely some sort of professional firm, the door knob and letter box also polished to an impressive, mirrored shine. And two doors down there was a contemporary blue and white sign fixed to the front of Number 27, advertising Coleman and Smith, an Advertising and Graphic Design studio; all Apple Macs, millennials and 501s. Ross wasn't interested in either Dentists or Graphic Designers but they did at least confirm that the house in between was the one that he was looking for.

'You sure that's it?' asked Craven, still peering out of the window.

Ross nodded. 'Yep, that's it. Number 25.'

'And you're sure about this?'

Ross smiled to himself but said nothing, still staring at the front door and wondering what was waiting for him on the other side. He wasn't really sure about anything anymore. Of course, a weekend in a London safe house, courtesy of Vector had made him feel half human again, particularly the combination of a hot shower, decent food and a comfortable bed. But he wasn't stupid. A couple of days on his own and he'd be straight back to where he was last week. He had no money left and nowhere else to go. Limited options. Try and stay on the run or call it a day and come back in, either to the Company or to the Brits. And Craven was right. After the shoot-out in Argento Bank there was no better opportunity to go back home. A hero's welcome.

'I'm sure,' said Ross, still staring out of the window and then unbuckling his seat belt. 'Time to go.'

'Okay. Look after yourself.'

Ross turned and looked at Craven for the first time in several minutes. 'I will. Thanks for the lift.'

'No problem.'

'And for your help.'

'You're welcome. Sorry about the bruises.'

Ross shrugged. The bruises meant nothing. They went with the territory and anyway, it would have been the other way round if he'd had his way. All part of the game. He nodded at Craven, as if to acknowledge the apology and then opened the passenger door. 'Maybe see you again sometime.'

Craven nodded back and smiled. Two peas in a pod. 'Maybe. Good luck.'

Ross slammed the car door behind him and walked up the short path to the front porch, not bothering to look behind him as Craven slipped the gearbox into first and pulled away. Ross pressed the bell and then waited for what seemed like an eternity before the door eventually opened...

Forty-Two

'THE POINT OF THE STORY IS TWOFOLD,' CONTINUED Carlisle. 'One; to illustrate the risk of upsetting the American defence industry which is one of the most ruthless institutions in the world and two; to demonstrate that the CIA will stop at nothing to remove any threat or obstacle that gets in its way, no matter how famous or influential it is. There were a lot of people who wanted Diana out of the way in '97 but top of the list were the same people who removed Kennedy almost 25 years earlier. Not exactly the same people of course but the same institutions; the CIA and the US right-wing oligarchy.'

'But why?' asked Albert, racking his brains to recall the events of over 20 years ago. He more than anyone was familiar with the story of Diana and was trying to remember what she had done to upset the US establishment.

Carlisle smiled at him, slightly surprised that he hadn't already made the connection. 'By the end of '96 Charles was living openly with Camilla Parker Bowles at Highgrove, a situation which absolutely incensed Diana. And earlier in that year, in response to adverse press reports about his prospects of becoming King should he remarry, Charles announced that Camilla was now a non-negotiable part of his life. In response, Diana decided to raise her game and with unprecedented publicity launched her personal crusade; the emotional and passion-charged ambition to rid the world of anti-personnel landmines. In January, amid a storm of international media attention she arrived at Luanda airport, close to Angola's capital and declared the start of her crusade, promising that her campaign would save thousands of lives. You must remember the photos of Diana visiting Africa that year?'

The three of them nodded, one photo in particular of her walking through an active minefield, complete with blast-proof body armour and protective visor having been syndicated to the world's press. An iconic image from the last year of her life.

'At that time Angola's war-torn countryside was littered with millions of landmines and the country had the highest number of amputees per population anywhere in the world. 2,000 Angolans a month were losing their limbs by stepping on uncleared landmines and facts like that, plus the sight of innocent, disabled children gathered into Diana's arms created a movement and a momentum which the world could not ignore. Over 70 countries were plagued with landmines in the mid-90s and so many were killing innocent people around the globe every day that the problem had become an epidemic. In highlighting the tragic cost to human life Diana had carved out a dynamic new role for herself on the international stage. It was a campaign that embroiled politicians of all persuasions and secured government support at the highest levels. She not only forced debate into the forefront of the political agenda but caused the Red Cross landmines appeal to soar beyond £1m, whereas the previous appeal had failed to reach even £50,000. By June her crusade was producing staggering results and Diana was planning further visits to Bosnia, Cambodia and Vietnam. But at the same time as all that success it was also incurring the wrath of global arms dealers and the US military.'

'But how could anyone possibly object?' asked George. 'Surely, anything which was going to save thousands of lives would have been received with universal support?'

'You would think so,' replied Carlisle, 'but object they did. Even the British objected. The UK Defence Select Committee accused her of taking political sides and of interfering with official government policy. Earl Howe, the then junior UK Defence Minister, accused her of being a "loose cannon" and Sir Nicholas

Bonsor, a former Foreign Office minister said that any campaign to deprive our soldiers of the use of landmines was, in his view, both dangerous and irresponsible.'

'And the Americans?' asked, Albert, pretty sure he knew what the answer was going to be.

'The Americans were incensed. Not only had she managed to convince the world's media but she'd also managed to persuade the US President. So much so that Clinton made a public announcement on 18 August that he was going to vote in favour of a landmines ban at an international conference in Oslo on 19 September. The response from the Pentagon and from his domestic opponents was outrage, much like the reaction to Kennedy's proclamation a generation earlier. Except in this case they didn't have an issue with the President himself but with the person who was influencing and manipulating his opinion.'

'Princess Diana,' replied Vinny.

'Exactly. Inevitably there was a period of frenzied lobbying but it was clear that Clinton had made a personal commitment to Diana that he wasn't prepared to break. Or wasn't able to, at least while she was still alive. There was also concern that Diana was about to champion the cause of Gulf War Syndrome, a hugely politically sensitive issue and one which the US military simply could not countenance. It was no secret in Washington that the Pentagon was violently opposed to Diana's meddling in international affairs but following Clinton's announcement the situation had spiralled out of control. Within days the intelligence community had put her under 24 hour surveillance and had started to contemplate ways of silencing her.'

'So it was the CIA who killed her?' asked Albert, his question largely rhetorical but still looking for confirmation. An old hack's instinct for nailing the facts.

Carlisle nodded. 'Yes, it was. Within ten days of Clinton's announcement Diana was assassinated in Paris. It was just three weeks before the Oslo Conference at which Britain and most of the western world would agree to sign the landmines treaty. The only major power who refused to sign was the United States, the President having been persuaded by enormous political pressure to finally renege on his promise to the late Princess. An outcome that would have been unthinkable had she still been alive.'

'That's outrageous,' said George, still trying to comprehend the scale of the CIA's involvement.

'Yes, to you, and to the world at large, it is,' replied Carlisle, turning around to glance at Buchanan, 'but not to the intelligence community. There was a larger, more binding treaty signed in Ottawa in December of that year which was agreed by 122 countries but which again, the US was the only major power not to sign. The CIA is an organisation that routinely gets involved in international terrorism, the assassination of political leaders, inciting civil wars, election rigging, drug trafficking, money laundering. You name it, the CIA have been involved in it. The murder of a British subject, albeit someone who was once a high-profile member of the Royal Family would be nothing to them.'

'And the Royal Family,' asked Vinny, unable to hide the disappointment in his voice. As conspiracy theories went that would have been much more interesting than a story about the CIA. 'They had nothing to do with it?'

Carlisle smiled. 'Absolutely nothing. Diana was an irritant to the Royal Family and an embarrassment at times but no more so than some of the members of their own family. They knew nothing about it. And it had nothing to do with the fact that Diana was going out with Dodi Fayed or because of some supposed pregnancy. The proposition is frankly, preposterous. It was all about power and money. Always has been, always will be. She was assassinated by the CIA and the only help they had was some operational support from Mossad.'

'Mossad?' said Albert. 'What did Mossad have to do with it?'

Carlisle shrugged. 'The Israelis have always been hand in glove with the Americans. The Israelis protect western interests in the

Middle East and in return the Americans provide coalition support to Israel. The CIA needed some help on the ground in Paris and Mossad were only too happy to oblige. Of all the countries in the world, the one that was really concerned about Diana's relationship with Dodi was Israel. Anything which promoted the acceptance of Islam and the agenda of the Arab nations was seen as a threat to their security.

Vinny slumped back into his chair. 'So is that it? Nothing to do with MI6?'

Carlisle shook his head. 'Or MI5. The conspiracy theories were all a clever smokescreen created by the CIA. And frankly, the gullible reporting by the British press has helped them perpetuate that. '

'So what about the last few weeks?' asked George. 'The crosswords and the events in Francorelli's last week. What was that all about?'

'There were some photographs,' replied Carlisle, reaching into the right hand drawer of his desk and pulling out a brown, A4 envelope. 'Photographs taken in Paris on the night that Diana was killed.'

'What's on them?' asked Albert, intrigued by the prospect that they could be pictures that had never seen the light of day before. He'd worked on the Diana story long enough to recognise all the photographs that were ever taken. At least that's what he thought.

'The actual content isn't important,' replied Carlisle, passing the envelope across the desk to Vinny,' but to say that they're incriminating would be an understatement. The Russians managed to get hold of them and were using them to blackmail the Americans. Thanks to Mr. Buchanan we have them now.'

'So what are you going to do with them? asked Vinny, turning the envelope over to see if there was anything written on it.

'Nothing. We're going to give them to you. For safe keeping.'

Vinny, George and Albert all looked at each other and frowned. That didn't make sense. What was the point of them having the photos if they couldn't use them? And besides, surely they would be in much safer hands if held by Carlisle or by Buchanan, whoever he was, rather than by a national newspaper.

'Westminster leaks like a sieve,' continued Carlisle as if reading their minds. 'Always has, always will. Too many ministers with political agendas. And Whitehall is no better. Full of civil servants with so called principles and a distorted sense of moral duty. Much safer with you.'

'So why don't you just destroy them?' asked George, still confused by the proposition.

'Because they may come in useful one day. There might come a time when we decide to publish them. Or at least threaten to.'

Again, Vinny, George and Albert looked at each other, not quite sure what to make of that last remark.

Carlisle looked at his watch and then started to stand up. The questions were getting difficult now and he had already disclosed more than he probably should have done. It was time to call an end to proceedings. 'Anyway, as much as I would like to continue our discussion,' he said, 'I'm afraid I have another appointment. Thank you for coming and for giving up your time. My secretary will show you out.'

'Could I ask one last question?' asked George, conscious that there was one answer from the crossword which they still didn't understand. 'Could you tell me the significance of the word VECTOR?'

Carlisle glanced at Buchanan who stared back at him, his face absolutely expressionless. Then Carlisle looked back at George, holding his gaze for a second to emphasise that the response was unequivocal. 'No Mr. Wiggins, I'm afraid I can't.'

—ᴍ—

Eventually the door opened; a middle-aged guy, thirty-something, in a dark blue suit and white shirt, the tell-tale bulge by his left ribcage confirming that he was carrying.

'I'm here to see Christine Michaels,' said Ross, not sure how else to announce his arrival.

'Damien Ross?' enquired the guy, as if they were on first name terms already.

Ross nodded. At least he was expected.

The guy nodded back and opened the door fully. 'Come in. Take a seat and I'll let her know you're here.'

He led Ross into a room on the right; a once upon a time front parlour of a family home but now a cold, soulless room with a few spartan chairs and a couple of small side tables. Like a dentist's waiting room. The guy disappeared to make a phone call while Ross decided to remain standing, pacing up and down a few times before staring out of the large bay window at the road outside, watching the traffic ebb and flow. Real life. The whole thing seemed surreal. One minute he was living below the radar in an anonymous Moscow suburb and then the next minute he was standing in a CIA safe house, about to meet the Head of London Station. He shook his head, as if waking himself out of a dream. Now was not the time to get sentimental. There was nothing left for him in Russia any more. It was time to focus on the future, not the past.

'Damien?'

'Yes.' Ross wheeled around and found himself facing Christine Michaels, not someone that he had ever met before but nevertheless exactly as he had imagined her. Slim, poised and slightly cool in a detached, superior kind of way. She stepped forward a couple of paces, holding out her hand to complete the formal introduction, the dark charcoal trouser suit and crisp linen blouse adding to the sense of understated authority. Ross took her hand and shook it gently, conscious that it was small and delicate, almost as if he wanted to pull it to his lips and kiss it softly, like a medieval knave being presented to a queen.

She held his grip for a second and then squeezed her hand and gave him a warm, genuine smile. 'Welcome home Damien. It's good to have you back.'

Ross smiled back, a sudden sense of relief surging through his body. 'Thank you. It's good to be here.'

'How are you?'

Ross blew out his cheeks, not sure whether to give a one word answer or tell her the truth. The latter would have taken several minutes and sounded like a confessional so he opted for somewhere in between. 'I'm fine thank you, although a little tired. And a bit apprehensive to be honest about coming in. It's been a long time.'

Michaels squeezed his hand again before letting go, trying to convey that she understood how he felt. 'There's no rush Damien. We can take this as gently and as slowly as you like. The important thing is that you're back.'

Ross let out a sigh, the stress of the last few weeks finally leaving his body. 'Thanks. So what happens next?'

'Well, at some point we'll need to fly you back to Langley but I thought we'd do an initial debrief in London. Get the basics out of the way. Is that okay with you?'

Ross nodded. He knew he didn't have any say in the matter but appreciated that she was trying to make him feel comfortable.

'I've commandeered a room on the top floor. It's more discreet.'

'Okay,' said Ross, giving her a nonchalant shrug. 'Ready when you are.'

'Good. Let's get started then. Lots of stairs I'm afraid but they keep you fit.'

Michaels led the way into the hall and then up the first flight of stairs with Ross a couple of steps behind, trying to maintain a conversation as she periodically twisted around to look at him. They eventually went up four flights to the top of the building, Michaels having no problem with the exertion, a product of early morning gym sessions and regular weekend jogging. Ross on the other hand was out of condition and struggled to keep up. By the time they got to the top he was half a flight behind and breathing hard.

'Sorry about that,' he said, climbing the last few stairs. 'Not as fit as I used to be.'

She smiled in sympathy, happy to wait for him to catch up. 'We're just through here,' she said, pointing towards a door at the end of the short landing. 'Would you like a coffee Damien before we start?'

'Yes, please. That would be great.'

'How do you take it?'

'Black, no sugar.'

'Good.' Michaels rested her hand on the door handle as if to open it and then suddenly paused. 'Everyone has heard about Tom Draper by the way. The Company owes you a huge debt of gratitude.'

Ross shrugged nonchalantly again, slightly embarrassed by the deception. 'It was nothing really. It was either him or me.'

'Nonsense. You've probably saved a lot of lives. A lot of people are going to be very grateful.' Then she opened the door to show him into the room. 'You make yourself comfortable and I'll organise the coffee.'

Ross stepped into the room, slightly surprised to hear the door close behind him. He turned around to check, just in time to catch a glimpse of a guy standing behind him wearing a black bomber jacket and a grey baseball cap. Plus the front sight of a muzzle and silencer pointing straight at him. A split second memory of a scene from *Goodfellas*, Joe Pesci walking into a room and not coming out. He hardly had time to mutter the words "oh no" before the three rounds of ammunition hit him, two in the chest and one squarely in the middle of his forehead. A second later he hit the floor, dead on impact. *Target down. Mission accomplished.*

Michaels put the empty cup in the coffee machine and pressed the display screen. Normally she had decaf, or just hot water for a herbal tea. Then she pressed the button for double espresso. Today was going to be a good day.

'Well, I think that went rather well,' said Carlisle, plonking himself back in his chair and swivelling round to look at Buchanan. 'What do you think?'

Buchanan stared back, his face expressionless, not entirely swayed by Carlisle's smug optimism. 'As well as can be expected, I suppose.'

'Are you going to call Michaels?'

'As soon as I get back to the office.'

'And say what, exactly?'

Buchanan shrugged again. 'I'll tell her that the British press have let us know that they've got the photos but that in the interests of national security they've agreed not to publish...'

'Good.'

'...but that in the event that international relations with the US look like deteriorating into serious conflict, they reserve the right to review their position on that.'

'Perfect. That should do it.'

Buchanan gave him a thin smile. 'Let us hope so.'

'Do you think they'll open the envelope?'

'Probably.'

'I assume you took a copy of everything?'

'Of course.'

'Good.' Carlisle swivelled his chair around, turning his back on Buchanan to signal that the meeting was over. 'We must do lunch sometime.'

Buchanan ignored the offer and stood up and walked out, shutting the door behind him. He had things to do and besides, he'd had a stomach full of Carlisle over the past few days. The last thing he wanted was to go to lunch with him.

Carlisle watched Buchanan leave and then stood up and walked over to the window. Outside the day was postcard perfect. The London sun shimmered above like a polished shield and in the distance the office blocks and skyscrapers shone silver against an unbroken backdrop of cornflower blue. Carlisle stood there, taking in the view, the city with all its familiarity unfurled in front of him, like an old reliable friend. Nelson's Column, Trafalgar Square, the Houses of Parliament, the London Eye; a sweeping panorama from a high definition movie screen. Beneath him, the buildings of Whitehall rose majestically above the hordes of people, the landscape constantly moving but the sequence always the same. The hustle and bustle of commuters, the crowds of tourists, red double-decker buses, black cabs, blue-uniformed policemen, broad, stone churches, historic monuments, flocks of pigeons. Life, movement, noise. And all around it London crouched; gas towers and apartment blocks, endless rows of shops and houses, tube stations, street lights, roads and traffic jams twisting and curving as far as the eye could see. And bridges and railway lines stretching away on both sides, separated only by the bright, shining flow of the river Thames glimmering in the distance. Carlisle smiled to himself. Up here he was king of the world. Master of all he surveyed. Untouchable.

Inside, the late morning sun streamed through the window, casting a warm glow of amber onto the dark, walnut floor; a chequer board of soft light and shadow. Carlisle turned to look at it, the dust particles dancing around him as his body broke the beams of sunlight. He stood there for a moment, mesmerised by the pattern. As the day moved on the squares would elongate into faded rectangles, stretching and yawning towards dusk before eventually surrendering to the night. He turned back to look at the view again when suddenly the telephone on his desk started to ring. He walked over and picked up the receiver, the efficient, familiar voice of Joyce Wilson at the other end.

'St. James's Palace for you. Can I put them through?'

'Yes, of course.'

Carlisle heard the call connect and then another familiar voice on the line; hesitant, slightly anxious and apologetic. He listened for a moment before responding to the question.

'Yes, they've just left.'

Again, another pause as he listened to the next question, the inevitable follow-up. Something which he could now answer with more certainty.

'No, it's all resolved.'

And then a third pause. The final question seeking final reassurance.

'Absolutely. No one will ever know.'

"Our revels now are ended. These our actors,
As I foretold you, were all spirits and
Are melted into air, into thin air:
And, like the baseless fabric of this vision,
The cloud-capp'd towers, the gorgeous palaces,
The solemn temples, the great globe itself,
Yea, all which it inherit, shall dissolve
And, like this insubstantial pageant faded,
Leave not a rack behind. We are such stuff
As dreams are made on, and our little life
Is rounded with a sleep."

William Shakespeare

Acknowledgements

Frank and Edna Olohan, for their support,
editorial advice and wise counsel

This novel was written in Tenterden, on journeys to London,
in Charles Dickens's private study at Bleak House,
and on the magical island of Herm

In memory of Frank Olohan